BADWATER

Also by Clinton McKinzie

THE EDGE OF JUSTICE

POINT OF LAW

TRIAL BY ICE AND FIRE

CROSSING THE LINE

BADWATER

CLINTON McKINZIE

DELACORTE PRESS

BADWATER
A Delacorte Press Book / May 2005

Published by
Bantam Dell
A Division of Random House, Inc.
New York, New York

This is a work of fiction. Names, characters, places, and incidents either are the product of the author's imagination or are used fictitiously. Any resemblance to actual persons, living or dead, events, or locales is entirely coincidental.

All rights reserved
Copyright © 2005 by Clinton McKinzie

Delacorte Press is a registered trademark of Random House, Inc., and the colophon is a trademark of Random House, Inc.

Library of Congress Cataloging-in-Publication Data
McKinzie, Clinton
Badwater/Clinton McKinzie
p. cm.
ISBN 0-385-33847-3
1. Burns, Antonio (Fictitious character)—Fiction. 2. Government investigators—Fiction. 3. Drowning victims—Fiction. 4. Trials (Murder)—Fiction. 5. Wyoming—Fiction. I. Title.

PS3613.C568 B33 2005 2004065514
813/.6 22

Printed in the United States of America
Published simultaneously in Canada

www.bantamdell.com

BVG 10 9 8 7 6 5 4 3 2 1

For Mom and Dad,
with love and gratitude

ACKNOWLEDGMENTS

A portion of this story is based on a real tragedy that occurred in Wyoming. I have entirely fictionalized the people and the events in my version. I deliberately learned as little as I could about the facts of the actual case so that I could tell the story my way, with my characters. That said, thanks to Taylor Reed for first tantalizing me with the germ of an idea while we were climbing in Sinks Canyon. Thanks are also owed to Jay Anderson and his wonder dog, Alobar, whose epic ten-year bare-knuckle brawl with a Vedauwoo crack called Lucille inspired another part of this story.

Once again I relied heavily on the first reader of everything I write, my wife, Justine, for her wise counsel. My agent, John Talbot, was always available to encourage and assist. Danielle Perez, my editor at Bantam Dell, helped steer this story back on course when, more than once, it threatened to plunge off a cliff. And finally, thanks to Robin Foster, who did the extraordinarily difficult job of making my original manuscript consistent, coherent, and readable. All errors that remain are a result of my managing to screw up her wonderful copyedit.

BADWATER

1

June 2004

one

The day it all began, I was doing the same thing I'd been doing nearly every day for the past year: beating the bushes in the state's vast forests and trying like hell to stay out of trouble. I was intent on lying low, minding my own business, and bothering no one but the shitheads who were cooking meth in the woods. This had been my sole occupation ever since an agency already inclined to be suspicious of me had become positively paranoid about my methods of investigation.

Now I was determined to give them nothing to suspect. As far as I—and my office—were concerned, I was out of the investigation business entirely. I'd been essentially demoted from a top-rated undercover agent to the role of a mere scout.

Under this new, unofficial job description I would drive each day along remote logging and mining roads in the wilder portions of the Lower 48's least-populated state. The rusty Land Cruiser I called the Iron Pig prowled the backcountry in low gear, my wolf-dog Mungo drooling out one of the backseat windows. Both beast and driver scanned the roadsides for items such as "death bags," strewn kitty litter, cold-medicine wrappers, lithium batteries, and glass jars filled with murky liquids. All of these were signs that somewhere nearby we would surely find a clandestine methamphetamine lab.

Meth—also called crank, speed, ice, glass, crunch, and crystal—had become the number one societal problem in Wyoming, surpassing even the red-faced shouting war between the extraction industries and the environmentalists. Ninety percent of crime in the state could be traced back to meth. Something like 40 percent of kids admitted to having tried it, and a lot of them swallowed the hook. They traded normal lives and desires for multiday psychotic binges, permanent brain damage, oozing sores, nowhere futures, and an overwhelming need for more.

I had seen it hundreds of times in the course of my eight-year career in law enforcement. I'd come to consider giving a kid a little tinfoil-wrapped packet of yellow crystals a crime far worse than handing one a loaded gun. The stuff is so addictive and mind-warping that it makes whiskey and pot seem as harmless as gummy bears. Bikers started cooking this scary shit in the late eighties and early nineties, but in the new century it's being produced by grade-school lab nerds, trailer-park yokels with Internet access, and some very well-organized Latino gangs.

It was the gangs and their so-called superlabs that were my primary prey. Or had been, anyway. A year ago I'd broken up the biggest one in the history of the West. But it was that very same bust that, for the second time in my career, had gotten me reprimanded and very nearly arrested myself. It had also utterly devastated my personal life, costing me just about everything but the dog and the truck. My job was still to hunt the drug and its dealers, but the subsequent investigations and arrests were handed to federal agents or local police who had less "colorful" backgrounds than Special Agent Antonio Burns, officers who could testify in court without a famously disputed shooting and a drug kingpin's odd disappearance following them around to cast doubt upon their credibility.

Although I hated to admit it even to myself, and despite the badge I still carried in my wallet, I'd become little more than an informant—the lowest of the low in the law-enforcement pecking order. A rat. I'd long since stopped blaming bad luck or bad judgment for my predicament. Instead I'd come to believe it was an arbitrary result of a flawed and often corrupt system. And I wasn't sure how much longer I could remain a participant in a system that had first disappointed then betrayed me. Or maybe, just maybe, I'd disappointed and betrayed it.

The afternoon of June 17 began with Mungo and me spotting three black trash bags in a roadside ditch. This had become an almost everyday discovery. Either there was more cooking going on or I was becoming very good at guessing where we would find the clan labs. Mungo wrinkled her snout at the plastic sacks and gave her signal; she coughed in a very unladylike manner, as if she had a hairball lodged in her throat. The ammonia scent was so strong that I could smell it myself. My eyes watered as I got out of the truck and pulled on a pair of rubber gloves.

All three bags were partially inflated. Full, I knew, of nasty gases and liquids. Phosphine. Anhydrous ammonia. Crystal iodine. Hydrochloric acid. Stuff that even the dumbest crankers are smart enough to keep the hell away from themselves and their lab. So what the motherfuckers do is dump them in a place like this, where maybe a little kid can find them and wonder what's inside.

I gently lifted the sacks by their tied-off necks and carried them deeper into the woods. There I concealed them as well as I could. It pissed me off that I didn't have the equipment and protective gear to deal with them properly. In the unlikely event the state or federal government would somehow scratch up the funds to do proper sanitation, I recorded the location on my handheld Global Positioning System.

A little ways farther down the road we came across a fresh double-track leading into the trees. The path had obviously been made by an all-terrain vehicle—it was too narrow for the Pig, and the torn earth had obviously been the victim of some very knobby tires. This in a place where no one—not even poachers or asshole off-roaders intent on tearing up a meadow somewhere—would have a legitimate interest in going.

I stopped and listened carefully. When I didn't hear the banshee wail of a two-stroke engine, I let the Pig creep on down the road for another quarter mile then parked in a turnout. Mungo leapt out and sniffed around while I laced up my running shoes and slung on a small pack. Consistent with my mantra of avoiding trouble, I left my duty weapon under the Pig's front seat. Trouble was all the .40 Heckler & Koch had brought me.

I looked, and wanted to look, like a grad student on summer break. *Just hanging out, dude, doing a little tramping through the woods.* If I looked anything like a cop, then I knew there was a pretty good chance I'd be shot on sight. So my hair was a little long, my face unshaven, and my shorts and T-shirt appropriately baggy and torn. Mungo was disguised, too, with a bright red bandanna around her neck. But she looked away disdainfully when I offered for the hundredth time to enhance her costume by letting her carry a floppy dog disk. She had her pride.

The disguises were good, though, even without the toy. It was only with a very close look that someone would notice the creases around my eyes, suggesting I might be a little old for a grad student, or that Mungo was no oversize shepherd-malamute mix but actually half Mackenzie Valley wolf.

"Vamonos," I called to her.

On foot we headed back down the road and then turned onto the double-track.

Within a few minutes we were hoofing it through a forest of lodgepole pines, with Mungo bumping her bony shoulder against my thigh. The sun cut through the needle canopy overhead in dusty rays and the trail wound around trees, drop-offs, and boulders. Mungo stayed at my side even when a squirrel taunted us from a high branch. We moved easily together—at least one of us was well trained. Her light-footed tread was something I tried to emulate, and I swung my head as often as she did, smelling, looking, listening.

Mungo's vigilance was due to a genetic instinct that had her always searching for something she could kill. My awareness, however, was defensive. It came from too much experience with booby traps.

These came in many forms—fishing line connected to detonators or mounted shotguns on the trailside, punji stakes in concealed pits, bear traps, poisoned hypodermic needles hidden in brush, fishhooks dangling from branches at eye level, and once, quite memorably, a half-starved mountain lion chained to a tree. Then there were the crankers themselves to worry about, as they were almost always armed a hell of a lot better than I would ever be, even with my duty weapon. The labs they protected could be anything from fancy trailers to canvas tents with crates of cold medicine and lithium batteries stacked under tarps. Dead or dying trees were always nearby, though—killed by the by-products that then sank down into the groundwater. The cooking process produced six pounds of highly toxic waste for every pound of meth. Poured in a trout stream, it would kill every fish for miles downstream. A lot of it seemed to get sucked up into the brains of the crankers, making them meaner and more prone to violence than a sackful of rattlesnakes.

Once I found the lab, and if it was unguarded, I intended to snap a few pictures with the digital camera in my backpack, record the longitude and latitude on the handheld GPS, and later E-mail both files back to the main office in Cheyenne. Maybe they would send out a SWAT team with a Hazmat disposal crew. Or maybe not.

Not was most likely, I had learned. There simply weren't the resources to bust up and then clean up every lab I'd found in the last year. Each site, it was explained to me the first few times I'd complained (later they just ignored me), could cost from $5,000 to $150,000—an amount of money that was sorely lacking in this economy, especially in a state with no income tax. I understood this, but it still pissed me off. This shit was killing people, after all. I even knew about it firsthand—and not just through my undercover observations. My one and only brother was among the hundreds I'd seen wrecked by drugs.

So far, though, I had managed to keep from firing the extremely flammable labs I'd found with flashbang grenades, managed to keep from arresting the cooks after encouraging them to "resist," and even managed to keep from screaming and pushing the office suits into walls, although sometimes it had taken deep breathing and seated meditation to cool the impulses. *I will be nothing but a good scout,* I constantly reminded myself. No trouble. *Just do your damn job—nothing more!* as my boss commanded me each time I reported in. Find the labs, turn them in, and do nothing.

Then wait and watch as nothing was being done.

I tried to be philosophical about it—*Hey, Ant, you get to spend your days wandering around in the woods with Mungo. You even find and get to rope up on cliffs no one's ever been on before. C'mon, man, a lot of people would kill for this job*—but the frustration had me grinding my teeth day after day. Pumping some chemical through my veins that was even meaner than meth. It had polluted me. It kept me from driving down to Denver and trying to win back the woman I loved, not to mention the daughter she'd given birth to six months before.

It wasn't just that the shitheads were getting away with it; it was that they *knew* they were getting away with it. And that other people knew—my own office, for God's sake, the state's chief law-enforcement agency—*knew* that they knew and let them go on laughing at the law. That was what really pissed me off—it actually enraged me.

But—*deep breath, center yourself, Ant*—I was being a good boy. I was becoming adept at avoiding trouble. Until this day, when trouble came looking for me and demanded yet another confrontation.

two

It was Mungo, of course, who first sensed its presence.

We were moving down the double-track at an easy pace, our noses, eyes, and ears taking in everything that our vastly unequal senses were capable of, when Mungo suddenly whipped her hatchet-shaped head to the left. Ears pricked in that same direction, she lifted her nose high and snuffed the air. I watched her eyes—in them I was pretty sure I could read whatever she was smelling, whether it be a moose, an elk, a bear, a stranger, or a booby-trapped clan lab.

The yellow eyes narrowed. Like she was frowning; no, confused. She confirmed this interpretation by glancing up at me, cocking her head, then going back to testing the air with quivering nostrils. Her big, pointed ears working, too, like some sophisticated radar system, her head moving this way and that. I waited for her to lock on.

"Qué pasa?" I asked when she did.

Mungo kept staring into the trees, straining her neck forward a little. She let out a soft whine. What the hell? I still didn't know what she'd locked on to. What was weird was that I didn't think she knew, either. All I could hear was the touch of a breeze in the treetops and the faraway rumble of a lot of water moving fast over stone. All I could smell was pine needles. I finally got impatient.

"Okay, Mungo. Whatever it is, let's check it out. *Vamonos.*"

I lifted my hand and flicked my fingers in the direction she'd focused on.

Mungo took a few hesitant steps off the double-track and into the trees—head still high, examining the air, not the ground—and then she shifted up into a higher gear. Within twenty feet she was moving at a fast trot.

Even just loping along, she traveled at a speed that I could only keep up with in an almost-sprint, something I wasn't willing to do when chasing the unknown. Mungo was aware of her master's shortcomings, however, and paused every hundred yards or so to wait for me. Her tail waved me on like a beacon. The forest's undergrowth wasn't particularly heavy, as the high canopy above only allowed light to enter in dusty beams. I was able to move pretty fast through it, not worrying too much about breaking an ankle but still imagining hanging fishhooks and punji pits.

I'd only been running for four or five minutes when I heard the first faint strains of what had undoubtedly been a cacophony in Mungo's ears. It sounded like yelling. Coming from not one person, I guessed, but several.

I slowed, holding my breath so I could listen. The forest had gone silent but for the rush of blood in my ears. The usual birds were quiet, the squirrels not chattering at all. Only the river was still rumbling away as a bass background for the distant screams. Then I picked up the pace until I was actually sprinting. As I ran, vectoring in on the sounds myself now, I mentally unfolded a map in my head.

The way the sunbeams slashed across the forest told me that I was heading west. Toward the Badwater River, which couldn't be more than a quarter mile away now. Just beyond the river—on the other side—ran a state highway. Maybe a car had plunged through a guardrail and gone into the river. Or maybe a raft had flipped on the rapids and the survivors were screaming for missing raft-mates. But, no, some of these screams, growing in volume as I neared, sounded angry. Others were pleading.

"I'm going to kill you!"

"You killed him! You killed him!"

"Do you see him?"

"Oh God, can you see him? Where did he go?"

"You're dead, you fucking fag! You're dead!"

What the hell? I asked myself again. Then I could hear a siren. Good. Somebody else's problem now, whatever it was. But I didn't—couldn't—slow.

Mungo was out of sight. When I'd begun sprinting, she'd blasted on ahead. Following the shouts, the siren, and the rumble of the river, I came to the edge of the forest. It ended so abruptly that I had to hook the trunk of a tree with one arm to avoid running right off a ten-foot bank and falling into the water. Mungo wolfishly grinned at me—*ha-ha*—from a few feet to one side, where she had stopped under the cover of some willows.

Despite the constant boom of white water both up- and downstream, the water below was slow and peaceful. Directly across the river, though, there was anything but peace.

Two highway patrol cars, lights still flashing but sirens now silent, were parked on top of a hill a little ways back from the river. That hill met the river with a rounded cliff that was twice the size of the opposite one I stood panting on. The cliff was actually an enormous boulder. To the south—left—side of the cliff was a beach composed of round stones, and on it raged two screaming boys. Both were being physically restrained by a beefy state patrolman. The other trooper—a tall, thin guy—was thigh-deep in the river, his head pivoting rapidly as he stared into the gold-and-green water in front of him. There was a pale young man in an orange life jacket in the river, too. He was charging around in the water like a maniac. Downstream floated a raft that was fighting the current—a man on board rowing hard, and a passenger, a woman with black hair, who was sobbing.

"What happened?" I yelled over the shouts of various people.

The tall trooper in the river jerked up his head.

"Who the heck are you?"

"Antonio Burns. DCI." DCI is my employer, Wyoming's statewide Division of Criminal Investigation.

The trooper, who'd immediately gone back to scanning the water after asking his question, popped his head up again. He looked at me with surprised eyes and an open mouth. Then the eyes narrowed suspiciously. I knew it was my name, not the name of the agency I worked for, that caused the reaction.

"They call you QuickDraw, right?"

I stared hard at him, not answering, as a bloom of heat spread outward from my chest. He quickly looked back down at the water, muttering, "Oh. Sorry."

"What happened?" I yelled again in what I hoped was an even voice.

"Kids say that guy in the life jacket pushed their cousin—a ten-year-old boy—off that cliff over there."

The maniac in the life jacket stopped splashing around. Now he looked up, and I saw the silver flash of a pierced eyebrow, gelled spikes of blond-tipped hair, and noticed the tattoos on the man's neck and arms.

"It was an accident! I told you! He went in right there!" He pointed a thin arm at what looked like deep water beneath the stone cliff. "Yell if you can see anything from that angle, okay?" Then he went back to splashing and peering through the golden shallows that rimmed the darker water beneath the cliff.

I didn't try to make sense of it. The most basic fact was obvious.

"How long's he been under?" I yelled as I shrugged off my pack and kicked off my shoes.

"Don't know," the tall trooper said. "Ten minutes, maybe. Might be fifteen."

"Oh my God!" the other man cried.

I turned around and began to lower myself down the bank,

holding on to loose rocks and roots. I paused to hiss, *"Paranda que!"* to Mungo where she was still concealed by the willows. I didn't want her jumping down after me, or getting shot by the cop, who might be surprised to notice a wolf on the bank. The water below looked fairly deep, but I knew better than to dive. Looks can be deceiving, and I was trying to be very careful about my neck these days. Both figuratively and literally.

"We got a 911 call maybe five minutes ago from the lady in the raft," the cop was saying. "She saw the whole thing and has a cell. We were running a trap on the highway just a mile away—"

I didn't hear the rest. Halfway down the bank, a stone I was gripping with one hand ripped out of the dirt at the same time a slippery root did in the other. I fell five or six feet, landing first on my bare feet and then my ass as I rolled all the way onto my back in ankle-deep water, banging both elbows hard on submerged stones. Embarrassing for a climber, but it was a good thing I hadn't jumped. The depth certainly was deceptive. And the water was outrageously cold—pure glacial meltwater running out of the Absarokas, its temperature only a degree or two above freezing.

But that's good, I told myself as I struggled to reclaim my breath and scramble to my feet on the slippery rocks. *Ten minutes, maybe fifteen.* I thrashed forward into deeper water near the river's center, thinking that the frigid water would slow oxygen-starved blood, and remembering a case where a young girl had been under the ice for forty-five minutes before being hauled out and resuscitated. Hypothermia when drowning can be a blessing. Lessens the amount of potential brain damage caused by prolonged submersion. There was a chance, anyway. Thigh-deep now and pushing a wake that splashed all the way up to my chest, I could see before me the dark green water in the pool beneath the big boulder.

I could also see a thin branch floating *upstream,* beginning to turn a slow arc back in the direction it should be floating.

Whirlpool! I thought too late, just as I jumped up then porpoised headfirst into the deep water.

three

The water was so cold I had to fight to keep the air from being torn out of my lungs. The cold was so intense that it burned my eyeballs as I stroked downward. The big boulder shaded this part of the river, so it was dark and getting darker the deeper I dove. I could still see a little in the green-black murk, but I couldn't see what I most wanted to see—the bottom. I could, however, feel the current now. It was gathering strength with each foot I clawed into the depths. It seemed to be moving sideways, trying to spin me.

It was a whirlpool all right, swirling down in a sideways funnel and drawing me under the cliff. It was getting tighter. Getting stronger. Getting so strong that I couldn't keep it from beginning to turn me around. But I forced my way deeper, fighting to hold my course and find a solid bottom that I could push off of. My ears ached with pressure and I moved my jaw to clear them. In the gloom I could make out huge, long shapes below me. They looked like coffins all piled together haphazardly. And there were some white sticks scattered over them. I could hear strange sounds, too. Pops and clicks and cracks like gunshots. And, far louder, a roar like a train passing just underneath. It was the sound of thousands of gallons per second being sucked through wood and rock.

Shit!

I belatedly realized what the current meant, what a whirlpool in this place indicated. There was a sink under the boulder, an underwater cavern gulping down a large portion of the river. Like the Sinks and Rise near Lander, where you can watch an entire river disappear then rise up a quarter mile later. The dark coffin shapes were shattered tree trunks that had been pulled under then wedged over the cavern's entrance. The white sticks were the arms and legs of a child.

What if he gets sucked through? What if I do?

Panic was suddenly an even stronger force than the cold or the current. I'm someone who has always reveled in the rush of adrenaline, but that's in high, airy places, a thousand or more feet off the deck, where the pull of gravity is familiar, where you can pant and curse all you want, and where a rope is always there to back you up. Here, under the river, there was no air. No light. No rope.

The panic was just too strong.

I arched my back and thrust for the surface with everything I had, shaking with cold and exertion and fear. Ashamed of turning around, giving in, but succumbing to the necessity. The whirlpool pulled me back and fought to hold me in its grasp. I had to angle for its center in order to weaken the hold. My lungs were starting to scream. Then I finally broke out into the light.

The tall trooper was still standing in the river just thirty feet away, staring at me with an expression of fear that I think was probably magnified a hundred times on my own features.

"Jesus! You okay? You okay?" he shouted.

I bobbed my head once, then forced the cop from my mind and instead concentrated on just filling my lungs.

I gasped three times. The first two were shaky, but the third inhalation was deep, all the way to the bottom of my gut. I scissored my body and dove again into the whirlpool.

This time I allowed the current to spin me as I swam, corkscrewing me down toward those dark shapes. This time I didn't let the panic blare any louder in my head than a warning chime, like the stall indicator on an airplane that's being pushed too hard. And I didn't let the cold get to me, or the pressure in my ears, or the burning in my chest. All I focused on was those white limbs stretched over what I still thought of as jumbled coffins.

I was being pulled downward so hard that I slammed into the logs. I slammed into the boy, too. A single big bubble rose out from behind a swirl of hair. His skin was cold and slimy to the touch, as were the tree trunks beneath him. The sensation was a little sickening, but it was nothing compared to the noise and friction of the horrendous volume of water sucking down past me. Praying I wouldn't get pulled through the gaps in the logs, I placed my feet on each side of the boy and wrapped my arms around him.

I pulled. There was only a tiny bit of give, then the body was yanked back as if the boy didn't want to come with me, as if he were determined to cling to the logs. No, it was the whirlpool—it was unwilling to release its prey. I pulled again. More give, and a harder tug back. My lungs were on fire. And my body was frozen numb except for where burning needles were spreading over my skin. And not only would the fucking whirlpool not let go, it kept spinning me off balance, trying to rip me into the abyss beyond the screen of logs. My vision was starting to go black around the edges, blacker even than where the current wanted to take me.

I let the current pull me down again until I was lying on top of the boy. He was so small. And as cold as a block of ice. I wrapped my arms around him as tight as I could. Then I planted my feet again on the slimy logs. I shoved for the light with all the strength I possessed.

This time the river decided to let the boy come with me.

There was a brief moment of elation—*Fuck you, whirlpool*—then the current rearranged its grip and began to pull again. As if it had just been screwing around with me, making me think I'd won. I battled for the surface, kicking weakly, feeling myself losing momentum. The current was again spinning me, drawing me back down.

I released the child's body from the bear hug I'd enveloped it with but didn't let go all the way—instead I put my open lips on his shoulder, taking in a mouthful of shirt and hair and flesh. *It's like a street fight,* I told myself as I bit down as hard as I could, *you do what you have to do*. Even if it's biting a kid on the neck.

Shooting out my arms, I stroked once, twice, three times, before feeling the body start to tear out of my mouth. I wrapped my arms around him again, thinking maybe those three strokes had freed me and my burden from the worst of the whirlpool's grasp. But when I looked up, the light above was growing smaller instead of larger as the blackness swelled over my vision.

In a second I was totally blind. Even the pinprick of light had disappeared. Some instinct urged me to inhale, to breathe the oxygen in the water—*H_2O, after all, is one-third oxygen, right? You can do it.* The urge was almost overwhelming. I fought it, believing it would be the final gasp of a dead man. The acceptance of water into my lungs would be the acceptance of an irreversible fate.

But I wasn't deaf. I could hear voices, not just the hollow snapping and popping and cracking sounds of the river. Only these weren't the voices I expected to hear when this moment finally came. I'd always thought that if death was anything but a ground fall on a slack rope, that the voices calling to me would be those of fallen climbing partners. But they wouldn't be greeting me with yells and screams. They'd been my friends, after all.

But what I heard were yells and screams. *Uh-oh*, I thought almost giddily. *Maybe there is another place.* A place where the inhabitants believe the lies that had given birth to the mocking nickname QuickDraw.

I opened my mouth and took the breath. I had no choice. There was no more resisting. The fight was over.

But suddenly it wasn't. Light bloomed before my eyes. And strength—a very little strength—returned to my cold-numbed and oxygen-starved muscles. I realized I was staring through a film of running water at the river and the canyon walls and the state trooper just ten feet away, waist-deep in the water.

I kicked and coughed and pulled desperately toward the cop, all the while clawing and clinging and even again biting the boy. Like he was some enormous goose a Labrador retriever had recovered. For a moment my perspective on death changed yet again. Maybe I'd been reincarnated as a big, wet Lab.

The trooper was yelling at me. He charged forward, into the deeper water, the river rising over his gun belt and then stomach. I was kicking rocks with my toes. Breaking toes, the way it felt. But the pain caused an agony that was strangely reassuring. It actually felt kind of good.

The trooper grabbed hold of my burden and together we wrestled it toward the beach. I was stumbling and thrashing and shaking, but I managed to keep my grip on an arm. A small, ridiculously thin arm. Looking down, I saw that I'd been biting the collar of a T-shirt as well as the muscle that runs from neck to shoulder.

There was no blood flowing from the wound.

With the added help of the punk rocker in the life jacket, we dragged the body onto the beach. The boy was so white he looked blue. Right away the punk rocker, who I now saw was not much more than a boy himself, dropped to his knees on the smooth stones next to the body.

While I vomited up a stomachful of water, he arced the boy's neck and put his mouth against the blue lips. He blew two quick breaths; the boy's chest rose and sank. I didn't bother checking for vitals, either. I just straddled the body and clasped my hands together over the boy's breastbone. I began pumping with numb arms that felt like wet noodles. Counting, "One, two, three," all the way to fifteen, then choking out, "Breathe!"

The punk rocker knew what he was doing. Instantly he locked lips with the boy again and held his fingers over the boy's nose. The fragile chest rose twice more beneath my hands.

We did this for two or three minutes, me still gasping and shaking as I pushed. Feeling a rib snap beneath my locked palms but not hesitating. I'd already bitten the kid like some kind of vampire, so why not break a few bones? You do what you have to do and you do it full bore—my dad's first rule. For some reason the trooper kept looking out across the river with a strange expression on his face, as if he might be seeing things. I stole a quick glance in that direction, wondering where Mungo had gotten to.

"Breathe," I again ordered the punk in the life jacket.

He bent again over the lifeless shape, but was torn away before his lips could make a seal. It was the two boys. I had forgotten about them, although I'd been dimly aware of them screaming and crying in the background. Now they had attacked the man in the life jacket, tackling him, then trying to drag him away from the body, still crying and yelling and flailing with their fists.

"Get them off him!" I shouted to the tall trooper.

I lunged forward to pinch the small, cold nose and press my own mouth against blue lips.

"They're the vic's cousins," the other trooper said, wading into the dogpile. As if that explained why they were attacking the punk rocker, and why he—a 250-pound cop—was having such a hard time pulling them off him.

I heaved backward and again began pumping away on the boy's chest. "Get-them-out-of-here!"

The tall trooper finally came out of his across-the-river stupor. The two patrolmen together subdued the boys by lying on top of them. The boys were still yelling and fighting, but the punk rocker was back in position, kneeling over the boy's head. *One, two, three, four, five,* I counted.

"I'm sorry," he was muttering between commands to *breathe!* "I'm so sorry," he whispered to the boy's face.

"What do we do with them?" one of the troopers asked.

"Cuff-'em-shoot-'em-I-don't-care," I said as I counted out my compressions. "*Breathe!* Just get them the fuck out of here!"

four

I think I've treated you before," the paramedic said as she handed me a rough wool blanket.

I wrapped it around my torso. The nausea and adrenaline were beginning to wear off. I finally realized how cold I was, how hard I was shivering, even with the afternoon sun so hot in my hair. I had to keep my jaw clenched to stop my teeth from chattering. My bare feet were starting to ache on the beach's smooth stones.

"Let me get your temperature."

She tried to stick something in my ear. I pulled away. "I'm all right."

"C'mon. You could be hypothermic."

I opened the blanket to show her the goose bumps on my chest. "If I was, I wouldn't be shivering like this. Okay?"

She frowned, but her eyes were smiling. "I *have* treated you before. Or tried to. Last year, at that mine where those people died. You were bleeding from a scalp wound. You wouldn't let me help you then, either."

"I think you're confused," I said, shaking my head.

But I knew she wasn't. And I'd liked her then, just as I liked her now. Big hair, makeup, strong-looking body and all. She was probably only a few years younger than me, in her mid to late twenties, but not my type. I always seemed to go for thin, natural women, and I always liked them best when their hair was wild and their features unadorned. But, even so, I really liked the humor and compassion in this woman's eyes. Someone who did a job like hers and still had all that light had to be something special. Of course, I might not like her so much if I hadn't won my two battles with her, now and that other time.

I wondered why death, or near death, always made me horny. It was only minutes earlier that I'd been helping to lift a stretcher bearing the boy's unmoving form up to the top of the giant boulder. Now the ambulance's siren squawked twice. The driver leaned out the window and yelled, "Jo!"

"Gotta go," she said. "I'll get you next time!"

She had to scramble up the slope to the top of the rock, not far from where the modified van with its flashing lights waited impatiently for her. It was in the middle of the highway, blocking it. Other vehicles were backed up on both sides of the highway.

The ambulance took off with a wail as she dove in. The tall trooper was trying to deal with all the people who were getting out of their vehicles and wanting to know what was going on. The beefier trooper had finally managed to herd the two other boys into the back of a patrol car, where they were still screeching like cats. I watched until I saw another police car, this one a county cruiser, pull up.

The punk rocker in the orange life jacket was sitting on the stones. The girl from the raft, which had finally beached, was crouched over him, her arms wrapping him protectively from behind. He looked pretty out of it. He was just staring at a random place on the ground a few feet in front of him. The girl was crying with her face pressed into the side of his neck.

I gingerly picked my way across the rocks to them and squatted down so that I could get my bare feet on the corners of the blanket. The guy seemed to have a hard time focusing on me.

"You okay?" I asked.

He nodded, but didn't look as if he was entirely sure.

"You did a good job with the CPR," I told him, meaning it. He hadn't panicked or forgotten how to perform. "Where'd you learn to do that?"

"I, uh, took a class."

"Must have had a good teacher. Where was that?"

"New York. Back in high school."

He was taking his time answering my questions. It was like talking to someone who just couldn't keep their thoughts together, not like someone who was being deliberately evasive, I decided.

"The kid, uh, did they say if he's going to be all right?" he asked after another long pause.

"No way to know yet. The cold water sometimes can help. His age, too. Children have something called a mammalian diving reflex, same as seals. It lowers their heart rate and shunts blood to the brain. For some reason adults lose the ability. Anyway, because of it, kids stand a better chance of surviving a prolonged submersion."

They both looked at me like I was speaking Greek.

So I just said, "What's your name?"

He licked his lips, probably tasting the same wet river breath that I was. Feeling the touch of those cold lips.

"Jonah. Jonah Strasburg."

"Mine's Antonio Burns. Call me Anton."

I stuck out my hand and, after a moment, he shook it limply. The tattoos on his arm seemed to be Chinese symbols. I thought I recognized one that my ex-fiancée, Rebecca, had on a framed scroll. It was supposed to mean *harmony.*

"Where are you from, Jonah?"

"New York. The city. We're, uh, out here on vacation. This is my girlfriend, Mattie Freda."

"Hi, Mattie. So what do you guys do when you're not vacationing?"

She answered, her voice a little choked by her tears. "I'm in school. At Columbia. He's a musician."

That explained Jonah's spiky hair, the tattoos, and the pierced eyebrow. And she looked like a clubber, too, with her black dye job and pointed bangs. She was wearing a sleeveless T-shirt but didn't have any tattoos that I could see.

"Rock and roll?" I asked Jonah.

"It's like that. But faster."

There was a lot of noise coming from the road. I turned and looked. People were moving around up there, on top of the hill where the highway veered closest to the river. Some of them seemed pretty angry. They were shouting things, both at the cops and down toward us. Locals, not tourists, judging by their manner of dress and the type of vehicles they were climbing out of. But a few tourists, too, in motor homes on their way to Yellowstone and the Tetons. They all wanted to know what was going on and the cops were apparently telling them something.

I wanted to know, too.

"You sure you're all right, Jonah?" I asked.

He'd been following my gaze up the hill. And now, as he met my eyes again, his pale skin was turning a greenish shade, and his eyes were again losing their focus.

"Hey. You okay?"

Jonah closed his eyes and nodded.

I felt a little lousy, interrogating him like this. But somebody needed to get a voluntary statement out of him, and I figured I could do it better than either of the state troopers. They did traffic violations, accidents, drunk drivers, stuff like that. DCI did mostly drugs, but serious stuff, too. Besides, I'd once been very good at this. Likability had once been my greatest asset as a cop. It enabled suspects to tell me things they wouldn't even tell their own lawyers, and it got me deep inside everything from outlaw biker gangs to hippie dope rings. It was a skill that came, I supposed, from having grown up as a military brat, a different school on a different base each year, and an urgent need to fit in.

"Can you look at me, Jonah?"

He opened his eyes.

"Tell me what happened."

Jonah licked his lips.

"We were on the river. Rafting. With a guide we hired."

"Okay, good." I gestured out toward the river. "Tell me what happened here."

Jonah cleared his throat and swallowed another breath. It looked like just breathing was a conscious act for him. This guy was really out of it.

"We came through those rapids. Upstream. You can hear them. They were, uh, really wild, and I guess I was pretty shook-up. First time I'd ever done something like that. Rafting, I mean. We came into this slow section here and those kids were on top of the cliff. We waved at them."

Mattie's teary face lifted off his neck. It was an angular face with a hawk's nose, but probably quite pretty without the blur of mascara beneath red-rimmed eyes.

She whispered, "They started throwing rocks at us."

Still squatting, I touched a finger to my lips. "Let Jonah tell me."

"Yeah, they started throwing rocks at us," he said. "I don't think they were trying to hit us. Not at first, anyway. They were just splashing us."

"Did you know them?"

"No. I'd never seen them before."

"You sure?"

"Yeah. We just got into town yesterday."

"Go on."

"Well, the guide, Pete, he yelled for them to cut it out. They didn't. They just laughed. Called us some names. Then, as we were going under the cliff, one rock almost hit Mattie."

He paused for a long time.

"Okay. What happened next?" I prodded.

"Before I knew what I was doing, I'd gotten out of the raft."

"We told him to get back in," Mattie whispered. I supposed she meant her and the guide. He was now talking to one of the troopers up on the hill.

I frowned at her and touched a finger to my lips again. "Go on, Jonah."

"I thought I could scare them. I tried to get back in. But I slipped, and the raft was moving away. Pete had put down the oars, I guess, now that we were in this slow part. The raft drifted farther away. There was nowhere to go but onto the beach. But the kids up above it were still yelling stuff and throwing rocks."

"So you went up there?"

"Hey, man, I couldn't just stand on this beach and be a target."

He was striving to sound defensive, but it came off hollow. His words started coming faster.

"I scrambled up the slope there. I honestly thought they'd run when they saw me coming. They were just kids."

The slope was one side of the big boulder, and it topped out onto a flat area. I'd run up that way, helping to carry the stretcher up the steep incline to where they could roll it toward the ambulance on the road. Although the ground was granite, some spindly pine trees grew in clumps out of the crack in the rock. There'd been three bikes in a heap. In my head I could see where the overhanging edge fell away into the river. It was maybe fifteen or twenty feet straight down. Into the deceptively calm waters that concealed the sink.

"But they were still there?"

"Yeah."

Jonah, talking even faster, told me the basic facts.

five

Jonah crested the slope. The three boys were just standing there. All dressed in jeans and T-shirts, some bicycles lying nearby. One of them was grinning. The grinner was bigger and older-looking, so Jonah spoke to him.

"Hey, you brats. What the hell do you think you're doing? You could kill someone, throwing shit like that!"

He expected to intimidate them with his tone, his age, and his tattoos. The tattoos were particularly impressive, running down both arms. When they were exposed in the summertime, people on the street would give him nervous sidelong glances even though Jonah was anything but aggressive. They were just for show, part of his image. But the bright orange life vest he was still wearing also made him feel a little ridiculous.

Maybe the kids were able to sense it in him. The niceness, the foreignness, because the fat kid snickered.

In a surprisingly deep voice he asked, "Where you from, man?"

A memory of some obnoxious late-night TV commercial for Tabasco sauce flitted through his mind and stopped him from answering "New York City."

What was wrong with these kids? They weren't running. They weren't cowering. And they certainly weren't apologizing. Jonah reached into his pocket and took out the Ziploc bag he'd put his pen and notebook in. He kept them with him everywhere for writing down lyrics.

"I want your names," he demanded. It was all he could think of to say.

This made the fat boy laugh. As soon as he started hooting, the two other boys started to laugh, too. Theirs were sneering laughs, half giggles and half grimaces full of sharp teeth.

"You gonna call our daddies?" the fat boy mocked.

Yeah. That was exactly what he intended to do. Suddenly it didn't seem like such an impressive threat. While Jonah stood there dumb, considering, the fat boy spoke again.

"Hey, Cody, why don't you whack this yuppie dipshit with a stick?"

A yuppie? Me? Jonah thought.

And while Jonah stood there, dumber than ever, one of the kids—the littlest, who couldn't be more than ten and couldn't weigh more than a hundred pounds—picked up a long stick. The little guy snapped off a few of the branches until he held a thin piece of wood that was maybe three feet long. Jonah was almost fascinated. He'd never seen children this outrageously cocky. He sort of admired them—it really was a little bit awesome. He almost couldn't believe this was happening. He realized he was half smiling, acting amused rather than intimidated.

Then the stick swatted him in the ear.

"Hey!" he'd yelled, jumping backward. The little brat had whacked him! He touched his ear. His fingertips came away with a smear of blood. Looking at the kid, he tried to think of what to say, what to do. The kid was grinning nervously. Fat Boy was hooting louder than ever.

"Hit him again! Whack the tourist piece of shit!"

The kid stepped forward and swung again.

Jonah grabbed the stick. It was so thin and brittle-looking that he tried to twist it, to break it. But it was too green to break. And the brat hung on—Jonah wasn't able to twist it out of his grasp.

The kid stepped back and tugged. Jonah held on. The little brat tugged harder, leaning back with all of his insignificant weight. The edge was just a couple of feet behind him. Below that was twenty feet of space and then the water. Fat Boy was howling with laughter. Jonah wanted to let go just so he could punch Fat Boy in the face. But he didn't let go. He couldn't do that. No, he couldn't hit a kid, no matter how obnoxious he was.

He remembered the way the cliff overhung all the way down to the still water. He remembered the deep pool beneath the cliff. That's what these brats needed, he thought with sudden inspiration. A serious soaking. A cold, wet lesson. Beyond the kid, in the river, he could see Mattie and Pete rowing upstream toward the beach.

The kid tugged again, really putting what little weight he had into it. Jonah smiled and let go, even giving it a little push. The brat staggered back two steps and tried to regain his balance. With his arms windmilling, the stick waving frantically in the air, he glanced over his shoulder and the uneasy snarl left his face. Then slowly, very slowly, he began to topple over the edge.

"Ha!" Jonah had yelled in triumph. "Who's next, you little shitheads?"

"He can't swim!" the smaller boy yelled.

"What happened next?" I asked.

"I didn't know . . . I didn't think . . ."

The tall trooper began to slide down the slope toward us, now that other cops—county guys—had shown up to handle the crowd. I still needed to get his name. The guide's—Pete's—last name, too. And those of the other two kids, the cousins. Jonah was staring out over the river, so I made a little motion with my hand for the trooper to hang back. He caught it, but so did Mattie. She turned and looked up at the trooper.

"What did you think would happen when you pushed him with the stick?" I asked.

It was a critical question. Intent was everything here.

"I didn't really push . . . just a little, when I let go . . . I didn't think . . ."

Yeah, he didn't think. It was a stupid thing to do, to push a kid into the river. He didn't know the depth or any hazards that might be below—like a fucking sink. I could still feel its frigid grasp. My already-shivering body flinched, trying to shake it off, while Jonah searched for words.

"Who are you?" Mattie suddenly demanded.

She wasn't crying anymore. Her gray irises were bright and sharp.

"My name's Antonio Burns, like I told you," I said. "Jonah, tell me—"

"No, who *the fuck* are you?"

"I'm a special agent with Wyoming's Division of Criminal Investigation."

I saw her shiver now. Then she said into Jonah's ear, "Don't talk to him anymore. Don't say anything."

Jonah took a couple of deep breaths, looking like he was thinking, or trying to think.

Then he said, "Look, Officer, or Agent, or whatever you're called. It was an accident. Jesus Christ. I thought he was just going to get wet, you know? I didn't know he couldn't swim."

I believed him, for the most part. But God, it was a stupid thing to do, especially in hindsight. And Jonah, tats and all, really didn't seem like such a stupid guy. I had to wonder, what would I have done in that situation? What if some brat had nearly brained Rebecca with a rock? I wanted to ask again what he had expected to happen, and how angry had he been, but the voluntary part of the interrogation was over. If I wanted more, now that he knew he was being interrogated, I'd have to read him his rights. And with the people yelling from up on the hill, it wasn't the place or time.

"Jonah, I need you to stand up."

"What?"

"I'm sorry. But I need you to stand up," I repeated.

Jonah tried to push off the ground, but his legs crumpled, like they wouldn't support him. Mattie stood with him and helped hold him up.

"Now turn around, please."

"What?"

The first time he'd sounded puzzled. Now he sounded alarmed. He was finally getting it.

"What are you doing?" Mattie demanded. "What do you think you're doing?"

I glanced up at the tall trooper and gave him a nod. He clattered over the stones toward us.

As gently as I could, I put a hand on the life jacket and pushed Jonah around. I ran my hand down his arm and held the wrist out for the trooper. He ratcheted a handcuff onto it. Mattie grabbed Jonah's free arm and tried to pull him away from us.

"Step back, Mattie," I said.

"No!" she yelled. "What are you doing? It was an accident! A goddamn accident!"

"Step back. Accident or not, he's got to go to the sheriff's office. If you want to help him, then please don't interfere."

I stuck out an arm and put my palm to the upper part of her chest, pushing her away. She leapt back as if I'd tried to grope her. The trooper managed to get Jonah's other wrist into the handcuff. The young man's chin fell onto his chest—he wasn't resisting at all. Mattie backed off but was still yelling.

I said to the trooper, "Take him to the sheriff's for me. I've got to get my stuff on the other side of the river. It'll take me about an hour to get into town. Don't talk to him. Don't let anyone talk to him until I get there."

He nodded, then said, "Be careful over there. I thought I saw something moving around in the trees where you dumped your stuff. Could be a wolf or a bear."

I smiled, but I didn't feel like smiling. I was feeling pretty bad. This sucked. But I was determined to do this by the book. I was going to be a good cop. I could hear my boss saying, *Just do your damn job—nothing more!*

"It's probably my dog. *You* be careful up there. It looks like some of those people are getting pretty riled up. We don't want a lynching."

six

Although I was careful to keep to the shallows and far away from the deep pool beneath the boulder, picking my way across the river was still a little scary. The rocks were slippery with algae, and the proximity of the sink made me extra cautious. I nearly fell down once when I kicked something that squirmed; the dorsal fin of a goosed trout shot upstream like a torpedo. It was with relief that I crawled up the far bank, away from all that had gone on in the river and what was still happening on the other side.

Mungo had stayed just where I'd commanded her to. I told her that she was a very good wolf. She responded by dancing around on her oversize feet, shimmying with pleasure at the compliment. She very nearly knocked me back off the bank. Then she warmed my legs by licking them with her sandpaper tongue as I tried to put on my shoes.

It's hard to believe that people are afraid of wolves. Sure, it's true they can and sometimes will take down unwatched livestock, but they're no threat to humans. Unless it's domesticated like

Mungo, a wolf will always flee the far more dangerous two-legged predators or, if captured, usually just cower in abject submission. Yet some people in Wyoming still believe in fairy tales. They see wolves in Grandma's bed, coaxing children close so they can gobble them up. For this reason, even owning a dog tainted with wolf's blood is illegal in most states, including my own.

But I also knew that something about Mungo scared people. She might pass for a dog with the bandanna, but the predator was just a little too obvious with a closer look. She generally avoided strangers, but when confronted she would spread her long legs, lower her head, and watch the stranger's every move through flat yellow eyes.

The state's residents had taken to the federal reintroduction of wild wolves about as well as they would have if the government were sequestering soldiers in their homes. Some openly called for armed revolt. Now that the reintroduction had been a success, and the Feds were considering delisting the animals as an endangered species, Wyoming legislators had the opportunity to come up with their own plan for regulating the few packs in the state. Their official proposal: shoot on sight. And they were outraged when the plan was rejected.

I tried one more time to get Mungo to carry the floppy disk, but she wasn't biting.

For me, there was nothing that spoke about the freedom and wildness of Wyoming as eloquently as hearing a pack calling to one another under a full moon. It was something I'd only heard once, when I spent a week skiing alone through the nearby Absaroka Mountains, but it had stayed with me. I'd told Rebecca about it just as she was writing a story for the *Denver Post* about a wildlife refuge for abused animals. The refuge was about to be shut down by timorous neighbors. She'd adopted Mungo, without asking for my approval, and given her to me as a gift. *My wild things,* she'd called us fondly in better days.

Now I was a cop in disguise, partnered to a wolf in disguise.

Hiking out, we ignored the meth lab that was surely nearby.

Ignored it just as my office would when I reported it. Right now, anyway, I was more interested in a possible crime that was far different from anything I'd ever investigated. Unlike drugs and murder, there were some potentially intriguing moral implications. Thinking about such things might be refreshing; it might even renew my faith in the law. And God knows I needed that.

When Mungo and I rolled into town an hour later, I parked away from the main street where the sheriff's office was located. Instead I stopped the Pig down by the river, in some dirt beneath a cottonwood tree. I cracked all the windows for Mungo and checked to be sure that all one could see through the wrinkled tint on the glass was a big dog shape inside and a gray muzzle poking through the opening. I walked a few blocks to the station.

There were three grim-faced deputies standing silently in the lobby. I showed my creds to the cop at the desk.

"So you're Burns," the deputy said.

The others exchanged looks and began to sidle over.

"Where is he?" I asked, acting in a hurry.

I was given directions down a hall to an interview room. The cop looked like he wanted to say something else. The others looked like they wanted to listen.

"Listen, Burns—"

"Anybody heard from the hospital?" I interrupted.

"Few minutes ago. The kid's name was Cody Wallis. A lot of people know him, a lot more know his dad. Anyway, he was declared dead on arrival. They never got any vitals at all."

I nodded quickly and headed down the hall. The boy's river breath was in my mouth, my hands feeling the crunch of the small bones in his chest. *Shit,* I thought. *What about the mammalian diving reflex? Why didn't I get hold of him on my first try? Why did I chicken out and go for the surface?*

It was a small room, like a walk-in closet, with the standard one-way mirror on a wall. Jonah was sitting in a plastic chair at the scarred desk, his head on his arms. His back was to me. They'd taken off the orange life jacket. Now he wore just a sleeveless black T-shirt with a white picture of a snarling rottweiler on it. Beneath it was the word PURGATORY.

He lifted his head when I came around the desk and sat down on the other side. His eyes were still spacey, his expression weary, and his fingertips were blackened from the fingerprinting. I didn't say anything. I was still digesting the news and wondering how I should deal with it.

"Is he all right?" Jonah finally asked.

Should I come on hard or soft?

"No. He died." Soft, I'd decided. Not *No, you killed him.*

But I watched his eyes constrict as if my fist were coming at his face. Then they grew bleary. And his face grew even paler, if that was possible.

"Oh shit . . . oh shit," he moaned.

"You did what you could to make it right," I told him. "You and I worked on him for more than fifteen minutes. The paramedics did all they could, the people at the hospital did, too. But it didn't do any good. We tried, though. Everybody tried."

"Oh shit . . . that little kid . . . I didn't mean . . . I didn't mean . . . I just wanted . . ."

I let him ramble on for a few minutes, listening and gauging his sincerity. I'd seen a lot of people faking remorse, but I wasn't getting any bent signals from him.

"Where's Mattie?" he finally asked. The tears were beginning to roll down his cheeks.

"I don't know."

I hadn't seen her since I'd pushed her away at the river. I hadn't thought about how she'd get here, or back to wherever they were staying. I felt a little bad about that, too.

"Can you take me to her? I think I need to lie down. I need to go back to the motel."

"Listen, Jonah. I'm sorry, but you can't go anywhere for a while. The county attorney's going to have to be notified, and then he's going to have to decide if he wants to file any charges. You're going to need to stay here. For the night, at least."

"Just let me see Mattie."

His face was screwing up and his lips were quivering. No, he wasn't faking it.

"I'm sorry. You can't right now. But I need to talk to her in a little bit. I'll find her. Don't worry. I'll see if she has a message for you. If she does, and if it's okay with the county attorney, I'll bring it to you."

I didn't leave. And I didn't read him his rights and start asking him questions. I just couldn't. My plan had veered off course. It was quiet except for Jonah, who seemed to be having a hard time breathing. It took a while, but he finally started to calm down.

"What could they charge me with?"

I didn't want to say the word *manslaughter,* or even the somewhat gentler phrase *criminally negligent homicide,* and set him off again, so I just shrugged.

"I don't know. What's that mean on your shirt, 'Purgatory'?"

He looked down at his shirt. The front was plain black except for a smaller picture of the rottweiler, a reproduction of the one on the shirt's back.

"It's the name of my band. Actually, it's the name of the guitarist's dog—Purgy. That's what we named the band."

"What kind of music?"

"Speeded-up Clash and the Dead and stuff like that. A lot of it original, but a lot of covers, too."

"You do 'Mexicali Blues'?"

"Uh, yeah." Then he got it and gave me a wan smile. "All that jailhouse stuff. 'Friend of the Devil,' 'I Shot the Sheriff,' 'I Fought the Law.' And here I am." He closed his red eyes and took some very deep breaths.

After a minute he added, "Fuck. That poor kid."

"Have you ever been arrested before?"

"No. Just an open-container citation when I was twenty. And a jaywalking ticket a few months ago."

I believed him. But we'd find out soon enough if he was lying. "You guys any good? Purgatory?"

"We played at the 9/11 memorial for cops and firefighters, were on national TV for a few seconds. Mostly just clubs in the city, though. We've opened for a few big names."

I could see that the tough look—the hair, the tattoos, the eyebrow ring—was just a look. He wasn't tough or mean. It was meant to be cool, nothing else. It was a uniform, in a way. Like the uniforms the two grim-faced cops were wearing when they came in a minute later to take him away.

Later on I would learn about his introduction to the county jail.

The next thing Jonah was aware of was a different voice speaking close to his ear.

"Stop. I want you to see something."

Jonah was jerked to a stop. He hadn't even realized that he'd been walking. It took an effort to lift his head and see where he was being led. His hands were still cuffed behind his back and a firm hand gripped each arm. There was a man on one side, a woman on the other, both of them dressed in powder-blue uniforms. They were in some kind of hallway, like what you'd find in the basement of a large building. Windowless, all concrete and steel.

It was the woman who had spoken.

Jonah turned to her and tried to focus.

Her face was young, a little heavy, and he could see that it might even be pretty if it were smiling at him. But the lips were pressed together and the blue eyes were narrow. Everything about it was rigid.

"Look in there," she ordered him.

Jonah didn't move.

She let go of his arm and stepped out of his vision, moving behind him. Then her hands grasped the sides of his head. She turned it so that he was facing one side of the hallway.

It wasn't a wall, but it was as unmoving as a wall. There were at least twenty faces peering out at him from between rectangles of steel bars. A kaleidoscope of them—high and low, left and right, white and brown—all staring out like gargoyles.

Staring at him.

Jonah, who had been booed off a stage more than once, had never had an audience like this. He'd never seen such hate. Never, in his worst stage nightmare, had he imagined it directed at him. But at least one of them was smiling. A big guy—some kind of biker look—with a full blond beard framed by tattooed fists on the bars. Jonah sought solace in the grin, returning an almost apologetic smile, before he saw that the grin directed at him was nothing close to friendly.

"That's our jail, Mr. Strasburg," the young woman said matter-of-factly, still holding his head in her hands. "In there. With these gentlemen. That's where you're going to be staying tonight."

Although Jonah couldn't move his head, he let his vision drop to the cement floor.

Then, in a louder voice, she called out, "You guys got room in there for a tourist who killed a local kid?"

No one answered.

"You've heard what they do to child-molesters in jail?" the woman continued in a softer voice. "Just imagine what they do to child-killers."

seven

I stayed in the interview room after he'd been hauled out. I squared the notepad in front of me, picked up my pen, then just stared down at the paper. There was really nothing to add. There was nothing I *could* add. Unlike at the river, when Jonah hadn't even initially known that I was a cop, here he had pretty obviously been in custody. Since I hadn't had the heart to Mirandize him, any statements or acknowledgment of guilt he'd made would be inadmissible in court.

If it came to that.

I hoped it wouldn't. But I'd seen the outrage on the stiff faces of the jail deputies when they'd led Jonah away, and remembered the shouts of the onlookers at the river. It may have been more or less an accident, but that didn't mean no one would pay for it. A boy had died, after all. Someone would have to pay. Whether the real cause was bad luck or stupidity or even the boy's own partial culpability, the community would demand retribution from somebody.

Still, if it were permitted, what I would have liked to write on the pad was that I kind of liked Jonah. Or at least I felt sorry for him. Remorse is rare in this business. True remorse, that is. Not the usual *I shouldn't have cooked my shit so close to the road*, or *I shouldn't have sold to that narc*, or even *I should have whacked that fucking narc when I had the chance.* I thought Jonah truly regretted pushing the boy into the river. Not just because it had gotten him arrested, but simply because it had led to the boy's death.

I didn't write any of that. I was still determined to be a good cop, nothing more. To just do my job.

Blowing out a breath and standing, I smoothed the horns of my hair in the two-way mirror before heading out into the hall. I had to grin at my reflection. *You're getting soft, Ant.* No one would believe it. I was aware that the image I could see was very different from what others had been seeing lately.

I began to wander through the small building, seeing few signs of life on the upper floor of the sheriff's department. No one challenged what a guy dressed in sketchy hippie clothes—looking like a climbing bum living out of his truck, which was more than a little true—was doing in this protected domain. I guessed they were all in the lobby, waiting for the lynch mob to form. I trotted downstairs.

The radio/911 operator was at her station. She didn't notice me—she was too busy with a paperback novel. No one else was around. Not even the three deputies who'd eyeballed me when I first came in. I looked out the windows, but the street was empty except for some tourists idling outside the gift shop and the restaurant next door to it.

Walking deeper into the complex, I pushed through a swinging door and discovered where everyone was hiding. It was a large conference room that doubled as a break room, and everyone apparently was on break. No one said *Boo!* when I walked in, but they all looked at me as if I had.

Still no one challenged me. I supposed they all knew me. I was somewhat famous—infamous, actually—in Wyoming law-enforcement circles. It was obvious from the sudden silence that they'd been talking about me.

"Hey," I said, giving them my best smile.

Once it had been my likability, my coolness, that was my best professional asset. But, judging from the faces and the continuing silence, I'd definitely lost it. I focused in on the one face I recognized—the tall state trooper from the river.

"Can I talk to you for a minute, Trooper?"

"Sure. Here or somewhere else?"

"Somewhere else."

I beckoned him out into the hallway. No one else moved or spoke. It was like time had frozen for everyone but the two of us. He followed me down the hall, out of earshot from the room.

"What's your name?" I asked.

"Seth McFarland."

"I guess you know mine."

The trooper chuckled. "Yeah, I know who you are. Sorry about calling you that other thing in the river. I didn't know it wasn't a compliment. A lot of guys would be flattered."

I felt myself scowl. And my blood grew a couple of degrees warmer. A head popped out of the doorway. I seared it with a stare and it quickly withdrew.

"The guy who made it up, this reporter in Cheyenne—he didn't mean it as a compliment."

"Yeah, I heard that, too. Some of those guys in there were just talking about that. A few seem to think you're some kind of badass, and others think you might be dirty."

I knew what the trooper just said was true—I'd been hearing the same shit for three years now—but what I couldn't believe was that this near rookie had the audacity to say it directly to me. He couldn't be much more than twenty years old. Either he was mocking me, or he was cocky as hell.

Then he continued, "I really don't care which it is. What you did in the river—diving down there—holy shit. That was about the craziest thing I've ever seen."

Instead of responding, I reached into my pocket and pulled

out the notebook. I tore off the pages where I'd written everything Jonah had said to me at the river. I pushed them into Trooper McFarland's hand.

"For what it's worth, I think it was an accident."

I turned to walk away.

It had been interesting, and I'd certainly gotten some stimulation out of it, but I realized it wouldn't be my case. I was damaged goods.

"Wait a minute," McFarland called. "What are you giving this to me for? State patrol doesn't do this kind of stuff."

I stopped and turned back.

"Neither do I. I'd appreciate it if you'd just add my notes to the report you write up for the sheriff here. I've got to get going."

"Hey, listen. I already talked to the sheriff about twenty minutes ago, and he said he's going to be recusing himself. He doesn't want any part of this thing. Said he's a second cousin to the victim, or something like that. He's already called your office to ask that they pick it up. I bet they'll be calling you any minute."

The state's Division of Criminal Investigation handles mostly drug crimes. But they often step in when there is a conflict of interest or simply the appearance of one—something that is pretty common in Wyoming's small, inbred towns.

Shit.

For a long time I'd been wanting my old responsibilities back, but this was not the kind of case I wanted to be in charge of anymore. This wasn't one where you do everything you can to put the bad guys away for as long as possible. No, I was beginning to realize that this was more the kind of case where any outcome will be a bad one. If no charges were filed, then the community would choose another scapegoat—most likely me or the county attorney. If charges were filed and a conviction was achieved, then I'd have nothing to look forward to but the immense satisfaction of putting an arguably innocent man in jail.

Putting asses behind bars is a piece of cake, I used to joke with my liberal climbing buddies in the days before my brother became a regular behind bars. *It's putting the innocent in prison that's the real challenge.*

But I didn't let myself get too worried. There was no way the office would put me in charge of this mess.

Then my cell phone rang. The screen said the caller's number was blocked.

"What?"

"QuickDraw," said a deep, raspy voice. "I heard you got a little wet today."

It was my boss, Ross McGee—the only man I willingly allowed to call me that. He'd once been my mentor, protector, and best friend. But since a year ago, when things went so bad with the big lab bust in an abandoned potash mine and the disappearance of a certain Mexican drug lord, McGee had abruptly ended all of those relationships. He'd suspected me of no longer worshiping at the same altar of justice where he'd spent thirty years communing. He'd also been all too glad to end another relationship to me—he was my ex-fiancée's godfather.

"The boy died, Ross."

"So I heard," McGee said without a lot of sympathy or compassion. But the man had done five tours in Vietnam before becoming a prosecutor and trying capital cases, so I tried not to hold it against him. But what he said next I had a harder time forgiving.

"You're about to get a lot wetter. The criminal investigation is all yours, QuickDraw. I'm turning you loose, bringing you back from the wilderness. Try not to fuck it up."

"Thanks a lot, Ross."

He responded with a hoarse bark of laughter. "Don't say I never did you any favors." He grunted another chuckle, then added in a quiet growl, "This is your last chance, *amigo*. You screw it up and you're done. And I don't just mean fired."

After a suitable pause, assessing his threat and what it meant, I asked, "Just what do you want me to do with it?"

"Do the family notification, then report to the county attorney for further orders. You know who that is? Your old scumbag partner, Luke Endow. They actually let him practice law after I canned his ass. You and him can catch up on old times. I bet you'll have a lot to talk about these days. Birds of a feather."

More hoarse laughter, then the line went dead.

Luke Endow. Now, there was another tangled relationship.

eight

Night had already fallen when I left the station, and I cursed it. I'd intended to climb a few rope-lengths or at least get in a little bouldering before bedding down. I'd wanted to watch the sunset from atop something high and see the darkness filling in the land below. My training schedule and my nightly calls to my daughter were the only steady things in my life. It had become a routine, one that I strove to rigorously maintain.

But now I had a job to do. A shitty job, but a real one for the first time in a year.

The hospital admissions desk gave me the name and address of the deceased. First name Cody, surname Wallis, born only ten years ago—in the 1990s, for God's sake. It seemed impossible for someone already dead to be that young. The address was a number on a county road. A ranch or, more likely, a subdivided "ranchette." Despite the state's hype, there were few real ranches left in Wyoming.

Mungo stood on the armrest between the front seats and studied a well-used Wyoming atlas with me. She was drooling, as well as blocking the light from the dome lamp. Normally we'd be eating dinner at about this time and she was probably a little annoyed. The county road was a place well outside of town, near the foothills of the Absaroka range. Twenty minutes, at least—Mungo was going to have to suffer with me. I elbowed her into the backseat, wiped my slobbered forearm on my shorts, and headed for the hills.

A year before, I'd had to tell my parents that my only brother, Roberto, was all but dead. Broken just about everywhere he could be broken, burst where things rupture instead of breaking, and in a coma he wasn't expected to recover from. That had been an ugly, ugly thing to have to say to your folks, but Mom and Dad had been expecting something of the sort for more than a decade. What made it infinitely worse, though, was that I also had to say that it was my fault. I'd let two FBI agents put my felonious, drug-addicted brother into a dangerous sting. I hadn't stopped Roberto even though I was aware of the price he might pay if things went wrong.

The memories didn't improve my mood. Imitating Mungo, I stuck my head out into the dark wind and tried to clear it.

We pulled off the highway at the county-road marker, then crunched on gravel for six miles before coming to a mailbox marked "Wallis." There'd been no other mailboxes, so I guessed this wasn't a McRanch or a ranchette after all. I stopped before turning onto the long driveway, remembering that I was still dressed like a climbing bum. Some of these ranching families could be pretty formal. Not that they expect anyone out here but young Mormon missionaries to show up in a suit, but torn khaki shorts were out. They screamed environmentalist or something, which wasn't fashionable around here. And I didn't want to be obnoxious while officially notifying them of the death of their son.

I hopped out of the truck, popped open the back, and pulled some clothes out of a crate. The back end of the Land Cruiser was packed with stuff—camping gear, climbing gear, skis and axes, like I'd robbed an outdoor store—as well as a crate of miscellaneous clothes. In it I found a pearl-button Western shirt that wasn't too wrinkled. The last time I'd worn it was while impersonating a Mexican drug mule. I buttoned it most of the way up this time, and didn't accessorize with the gold crucifix. I found the pair of black jeans that went with it, as well as the well-worn buckskin boots. Good enough, I figured. Not quite respectable, but at least not obviously offensive.

The long driveway was dirt but graded smooth. The house was maybe a half mile from the county road, set in a dip between two hilltops. On three sides around it—the west, south, and north—had been planted cottonwoods to block the wind. They must have been around for a long time, as the trees were more than fifty feet tall. The house was a two-story with wooden shingles and dark windows. Parked all around it were dusty sedans, SUVs, and beat-up ranch pickups.

Despite it being a rare windless evening, and despite all the vehicles, there was no one outside.

"*Paranda que,*" I told Mungo before locking her in.

Then I walked toward the silent house.

The house was as well maintained as the driveway. The porch was freshly painted and had been swept clean of Wyoming's ever-present grit. More than a dozen pairs of boots and tennis shoes were lined up outside the door.

I glanced at the picture window by the door but couldn't see much because the front room was dark and there was a lace curtain on the inside. I bent and peered in, wondering what had happened to all the owners of the boots and vehicles. I jumped back when I realized there was a face, just inches away through the glass, staring back at me.

It was one of the boys from the river. The older one, judging by his chubby face. The one who Jonah claimed had told now-dead Cody to "whack this yuppie dipshit with a stick."

"Hello," I called out.

He didn't respond.

I motioned toward the door, but the kid just kept on staring at me. I mimed turning a knob, opening the door. Nothing. Finally I knocked on the door. Hard. The kid's face suddenly did take on an expression—the brat snarled at me like a wild animal then disappeared.

I stood there for more than a minute before the door opened. The man standing on the other side was big—tall, wide, and beefy. His whole face seemed droopy, though, following the bow of his walrus mustache. I could see that his eyes were red. He didn't resemble the small, cold figure I'd done my best to breathe life back into, but I knew this had to be the dad. And I wanted to crawl away.

Do your goddamn job, Ant, I reminded myself.

He looked me over, then asked, "What can I do for you?"

"I'm sorry to bother you. Are you Mr. Wallis?"

The big man nodded.

"My name's Antonio Burns. I'm a special agent with the Wyoming Division of Criminal Investigation. I, uh, believe you already know what I'm here to tell you."

The man nodded again, the face drooping even more. "My boy's dead."

"Sir, I can't tell you how sorry I am."

Another dull nod. Behind him was a dark living room, a TV playing quietly, all but naked men and women incongruously cavorting on a beach. Some bullshit "reality" show. Try this for reality. Beyond the room was a hallway, and it led into a sunken family room. There was light in there, a murmur of many voices, and a few faces peering down the hall at me. That was where everyone was. Mourning. Grieving. The snarling boy, though, was gone.

"Sometime in the next few days I'd like to talk to you and your wife. I realize that now's not the time. I do, however, need to talk to the two boys who were with your son as soon as possible. I believe they're his cousins. Are they here?"

"I'll get them," the man finally said. "Their parents will want to talk to you, too."

"That's fine," I said. "I'll wait here. We can talk on the porch."

The man started for the other room but stopped.

"Are you the fellow who went into the river?"

Now it was my turn to just nod.

The man stood very still, looking past me, his red eyes slowly filling with liquid. The drooping face began to crumple.

"Thanks," he managed to say on his second try with a breaking voice. Then he turned and staggered like a blind drunk toward the other room.

It wasn't the boys that came toward me, though, but another man. He was squat and bald and short, maybe five-six to my five-ten. In Wyoming, a state that seems to breed big people, he made me feel tall.

He planted himself in the open doorway and grinned up at me.

"I can't fucking believe it. Antonio QuickDraw Burns. And looking good, too. What are you supposed to be tonight? A pimp?"

I looked at his rumpled suit and his wide, untidy tie.

"Hey, Luke. What are you supposed to be? A citizen?"

He came out, closing the door behind him.

"Didn't you hear?" he chortled happily. "I'm the goddamn county attorney. I run this town. I'm here commiserating with my constituents."

Luke dug in his coat pocket and came out with a pack of budget cigarettes and paper matches.

"These people actually elected you? There must be some really bad water in Badwater."

Wearing only his socks on his feet, the lawyer gingerly stepped down onto the dirt and waved for me to follow him as he lit up. We walked a little way away from the house and stood between some cars.

"Shit, I can't believe they're still letting you run around with a badge and a gun. But the old man was always in love with you. He must be, to let you get away with all that shit. The things I've heard about you . . ."

I had to laugh at the irony. Luke, my very first partner, had been fired for tiptoeing across the line. Some warrantless searches, some roughing up of suspects during interrogations, some "personal use" of contraband. My alleged transgressions were far more spectacular. But it was Luke who had gotten the boot. He made up for it, though, by going to law school, getting a degree, and becoming a criminal prosecutor. Now he got to order the investigators around.

He was aware of it, too. He grinned at me.

"Don't go thinking you're such a hotshot, Ant, now that you got this badass rep. I'm looking forward to having you as my whipping boy. It's gonna be like old times."

"You think this thing is going to get that involved?" I asked. What I meant was, *Do you really plan on charging Jonah?*

"It's a terrible thing," he said, shaking his head. But I thought I could also see a bit of the grin still on his face. He struck a match and fired up a bent cigarette. After huffing on it a couple of times, frowning deliberately, he added, "You never saw this. My wife hears I'm smoking again and she'll be all over my ass."

I waited to hear about her, or even be told her name, but he said nothing. So I tried again.

"Do you think it's going to take much time? From what I can tell so far, this whole thing was an accident."

He sucked deep on his cigarette again and blew it out hard. Then he held the cancer stick out from his body, as if trying to avoid the smoke.

"You think so, huh? Those people in that house, I represent them now. Right now they're thinking that Cody was murdered."

Murdered? That requires intent to kill or do great bodily harm, and I hadn't seen any evidence of an intent other than to give an obnoxious kid a soak in the river. But before I could express my skepticism, the front door opened then banged shut and a pair of feet hammered down the dark steps.

The man who was immediately in my face was short, too, by Wyoming standards. About my height, that is, and about the same age as Luke and Mr. Wallis. Unlike them both, this guy was rawhide thin. But his intensity made him seem bigger.

"You the cop who wanted to shoot my boys?" he demanded.

"Excuse me?"

"You heard me."

I looked to Luke. I expected him to at least roll his eyes, in order to indicate that this guy was a wacko, or to step in and say or do something if he wasn't. But my old partner was looking away. Like he was deep in thought or something. He wasn't smiling anymore.

"Sir, I don't know what you're talking about. I never told anybody to shoot anyone else."

"Now you're calling my boys liars," he said without raising his voice. His eyes, however, and the pressed whiteness of his lips, indicated that his temperature was rising to the boiling point. Luke was still doing nothing.

"Your boys . . . were they the ones at the river? The ones with Cody?"

"His cousins."

"Okay, now I know what you're talking about. Your boys, they were upset. While I was doing CPR they attacked the man who was assisting me—"

"Guy who killed Cody, right?"

"But I didn't know that at the time. All I knew was that he was trying to help. With the CPR. So when your sons attacked him, I asked the other officers present to restrain them—"

"Cuff 'em or shoot 'em, that right?"

I felt warmer remembering my own words—from shame, not anger.

"Yeah, that's probably what I said. But I didn't mean it literally. I was just trying to emphasize the need—"

He wasn't listening. He was looking at me with disgust and barely concealed violence.

I held up my hands in a gesture of surrender.

"Look, I'm very sorry. It was a dumb thing to say. But at the time I didn't know what was going on. Just that a boy—your nephew, I guess—was dying. And that I was trying to stop that from happening. I'll apologize to your sons if you like."

The man's temperature seemed to drop a few degrees. After staring at me for another few seconds, he blinked. Then he glanced back at the house.

"I'd appreciate it if you'd do that," he said. "Make it in a day or two. The kids are pretty shook up."

He spun and walked back toward the house. Going in, he managed to close the door softly.

My tension eased and I could once again hear the crickets in the night.

"You handled that well," Luke told me, his grin returning. "Given your rep these days, I half expected you to just shoot him."

I swallowed a *Fuck you, Luke,* and said instead, "When something like this happens, it's always easiest if you've got someone to blame. Or at least to vent on." I knew from firsthand experience. I'd once desperately felt the need, only I'd had a better target. Pushing away the thought, I asked, "What's his name? And his kids'?"

"Ed Mann. The boys who you threatened to shoot are Randall and Trey. You're going to talk to them, right?"

From Mann's appearance—very dissimilar to the far brawnier Mr. Wallis—and his different surname, I guessed that the boys were related through their mothers.

"I said I was. But, like he said, I'll wait a day or two."

"And you already interrogated the perp?"

Calling Jonah the perpetrator sounded a little strong, but I nodded to this, too.

"His name's Jonah Strasburg. He's a tourist, a musician from New York."

"Did he confess?" Luke asked, pausing for an answer before taking another hit.

"Well, he said he'd gotten in an argument with the kids after they'd thrown some rocks at the raft he was on. He confronted them. One of the kids—Cody—picked up a stick or something and swatted him. They had a kind of tug-of-war with the stick, and Strasburg let the kid fall into the water."

"Did he push him?"

"Yeah. He says he kind of pushed when he let go of the stick."

Luke took his hit and thought for a minute.

"Did he know the kid would fall into the water?"

"Yeah. He said he did. He thought the kid was just going to get wet, teach him a lesson, he said. He's feeling pretty lousy about it."

Luke smiled, the admission settling happily into his lawyer's brain. "Sure he is. He's going to feel a lot lousier, too. They're not going to make him too welcome in the jail. 'Spect he's going to have a rough night."

I thought about arguing, but I made myself keep my mouth shut. It wasn't my job to give a legal—much less an ethical—opinion. Not even to my old partner Luke, who'd once taken a bullet that was meant for me. Taken it in the ass, as a matter of fact. No, I just gathered the facts and evidence and presented them to the prosecutor. I wasn't qualified for anything else. Not according to the main office, and, lately, not according to myself. *Just do your job, Ant. Nothing more.*

Luke flipped his cigarette onto some dry grass beside the drive. Taking out a small cylinder from his pants pocket, he sprayed a blast of wintergreen Binaca into his mouth. Then he sprayed it on the shoulders of his suit.

"Be at the courthouse in the morning for Strasburg's appearance, okay? I want you with me every step of the way. The community needs to know we're taking this one seriously."

He gave my shoulder a whack, adding, "Glad to have you back on board, Ant. We're gonna have some fun."

Before heading back to Mungo and the Pig, I carefully ground out the orange ember in the grass. That family didn't need another tragedy that night.

nine

He's going to feel a lot lousier. The words kept intruding into my thoughts as I drove up the highway, higher into the mountains. *They're not going to make him too welcome in the jail.*

All I wanted to do was get to my camp. Stronger than the grind of hunger in my belly—a hunger Mungo shared and was expressing by repeatedly pressing her cold snout into the side of my neck—was the need to get away from all this. From the job. From the tragedy. From people, too. Even people I knew and liked.

I'd had more contact today than I'd had in weeks. Maybe months.

The place where I'd been camping was no more than twenty or thirty minutes away. It was in a seldom-visited canyon, beneath an overhanging granite wall that concealed what just might be the hardest wide-crack climb in the world—a crack I was determined to be the first to climb. The secret project had been a gift from an old friend, who had decided to give it up after more than a decade of torn muscles, ruptured ligaments, and flayed skin.

He'd refused to name it until it was climbed, but I was less modest. I named it before I even saw it. I called it Moriah, after my six-month-old daughter. Both Moriahs were proving to be the greatest challenges I had ever faced. I figured maybe if I could win the heart of one of them, I might learn the secret to the other.

We could be there in just a half hour, then I could cook a late dinner of rice and beans and tofu dogs over an aspen fire. I could drink a little wine. I could howl back at the coyotes. And, most important, I could make the phone call that was the culmination of my dedicated daily training.

But I turned the truck around. I wouldn't be able to sleep, much less phone my infant daughter, with Luke's veiled threats about Jonah's "welcome" echoing around in my skull. Mungo, who seemed to understand that dinner had been again postponed, let out a long, low groan.

"I'm sorry," I told her.

I reached back to pet her, but she shied away from my touch.

The men's jail in the sheriff's department basement was more than fifty years old and contained only six cells. The overflow—caused by an increase in population and the availability of cheap narcotics like meth—was housed in bunks around the central "rec" room. All of it was dark and quiet when I walked past in the corridor outside the bars.

Two deputies were in the monitoring station. One was the blonde woman who'd escorted Jonah from the interview room earlier, and the other was a gray-haired man with a buzz cut. They were playing chess and eating microwaved popcorn. The butter smell was so strong it made my stomach cramp. I had to wonder what it did to the inmates. To one side of the deputies was a table with a coffeemaker, a microwave, and a large TV. The screen showed an angle of the darkened rec room. The speakers crackled with only the occasional inmate's cough.

"Hey. This is that guy I was telling you about," the young

deputy, seeing me, said to her partner. "His name's Burns. He might not look like it, but he's with DCI."

"Hi," I said.

"I'm Sally, he's Tom."

Her voice was friendly. Actually, more than just a little friendly. And her grin was too wide. It set me on edge as much as the fact that I couldn't hear any snores coming from the rec room. Not when I passed, and not now, coming from the TV's speakers. Dope fiends, alcoholics, and inmates tend to snore. Loud. It was as odd as a good cop being pleased to meet me.

"Call me Anton."

"You the guy people been talking about?" Tom said, looking me over and frowning. "The famous narc?"

"I don't know about that."

"What's up, Anton?" Sally asked, saving me.

"I need to see your new guy. Jonah Strasburg."

"Uh, right *now*?"

"Yeah. I'm sorry, but—"

Buzz-cut Tom was shaking his head.

"No can do, Agent. We can't go in there tonight. It would wake everybody up. Most of these guys are good fellows, but they'll be grumpy as hell all day tomorrow if we stir them up in the middle of the night."

"Well, at least your shift will be over by then, right?" I tried a smile, but Tom didn't return it. "I need to see him now. Really. I just came from a meeting with Luke Endow, your county attorney."

I hoped that would spur them into action. It made it sound like the county attorney had requested my visit. But Sally just laughed.

"That perv? I'm surprised he didn't come with you. He never misses a chance to try and grab my ass."

"He was pretty busy. We were out at the Wallis place—the family of the boy who died. Luke is still out there."

The two deputies exchanged looks. Then Tom joined Sally in grinning slyly at me.

Tom said, "Oh yeah. I get it. You want to make sure Strasburg gets a little special treatment, eh?"

Sally laughed. "You don't have to worry about that, Anton. I think it's probably being taken care of."

I didn't like their smiles. I didn't like their words. They obviously believed the things that had been said about me, and they thought I would gladly be a party to whatever was going on. Neither of them looked like the kind of cops who would allow a young man to get hurt on their watch—Tom looked gruff but solid, Sally looked smart and impish. But you never knew. I'd known jailhouse deputies who watched criminal after criminal placed in their care walk out with lightweight pleas and dismissed cases. Other longtime inmates spent their time amusing themselves by filing frivolous complaints about their wardens, dragging them into federal court for supposed cruel and unusual punishment like serving creamy peanut butter instead of chunky, attempting to secure their jailers' mortgages and other assets. Some deputies came to think that the punishment inflicted by inmates on one another was the only punishment they'd ever see.

"C'mon. Let's go," I said.

Still grinning, both of them shoved back their chairs and stood. Leading the way, they simultaneously adjusted utility belts heavy with the tools of their trade—radios, handcuffs, gloves, Tasers, and batons. Even in this relaxed small-town jail, the deputies knew better than to take a gun into the jail itself.

All was still quiet in the corridor. No snores. No nightmare groans. No complaints, even, when Sally unlocked and rolled back a squeaky steel door. But I thought I could detect the soft rustle of sheets and blankets as bunk-bedded inmates rolled over to look our way.

"He's in there. We put him in with Russell Smit."

Sally grinned like I should know Smit's name. Tom pointed to a cell that was the farthest from the hall.

That was even more wrong. The new guy should have been assigned a bunk. The worst in the place, up against the corridor bars, where the lights would be on him all night. No way was he going to get for himself the greater privacy of a cell while men with more seniority slept on the open bunks. Not unless he was a lot bigger and tougher than I knew Jonah to be.

The rec room was large, but not all that dark. The lights from the corridor, although dim, penetrated the room completely. I passed tables and benches and even a couple of second- or third-hand La-Z-Boys that faced a black TV screen mounted high up on a wall. Life in a county jail was not all that bad. Most of the men would be drunks or wife-beaters serving misdemeanor sentences. The others would be awaiting trial. Anyone convicted of a felony would be sent to far less comfortable housing at the state prison in Rawlins.

The cell door was open, as were the other five I had walked past. It was darker in there, but not dark enough. Sally stepped up next to me, peering in. Tom stayed back to guard the open gate.

There were two cots inside. On one of them lay the form of a man far larger than Jonah. Smit, I assumed. In the second or two it took my eyes to adjust to the diminished light, I made out a heavy blond beard and a pair of close-set eyes glinting at me. Some white teeth, too. He was flat on his back, his fingers laced together innocently across his heavily tattooed chest.

On the other cot there was a shape that was far smaller than Jonah's should have been.

He was on his side, naked except for a pair of white jockey briefs. His arms were tied behind his back, his feet tied to the same restraint. Hog-tied, the way you do a calf in a rodeo. With strips of shirt, apparently. Beneath his bulging eyes was another shirt that was serving as a gag.

At least he was still alive. I could tell because his body was trembling and jerking.

The big man reclining on the other cot lifted his head.

"Sal, I don't want this faggot in my crib anymore. He made a move on me—"

But Smit didn't get to finish his bullshit complaint.

Without thinking or really being aware of what I was doing, I'd lifted the gun-shaped Taser out of the holster on Sally's utility belt. I pointed it at the broad, bare chest and depressed the trigger. A tiny red dot appeared just below the man's wide neck. Then I pulled the trigger all the way.

With a pop of compressed air, two barbed darts trailing insulated wires shot out of the muzzle at 120 miles per hour. They embedded themselves among the dark etchings on Smit's chest. Tiny pieces of confetti scattered in the air as proof that the weapon had fired.

No such proof was needed, though, because for the next five seconds the big man's body bucked on the bed, flopping like a fish, one arm beating without rhythm on the concrete wall. His mouth opened and snapped shut with audible force.

"Hey!" Sally was yelling. "Hey!"

I stuck the gun back in her holster and scooped up Jonah in my arms. I wanted him out of the way before Smit regained his senses. I used him to push the deputies out of the cell. Back in the main room, I dropped Jonah on a Ping-Pong table then turned to slam shut the cell door.

"Are you crazy?" Tom demanded angrily. "What the hell did you do that for?"

Sally shoved me. "Shit, man! Why'd you do that?"

Amazed and excited prisoners were sitting up in their beds and beginning to chatter.

I had done what anyone would do. Anyone, that is, but a cop. I'd Tased a man who was showing no resistance. Good cops don't do that. They stick to the use-of-force rules and leave to the courts any question of punishment. I hadn't even had the presence of mind to shout the way bad cops are supposed to—*Stop resisting! Stop resisting!*—long after you've wrung the last bit of resistance out of them.

I used my pocketknife to cut the T-shirt gag out of Jonah's mouth. Still tied, he began to take huge, shaky breaths.

Just behind us, a bellow of rage exploded from the locked cell. Something with the mass of a piece of chewed gum struck my back, accompanied by a spitting sound. Turning, I saw the shirtless, bearded giant gripping the bars as he snarled at me. What looked like blood was running down the beard.

The chewing gum, I realized, was a hunk of tongue that he'd bitten off while convulsing on his cot.

ten

It was after one in the morning when I finally reached my isolated camp below the overhanging cliff. It was cold, too, up at well over nine thousand feet. I was too exhausted to build a fire, so I just heated a can of beef stew on my little blowtorch of a stove. Mungo received her usual share, dumped over dry dog food. She was still angry and gave me a baleful stare before gobbling it up.

"I read that wolves in the wild can go weeks without food. What kind of chickenshit wolf are you, anyway?"

Mungo didn't reply.

There were a million pinpricks of light in the black sky. With no smog and no light pollution in these mountains, the stars were so numerous and bright it was almost impossible to make out the individual constellations. Directly overhead, though, was only blackness. Up there, three hundred feet above my head, the cliff jutted out with a roof that I was coming to know very well. On its underside was the forty feet of never-been-climbed rock that I'd made my goal.

Actually, it was forty feet of never-been-climbed *not* rock. The hardest crack in the world. It was parallel-sided, flaring outward, and stuck straight out from the cliff face where the massive overhang topped it like the long brim of a ten-gallon hat.

My Moriah. One of them, anyway.

I spooned up my stew and contemplated the fact that it had been a bad day. I'd risked my life for nothing, let a kid die with my hands over his heart, failed to get in any training, gotten a tourist locked up and tortured, and violated my oath as an officer of the law. Far worse, I'd failed to make the daily phone call that was the one thing in my life—other than the fat crack over my head—that gave me hope.

My phone, a little Motorola Iridium that was the only thing that got consistent service in Wyoming's mountains, lay on my lap. I kept looking at digital numbers on the phone's screen that told me the time. It never got any earlier. And it was far, far too late to call.

Instead I got a jug of cheap red wine out of the back of the truck and took a long draw. With the heavy taste in my mouth, I thought about calling Roberto. He was the only one I knew who would be pleased with my actions. He'd absolutely love the story of me Tasing the defenseless Mr. Smit. But, as usual, thinking about my big brother brought me no solace. I took another swig from the jug to try and keep down the sudden but familiar nausea. I couldn't afford to lose the stew, since I'd need the calories for climbing tomorrow. A cold sweat broke out on my skin as I thought of my brother's once-magnificent and now-wrecked body—the wasted legs, the cracked spine, the myriad scars, and, worst of all, the long grin of puckered white skin across his throat from the blade of a machete.

All of them my responsibility. I'd let him go in there, to the narcos' compound.

I dug deeper in the back of the Pig and came up with a small Tupperware container. In it were an eighth of clumpy weed and a small metal pipe. It worked for chemo patients suffering from chemically induced nausea—why not me? I packed the bowl and took a few hits. It was good stuff. Indigo Red. There were purplish hairs on the sticky buds, a sure sign of potency. As a narcotics officer for eight years, I was adept at telling the good from the shake.

Mungo watched me, still bitter. Or maybe shocked at my behavior.

"It's been a bad day," I tried to explain. "A really bad day."

After cutting Jonah loose with the blade on my pocketknife, I'd half-carried him into the officers' lounge and dumped him on the sofa. He wouldn't talk at first. He didn't trust me, and I didn't blame him. It had been me, after all, who'd put him in there in the first place. I had to spend a lot of time explaining. And apologizing.

I chased the deputies out of the room, got Jonah a new shirt and pants, and apologized some more. I closed the door, too, to muffle the outraged roars of Smit and the complaints of the other inmates. I promised Jonah that he would be locked each night in his own cell, and that he could remain there during the day, too, if he chose. That I would do everything I could to see that he was protected from now on.

Finally he talked.

He hadn't been sexually assaulted, it turned out. Not yet. Apparently Smit had been working up to it when we came in. Jonah had been bound and gagged by Smit alone, he said, then was used as a punching bag. There were red swellings on his face, stomach, chest, and lower back that confirmed this. By the morning, I knew, the contusions would turn black-and-blue. Jonah said Smit kept calling him a faggot, getting more and more excited, and telling him he was going to teach him a lesson he and his kind wouldn't soon forget. Rape, I knew, was a crime of violence and domination, very much a part of prison life even if few admitted to either perpetrating it or being victimized. Smit would see Jonah as "fresh meat" that needed to be brought under control. The big man might even see himself, like the guards had, as assaulting Jonah for a just cause, to punish him for the killing of a local boy.

The sheriff, whom someone had awakened and notified about the ruckus in his jail, barged through the door. He didn't need to ask who the hell I was. He just demanded to know what had happened.

While Tom said he hadn't seen anything, Sally unexpectedly backed me up.

Sally said, "It was really dark, so it was hard to see, but old Smit suddenly started up. Like he was jumping out of bed or something. Coming at us, I guess. Lunging. I was reaching for the juice myself, but Anton here beat me to it." She laughed, a little nervous. "They don't call him QuickDraw for nothing, you know."

"I know," said the sheriff glumly.

He looked at me, making it clear that he knew very well another reason for the nickname.

The sheriff, of course, had also known Sally was covering for me. But he didn't want a scandal coming out of his jail. It was bad enough that an inmate had been beaten by another inmate. It would look much worse if an officer was charged with beating the inmate who had been allowed or encouraged to beat the first inmate.

Because of Sally's adherence to my side of the blue line, there was no case to file, no statements to make. Only a use-of-force form to fill out that contained mostly fiction and conjecture. Smit could make a complaint about me, but no one would believe an inmate over a cop. Not even over this cop. Not, at least, with Sally backing me up. Jonah could file charges against Smit, but Smit would repeat his story about Jonah having "made a move" on him, and no jury would likely find one inmate credible over the other to the point of "beyond a reasonable doubt."

It was an impasse.

I felt pretty bad about having violated my oath, just as I was violating it now by smoking some high-grade dope in a remote canyon. The oath about being good, staying out of trouble. But, at the same time, I felt pretty damn good, too. The stars were beginning to pulse. Gravity was losing a little bit of its influence. And I was smiling into the night.

God, but that had been fun. A much-needed outlet for all my other failings during the day. It wouldn't teach Smit a lesson, it wouldn't make him law-abiding or compassionate, but it had been a nice bit of payback. And fun—I couldn't forget that. No. I'd gotten to pump fifty thousand volts into an unarmed, non-threatening criminal for free.

I heard myself laugh. Good cop, my ass.

And it was only for free until Smit got out. Then there might be a price.

"You'd better watch your back when he gets out," the sheriff had grumbled. "That fellow tends to hold grudges."

Smit had emphasized the sheriff's point by bellowing from the rec room throughout our conversation, "Who was that little motherfucker? I want that motherfucker's name! I want his ass!"

Only because he was missing the tip of his tongue, it sounded more like "Who was wat moffa-fucker? I wanh wat moffa-fucker's name! I wanh his ass!"

Remembering, I laughed some more.

Since I knew he would find out who I was soon enough, there hadn't been any point in hiding from him. I knew that it would be the very worst thing I could do. To show fear would only fuel his desire for vengeance. So, after finishing up with the sheriff, I walked out into the corridor and stepped up to the bars.

The big man was gripping them with his fists, tattooed knuckles at almost the level of my head. There was snot in his mustache and a red stain in his beard. His cheeks and eyes were filled with blood.

"Stop lisping like a little girl, Smit. The name's Burns. Antonio Burns."

* *

Getting sleepy and too tired to deal with the tent, I had just thrown my sleeping bag in the dirt when the phone on my hip chimed. My heart leapt, but then settled back down when I realized it could only be work related. Someone calling to chew me out in the middle of the night. Probably Ross, who had an uncanny ear when it came to hearing about me getting into trouble.

So it was without enthusiasm that I put the phone to my ear.

"Yeah?"

"Are you all right? You didn't call."

It was Rebecca. My heart rode the roller coaster right back up.

"I was just, uh, busy."

"Oh, yeah? You seeing someone finally? Never mind, forget I asked." She sounded amused, not angry. "So how was your day, Ant?"

"Good," I lied. "Just busy."

"I bet."

"What are you doing up this late?"

"Feeding your daughter. She's biting my boob as we speak. The little monster has got teeth like Mungo's."

"Let me talk to her."

The phone moved so that I could hear small sucking sounds.

"This is your dad, sweet thing. You doing okay? I miss you. I love you." The sucking sounds stopped. "You may not see me all that much, but I think of you all the time." A whimper could be heard. It quickly began to escalate to a wail. I added quickly, "Sleep well, honey. Have sweet dreams."

Rebecca came back on the phone after murmuring to make the crying stop. "It's late, and she's tired," she tried to explain.

"Sure. I understand."

But I didn't. She always cried when I held her or talked to her. It was as if she could see right through me with her penetrating blue eyes, see all the stuff I tried to keep inside. Instead of just a father's love, she saw something that scared her.

"Hey, Ant. It's okay. Dads can't really do a lot for kids this age. Some friends of mine say their kids act like this, too. Unless you're going to grow some boobs, you'll just have to wait until she gets older. And you need to hang around some more. Speaking of which, are you coming to Denver tomorrow like you said?"

"No. I can't. There's a hearing in the morning I have to be at. A thing here in Colter County. Then I have to do some stuff after that. But I should get there on Saturday."

I wondered where I'd sleep. In a motel, in Rebecca's bed, or on her couch. It was different on each occasion, depending on her moods and other romantic interests. Rebecca, even six months after giving birth and still breast-feeding, had little trouble getting dates.

"Anything interesting?"

There was more than just normal curiosity in her voice. She had left her full-time job as a newspaper reporter to cohost a morning news show on TV. I knew she missed doing her own investigations—now she pretty much just read off a TelePrompTer and conducted inane five-minute interviews with local authors and chefs. But she made a lot more money this way and worked far fewer hours.

I assured her the court hearing wasn't about anything interesting at all.

That made her chuckle.

"Then you're slipping, Ant. Good thing, too."

"Have you seen Roberto?" I asked.

Pretty high now, and no longer queasy, I could actually speak his name without wanting to vomit.

"He was here this morning to take Moriah for a walk."

Roberto's legs were almost entirely paralyzed, but he liked to put our daughter in a backpack and hobble on his steel crutches around the homeless and the executives on Denver's 16th Street Mall. It wasn't something I was particularly enthusiastic about—my brother, handicapped and with his addictions and his criminal record, wasn't exactly the best role model for my daughter. But how much better was her dad? And for some reason Rebecca had grown fond of my brother. A year ago, before the accident, she couldn't stand the sight of him. Just the mention of his name had made her back go stiff.

"Mary's back?" I asked.

Roberto couldn't drive and didn't own a car. His girlfriend, a former FBI agent, was supposed to be out of town doing private protection for some Fortune 500 big shot.

"No, she'll be gone for another week at least. A monk brought him."

"A monk?"

"Tibetan, I think. He had a shaved head, saffron robes, and everything. A little VW, too. He was very sweet and very shy, so I let him drive my Porsche with the top down while Roberto took Moriah out. He seemed to really like it."

My daughter was certainly getting exposed to a lot of diverse lifestyles. Just not mine.

After a few more minutes of talking inanely, I asked to speak to my daughter one more time. The phone moved and the gentle slurping could be heard again.

"Good night, Moriah," I said quickly while staring up at the dark blot in the sky I'd named after her. "Sleep tight. Have sweet, sweet dreams."

I hit the END key just as I heard the first whimper.

eleven

At 9:00 A.M., four orange-clad inmates shuffled into the courtroom through a back door next to the judge's bench. The deputy leading this mini chain-gang directed them to seats in the front of the jury box. Jonah entered last, shackled like the others by his wrists to the steel cord that connected all four inmates. He took one look around the packed courtroom then dropped his eyes to the rail before him. Without his spiked hair and facial jewelry, and without his tattoos displayed, he looked not much more than a teenager.

A rumble of interest rose up from the gallery. I couldn't catch complete sentences, but the general tone seemed to be a sense of satisfaction over the bruises swelling Jonah's face. Mr. Wallis, the dead boy's father, was not there, but feisty little Mr. Mann was.

One gaze was directed at me rather than Jonah. It came from the rear corner of the courtroom, far away from where I leaned against the wall next to the prosecution table. But even from the distance of thirty feet, I could feel its heat. Mattie Freda was huddled alone there, her pale skin turning an angry pink from having seen Jonah's battered face.

I considered walking through the low swinging doors dividing the well of the court from the gallery, excusing my way down the last aisle, and attempting to make an explanation. To tell her what had happened. That I wasn't responsible. The look on her face told me she would need some convincing.

But I didn't move. I was responsible, in a way, and I didn't want to draw attention to her like that. Plus, having already seen how high-strung she could be, I didn't want to risk another scene with her. Instead I looked away and watched the county's public defender shove up from his table and hike across the well to stand before the prisoners. He was a fat man, dressed slobbishly except for well-styled silver hair.

I was close enough to hear what he said to them in a low voice.

"Gentlemen, I'm Jake Henning, the public defender in this county. I'm probably going to be serving as the attorney for most of you. None of you, frankly, looks like you got a pot to piss in, much less the cash to hire an attorney of your own. Anyway, the judge is going to tell you why you got yourselves hauled in here. He's going to tell you what rights you have, and ask you if you want to talk to an attorney. Provided you qualify, you can have me represent you on the county's dime, and I'll probably be able to work out some kind of deal with the county attorney."

Then he pointed to Jonah.

"Excepting you," he said. "You're Jonah Strasburg, right?"

Jonah nodded, his eyes still down on the rail.

"Yeah."

"Look at me when I'm talking to you, son."

Jonah looked up.

The lawyer leaned in close to him, but when he spoke his voice was loud enough to be heard in the gallery.

"I'm not going to represent you, whether you qualify or not. Understand? I've got a conflict that's going to prevent that."

"A conflict?" Jonah asked softly.

"That boy you killed—excuse me, allegedly killed—he was my wife's cousin's son. So I'm not going to have anything to do with you or your case except to hang around here as a spectator. And to do some serious celebrating when they convict your sorry butt. Now, I've already talked to the judge, and he's going to find some other fool to take your case. If the poor sucker's willing, he might come see you next week."

The fat lawyer gave Jonah a long, contemptuous look then stalked back to the defense table. Several men in the gallery gave him clenched-jaw nods, approvingly.

Luke, who had come into the courtroom just before this and was arranging papers on the prosecution table, motioned for me to bend over.

He whispered, "Don't think old Jake's all that noble. He's just running for my job next term. Wants to show everyone he can be a hard-ass even when he's on D."

I looked at Jonah again, expecting to see him looking down again, his expression as hangdog as it had been last night. I was surprised to see him glaring at the defense attorney, his damaged face as hard as the faces of the men and women in the gallery.

Good for you, I thought. *Being mad beats being sad.*

An elderly woman came in from the door behind the judge's bench. She called, "All rise!"

There was a rustle of clothes, a rattling of chains, and the stomping of boots as everyone complied. The judge then entered through the same door. He was old, too—a shrunken, bent figure with flapping wisps of white hair and a robe that billowed around him as he marched to his chair. He glared at all of us, lingering for a long moment on me and Luke. I wondered what I had done. Maybe he'd somehow heard about the ruckus in the jail.

The judge didn't sit right away, or allow us to sit either, with the customary muttering of "Be seated." Instead he issued a warning in an angry voice.

"Ladies and gentlemen, I understand why so many of you are here. I empathize with you, too. But this is a court of justice, not public opinion." He glanced meaningfully at Luke and me again, then continued, "I won't tolerate any outbursts, and there's going to be no screwing around. That includes the parties to these cases. Anyone makes so much as a peep without my permission and I'm going to clear the room. Do we understand each other?"

No one made a sound.

"Then please sit down."

The judge's threats seemed to me as inappropriate as the defense lawyer's comments to Jonah. No one had said anything. If there'd been a hint of a coming outburst, I hadn't seen it. And I wondered about the reason for the stink eye directed at Luke and me.

I sat down next to the county attorney, as uncomfortable in my role as advisory witness as I was in my navy suit. After what had happened last night, I'd gotten dressed at my camp instead of coming in to shower in the jail and adjacent deputies' locker room. It felt a little weird to be dressing so formally in an isolated canyon thirty miles from town. The temperature was only a little above freezing when I splashed myself clean in the river, and I still had a slight headache from dunking my head.

One by one Jonah's fellow inmates were called to stand at the podium between the prosecution and defense tables. The judge recited a list of their rights, asking if they understood after each statement. They would answer "Yes" or "*Sí*," although even I, with eight years of experience in law enforcement and a master's degree in criminal justice, couldn't fully comprehend all the nuances that went along with each constitutionally protected right. Luke then read the charges against them and the potential penalties if convicted. The judge asked if the inmates wanted to consult a lawyer before entering a plea. All did, and all indicated that they would like to have the county pay their legal costs. Jake Henning, the PD with the nice head of hair, stood and gave each man a form and a business card. I grew close to drifting off.

"Jonah Strasburg."

He stood as the guards unhooked him from the chain. Unlike the other prisoners, he remained handcuffed. Everyone watched him stumble as he came out of the box, then he had to cross the well under the weight of all those hostile eyes. I felt even sorrier for him than I had before. He glanced at me, but I couldn't read what was in his gaze. Probably wanting to ask me to save him again, like I had last night. But I stayed stone-faced, sitting next to the prosecutor. Like a good cop.

Luke climbed to his feet.

"Luke Endow. For the People," he announced for the spectators and the tape recorder.

His voice was stiffer, more formal, than it had been when he'd entered his appearance on the other cases called that morning. He slapped a document on the podium in front of Jonah, then studied the young man's face for a moment. When he turned back to me, Luke's own face was grave but his eyes seemed to be twinkling with pleasure. I was beginning to understand why. With a disputed election coming up, this case would keep him in the spotlight. I cynically assumed that the public defender, Luke's opponent, with his tenuous familial connection to the boy who'd died, had recused himself so as not to be sharing it, but for the wrong side. Jonah was going to be the main course in this election meal.

I really didn't want to be here. For the first time in a long time, I wanted to be performing my absolutely useless duty of tramping through the woods, scoping meth labs. This wasn't an arraignment but a campaign event.

"As you can see from the papers before you," the judge said, "you are charged with a felony. That means it is a crime for which, if convicted, you could be sentenced to more than a year in prison."

He proceeded to read Jonah his rights. Any statement he made could be used against him. He had a right to an attorney even if he couldn't afford one. Any plea he made must be voluntary. He had a right to a jury trial. And so on, all the things anyone who watches TV is aware of. Then, in a voice that seemed equally resigned and disgusted, he finally told Jonah the nature of the charges against him.

"The crime you are charged with having committed on Thursday, the seventeenth of June, in Colter County, Wyoming, is the crime of murder in the first degree."

My head snapped toward Luke, who was sitting next to me. He was staring down at his papers, a faint grin on his mouth.

"You got to be kidding me," I started to whisper. Now I knew why the judge was so pissed.

Luke put a finger to his lips.

"For you to be found guilty of this crime, it must be proven that, after deliberation and with the intent to cause the death of a person other than yourself, you caused the death of the person. Or it may be proven that, under circumstances evidencing an attitude of universal malice manifesting extreme indifference to the value of human life generally, you knowingly engaged in conduct which created a grave risk of death to a person, or persons, other than yourself, and thereby caused the death of another, namely Cody Wallis, age ten."

There was a rumble from the gallery, and an angry shifting of boots. The judge glared and raised his gavel—almost as if he might throw it—but didn't strike. The gesture was enough. The noises subsided. I expected that if he were to throw it, it would be toward Luke and me. The judge clearly knew the first-degree murder charge was politically motivated and didn't like it.

I turned and looked back at the citizens. The concentrated gazes of all but Mattie were trying to light Jonah's back on fire.

I'd once been in a similar courtroom where such mass vengeance had been directed my way. Only it wasn't a criminal courtroom—it had been civil. And the supposed "victims" hadn't been children. But the faces had hated me just as much. One of them belonged to the prick of a reporter who had dreamed up the nickname QuickDraw.

Mattie was the only one deviating from the hatred directed at Jonah. Her hatred was still directed at me, intensified now. I quickly turned away again because Mattie obviously wanted to see me spark up.

Instead I watched Jonah, feeling real sympathy for him now. Shit, I'd been there. Almost—my life hadn't been at stake, only my job and reputation. Jonah seemed to be bearing up to the higher stakes as well as could be expected. He was standing rigid and pale, his fists clenched while his hands were still cuffed. But I suspected the muscular contraction was due to an attempt to keep from fainting rather than defiance. The breeze from an open door might knock the kid over.

For Luke, the game was high-stakes poker. For Jonah, it was Russian roulette.

The judge read on, outlining all the lesser included offenses Endow had thrown into the charging document just to make sure something heavy and hard would stick. Murder in the second degree. Manslaughter. Assault. Menacing. Criminally negligent homicide. He'd really piled it on. The only thing lacking from the Wyoming statute book was "sheepherder abandoning his flock." The stacking of charges was usually intended to intimidate the defendant into accepting a plea.

"Now, I'm not going to ask you to make a plea at this time," the judge said. "I'm going to wait until you've had a chance to talk to counsel. As I said earlier, if you can't afford to hire your own, the court will provide one to you. But at this point I need to ask you if you have an attorney, or anticipate hiring your own, because our public defender has recused himself from this case."

Jesus, I thought, *I shouldn't have arrested him. I should have given him a shove and shouted for him to run!*

Jonah cleared his throat, the microphone on the podium picking it up. Then he cleared his throat again.

"Um," he said in a quiet voice, "I, um, don't think I can afford to hire an attorney."

"Then the court will appoint you one. I'm going to reschedule this hearing for five days from now."

The judge abruptly stood and concluded the hearing by leaving the room. No one moved for a moment, then the deputies grabbed Jonah and led him back to the jury box. The prisoners were rehooked to the chain and pulled out, Jonah leading this time. At the rear door, just before disappearing, Jonah looked back. His eyes sought out Mattie in the far corner. The slack, numb expression on his face was heartbreaking.

twelve

Luke shuffled papers while the courtroom emptied. Occasionally someone leaned over the rail and clapped his shoulder. Luke would turn, and the man or woman would say "You get him, Luke," or "You make him pay for what he did to our Cody," or, once, "Hang him high, Luke. Hang him high."

The county attorney would nod solemnly by way of reply and go back to shuffling, the same surreptitious gleam in his eye. I suspected he was about as sorry over the boy's death as he would have been if he'd won the lottery. It was manna from heaven for a politician, especially a struggling one. Everyone would be talking about how tough he was on crime, about how hard he went after an outsider who had the audacity to kill a local child. I stayed in my seat even though the urge was strong to get away from him.

I really hated politics and the way it could pervert justice.

But I stayed not only because it was my job but also because I owed it to Luke. He still had a limp from the bullet he'd taken for me. I wondered if the wound still pained him very much. I wondered, too, if the bullet might be the reason he'd gotten so damn fat. Not that he'd ever been skinny, but he was so fat now he'd probably die of a heart attack at an early age, and in a way, it might be my fault. But at least I couldn't blame myself for the loss of his hair. It had already been thinning when we first met. I could still picture him as he'd been that day eight years ago—he'd been trying to infiltrate an Earth First! rally near Jackson Hole and was dressed as an over-the-top hippie from a quarter century earlier, complete with beads, bell-bottoms, and granny glasses. The idiotic outfit exposed him as a narc as fast as the obvious calculation in his eyes. I would learn over the months we spent together that he was far more effective at running CIs—confidential informants. Kicking their butts and always sending them in for more and more evidence. He was also known for protecting them from overly curious judges and defense attorneys, and for building rock-solid cases that the prosecutors would too often give away so they wouldn't have to bother with another trial that would take time away from their fishing and hunting trips.

I had still been an FNG—a trainee—when he caught the bullet. I hadn't even gone through the academy in Rock Springs yet. Luke was my partner and training officer. One night we were in the mountains outside Story, Wyoming, surveilling a house whose owner we intended to arrest. At 3:00 A.M. a car finally drove up with our suspect inside. Luke covered me as I jogged up the driveway behind it, intending to be in the driver's face as soon as he stepped out of the car. Only he somehow saw me in the red glow of his taillights. Without even stopping, he opened the driver's door, twisted halfway out, and started shooting.

I dove into the trees on one side of the driveway. My desperate lunge for cover was so sudden and so spastic that Luke thought I'd been hit. He returned fire then yelled my name. Since our suspect was still sporadically firing back with vicious little small-caliber pops, I thought it wise not to answer and give away my position. Luke took my silence for mortal danger—he probably pictured me with blood spilling out of holes in my flesh. He charged out of the trees like a short, balding Rambo. He was emptying an entire fifteen-round clip as he ran in a weird sideways scuttle, trying to make himself a skinnier target, I guess, which might have been a good strategy if he weren't already showing signs of his current chubbiness. The suspect somehow wasn't shot, but his very last bullet struck Luke in the meat of one cheek and passed through both it and the other. It was lucky for him that he disabled Luke in this way. If he hadn't, I had no doubt Luke would have killed him, whether the poor idiot who'd shot him had any more ammunition or not.

I was following the rules in those days, just as I was trying to now. I didn't even take a cheap shot for my partner—not even a little kick to the groin of the man who'd tried to kill both of us—when I tackled the asshole as he tried to run from his car. Luke had given me shit about that for months. *Goddamnit, Burns, the fucker pops me and you cuff him like he's your mom and take him in without a scratch while I'm lying there bleeding out of my ass.*

Things sure had changed. With me, at least.

The courtroom's doors banged shut a last time and the room was silent.

"What did you think, *amigo*?" Luke asked, finally letting the grin lift up his jowls the way he'd been aching to all through the morning.

I thought it sucked.

But I forced myself to recite my mantra. Besides, it really wasn't any of my business. I just gave him the facts and he made the charging decisions. That's what good cops do. I couldn't stay totally silent, though.

"I'm not sure I see the factual basis for murder, Luke. The intent element, I mean. I don't think I put anything about that in my report."

The smile dropped along with the jowls.

"What are you talking about, QuickDraw? You were there at the scene. You arrested the son of a bitch. He threw that kid off the cliff into the river."

"But did he really intend for Cody to die?"

Luke drew back and studied me.

"Christ, have you gotten limp-wristed or something? Of course he intended for him to die. Strasburg had just come down the biggest, baddest rapids in the river and then he pushes that kid into the same water?"

The fact that it was downstream from the rapids didn't register with him. He continued. "And you just saw our potential jury pool—do you think they're going to believe it was an accident? They'll buy extreme indifference, at the least."

I shrugged. It was probably true. It depended on the abilities of the defense. Not, as justice should, on the actual facts.

Another smile crept onto Luke's face, this one sly.

"Besides, this is just for openers. I'm not going to have to prove anything. You know the game, QuickDraw. That kid and whatever putz the judge rustles up to represent him will fall all over themselves to plead to any lesser I can name. They'll take anything, anything at all, just so long as they don't have to risk mandatory life under Murder One."

I'd always hated plea bargains. It seemed to me that if you commit a crime, you should be convicted and sentenced for your actions. Not some other, sometimes unrelated, offense, just so the state didn't have to go through the effort and uncertainties of an actual trial.

I wasn't stupid, though—I understood that in a wildly overcrowded and underfunded judicial system, you can't take everything to trial. And that each year lawmakers make it a thousand times worse by trying to look "tough on crime" and passing new laws and mandatory sentences. Deals had to be made—the system had long ago been overwhelmed. What I really objected to was the politicization of the process. Prosecutors were elected, and their first priority was always to stay in office. The pleas they offered—and the charges they filed and overfiled—were far too often based on that priority. A county attorney had to have a politician's instinct for the sound bite and know who to hammer and who to soft-sell to keep the money and votes flowing.

It had little to do with justice. Less and less each year.

Luke chuckled.

"I bet they'll be so scared of the murder charge they'll jump for criminally negligent homicide and a ten-year minimum."

"That's what you're going to offer?" I asked.

But Luke didn't answer. We were interrupted by a voice from the back of what we'd assumed was an empty courtroom.

"You're disgusting," a voice said, not much louder than a whisper but with enough emotion behind it that it carried like a scream.

I turned around in my chair. Luke did, too. Mattie Freda was still huddled in the far corner, her black bangs above dark eyes looking as sharp as Mungo's fangs. I noticed that she'd taken out the facial jewelry she'd worn on the river. Her blouse was some black, shiny material. If it weren't for her dyed hair, she'd look almost respectable.

"Who the hell are you?" Luke demanded.

"Mattie . . ." I called to her.

"Don't even fucking speak to me, you goddamn Nazi!"

With jerking movements, she grabbed her bag, lurched to her feet, and almost ran out of the room.

Luke chuckled.

"That's the girlfriend? Bet she wouldn't be too bad in the sack if you like a little strange. Looked like she has a body on her. Anyway, she'll be fucking great if we ever get her on the witness stand. Piss off everyone in town with that attitude."

I wanted to go after her but didn't. I rationalized that it would be good to give her a little time to cool off. It was also true that I didn't want to chase her down, apologizing, in front of Luke.

Instead I asked, "Did you hear how Strasburg got those bruises?"

Now he laughed. "Sounds like my old buddy Smit was angling for early release. He sure opened a can of whup-ass on Strasburg, all right. I didn't think that big bastard would beat up anyone but his girlfriend—all we ever seem to get him on are piddling little DV charges, even though he's the ringleader of half the tweakers in this county. But you'd better be watching your back when that boy gets out—he'll probably try making another exception for you. I heard he had to get six stitches in his tongue after you zapped him."

Then he turned serious. "By the way, I met with the sheriff about it before court this morning. He wasn't too happy with you for stirring things up in his jail. He wants you to stay out of there, understand? Putting Strasburg in solitary will be a big drain on his resources, and if we piss the sheriff off too much he's not going to endorse me when the campaigning starts." He shook his head, remembering, and frowned at me. "No, he wasn't happy at all."

I said, "I wasn't too happy that his deputies allowed our suspect to get the shit kicked out of him."

"Come on, QuickDraw. What did you expect when you put him in that jail after he killed a local kid? In this town, there's always going to be a little unofficial payback. Might even make him a little malleable, if you know what I mean, when it comes time to do a deal. After what I heard about you in Cheyenne, I'm surprised you'd be so squeamish about something like that."

I decided to reason with him in a language he'd understand.

"Do you want him coming into court looking like a victim instead of a perp? Do you want him filing lawsuits against you, the sheriff, and the county for violating his civil rights?"

Luke considered it and scowled. "Yeah, I guess that's right." Then the scowl changed into a leer. "You know all about those kinds of lawsuits, don't you, QuickDraw?"

I ignored the question and the old pain and anger that flared with the reference.

"I hear you've got some experience with other forms of retaliation, too," Luke said. "Perpetrating it, I mean. I bet there's some stuff nobody even knows about, right? Took you long enough to figure it out, *amigo*. But it's the way the real world works."

The pain and anger turned suddenly to fear. I found myself staring into his piggish eyes, feeling my own eyes growing hard and sharp until he looked down at his papers.

What did he know?

He was just a small-town prosecutor and former Wyoming cop—he couldn't possibly know anything about a botched FBI operation, my brother's "accident," or my role in the disappearance of the Mexican drug lord who'd been responsible for it all. He couldn't know. McGee just wouldn't betray me like that. And no one else knew, or at least no one had any evidence.

But for a moment my world was thrown off-kilter, and I could see myself standing in a moonless Baja desert, a wounded man crawling at my feet, the boom and kick of the shotgun in my hands, and the splash of hot blood on my bare legs. I remembered feeling no pity, no remorse. And, sick as it was, I still felt none.

Luke was shuffling his papers a final time, this time organizing them into a neat pile and stuffing them in his briefcase. He stood and hefted the case.

"I want you to interview those kids today, okay?"

"Who?" I asked after a pause.

"The Manns. Wake up. And quit giving me those cold snake eyes."

thirteen

Having met the brothers and their dad once already, I wasn't looking forward to meeting them a second time.

The desk sergeant at the sheriff's office who gave me directions seemed to share my concern. After he drew me a map on the back of a complaint form—diagramming several unsigned roads and turns off the main highway—he gave me a funny look.

"You going out there alone? About this river thing?"

"Yeah. Why do you ask?"

He shrugged.

"Just curious. There could be a lot of reasons for a DCI guy to head out that way."

"Oh yeah? Like what?"

"The family's a little high-strung, you might say. Not a lot of respect for authority. The father used to be a regular customer in here when he was a young buck. The two older boys—a pair of twins—are doing their damnedest to follow in his footsteps. I've got a daughter their age, and she thinks that they're getting into meth pretty heavy. It's becoming a real problem around here. But being with DCI, I guess you already know that. Anyway, I suppose the younger boys are still nice kids."

I thanked him for the information. And I decided it would be a good idea to call ahead instead of just dropping by.

On the phone I talked to a woman who identified herself as Elizabeth Mann, the boys' mother. She sounded surprisingly friendly.

"Sure, come on out," she said. "We're all lying pretty low this morning, feeling blue about Cody. I'll send Ed or one of the boys down to meet you at the gate."

In the late-morning heat, Mungo and I headed out of town. The route took us west along the highway beside the river. There were several vehicles parked on top of the hill above the big boulder. I didn't slow to gawk. Past the turnout, we forked right on a county road and rose up into the foothills. It was a pretty drive. The sagebrush was still a little green from the spring, and the peaks of the Wind River range gleamed with fresh white snow. I could make out some of the distant couloirs, ridges, and faces, and took note of the ones I had climbed, remembering good times in simpler days.

Ed Mann seemed even smaller in the daylight than he'd appeared last night in the darkness. Maybe it had something to do with having vented his anger on me already. He was leaning against the bumper of a ranch truck at the last turn that was marked on my hand-drawn map.

Seeing me, he nodded without smiling, tugged on the brim of his dirty baseball cap, and climbed into the cab of his truck. He stuck out an arm and waved for me to follow. I quickly saw why Mrs. Mann had thought it necessary to send out her husband as a guide. After passing the gate and entering the Manns' property, there was a maze of double-tracks leading off in all directions.

I followed close to the ranch truck's bumper, observing the gun rack and the sticker in the back window that read:

"Freedom at Any Cost"
—Randy Weaver
Ruby Ridge, Idaho

Nice. Really nice. Especially for a cop already apprehensive about making this trip. I was glad, at least, that I didn't wear a uniform or drive a police cruiser. If Mungo could read, she wouldn't have liked a sticker on the tailgate: "Shoot a Wolf, Save a Rancher." And then there were the usual round decals proclaiming the driver's affiliation with the National Rifle Association. I rolled up the back windows so Mungo couldn't stick her big head out.

As expected, the house wasn't much. Just a regular ranch house, unlike the Wallises' fancier residence. A functional place that had been added to many times over the years with unprofessional labor, surrounded by dirt, sage, and weeds. But it was relatively neat—there was none of the usual ranch junk in the yard. An L of tall cottonwoods screened it from the west and north winds. The height of the big trees indicated the house had probably been here a very long time. Mann didn't stop in front of the house, but more than fifty feet away, behind the line of trees. Here I found all their junk—old pickups, tractors, and appliances all in various stages of either deterioration or reconstruction. He parked and I did, too. I expected that someone, probably the missus, didn't want all the crap in front of the house. There it would ruin what was an impressive view of high, rolling plains leading up to the peaks.

She met us on the porch. Tall and powerfully built, she resembled Cody's father, and this, along with the different last names, led me to assume that the familial connection went through her. She wore a clean white uniform. It turned out that she was a nurse in Badwater's emergency clinic.

"I was there when they brought him in," she told me, shaking her head sadly. "He looked so tiny I almost didn't recognize him.

We worked on him for almost an hour and did everything we could think of. But he'd been under for too long."

I bowed my head, feeling again that maybe I'd really screwed up by chickening out on that first dive. Maybe a single minute would have made a difference.

"Our boys told us what you did. I want to thank you for going into that river after my nephew. For trying to resuscitate him, too."

"Thanks," I mumbled. "I wish I'd gotten there sooner."

She turned to her husband. "Make sure the boys don't give this young man any guff." Then she marched out to her car to start her shift.

I was sorry to see her go. Her forthright, appreciative manner contrasted with what I already knew of her husband and at least his younger sons.

Ed Mann silently escorted me upstairs. He hadn't yet spoken but a few words to me. Randall and Trey were waiting in a shared bedroom. It was a disaster—what you'd expect of kids their age—but not particularly dirty. The only offensive things about the surroundings were the posters on the walls and the related music that was playing too loud.

I was familiar with it, although I'd rather not have been. The group was called the Insane Clown Posse. White guys dressed up in leather, spikes, and clown makeup like Kiss, but playing shock rap-metal, singing about graphic violence in terms full of expletives. Their music had been pulled from one Wyoming store, and a school district banned their apparel, after a few concerned parents connected it with an uptick in teen shootings and suicide. This, of course, only added to that band's luster among the tasteless kids who were really only looking for a way to jerk around their parents.

"This is the fellow who wants to talk to you about what happened yesterday," their dad said. He pointed to the larger boy—"That's Randy"—then to the smaller one—"That's Trey."

I walked uncertainly into the room, feeling out of place in my suit and tie. And I suddenly felt old. I had nothing in common with these sullen kids and their shitty music. A trained and experienced undercover investigator, I'd always assumed I could get along with anyone, from any segment of society. I'd always been athletic, smart, and cool. But I could tell there was nothing I could do that would impress these two.

"I was at the river yesterday, too," I said. "I need to hear from you two what happened before your cousin fell into the river."

"He didn't fall," Trey said. "He was pushed."

"You're the guy who told the cops to shoot us," Randy said.

I sighed and looked at Ed Mann before addressing his kids.

"I didn't mean for him to really shoot you. All I wanted was for you guys to stop interfering with my attempts to do CPR on Cody. I'm sorry I phrased it that way—I didn't mean it literally. And I'm really sorry about what happened to your cousin."

Neither of them replied. Both boys were glaring at me with more than the usual teenage hostility. Randy, the big one, was older and fatter than his brother. In fact, he was probably heavier than his dad. I knew he was fourteen years old, but he looked even older than that. He had a spiky flattop hairdo but wore it long in back, a country style known as a mullet or the Missouri Compromise. He wore a T-shirt and a pair of saggies big enough for a cow. Trey was still skinny and two years younger, but he was groomed and dressed about the same. They were each seated on their own beds.

I spotted a rocking chair under a pile of clothes. After surreptitiously patting it for sharp objects, I sat down on top of the clothes and took out my pad.

"Okay. What were you guys doing by the river?"

They looked at their dad, who remained in the doorway with his arms folded, before deciding to answer me.

"Riding our bikes," Randy said.

"We were grounded from riding our four-wheelers," Trey added.

"You were riding along the highway?"

"Yeah."

Their dad said menacingly, "You guys better have been staying on the shoulder."

"We were, Dad," Trey, the younger brother, whined. "We were just riding into town to hang out. We took a break on that big rock above the river. You can sometimes see the rafts coming through the rapids. We saw one coming down."

"So you stayed and watched?"

Trey looked at big brother Randy, who, after a moment's reflection, nodded permission for him to answer.

"Yeah. There was the long-hair from the outdoor store in it and a couple of tourons."

"Did you yell anything at them?"

"No."

"Did you throw anything at them?"

Trey gave Randy another glance. Randy didn't nod this time. Instead he was staring back at his little bro.

"Did you throw anything, Trey?" I asked again.

He looked back at me.

"Nah. We were tossing some rocks in the water, but we didn't throw anything near the raft."

"How about you, Randy? Did you or Cody throw anything at the raft?"

Randy stared at me before answering.

"What are you accusing us for? It was that tourist fucker that killed Cody."

"Randy!" his dad snapped.

I assumed that this was a house where corporal punishment wasn't unknown. I wouldn't have minded a demonstration, but I reminded myself that these boys had just lost their friend and cousin.

"Listen, you guys, I'm building a criminal case against that tourist, a guy named Jonah Strasburg. To do that, I need you and your brother to tell me everything that happened. If you did throw some rocks, I need to know. You won't get in any trouble for it."

Mr. Mann, though, disagreed. "You better not have been chucking rocks at people," he said. Which didn't help me get them to admit what I was pretty sure was the truth.

"We weren't throwing rocks at nobody. We dropped some in the river, but nowhere near the tourons."

I considered asking their dad if I could talk to them alone, but decided to drop it. Without Dad standing by they probably would just tell me to stuff it.

It took a while, but I finally got the rest of their sanitized version. For no reason at all, the "skinny tourist dude" had gotten out of the raft, charged up the slope to the top of the rock, and started yelling at them. They thought he was crazy, that he might attack them. Cody picked up a stick to defend himself. The tourist went crazy and shoved him off the cliff.

It was bullshit, and I tried one last time to get them to admit it.

"Do you know how he got a cut on his ear?" I'd seen the small wound, and Jonah had told me that it was Cody striking him with the stick.

But the kids just shrugged sullenly. Realizing I'd probably gotten all I could out of them—enough certainly to make Luke happy—I wanted out of there. The whole case, their attitudes, and the terrible music, were beyond grating.

I wondered if my brother and I had ever been this obnoxious. The answer was probably yes. I remembered the music that had influenced us, from our clothes to our attitudes—Led Zeppelin, the Clash, Suicidal Tendencies. We'd shaved our heads to create Mohawks and torn the sleeves from all our T-shirts. It was a wonder our folks hadn't resorted to some serious corporal punishment themselves.

Who knows—things might have turned out better for Roberto and me if they had.

When I was done, or, more accurately, had given up, Ed Mann led me back downstairs. The bedroom door slammed behind me and the music cranked way up.

Out on the porch, I guiltily made the usual police suggestion to potential prosecution witnesses, intended to hinder any defense.

"There may be a defense lawyer or investigator who'll want to talk to Randy and Trey, too. You can talk to him if you want, but it's your choice. You don't have to."

Mann took my meaning. He nodded and scratched his chin.

"Nobody in my family's going to be talking to anyone who's trying to get that murderer off."

"Like I said, it's up to you. I'm only telling you that you have a choice because sometimes the defense guys try and make it sound like you *have* to talk to them."

He gave me a bleak smile.

"Don't worry, Agent Burns. No one can make me or my boys do anything we don't want to."

Thinking of his bumper stickers and guns, I believed him.

He added, "Now you tell Luke that I want this asshole from New York prosecuted to the full extent of the law. And beyond."

Then he closed the door.

Relieved to be away from Ed Mann and his young sons and the sullen anger all three shared, I crunched across the gravel toward the informal parking lot/junkyard behind the brake of cottonwoods. It was getting hot. When I'd woken at dawn, it was close to freezing, and now, at only eleven-thirty, the temperature had increased by at least fifty degrees.

I stepped into the shade the large trees offered, passed between the solid gray trunks, and found two men standing beside the Pig. One of them was leaning against the driver's door, peering in with hands cupped to the tinted windows. The other one was poking in the cracked rear window with a long stick. I froze for half a second then picked up my pace.

The one with the stick jerked it out suddenly.

"Look at that!" he said, holding up the jagged end for the

other one to inspect. White wood showed bright where the bark had been stripped from the stick's tip.

"Fucker tore it in half!"

Both of them turned as they heard me coming.

"Get away from my truck."

They looked at each other and grinned.

"Who do you think you are, man? This piece of shit's on our property and we'll stand wherever we damned well please."

So these were the twins I had been warned about. Both of them resembled their mother in height, their father in physique. Only they had enhanced their dad's whipcord muscles with oversize balloons. It was an artificial enhancement, judging by the red bloom of acne on their shoulders and cheeks—a side effect of steroids. Both were dressed in jeans and tank tops that showed off their ill-gotten muscles as well as long, skinny necks and thighs. To me they looked ridiculous—all meaty delts, twin slabs of pecs, and bulging biceps. Nothing that would do them any good in any conceivable sport or occupation. Both had short brown hair. The only thing that distinguished the two was that one had a scraggly soul patch on his lower lip and the other had an upside-down horseshoe mustache.

I pushed between Hairlip and Horseshoe and looked through the two inches of open window. Mungo was crouched inside, her yellow eyes slitted. She was growling, but when she saw me she stopped and licked at her clenched and exposed white teeth. She didn't appear to be hurt.

"I'm a cop. And you better not have hurt my dog."

I walked around the truck so that I wouldn't have to open the door with the two brothers at my back. On the other side, I unlocked and opened the door. Mungo stayed where she was, lips still raised and muzzle pointed like a gun at the men on the other side of the glass.

"We didn't hurt her, man. Just trying to see what kind of dog it is."

"And that ain't no fucking dog."

"You okay, Mungo?" I asked, reaching between the seats and patting her hip.

Mungo licked her fangs again but didn't take her eyes off the opposite window. I took that for a yes. I slammed the door shut.

"She's a shepherd-malamute mix. You want to know anything about her, just ask me. Don't try to spear her."

"That's a wolf, man. I know a wolf when I see it. Shot two of them from my snow machine last year."

I stared across the hood at the one who'd said this. Hairlip. He was grinning broadly.

"Oh yeah? Did you report it to the Feds?"

"Nope."

"Too bad. I might. Shooting an endangered species is a felony."

His grin widened.

"Too bad you don't have any evidence, pig. I know the law, and a 'criminating statement don't mean shit unless you got something to back it up with."

Well, he did know the law. From much experience on the wrong side, no doubt. I could threaten to execute a warrant based on his admission and I'd bet I would find the hides hanging proudly somewhere. But I wasn't going to stand there and dance with these muscle boys. I had other things I needed to do.

I walked back around the bumper toward them and had to reach between them to open the driver's door. When I tried to pull it open, Horseshoe caught and held it with his hand. He kept me from opening it all the way.

"What's your name? I'd like to know the name of a guy who thinks he can bust me for shooting vermin," said Hairlip.

Still holding the handle, I said, "It's Antonio Burns."

"That doesn't sound like a spic name. And you look like a spic."

I didn't say anything. I wanted to pull my gun. It was on my right side, in its plastic paddle holster, clipped to the inside of my belt, just underneath the silk-lined fold of my suit coat. I knew how smooth and quick it would come out. But I also knew the trouble that simple, enticing action would cause. An incident report. Complaints. A lack of cooperation from the grieving Mann family. I couldn't afford any more trouble.

"You the wetback who was at the river where Cody got killed?" Hairlip asked.

"Yeah."

I guess I expected some grudging appreciation then, even a curt thanks, for what I'd done to try to save their cousin. For risking my ass by swimming down into that sink. But I was mistaken. The one holding the door lowered his head so that his face was very close to mine.

"You make damn sure that fucker gets the chair. You understand? Else you're going to have to answer to us, spic."

Mungo chose that moment to launch herself at the rear seat's window. Her teeth hit the glass with a crack that made my own teeth ache. I pulled on the handle hard, surprising Horseshoe, the one holding it, some more with the strength with which I yanked. He was already off-balance from Mungo's sudden lunge and my jerk smacked the door into his hip. It made him stumble and fall. The other brother, Hairlip, leapt away from the truck, as if the big animal might somehow fit herself through the little two-inch-wide opening.

I hopped in, barely waited for the engine to catch, and tapped down on the accelerator. The Pig rolled forward fast enough to be out of their reach, but not so fast as to look like I was fleeing in terror. One brother took a couple of quick steps and attempted to kick the rear gate. Watching him in the rearview mirror, I goosed the accelerator harder this time. Twin rooster tails of gravel shot into the air, sending both brothers reeling and adding pocks to their already pockmarked skin.

I was rewarded with a total of four upraised middle fingers through the lingering cloud of dust. Some shouted epithets, too.

"Nice move, Mungo."

I grinned at her in the rearview mirror and she seemed to be grinning back.

Nice move, Ant. It had been fun, but I knew I would have more trouble from the elder Mann brothers.

fourteen

Instead of escaping the rising heat and running for my high canyon camp for another bout with Moriah, I drove slowly back toward town. There were a couple more interviews I needed to do, a little more investigating. Then, I hoped, I could put everything behind me—Badwater, politics, my slippery grasp on my job, the good man I'd jailed, and the taste of snowmelt on a dead boy's lips.

Badwater Adventures was located, appropriately, on a bank of the river just outside of town. I pulled into a parking space and paused with the air conditioner blowing to write down the statements of the younger Mann brothers, including a brief and self-serving account of my run-in with the twins. *Elder Mann bros approached as RO* (reporting officer) *exited the property. Bros appeared angry and aggressive. RO entered vehicle and left premises to avoid a confrontation.* I wanted to document everything, but I wasn't going to mention that the brothers suspected that I was in possession of an illegal "predatory" animal. Nor was I going to mention intentionally pelting them with rooster tails of gravel. I was still trying like hell to avoid any of this from coming back to haunt me.

Given my luck, of course, this was an absurd fantasy.

The store looked like a ramshackle log cabin from the outside. Inside, it was big and brightly lit, jam-packed with everything you might need for nonmotorized play in the Wyoming outdoors. There were racks of clothes and kayaks and skis, hooks from the ceiling that suspended ropes and assorted climbing gear, and shelves of guidebooks and instructional texts. Covering the walls were posters of mountains and rivers and the hardy, attractive people who conquered them.

Pete the Guide was the only one manning the floor. He was everything you'd expect a river guide to be—big and tan, with blond hair that was pushed back except for where one curly lock lay across his forehead. Three middle-aged tourist women were chatting with him, flirtatiously debating whether they should sign up for a river trip.

Pete looked my way and gave me a nod that said, *Be with you in a sec, dude.* I idled by a glass counter that displayed Big Bros and Number 5 Camalots, wondering whether I had enough gear for Moriah. The $75 price of the big cams convinced me that indeed I did. That money would be better spent on the real Moriah's educational trust, where I was putting every spare penny.

Behind the counter of climbing protection, there was a faded poster that caught my eye. It showed a shirtless man with longish black hair sitting precariously on a ledge no more than a foot wide. A thousand or more sheer-to-overhanging feet below him was a gray smear of broken stone—I recognized it by the color of the rock as the Black Canyon of the Gunnison. It was not an unusual big wall photo except for two things: There were no ropes in view, not even a harness, and the smile on the man's face and the bright blue light of his eyes gave the distinct sensation of rapture. The caption in the corner read: "The notorious Roberto Burns letting it all hang out, free solo on the Stoned Oven, V 5.11d."

I'd never seen this one before. I quickly turned away. The photographer had captured too perfectly how I always pictured my brother in my head—and nothing like the way he'd looked since his accident.

The three ladies walked out, tittering over Pete and casting little waves back at him. I was the only one left in the shop.

He bounded over and stuck out his hand like he meant it.

"You're the guy who went in the river."

I nodded and told him my name and occupation.

"That was ballsy, dude. Very ballsy. I've seen that river real low, and knew there was a big-ass sink there. We call it Satan's Suck. You have to avoid it like herpes in low water. But yesterday, it was totally invisible. I saw you heading that way and tried to shout a warning. Next time I looked, you were just gone, dude."

"Thanks anyway, for trying to warn me."

"Poor kid." He shook his noble head, an awkward but probably well-meant attempt at concealing his natural enthusiasm. "Never even came up for a breath. The Suck just grabbed him. Took him down."

"I need to ask you some questions about what happened."

After getting his full name, address, and birth date, I started with how he'd first met Jonah and Mattie.

He told me they'd come in yesterday morning, apparently just looking around like those ladies. They'd seen the river posters on the walls, and Mattie asked how much to do a float trip. It was a nice day, and Pete didn't want to be indoors, so he'd offered to take them right then for half price. The girl had agreed, but the boyfriend, Jonah, seemed pretty reluctant. Still, he'd signed the releases, and Pete had called for another girl to come in and take over the shop for the day. They'd headed out. His roommate had dropped them off at a put-in twelve miles upstream.

"How was the water?"

"High and fast. I was a little worried. Wasn't sure we'd make it without someone taking a swim. Mattie was having a blast, totally stoked, but that dude Jonah seemed freaked by the rapids. Kept saying he'd never done anything like this before. She kind of teased him about it, but I don't think he was real happy."

"What happened when you got to the sink?"

"Well, we'd just come out of Rinse Cycle, the biggest waves on the river. Full of head drops and standing waves. It's a really tricky stretch, especially when the water's this fast. Mattie was screaming her head off. Jonah was just hanging on, I think. Hell, I was, too."

"What happened next?"

"Well, when we came out of the rapids, Mattie was whooping and talking a mile a minute. Jonah was real quiet. I just let us drift in that slow water, letting the waves drain from the boat. Then there was a plunking sound and I got splashed. Thought it was a trout at first. Then I looked around and saw those three kids up on the cliff. I waved at them, maybe smiled or called out something, then I saw one of the little bastards throw a rock. I yelled at them to knock it off, but they just kept throwing. The closer we got to the cliff, right underneath them, the closer they were getting with the rocks. They were practically just dropping them on us. Big rocks, too, like Frisbees. I picked up the oars and began to row downstream. To get out of the way. Then one of the rocks hit the gunwale right next to Mattie. That's when the guy, Jonah, hopped out of the boat."

"The boys claim they weren't throwing rocks at you."

"Then they're lying, dude. I can't swear they were trying to brain us or anything, but they were definitely winging them in our direction."

"So what happened when Jonah got out?"

"I told him to get his ass back in the boat. Mattie did, too. And he tried, but it looked like he slipped on the bottom. We were moving by then, picking up speed a little, and then he lost his grip on the gunwale and fell down. I started backing about then, but we were already twenty or thirty feet away and losing ground. Another rock splashed down right next to him. The kids were laughing and yelling stuff. Jonah turned and began to slosh for the beach."

"Would you have done that? Gone for the beach?"

It was speculation, and wouldn't be admissible in court, but I was curious.

Pete barely paused to think about it. "Sure. Dude couldn't just stand there and wait for me. Heck, I didn't even know if I'd be able to get the boat back to him. And I surely would have kicked those kids' little butts for what they were doing."

"But you wouldn't have pushed them off the edge?"

He looked shocked.

"Hell no."

"Because you knew about that sink."

"Yeah."

"What if it was just deep water under there?"

He rubbed the blond stubble on his chin and thought about it.

"I might have been tempted, but I didn't know if those kids could swim or not. They weren't wearing vests, you know. And I've got a license to protect. But they deserved a dunking."

What would I have done? I wondered. What if it had been Rebecca or Moriah they'd almost hit with a rock? I was pretty sure the little bastards would have more to worry about than just getting wet.

"Okay, so what happened after Jonah got to the beach?"

"I couldn't hear much of anything, because we'd gotten down to where the river was rumbling again, and I couldn't see because my back was turned so I could haul on the paddles. I just kind of looked over my shoulder every now and then. I saw Jonah on the beach, and saw the kids above him, maybe shouting down at him. Next time I looked Jonah was just standing there looking sad, like a drowned rat. When I looked a minute later he was starting to climb the cliff. Real slow, like he didn't want to be doing it."

"Were the kids still throwing rocks at him?"

"Not that I could see. But they could have been. Anyway, I expected them to run. They were just kids, right? That dude Jonah's not that big, but he looks kind of tough with all those tattoos and studs. But the kids didn't run. Jonah got to the top and it looked like he was talking to them. When I looked again, one of them—the one that ended up in the river—had a stick and was swinging it at Jonah."

"Could you see if he hit him?"

"Looked like he nailed him, dude. I saw Jonah reach up and grab the side of his head."

"How big was the stick?"

"I don't know. I couldn't really see it all that well. But like this, maybe?" He spread his arms all the way, then bent his elbows a little, shortening the span. "That's the way it looked, anyway."

"Then what happened?"

"Next time I looked, there was a tug-of-war going on. Then the kid went off the edge." After a somber pause, he went on: "The other two, they sort of rushed Jonah. I could hear them then. Screaming and all that. Couldn't hear what they were saying, but I could tell they were pissed. Jonah ran—no, he slid or fell—back down to the beach and went into the water. Like he was trying to find the kid. But the little dude was just gone."

"Did he come up for air, or call for help, or anything like that?"

Pete shook his head.

"The girlfriend, she started screaming. Then she got out her cell phone and called 911. Said a kid was in the river and hadn't come up, and that they needed help. Had me stop rowing to tell them where we were. It was just a couple of minutes later when the cop cars showed up on top of the hill, then a minute later you came out of the trees." He gave me a grin. "Just jumped right in. Like it was a swimming pool. That was something else, dude."

"I didn't know there was a sink."

I wasn't happy. Pete had confirmed everything Jonah had told me. He'd verified that my hunch was correct that the Mann boys were lying about the rock-throwing and stick-swinging, which would make the case messy if it ever went to trial. Worse, he'd convinced me that Jonah didn't deserve what was happening to him. And I, the good cop, was the one doing it to him.

That fact made what I had to do next even more unpleasant.

The motel where Mattie Freda and Jonah Strasburg had been staying was called the Wagon Wheel. It offered the usual amenities—cinder-block construction, vending machines prominently displayed, a parking lot full of minivans, a swimming pool jam-packed with bladderless kids, and exorbitant summertime prices. As much as I tried to dislike the "tourons" and their crowd-loving, littering, give-the-bear-a-Twinkie-and-smile-for-the-camera habits, I had to bless them, too. Their loose dollars were the biggest barrier to the state's desire for drilling or chopping down everything in sight and implementing its shoot-on-sight policy toward the recently recovered wolf packs.

No shade in sight, so I locked Mungo in the truck and left the engine running and the air conditioner blasting. I headed for the front desk but diverted when I spotted Mattie by the pool. She was sitting stonily amid splashing, running, screaming children and the mothers who were trying to restrain them.

With her pale skin and fanglike bangs, she looked even more out of place here than she had on the river. She was dressed entirely in black, sitting rigidly on a deck chair beneath an umbrella. A book was open on her lap, but she wasn't looking down at it. Instead she was just staring into space like a gargoyle from behind a pair of dark lenses. There seemed to be an invisible barrier around her. Not one of the children crossed its line, nor did any thrown balls or flung water seem to penetrate.

Seeing all the small, wet bodies made a lump rise in my throat. The dads were probably all off fishing. I swore I would never leave Moriah behind like that. An irritating voice in my head laughed at that. *Look at yourself, Ant. What the hell do you think you're doing?*

"Mattie?"

She jumped. Her expression hardened even further when she realized who it was who had spoken her name.

"What do you want?"

I sat down on the empty chair next to her.

"I need to get your statement. And I need to apologize for what the county attorney said after the hearing this morning. Sometimes all lawyers think about is winning the case, not the people involved."

She stared for a moment, then looked off into the distance again.

"I need to apologize, too. I got in to see Jonah. After court. I'm sorry for what I said to you. For part of it, anyway. I thought you were the one who beat him up. Now I know you weren't. He said he heard the guards bitching that you insisted he be put into protective custody."

She said it formally, without real sincerity or appreciation for what I had done. I was the enemy. Just because I had done something decent, it didn't mean my enemy status had changed.

"Has he talked to a lawyer yet?"

She laughed, but not very cheerfully.

"The public defender won't represent him."

"I know. You should probably hire someone good."

"Yeah, right. I went through the town's yellow pages, which is about the size of a take-out menu. Do you realize there's more than twenty frigging lawyers in this shitty little town and that only two of them were willing to take his case? Both of them said it would require a large retainer. I was quoted a minimum of ten thousand dollars."

"Do you have it?"

She looked my way again through her black lenses.

"Do I look like I have ten thousand dollars?"

"What about your car? Maybe you could sell it."

She pointed to a 1970s Oldsmobile sedan in the parking lot. It made my Pig look like a shiny Mercedes. The windshield was cracked, the tires bald, the vinyl roof pilled, and the most visible color was gray primer.

"You think somebody would give me even a hundred bucks for that? Besides, it's not even ours. We borrowed it from a guy in Jonah's band."

"I thought the band, Purgatory, was supposed to be pretty good."

"They do okay, for a band. That means maybe eight or ten shows a month, a couple of thousand bucks split four ways, and after the manager takes his fifteen percent. It's not enough to even cover my tuition or our rent. Purgatory isn't ever going to make any serious money unless they sell out. Start doing pop."

I asked some more questions and learned that she hadn't spoken to her parents in years and that they didn't have any money anyway. Jonah's parents had both moved to Israel two years ago and he had barely heard from them since then. Mattie was financing her education with partial scholarships and loans. She and Jonah had about five hundred dollars to fund their remaining vacation.

"Okay," I told her, trying to sound reassuring. "So you'll qualify as indigent. The judge will appoint someone. He has to. You won't have to pay a dime."

I knew that sometimes you're a lot better off with court-appointed counsel. A good public defender—a true believer—can be better than a dream team. The True Believers care about more than just money. It's a calling for them. A crusade against cops and prosecutors, which, having seen things from my brother's side of the law, I didn't really begrudge them. Unless, of course, their swords were hacking at me. Plus the state will pick up the tab for experts and investigators, something a defendant himself has to do if he's represented by private counsel.

But it's hard to convince defendants they're usually better off with a public defender or appointed counsel. It was even harder in this case.

"Luke—the prosecutor—told me the judge is going to call around. There's bound to be someone with the free time and willing to accept the court's rates."

Mattie's look, even concealed behind sunglasses, told me just how bad that sounded.

I sighed and decided to get down to business.

"Are you willing to talk to me about what happened yesterday? About the river trip, and how the kid ended up in the water."

"Why should I tell you anything? You're the guy who put Jonah in jail."

I wanted to tell her that I'd had no choice. I'm a cop, and that's what cops do when it's apparent a crime may have been committed. Especially when it involves the death of a child.

But all I said was "Because it might help Jonah if we can learn all the facts."

Her version was pretty much the same as the guide's. And Jonah's. The kids', too, although like Pete and Jonah she was emphatic that the kids were throwing rocks at them. Trying to hit them, she believed. And she'd watched Cody Wallis pick up the stick and swing it at Jonah's head.

After hearing her out and making my notes, I put my card on the plastic table next to her.

"Call me if you think of anything else. Or if you hear that someone's giving Jonah a rough time in the jail."

She said nothing, and she didn't touch the card.

"Look, Mattie. I'm sorry about all this. I had no choice but to arrest Jonah. If I hadn't, the state troopers would have. Or the people up on the road would probably have torn him to pieces. My only job now is to collect all the facts and evidence and turn it over to the county attorney. He's the one who files charges and decides what those charges should be."

In other words, the biggest cop-out for a cop: *Just doing my job, ma'am.*

She still said nothing. She just watched me squirm, through her dark lenses.

I sighed, closed my notebook, and stood up. I was halfway to the gate in the iron fence surrounding the pool, weaving among the milling children, when she called out.

"Hey!"

I turned around and went back to her.

"I saw in the paper that the funeral's going to be on Sunday. Should I go?"

Now it was my turn to stare blankly at her. All this trouble, all this anger and resentment, and the woman thinks she ought to go to the funeral. Yesterday I'd suspected that Jonah was truly remorseful, that he was probably a good guy. The same was clearly true of her. I wasn't used to dealing with these kinds of people.

She looked away from my stare.

"I'd really like to go," she said softly.

I remembered the clenched jaws I'd seen in court that morning among the relatives and spectators. The slaps on the prosecutor's back and the "Hang him high, Luke. Hang him high."

"Don't," I told her. "The family's pretty upset. The whole community, too. It would be better if you didn't. Your presence there might just make it worse. You should lie low, stay out of sight until this all gets sorted out."

God knows it can't get any worse, I thought. *Or can it?*

fifteen

I was hanging in space at eight o'clock on Saturday morning. It was exactly where I wanted to be.

Two hundred feet off the deck, the right half of my body wedged in a fat crack splitting the underside of a forty-foot roof, my muscles shaking with an overdose of lactic acid, and my breath coming in ragged gasps, I was happy. It didn't matter that sharp crystals were grinding into my shoulder and forearm and knees, or that there was a very good chance I was about to drop like a bomb and take the big swing—a swing that would end in an explosion against the rock face below. I'd made it out almost twenty feet from the little cave where the roof began. Halfway. Farther than I'd ever made it before. Now if I could just get some protection into the crack, I'd be safe.

The rope ran back to the anchor in the cave from where it was tied to the self-belaying device on my harness. Only one piece of pro kept it from drooping all that way: a Number 5 Camalot whose expanded quad cams I'd placed by standing in the cave and reaching out as far as I could. But that was still fifteen feet behind me.

If—when—I fell, I would drop straight down at first, toward

the green blur of aspen leaves that grew up to the side of the cliff. Then, as the rope caught my weight, it would swing me toward the smooth granite face below the cave. I would bash into it, just as I'd already done three times that morning. But this time, since I was farther out than ever before, I knew the cost of a fall would be magnified by the increased momentum of the swing. I would pay the price for progress with pain.

But I was determined to pay and pay until I couldn't lift my arms above my head, until the skin on my shoulders and hands was ripped clean off. Then, stripped bare, I'd load Mungo in the Pig and drive to Denver.

But I wasn't feeling the fear, or the pain, or even the anticipation of seeing Rebecca and my baby daughter. All my consciousness was focused on nothing but somehow freeing my left hand, snatching up the cam clipped to my waist, and cramming it into the crack. There was no other thought in my head. Some people call it flow, or being in the zone. What climbers and surfers and skydivers call it is feeding the Rat. The addictive joy of putting yourself in a situation so primitive and physical that your awareness of everything else in life is turned off completely.

I let go of the crystal I had been pinching with my left thumb and fingers and reached for a cam on my harness. Immediately, I felt myself on the verge of taking a dive. Gravity hung on to my back like a three-hundred-pound gorilla. I was suspended only by where my right elbow, palm, and both knees were jammed up into the flaring crack. Suspended, but barely—a feather could have brushed me out. My hand was shaking so bad I couldn't get the cam unclipped.

Then a shrill tone cut through the air.

And my world suddenly accelerated at warp speed.

I dropped in a great swoop, the wind roaring in my ears and the colors of sky, stone, and trees all running together. *Fall like a cat,* I reminded myself as I did the opposite and wrapped my arms around my head and brought my knees up to my chest. Then, just as the momentum reached its peak, I struck the cliff.

I hit the rock wall like some large, stupid bird smacking into a plate-glass window. A retarded pelican, perhaps. A long *aaaahhhhh* came from my mouth, and it didn't want to stop. It seemed like minutes before I could actually inhale a new breath. And by that time, of course, the phone in my pack in the cave had stopped ringing.

When the stars stopped dancing and I looked up to see where I'd fallen from, there was a surprise. The Number 5 Camalot swung there prettily, maybe twenty-five feet out under the roof. I'd somehow slapped it in before cutting loose. Next time, if I could clip the rope to it, I'd be protected. No more crashing into the wall. And only fifteen feet more to the lip!

I wanted to shout in premature triumph, but I was hurting too bad for that. I hollered in my mind, though—I was getting closer to climbing what had to be the hardest wide crack in the world. This realized, I began to wonder if Moriah, when older, would really appreciate having the world's hardest fat crack named after her. Maybe, I thought, I needed to think up a new name.

Then the phone began ringing shrilly again.

I grabbed at holds on the merely vertical face and hauled my battered carcass up into the cave. If my life were anywhere approaching normal, I would have left the damn thing in the truck. But when you've got an ex-fiancée you're still half in love with, a six-month-old daughter, and a handicapped, drug-addicted brother, you tend to want to stay in touch. Staring at the screen, though, I saw that it wasn't any of these reasons I had for carrying the phone.

"What the hell, Luke?" I asked after reluctantly hitting the button.

"The defense has arrived. And you aren't going to believe who they got to represent this scumbag." He sounded genuinely alarmed. "Get your ass over here and talk to them. Pronto. I don't want them to have any reason to try and continue this thing. I don't want them complaining to the judge that our lead investigator dragged his feet on this."

And then he hung up.

"The stakes have gone up," Luke announced when I walked into his office an hour later.

He was grinning, but it wasn't the shit-eating grin he'd worn at the arraignment the day before. This one looked strained. And a little sick.

"What happened? Who is this guy?"

He shook his head and stretched the shallow grin further.

"You'll see, Burns. You'll see. Just try not to piss your pants, okay?"

Walking stiffly in his well-worn boots, he escorted me down the hall to a closed door. Here he paused, forcibly settling his features into what was probably meant to be a friendly, slightly bored expression. I noticed he was wearing a suit even though it was Saturday morning.

The man and the woman in the conference room were wearing suits, too. They sat on the other side of a big table, with file folders and laptop computers laid out in front of them. Evidently they'd been working while waiting for me. The room reeked from an overdose of someone's cologne. The scent of chemicals, spice, and leather was too heavy for a woman, so it had to be the man's.

The woman—who I couldn't help but notice first—was more than a little bit attractive. She had blue eyes, blond hair, and a spray of freckles across her nose and cheekbones. Wearing no jewelry or makeup, and with her pulled-back hair cut prudently above her shoulders, she looked like an athlete. A hard-core athlete. A runner or a biker, I guessed. Maybe even a climber. We might have something in common. The way she looked up at me, though, was far from friendly.

The man was good-looking, too. He was probably twenty

years older, in his mid-forties. He had a lantern jaw and gray-black hair sculpted back from a high forehead. His dark green suit was probably the most expensive I'd ever seen. And he was wearing it on a hot Saturday morning in Badwater, Wyoming.

They were staring at me, not Luke; the man smiling, the woman most definitely not. Other than for the blonde's glower, I saw no reason to wet myself as Luke had suggested I might.

"This is Antonio Burns. He's acting as my lead investigator on this," he said. "Burns, meet William J. Bogey."

He said it like he was announcing the presence of royalty. Or introducing me to my executioner. The man's name was vaguely familiar—I knew I'd heard of him somewhere before.

I leaned across the table and held out my hand.

"Nice to meet you."

He rose halfway out of his chair to take my hand, then hesitated. I followed his eyes down to my outstretched paw and saw why. Dried blood caked my knuckles and the sticky residue of athletic tape made my hand look none too clean. Certainly not the kind of hand he'd want brushing his bright white French cuffs. But he swallowed and shook anyway.

"The pleasure's all mine," he said in a smooth baritone. "Let me introduce you to a former student of mine, Brandy Walsh. She just graduated last month and has agreed to act as my co-counsel in this matter."

"Hi." I smiled at her.

She didn't smile back or offer her hand.

Feeling persecuted by her gaze, I irritably wondered why Luke had agreed to meet with these people on a Saturday morning. Luke was, after all, fat and lazy. It would have been more his style to insist on office hours. But I figured it was a good thing that someone who so obviously made him nervous was taking Jonah's case. Maybe it would bring him to his senses, or at least pressure him to offer a reasonable plea deal. Maybe it would make this whole thing just go away.

"I was a student of Boogie's at UWyo, too," Luke said to me.

"That's what they call him: Boogie. Has to do with his seventies-style hippie politics or something. He was a pretty good professor, though."

"And Luke was a very good student. But I'm afraid any attempts to pass on my political or legal views utterly failed."

Both men laughed. Brandy Walsh didn't—she was too busy giving me the stink eye. For a few more minutes Luke and Bogey sparred with fake good humor, remembering old classroom debates, until Luke finally pulled out chairs for both of us.

"So, you ready to talk a deal?" he asked. "I'm not really sure what I can do for a guy who murdered a little kid. Not even for you, Boogie."

"Maybe we can talk about that after we exercise our due diligence, Luke," Bogey said with polite condescension. "I think perhaps we should try and discover a little more about what happened on the river."

Luke smirked.

"Oh yeah, that's right. A big shot like you needs to do a lot of research, then bill the county at your hourly rate. I forgot—but hey, I'm just a dumb hick prosecutor."

I was beginning to sense that the animosity between them was more than knee-deep.

Still smiling nicely, Bogey said, "We'd like to begin by asking Mr. Burns some questions. Brandy prepared a preliminary list last night."

Brandy flipped open her computer.

I looked at Luke, who shrugged.

"Sure, he'll answer your questions. But you could just wait and read his reports."

"I expect we'll want more detail than what will likely be in his reports," Bogey said diplomatically.

Brandy was still watching me. She gave me a grim, unpleasant smile. When she spoke her voice was fake-sweet.

"You don't mind, do you? We just want to make sure we get the same answers from you on the witness stand."

I did mind. What a bitch. I'd met her only two minutes earlier and she was already implying that I was a liar. In fairness, though, I'd already decided that *she* was a liar. She was a defense lawyer, after all, or at least training to be one. And most likely a True Believer like her professor. Luke's comment about Bogey's "seventies-style hippie politics" was something he'd often complained about in the old days when we'd be called to the stand and dragged over the coals by public defenders. They were often True Believers—attorneys who believed that anything, from misdirecting the jury to outright lying to slandering cops and prosecutors, was justified in the cause of getting their clients off. Over beers after one grueling trial, a PD who belatedly decided that I wasn't, as a cop, necessarily an emissary of Satan told me, "It has nothing to do with the search for the truth. Not for your side, and not for mine. A trial is war. Once it's declared, when the county attorney files charges against my client, all questions about right and wrong, the truth, and the reasons for the war in the first place get thrown out the window. There's only one thing both sides are focused on and that's to win. At all costs. Using whatever tactics are necessary. You challenge the arrest. You indoctrinate the jury. You annihilate the witnesses. Hell, you firebomb Dresden if you have to, you nuke Hiroshima."

"I don't mind answering your questions," I told Brandy Walsh.

"Good."

She plucked a mini tape recorder from where she'd apparently been hiding it in her lap and thumbed it on. Then she posed her fingers above her keyboard. She was going to record this two ways, just to be doubly sure she could prove any lies and to let me know that she expected nothing less of me.

"First, we need to know how to reach you in case we have later questions."

I gave her my cell-phone number.

"And your address?"

I recited the office's address in Cheyenne.

She looked up. "No, your address here in Badwater."

"I don't have one."

"Then where are you staying?"

"Here and there. Camping out, mostly," I admitted.

"Don't be evasive, Agent Burns. We have a right to know."

I looked at Luke, wanting to roll my eyes. He was slouched back in his chair, pretending to be bored again. I looked at Bogey, but he was watching his protégé with apparent pleasure. And she was still staring rudely at me, waiting for my answer.

"I'm not being evasive. I live out of my truck. I sleep wherever I want."

I'd always thought it was kind of cool, not having a fixed address. I liked sleeping under the stars far more than I did under a ton of beams, plaster, and injected-foam insulation. But the way she was looking at me made me feel like a homeless person. And homeless not by choice—a person no one would tolerate in their home.

"They don't pay these DCI fellows as much as they do us lawyers," Luke joked.

The questioning went on. I held back my annoyance and told them what I'd seen and heard and exactly what their client had said. I kept my opinion that the whole thing was a stupid accident to myself, as well as the fact that I thought their client was a pretty good guy. My opinions had nothing to do with the legal case; stating them would serve no purpose but to piss Luke off and get me in deeper shit with my own office.

It wasn't until we were past all my dealings with Jonah that she switched to leading questions. Lawyers love these, particularly with witnesses they deem hostile. They're a great weapon—with them it's so easy for a lawyer to trip a witness up, or make him look bad, or twist his words into something he never intended. Their sole purpose is to nail you in a tricky way, and trying to avoid them is like trying to dodge hurled knives while strapped to a revolving wheel.

"You never read him his Miranda rights, did you?"

"No. I never asked him anything incriminating once he was in custody."

That seemed to make her mad.

"You didn't read him his rights when you interrogated him at the river?"

"Nope. I wasn't interrogating him. I was just trying to find out what had happened. He wasn't in custody yet."

"Oh? So he was free to get up and leave?"

"No, but he didn't know that."

"So you admit to tricking him."

"Lady," Luke finally interrupted, "we're about done here. Those are suppression issues, and you can save 'em for the suppression hearing. And you probably don't know this, but it isn't real polite to ask leading questions like this in a courtesy interview. You'd better save that stuff for when you're putting on a big show for the jury. If you're foolish enough to take this thing that far."

While Brandy Walsh's tan turned a little pink and she let Luke feel her blue-eyed glare, Bogey spoke up.

"Actually, we intend to ask the judge to allow us to depose Agent Burns under oath. Prior to the suppression hearing."

Luke chuckled. "It must have been a while since you've done a criminal case, Professor. Depositions are for civil matters."

The professor chuckled, too. He responded to Luke's mockery by taking a poke at me.

"They're not unheard of in criminal cases, Luke. We'll be asking the judge to allow one. Due to Mr. Burns's reputation, of course. I think the fact that you've chosen him as your lead investigator in this matter will allow us considerable latitude in questioning him."

My face got hot. The only appropriate way to respond to a comment like that would be to leap over the table and grab him by the throat, but I held on to that impulse.

"And we'll need copies of all Mr. Burns's notes about this.

And any other notes or reports that you've received. Can you give us copies right now?"

Luke shook his head. "I'm no copy jockey. Don't even know how to turn the damn machine on."

"Perhaps Mr. Burns can handle it?"

Luke laughed.

"No. He's a DCI agent. Not in his job description. You can get your copies Monday or Tuesday, whenever my secretary can get to it."

Luke was keeping his cool. I was a little bit proud of him, tweaking the professor and his attack poodle right back, but I also knew that there was no good reason not to turn over everything now. The defense would get it all sooner or later—they had a right to it under the rules of discovery. But still, I could definitely understand his desire to screw around with these people.

"Luke, you aren't going to make me have to talk with the judge about this, are you?" Bogey asked in an amused but slightly scolding tone.

"You can talk to the judge until you're blue in the face. Only it had better be in open court, and the discovery hearing won't be scheduled until at least Thursday. You see, Boogie, this is just another case on my docket. It wouldn't be fair for me to treat it any different than anything else I've got on my plate. I can't give you priority just because you used to be a big shot."

Bogey went on smiling, but it was with his mouth only, not his eyes.

"Luke," he said slowly, "I think you're going to find that this is like no case you've ever seen before."

Now that threats were being made openly, it was pretty clear that the "courtesy interview" was over. We all stood up. Very reluctantly, I again shook hands with Bogey, who was still smiling. At me. Like I was some delicious meal he was about to eat. I turned toward Brandy, but she was ignoring all of us. She was bent over, packing away her computer in a briefcase on the floor.

If she hadn't been so unpleasant, and if I weren't such a gentleman, I might have admired the way her navy skirt was pulled tight across lean buttocks. Instead I looked at Luke, who wasn't being such a gentleman, and Bogey, who was now taking the opportunity to look down her shirt.

When she stood, she caught Luke's ogle. The look of disgust she gave him made me want to laugh and wince at the same time. With a wrinkling of her nose that was almost a snarl, she hefted the briefcase off the floor and marched out of the room.

Bogey followed, still smiling tightly, saying, "We'll be in touch, gentlemen."

I noticed that he, too, was wearing cowboy boots. They seemed to be de rigueur for lawyers in this state. Unlike Luke's, though, Bogey's were expensive ostrich skin.

When they were gone, Luke started to laugh.

"Woowee, that was fun. That little girl had your number, QuickDraw!"

"Yeah," I had to agree. "She did."

"What a hard-ass! And you can take that any way you want. Hell, she could crack walnuts with that ass. And bust balls with the rest of what she's got. Do you think Bogey's banging her yet?"

"I don't know, Luke."

"If he's not already, he will be, the bastard. When he was famous he was always banging his students."

"Including you?"

Luke laughed so hard he started coughing.

He seemed pretty pleased with the way things had gone, especially given how things had started. I could tell he felt good for having stood up to his former professor, a man who obviously intimidated him. They must have had some good arguments back in law school, and I imagined that Bogey had got the best of him each time. Bogey was so smooth, while even in the old days Luke had a hard time disguising his emotions and not letting them overwhelm him. Obviously, Luke was eager for a rematch on his home court.

"That guy's so damn arrogant," he said, still chuckling. "Dear God, I just love getting to jerk his chain. He was once a serious big shot, getting prime-time cases, and when he didn't get them, he was on TV to analyze them. But he's been a loser ever since some victim in a rape trial he was doing killed herself. People said he went after her too hard on cross. After that, no one would touch him. And it's still kicking his ass—you can see it. Let me say it again, QuickDraw; we're going to have us some fun on this thing."

sixteen

I did the math, and then felt ambivalent about the sum.

It would take nine hours to drive to Denver—even a gold special-agent's badge couldn't push the Pig more than ten miles an hour over the speed limit of sixty-five. That pace would put me at Rebecca's loft long after Moriah had gone to bed. And since Luke had ordered me to be present at Cody Wallis's funeral at two the next afternoon, I would have to leave Denver before Moriah even woke up. If I was lucky, I might get to do the midnight bottle-feeding in return for eighteen hours on the road—a feeding in which she would probably cry and punch and kick from the moment I picked her up until Rebecca took her from me. On top of that dismal prospect, Rebecca wouldn't be too thrilled about me showing up so late and bailing so early. It was very doubtful I'd be invited to share her bed.

So I opted to stay in Wyoming. There was plenty to do, even though my body was too burnt from the morning's exertions to crawl up into the world's hardest fat crack.

First I had to flush out the lactic acid with a long run on an old elk trail that meandered among the cottonwoods lining the creek at the bottom of the canyon. This also served to strip away any extra remaining ounces of fat that would weigh me down when I made my next attempt at levitating into the sky. Then there were backpack-weighted dips to do between two boulders in order to counterbalance the punishment I'd given the muscles in my back, shoulders, and biceps. And there were pots I hadn't scraped real well in a couple of days, tiny holes in my tent from campfire embers that needed patching, cam triggers that needed oiling, and a gun that needed cleaning.

I finished off the chores with a jump into my bath—a clear pond formed by a beaver dam. I gritted my teeth against the cold and hyperventilated for more than a minute until my body was willing to work in the water. While I shampooed with a blob of biodegradable soap, Mungo swam circles around me, huffing water and paddling madly with her oversize paws. She nosed every inch of the beaver dam but wasn't willing to dive to explore. I could almost hear the beaver laughing at this predator so out of her element.

At sunset we drove back into town for dinner. I wanted to eat in a restaurant—I was sick of my white-gas cooking and I felt a rare need to be around people, particularly people who didn't know me. Later, I planned to use the office key I'd gotten from Luke to run criminal histories on all our witnesses.

The restaurant I chose was a Mexican place called Cesar's. It looked run-down from the outside, but its parking lot was nearly full. It seemed like an indication of good food until I walked inside and found all the people at the dim bar, not around the tables. Apparently it was a local watering hole where the people drank but knew better than to eat. I was hungry, though, so I stayed.

After five minutes a chubby waitress with big hair finally escorted me to a booth in the back. The table was sticky with crumbs, the menu was slick with grease, and the tall margarita she brought me was nothing but syrup. By the time I actually ordered, I wasn't looking forward to getting my food anymore. Which was fine, because it took a long, long time for it to come.

There was entertainment, though.

The bar at the front of the restaurant was getting frantic with the Saturday-night crowd. Most of the customers appeared to be itinerant male roughnecks out to celebrate the opening of more public lands to drilling. They were all white, twenty to forty, and drinking hard to wash away the sweat, grease, and dust of a shift on the rigs. There were a few little groups of local women eyeing and being eyed by the men, a few older locals watching the fun, and above them all, glassy-eyed and superior, were the smoke-stained heads of deer, elk, and pronghorns.

The bar, and the crowd, brought on a strange sense of déjà vu. I didn't know where it came from until a crack of pool balls brought a cold sweat to my skin. It was exactly like the bar in Durango, Colorado, where my brother had killed a man. I'd visited the place one autumn night soon after he was charged, trying to ascertain just what he'd done and whether he was being treated fairly by the local prosecutor. To my dismay, it turned out he was.

Soon after being released from federal prison (for chain-sawing five miles of telephone poles in a drug-induced rage after the phone company had been late in installing his phone line), Roberto had hit the road on his motorcycle for a climbing trip fueled by speedballs, an injected combination of heroin and cocaine. In Durango he'd been sitting out a thunderstorm at the bar one night with a girl he met there. She was his type—a fragile recovering junkie and former runaway trying like hell to pull her life together. My brother worshiped such women, and they liked to try to mother him. While they were talking, a roughneck lurched out of a booth full of drunken friends and approached. "Take off, spic," he'd told my brother as he shouldered between them. Laughing and clowning for his buddies back at the table, he reached up between where the girl's legs were spread on the stool and roughly groped her.

Roberto had laughed, too. Laughed so hard, in fact, that he managed to smash off the rim of his beer mug on the bar's edge. When the roughneck turned back to him, Roberto had screwed what remained of the mug into the man's face. Then he'd taken him to the dirty floor and beaten him to death.

I began to get that queasy feeling again, started to breathe a little too fast, and I drank more of the margarita even though it only made the symptoms worse. After a few minutes I began to get ahold of myself. I forced deeper breaths and managed to push away the image of my brother now, no longer a semipsychotic defender of animals and women, but a cripple with a dented head and a scarred throat.

A distraction helped; into the bar came the paramedic from the river. She definitely stood out in low-riding jeans and a buckskin halter top. Attending to her were three men who, judging by their short hair and mustaches, had to be either fellow paramedics, firemen, or cops. I watched her joke and shove at them and, laughing, get shoved back. They appeared to be celebrating something of their own tonight.

I ate a tasteless enchilada and watched. Sitting in the dim back end of the restaurant, it was disassociating, like watching TV. The show was about people I had nothing in common with, laughing at jokes that I probably wouldn't find very funny. Instead of feeling superior, it made me depressed. And homesick for the only real home I'd ever known, my grandfather's *estancia* on the Argentine pampas. On a Saturday night there, we'd be outside by the fire pit with all the vaqueros' families, eating *parrillada* from a freshly killed steer and drinking wine made from grapes grown just a hundred yards away. Laughing. Playing games. Maybe singing. My brother and I would be planning another trip into the Torres del Paine, or maybe just back from one. And here I was now, seven thousand miles away and all alone.

What the hell was I doing here? It was hard to remember.

So I was kind of happy to be distracted further from these thoughts when the paramedic noticed me as she came out of the bathroom. Jerking her body in exaggerated surprise, she grinned and veered toward my table.

"You're still alive! Man, that's a shame. Twice now you've made it look like I don't know my job."

"Sorry to disappoint you," I told her.

"Well, maybe you can try to make it up to me. You here alone?"

I nodded and she slid into the booth. She scooted so close that her hip bumped mine. She smelled of some kind of vanilla perfume.

She looked at me very intently, then said, "Well, Special Agent Antonio Burns, are you as big a pain in the ass when you're off duty as you are when you're on?"

Her breath was ripe with the fruity smell of hard alcohol.

"How do you know my name?"

She laughed.

"Everybody knows your name, man. All I had to do was ask some cops I hang around with. Half of them think you're some kind of hero, and the other half think you're Dirty Harry. One guy told me that they even talk about you at the academy in Rock Springs, a sort of teaching tool on what *not* to do in an undercover operation."

"That's nice to know."

"So which is it, Antonio? You a hero, or a bastard?"

"The only thing I do know is that *you're* obviously as big a pain in the ass off duty as on," I told her.

Her laughter made her blond curls shake. Her eyes, which were wet and bloodshot, stayed on me. Around them her skin was dark and sparkly with some kind of eye shadow.

Then she pretended to pout. "It's my birthday. I can be a pain in the ass if I want to. What I know about *you* is that you're interesting. Maybe dangerous, too. And I'm drunk enough to be interested in a little danger."

It had been a long time since I'd been approached so directly. And it took away some of the sting from the morning's interview with Brandy Walsh. I looked away and drained the oversize glass of yellow syrup that the waitress had claimed was a margarita. I belatedly realized that maybe there was some tequila in it after all, because I was beginning to feel off balance. The chubby waitress brought me another—it was two-for-ones all night, she said—as well as two screwdrivers for my new friend.

"What's your name?" I asked.

"Danger Girl. But I was born Jo. Jo Richards."

"Who are those guys you're with?"

She said they were friends, fellow paramedics. They were keeping a close eye on us, squinting our way in the restaurant's gloom. But none of them looked particularly pissed, so I assumed there wasn't a boyfriend among them.

"Why don't we go have a drink with them? Then maybe we can take off and go somewhere."

I shook my head.

"I can't. I have to work tonight."

"No, you don't. The only thing you have to work at tonight is making up for the fact that you've twice hurt my feelings by refusing to let me treat you." Jo leaned closer, until her lips almost touched my ear, and poked a finger into my ribs. "Tonight you're going to let me treat you, Antonio Burns. It's my birthday, damn it."

I smiled and sipped my drink. It was tempting. Man, it was tempting. I could imagine what her lush body would look like without the fringed halter and jeans. I could imagine what it would feel like. I looked into her blurry eyes and knew that the ride would be a wild one. And, God, I needed a ride into oblivion.

Her fingers slid down my side and gripped my thigh.

"Where should we do the examination?"

Then she laughed a little nervously, as if, even drunk, she realized just how badly she was behaving.

"I'm camping out," I explained. "More than a half hour outside of town."

"Well, I've been living with my folks since I broke up with my boyfriend. That won't work. They're nice, but they're foursquare fundamentalists. Dad would chase you out with his shotgun and Mom would make their whole church pray for our souls for the next ten years."

She stuck out her lower lip for a moment, then looked around and gave me a sly smile.

"Maybe we should just do the initial assessment in your car."

"Only if you don't mind sharing the backseat with a hundred-and-twenty-pound mutt."

Jo pouted again. And I pondered. I couldn't take her to the county attorney's office, could I? No. I wasn't ready to jeopardize my job like that. Plus I was still half in love with Rebecca. And Jo was just too wasted. I was enjoying the explicit flirting, I was flattered and tantalized by it, but I already knew it wasn't going to happen tonight. In fact, it wasn't going to happen ever. She just wasn't my type. But I let her thumb and fingertips massage my thigh just above my knee as I swallowed more syrupy tequila.

People at the bar looked toward the door, and I heard conversations pause then pick up again. I squinted through the dark and the smoke and saw that the Mann brothers had just walked in. Horseshoe and Hairlip, the twins I'd confronted by my truck and who were rumored to share a meth addiction.

To Jo I said, "I think we should schedule an appointment, Doctor. Maybe sometime when you're sober."

She laughed again, but this time it sounded fake. Some of the heat that had been building between us was blown away. The gentle pressure of her fingers stopped kneading my thigh.

"Hey, Antonio, I may be a little trashed, but I know what I'm doing. I've had a crush on you for a year now, ever since I tried to wrap your thick head at that old potash mine."

"You said you didn't even know my name until two days ago."

"Yeah, but that doesn't mean I wasn't interested. Nobody would talk about you at the mine. Or what had happened. All I know is what I read in the papers, about some kind of botched raid on an underground meth lab. Something the Feds said DCI had screwed up, but the word is it was the other way around. Your name was never mentioned. The FBI was running around squelching everybody, including yours truly. What the hell was going on?"

"I could tell you, Jo, but then I'd have to kill you."

She groaned at the joke and continued, "Oh yeah, then you got in that piece-of-shit truck that almost ran over the commander of the state patrol. Thought he was going to go into cardiac arrest, he was so mad. I liked that. That bastard's a friend of my dad's. He's been hitting on me since, like, I turned fourteen."

That gave me the opportunity to change the subject. I asked Jo about herself while I watched the men at the bar. The Manns were looking around, smirking at the other customers and staring back aggressively at anyone who met their eyes. They moved their heads and arms in little jerks, drinking from their beer bottles too often. Even from across the dark restaurant it wasn't hard to guess that they were tweaking.

Jo was still talking, telling me about growing up in Badwater, about being a junior regional rodeo champ as well as Miss Colter County, about trying to save up enough money by living at home to finish college in Billings, then maybe go on to medical school.

"I know you're supposed to talk about yourself when you're drunk, but I want to talk about you. Who the hell are you, Special Agent Burns? Why'd you risk your sexy little butt jumping in that sink after the Wallis kid?"

"I didn't know there was a sink there."

The one with the scraggly soul patch—Hairlip—finally locked in on me. He nudged his twin, said something, and pointed. Then they were both glaring my way with mean little smiles on their mouths.

"Uh-uh. That's not what I heard. Word is that you dove twice. The first time you maybe didn't know, the second time you had to."

"Do you know those two idiots at the bar?"

It took Jo a minute to focus that far and pick out which pair of idiots I was talking about—the ones staring hard at us. When she managed, she rolled her wet eyes.

"The 'roid boys. Wonder who let those freaks in here?"

Carrying their bottles, the brothers began weaving through the empty tables and coming our way. They walked stiffly, sticking out their puffed-up chests and holding their arms out from their sides. They both wore flannel shirts with the sleeves rolled high so everyone could admire their overbuilt biceps. I pushed the table lightly and discovered it wasn't bolted to the floor. Then I sat where I was but shifted my weight forward, over my feet.

"Maybe you should take off," I said to Jo.

She laughed, but didn't move to leave.

"Hey, Wolfman," Horseshoe called as they approached. "What the fuck you doing here? You're in some deep shit, man. Our friend Smit's gonna be looking for you before long."

"He ain't no Wolfman," Hairlip said. "He's a fucking rabbit. That's why he ran away yesterday before we were done talking to him. Ol' Smit is going to be sticking a boot up your ass when he gets out. That was a pussy thing to do, shooting him with that stun gun. Had to get six fucking stitches in his tongue."

They were definitely tweaking. It was as plain in the cadence of their speech and the way their jaws were clenched as it was in their pinprick pupils. It wasn't good, either, that they were obviously friends with the giant that I'd Tased in the jail. I wondered if they had encouraged him to further torment Jonah. Not good at all. In just forty-eight hours I'd apparently stirred up what must be the entire criminal underbelly of Badwater, Wyoming.

Before I could say anything, Horseshoe continued, leaning against the table now, "What the fuck you doing here anyway? You're supposed to be working, making sure that New York motherfucker gets the chair for what he did to our cousin. Make sure those fucking city lawyers come into town today don't get him off like O. J."

News sure gets around in a small town like Badwater.

Jo spoke up before I could.

"You boys use the word *fuck* one more time and I'm going to slap those grins right off your stupid faces. Then I'm going to stop by the clinic and have a word with your mom."

The brothers glowered at her, acknowledging her for the first time.

Horseshoe said, "What are you doing with this guy, Jo? He's a goddamned narc."

"Then maybe he should be taking a closer look at what you two morons have been up to."

"That's bullshit!" Hairlip howled. "We don't mess around with that shit! Anyone who says so is lying."

"Yeah!" his twin said. Then he tried to change the subject back to accusing me by saying, "This jerk told a state trooper to shoot Randy and Trey when they were going after the guy who killed Cody."

"Because they were interfering with CPR," Jo said. She'd really been checking up on me, too, finding out everything she could about what had happened at the river. "And he said it just to scare them off."

"It was a shitty thing to do," Horseshoe said, turning his glower on me. "You don't threaten our little bros."

Jo waved a hand dismissively, saying, "They're brats, same as the two of you. Always sneaking around the woods in back of my folks' place, just like you perverts did when you were in junior high. Hoping to see me in my underwear or something. Now get out of here. Go smoke your crank or pump your weights or masturbate into the mirror. Just get out of my face."

For some reason they took this from her. I guessed it was some leftover power from high school, where she had surely been older and undoubtedly popular. I tried not to laugh, knowing that adding my ridicule to hers would immediately escalate things.

"You're a real pain in the ass, Jo."

"Everybody's saying that tonight," she said, nudging my leg with hers.

As they turned to go, Horseshoe suddenly leaned across the table and stuck his finger in my face.

"You'd better watch yourself, narc. Don't mess with us. And you take care of that fucking tourist."

Jo knocked his hand away.

"Get over yourself, Ned. You aren't scaring anybody."

I hadn't said a word, but they were making me nervous. These idiots were too dumb to care who they were messing with. They were more afraid of this girl, and their mother, than that I was a cop with a nasty reputation. This stupidity made them very dangerous. If they were a little smarter, they wouldn't have bothered me so much.

The computers in the county attorney's office were all out of date. The software was ancient, the text on the screen a sickly green, and the modem connection to the FBI's National Crime Information Center still a screeching dial-up. It was as if I'd been transported back to another era—ages ago, at least eight years, when I'd been a brand-new agent with a master's degree, chock-full of enthusiasm and respect for the system of justice, learning about the real world from Luke Endow.

After the two large margaritas, my technological disdain seemed kind of funny. I slept in the dirt but could complain about old computers.

It was nice, at least, to have the office to myself. To not have to listen to Luke's tough-prosecutor talk, or endure the stares of his staff, who looked at me like I was an animal that had escaped from the zoo. At nine o'clock on a Saturday night, the office was totally silent but for the hum of old machinery.

Mungo sniffed around on the well-worn carpet. She'd already given me a thorough sniffing when I'd climbed in the Pig. The wolf-dog poked her head between the front seats and nosed my face, not licking, but picking up where Jo had kissed me before I could leave the booth. Then she caught the scent of Jo's perfume or hand lotion on my pants, and gave me a very dirty look.

"Don't even think of ratting me out," I told her.

Not that Rebecca would really care.

I typed Jonah's full name and birth date into the box on the screen. He had been cited for jaywalking in 2003, just as he'd told me. And for having an open container of alcohol in a prohibited place in 2002. The computer noted that he'd been fined for both crimes, in addition to a surcharge for FTAing—failing to appear—at one initial hearing date.

Yeah, Jonah was a hardened criminal, all right. Luke was going to be disappointed.

Next I typed Mattie Freda's name and birth date. Here I got a solid hit. She'd been arrested three times, all for misdemeanor trespass. But no convictions were listed, so the cases must have been dismissed. *Trespass* means different things in different states—it could be anything from burglary to shoplifting. But in her case, I suspected it was protesting. She looked like and acted like an activist for something.

I printed it out, because if Luke could trick her into denying ever having been arrested, he could use it to undermine all of her testimony, which was likely to be favorable to Jonah. It's the kind of nasty thing both sides do in a trial.

I checked Pete the Guide, too, not for impeachment material—his testimony was likely to be unbiased—but for any surprises in his background. He'd gotten a DUI in California and that was all. I printed it out, too. We'd need to share this stuff with the defense, anyway.

And that was all the witnesses, except for the two underage Mann brothers, who wouldn't have NCIC records. I checked them out by going into the file room, switching on the light, and scanning the juvie files.

As I expected, there was a wide shelf half full of Mann files. But all of the files were at least a couple of years old and dealt with Ned and Zach Mann, rather than the younger bros. Wondering if the twins had always been the scumbags they appeared to be now, I pulled out two identical-size stacks of folders and took them to a table.

Theft at age twelve, CDs from Kmart, charges dismissed in return for "parental correction." Theft again at age fourteen, this time a bottle of Jack from a local liquor store, resulting in a deferred prosecution requiring six months good behavior. Assault at fifteen, beating up a kid five years younger who'd picked on their brother Randy, reduced to harassment and eight hours of community service. Also theft at age fifteen, stealing a kid's skateboard, case dismissed, no reason given.

Age sixteen got even more interesting. Assaulting another kid—their own age this time—who they claimed made fun of them. Theft of more liquor. Cruelty to animals in dropping another classmate's cat out of the backseat window of a moving car. Sexual assault for getting another classmate so drunk she passed out and then taking advantage of her. The only thing they'd actually been "adjudicated" for was the theft. Either Luke's predecessor had been pretty lax, or the brothers had learned how to work the system.

Age seventeen had only one charge, arson, for starting a fire in the Shoshone National Forest. This had resulted in another adjudication, their third. Three adjudications and you're out—they were sent to a kids' boot camp in Utah for six months, which was presumably the reason why they stayed out of trouble for the rest of the year.

After putting the files away, I plugged the twins' names into NCIC on the computer. Nothing but some pending possession charges for a small amount of marijuana in another Wyoming county. They'd apparently been good in the three years since their eighteenth birthdays. But I knew that wasn't true—I strongly suspected them of using both steroids and meth. They just hadn't gotten caught. Or maybe their family had some pull with the sheriff and the county attorney. Small towns often dispensed their own informal justice, based on a combination of local values and politics.

Mungo rested her head on my sullied knee. I scratched her ears while I considered whether I needed to check up on anyone else. Finally I entered *William J. Bogey* into the box. Luke might appreciate a little opposition research. There were a dozen William Bogeys, but none that seemed to have the right dates or locations. Too bad. Some dirt on him would have made Luke very, very happy.

I tried Googling Bogey and had more success. A huge amount of it, actually—thousands of hits. Some apparently were legal filings, others opinion pieces he had penned, some announced his appearance as a pundit on CNN or MSNBC, and a huge amount were articles either about him or mentioning his name. I looked at a few that appeared to feature him prominently. They had headlines like "Attorney Bogey Alleges Planted Evidence," or "Bogey Accuses Police of 'Gross' Misconduct," and "Bogey: Prosecutor Lied." Reading the articles, I found that a lot of people felt he'd gone over the top when he'd served as lead defense counsel for a professional athlete accused of rape. He didn't just tear into prosecutors, cops, and hostile witnesses, but he went after the victim, too—a sixteen-year-old girl with a history of mental illness—and absolutely tore her to shreds. The girl had actually killed herself after the fifth day of cross-examination.

The articles, as well as the announcements of his TV appearances, were all at least a few years old. Maybe he was hoping this small case in Colter County would bring him back into the limelight. The thought made me groan out loud. I hoped like hell Luke would settle this thing fast.

Next I put *Brandy Walsh* into NCIC and got a hit—a string of busts for prostitution and possession of crack cocaine going back ten years. AKAs of "Brandywine" and "Big-Butted Brandy" and "Brandy Blow." This was great stuff. Unfortunately, there wasn't any way it could be the same young woman. The FBI's description had her as four feet ten inches tall and 240 pounds.

Damn. But I printed out a copy just for fun and put it with the stuff I was going to leave for Luke. He'd get a laugh out of it. He might even include it in the discovery.

Googling Brandy Walsh, I got another surprise. A relevant one this time. If it was the same person—and one close-up picture made it appear so—then she'd recently been a semiprofessional surfer. There were lists of contest results in Hawaii and California from 1995 to 2001. A brief biography said that she'd grown up in Kona and was attending college, as of 2000, in Santa Barbara, where she was studying history and criminal justice.

If it was the same Ms. Walsh, then, I wondered, what had brought her to law school in Wyoming? And how had she gotten hooked up with a onetime celebrity lawyer like Bogey, working on a criminal case?

I printed out the bio and picture and left them for Luke, too, along with the other stuff. My notes on the Mann twins I kept to myself. They weren't a part of the investigation, but those two losers worried me. I couldn't decide if they were truly dangerous or just fuckups.

seventeen

Nearly a hundred pickups and SUVs crowded the streets around a small church in the center of town. The majority were oversize four-door ranch vehicles, like Dodge Rams with three-foot-high chrome grilles and Ford Excursions and Chevy Surburbans that stretched to almost twenty feet in length. These monsters made my Pig look dainty. In Wyoming it's fashionable to own the newest, biggest, most powerful thing on the road. Particularly, for some reason, among the struggling farmers and ranchers—the same people who complain the most bitterly about rising gas prices, even in a state that has no fuel tax.

The locals gathered in clumps on the church lawn, talking in low, sometimes angry voices, shaking hands and hugging. The ceremony wasn't scheduled to start for another ten minutes and already there was an impressive turnout. I'd learned from Luke that both the Wallis and the Mann families had been in Colter County for generations. The Wallises were, in fact, sort of the county's First Family. Cody's grandfather had even served as county commissioner for nearly thirty years. Then his father had become one of the region's wealthiest homegrown businessmen through the leasing of heavy farm machinery. The Manns, on the other hand, had begun just as prosperously but hadn't done so well in the last couple of generations, as evidenced by what I'd learned of Mr. Mann's long-ago scrapes with the law as well as his oldest sons' lengthy juvenile records. Surly Ed Mann had been better lately—he was currently the president of the County Cattlemen's Association.

Luke had also helpfully explained why the Mann twins didn't have anything recent on them. Under his predecessor's reign in the county attorney's office, and under his own now, as well, it was deemed impolitic to harass the Mann family when it came to minor charges. Especially in the coming electoral season. Luke assured me, though, that if the twins ever did anything serious, he would clean house. I hoped so. Particularly if the "something serious" was done to me.

I moved quickly across the lawn, averting my eyes from anyone who seemed to be looking my way.

At the top of the church steps I observed Luke chatting up a white-robed minister. From the way the county attorney was talking—his usual shit-eating smirk veiled by an expression of somber wisdom—it was clear to me that he was busy politicking. I managed to weave around behind him without being seen. The minister, though, caught me when I glanced in his direction. He gave me a gentle smile and a saintly nod that conveyed a blessing. I almost laughed. He obviously didn't know who I was or anything about me. I scurried on into the church and found an empty pew three rows from the back.

Then I almost missed the bench when I turned to sit.

In the row behind me, tucked between two pairs of oblivious senior citizens, was Mattie Freda.

She was dressed all in black, which as far as I could tell was the only color she ever wore. Her lacy blouse covered her pale arms and vivid tattoos. For the occasion she'd even removed some of her facial jewelry and gone easy on the spiky hair gel. She actually looked exotic and quite pretty. But what the hell was she doing here? I'd warned her to stay away.

I fought the impulse to say something—to even acknowledge her with a greeting or a rebuke. It would inevitably lead to her moving to sit beside the only familiar face in the church. Then, sooner or later, someone would figure out who she was, the whispering would begin, more heads would turn, and my career would be over. It would look like I was escorting the supposed killer's girlfriend to the victim's funeral.

I stood up and started to move away, but I was pinned in on both sides by the arrival of families with squalling toddlers. I decided that it would create even more of a commotion to attempt an escape—better to sit tight and pretend ignorance.

After a few minutes in which Mattie did not attempt to speak with me, I began to relax and look around. My attention was immediately drawn to the varnished coffin behind the altar. Built of some heavy, dark wood, it was surrounded by candles and flowers. I tried not to think about the small boy inside, or how he'd looked when I'd dragged him onto the beach, or how his breath had tasted like the river. I tried not to think of Roberto, too—how it was a miracle he hadn't been placed in a coffin like this one, and how it might have been a blessing if he had been.

The church filled as the crowd outside was ushered in. Among them were many teens and preteens—schoolmates, probably, of Cody's and the younger Manns'. Most of the kids hadn't bothered to dress any differently than they would have for school. The boys wore baggy pants and T-shirts, with puka-shell necklaces around their throats; the girls were showing too much cleavage and abdomen. They all acted as if they were in school, too: whispering and signaling and giggling. I supposed they'd seen too much fake death on TV and in video games for this sedate ceremony to have any effect.

The parents, for the most part, didn't bother trying to correct their children's behavior. They seemed to have given up.

I had to wonder if I had been like this twenty years ago. I probably looked just as stupid with the Mohawk I'd sported for a while in the early teen years, but I would never have dreamed of acting like this at a funeral. It wasn't just fear of my parents' reproach; it came from some innate sense of respect and empathy. Even Roberto, the convicted killer, wouldn't behave this way.

Maybe we were just cooler.

The only time I could remember us ever being so blatantly disrespectful was the time we'd ditched school, "borrowed" a military Jeep, and gone cruising the streets of Manila in a rainstorm. We searched out the biggest puddles we could find and plowed into them, sometimes sending up fifteen-foot walls of water. Turning a corner, we'd seen a puddle as big and deep as a lake up ahead, filling the street with brown water from curb to curb. I was driving, and I floored it—somehow oblivious to the crowd of shopkeepers, chickens, pigs, and customers all huddled under awnings on both sides of the road. I'll never forget the shame I felt just as I noticed them—and saw their faces—before the twin waves of water leapt up and obscured my view.

"I know you told me not to come," a voice whispered in my ear, "but I had to. Jonah asked me to be here for him."

I didn't respond or turn around. I sat stonily facing forward, remembering that old shame, and feeling a little new shame, too.

The Mann family walked down the center aisle, Ed Mann looking mean and tough, his wife stern and grim. The younger brothers, at least, were dressed more appropriately in collared shirts and long pants. But they didn't look happy about it, and kept their scrubbed and angry faces pointed toward the ground. The older twins both wore ill-fitting suits and sunglasses. They looked even less happy—it was probably galling not to be able to show off their muscles. They stared all around in challenge, just as they had at the bar. I focused on the back of the head in front of me until they'd sat down.

Next came Luke with a large woman gripping his arm. His wife, I guessed. He'd gotten married while in law school, but no one I knew from his old life at DCI had been invited. They appeared to be leading Mr. and Mrs. Wallis to their seats in the first row. Apparently Cody had no siblings, or none that could make the service, because no one else accompanied them. The father, big and wide as he was, took each step as if his leg bones were made out of glass. Tears rolled down the mother's face as she stared at the coffin and staggered. Their obvious grief made my heart feel like a cold stone.

Everyone finally grew quiet.

The minister appeared at the altar and asked us to bow our heads. We prayed, then sang hymns, then half-listened to a sermon—something about it being a part of God's plan when life is brutally cut short. I wasn't buying it, and wasn't really paying attention. Then he said something that surprised me, and evidently many others in the congregation.

"I ask that you not only pray for Cody, but also for the soul of the man who took Cody from us."

This brought angry grumbles from the front half of the church. I saw Luke's head turn nearly 180 degrees in both directions, his political radar fully extended.

The minister continued on this unpopular theme, preaching about Jesus and love and forgiveness. The congregation was clearly in the mood for something a little more Old Testament.

The grumbling intensified. One person turned to look at me. Not me, I realized after an uncomfortable moment, but through me, to where Mattie Freda sat just behind me. Other faces began to turn, too, as a message was whispered from ear to ear throughout the front of the church. I resisted the urge to turn myself and see how Mattie was holding up. The eyes were withering. The heat of the gazes passing by me made me want to squirm in my seat.

Unaware of how his message of love and absolution was being twisted into two hundred laser beams of hate, the minister rambled on. I heard Mattie rustle in her seat behind me. Then I heard the quick taps of shoes fleeing down the aisle. I caught the additional sound of a single muffled sob.

I'd warned her not to come. But I still felt like shit. Like a coward.

And yet I couldn't despise the people whose stares had just ejected her from the church, either. They were mourning, they were angry, they couldn't yet accept that the kid's death had just been a mindless accident. Nothing alleviates grief like causing it.

I know. That kind of grief had taken me to Mexico one year ago. And the best part of me, the good cop, had stayed there.

With the exception of the Mann twins, these locals were probably good people. They were just irrational with sorrow. And too stubborn to ever admit that irrationality. In desperate times, they clung to desperate ideas. Like the fantasy that their ranches and farms are the backbone of the American economy. Or that environmentalists will stop at nothing until they've eradicated mankind altogether. Or that wolves—or even half wolves like Mungo—want to carry off their children.

When it was finally over, after we'd followed a hearse to the graveyard and the boy named Cody Wallis had been lowered into a hole in the ground, the kids bolted first. Then the elderly wandered away. In a few minutes the cemetery had been stripped of anyone not between twenty and seventy. The grown-ups who remained gathered in small groups on the grass. The largest of these groups was centered around Luke.

They were asking him some questions, but seemed mostly to be giving him their opinions. They were pretty much the same opinions they'd given him at the arraignment: *Hang him high.* Only now there was more fever to the demands, as many people were crying or tight-jawed from just having watched the burial of Cody Wallis.

And the county attorney of Colter County nodded solemnly as he listened to the voices of his constituents.

My boss, Ross McGee, called soon after the service.

"Working on a Sunday, Ross?" I asked lightly.

"You bet your ass. And you'd better be, too," he growled.

I could picture him in his office at the attorney general's building in Cheyenne, the blinds shut against the sunlight, hunched over his paper-strewn desk. He resembled an aging Viking warlord with his long white beard, bulldog body, and fierce blue eyes. Since the death of his wife the previous year, he never stopped working. Managing the affairs of the state's premier law-enforcement agency was all he did these days. And, where once he'd run interference between his agents and the state's politicos with devilish humor, gleefully sticking it to the suits with me—his protégé and acolyte—at his side, it was now all business. At least when it came to me.

"I am," I said. "I was just at the boy's funeral. The defendant's girlfriend was there, too."

"Did they lynch her?"

"No, but it looked like they were thinking about it." I couldn't help adding, "I guess they didn't because Luke is doing all he can to lynch the defendant in court."

McGee's voice was sharp. "That's none of your business, Burns. You don't make the charging decisions. You're there to do nothing but build a case."

"I know, I know."

"You do what Luke tells you and nothing more."

"I know, Ross. You already read me the riot act."

"I'm going to read it to you again. I get a single complaint from Luke and you're history. Got it? You do anything on the side and you're gone. This is your last chance, QuickDraw."

I know he wanted my vow of fealty, and maybe even an expression of appreciation for being allowed this final opportunity, but I couldn't utter either one.

Instead I said, "You know this whole thing's bullshit, don't you? Luke's going to nail this kid just because it will get him re-elected."

There was a long silence over the line.

"So now you're a pussy, Burns? For the last eight years I've heard you do nothing but bitch about how the suits didn't let us really hammer the bad guys. You whined that the sentences were too light, that the pleas didn't match the crimes, that the scumbags you arrested were getting paroled early. You got so jammed up about it, you started taking things into your own hands, didn't you? Like when you went down to Mexico last summer."

Now I hesitated. I had a nasty thought—this call was being recorded. My onetime friend and mentor was trying to get me to make an admission. Would he really do that? What he suspected I'd done in Mexico had twisted him, as well as Rebecca. It had turned them both against me. For Rebecca, it confirmed all the dark things she'd previously said she sometimes saw in me. For McGee, though, my trip to Mexico was even worse. I had broken his most fundamental belief, that of the rule of law.

But what would he have done if Jesús Hidalgo had gut-shot *his* only brother, tortured him, then slit his throat and stuffed him in an abandoned mine? What if it had been *his* brother whose body was torn apart like that while the perpetrator walked free? I liked to think McGee would have gone down to Mexico with a shotgun, too. But maybe he was just stronger than me. Maybe his belief in the law was like a belief in God—all would be right in the end. The villains would be punished, the good would float among the clouds strumming harps. But I'd lost the faith.

"Fuck you, Ross."

"You watch it, QuickDraw. Watch it."

eighteen

It was already evening when I parked in the pullout near the river. The sun had just disappeared behind the snowcapped summits of the Absaroka Mountains, and the shadows of the pines were fading into the growing gloom.

There was only one other car on the side of the highway, a VW Jetta that was nearly as beat-up and rust-spotted as my Pig. No one was in it, but I could see only an expensive-looking mountain bike wedged tight in the backseat. The engine was cold when I put my hand on the paint-flaked hood. I decided the car had probably broken down. The driver must have hitched into town instead of pedaling.

It seemed safe to let Mungo out to play. She shivered with pleasure as she leapt out of the truck. It had been a long, truck-bound day for her.

I hopped over the guardrail as Mungo slunk under it, then we walked a short distance through the trees on the well-littered trail. It ended on top of the giant boulder above the river. It looked a lot different in the dusk than it had in the frenzied daylight, when I'd helped wrestle the stretcher up from the beach.

Then there'd been shouting gawkers, hustling paramedics, frantic police officers, raving young cousins, and one dead child. Now it was eerily quiet except for the distant thunder of the rapids upstream. All the adrenaline-induced brilliance of sound, color, and energy was gone.

But the memories of it all lingered in my mind like vengeful phantoms. The river had not released its grip on me. I could still feel its power. I could still hear it roaring in my ears. I could still see the blurry white shape spread over the darker, jumbled coffins. I could still feel the inexorable pull toward it.

My lungs tightened and, even though I was standing immobile, I found myself taking fast, shallow breaths.

Things were even eerier once I climbed up onto the flat top of the rock where the battle had taken place. Here, piled high on a flat space just shy of the edge, were stuffed animals, bouquets of flowers, and dozens of hand-drawn cards. The mound of tribute lay in a half circle around a crucifix someone had pounded into a crack in the rock's surface.

"Check it out," I murmured to Mungo.

I'd never seen this kind of spontaneous gesture. I had to fight to push away the thought that again twisted my gut—if I'd only gotten there sooner, if only I'd been brave enough to complete that first dive . . .

I realized I'd better get busy before it got too dark to see.

Unlikely as it was, what I'd come to find was the stick Cody had used to swat Jonah. Since the younger Mann brothers denied there being a stick, or even any rock-throwing, I figured that showing the stick to Luke might encourage him to cut Jonah—and Mattie—a break. It would help prove that there really was a struggle and that Cody and the Mann boys had instigated it. On a more practicable level, it would also prove that the best witnesses for the prosecution—the boys—had lied. Maybe it would be enough to get Luke to swallow his pride and political stratagems and just get rid of this whole thing. But the stick, I knew, had in all likelihood gone off the edge with the boy. There remained a chance, however slight, that it could have washed up on the beach below. I looked around on top of the boulder and all I could find were small twigs, rocks, and pine needles.

A crunching sound like a footstep made me jump. It came from over the edge that led down to the beach, where I was just about to go. Nothing followed it—just silence. I played the sound over in my head, wondering what it could have been. Some animal walking on the river stones was my best guess. A bear? A moose? Something attempting to be furtive, knowing Mungo and I were up here poking around. I looked at Mungo and saw her standing where the boys' bikes had been on that afternoon three days before. Her head was raised, her nostrils quivering.

I took three quick steps to the edge and looked down. Then I jumped again.

What was down there on the beach was scarier than any ghost, or even a grizzly. It was the lawyer, Brandy Walsh. Her hands were on her hips and she seemed to be glowering up at me.

"Hello," I called.

She didn't answer.

"It's Ant," I added in case she couldn't make me out in the twilight. "Antonio Burns. We, uh, met yesterday morning."

She looked very different than she had in the county attorney's conference room, but no less intense. She appeared to be wearing cycling clothes—tight black shorts and some lighter-colored sleeveless top. She must have gone for a ride before coming here. Something small, like a camera, hung around her neck. Her hair was pulled back in a ponytail, and there was a pair of sporty sunglasses pushed up in her hair. If it hadn't been for the familiar disapproval radiating in my direction, I might not have recognized her.

"Hi," she finally said, her voice flat.

"What are you doing here?"

She hesitated a moment before answering. When she did, her

voice was more strident. I realized I'd probably really freaked her out by showing up here just as it was getting dark. *Good,* I thought.

"Looking for the branch my client was struck with. It wasn't listed as evidence on the initial report your pal Luke gave us."

"That's why I'm here, too. Did you find it?"

The ponytail swung a little as she shook her head.

"No. Not yet."

I squatted, turned, then carefully scrambled down twenty feet to the beach. When I faced her, she still had her hands on her hips, but she'd moved back a few feet. I examined the beach with its smooth, round stones.

There were pieces of wood scattered everywhere. Most of the ones I could see were too short or too thick to match the descriptions I'd gotten from Jonah, Mattie, and Pete the Guide. Or they appeared to be bleached, like they'd been in the water, not up on the cliff. But it was hard to tell, it was getting so dark. Then I noticed a small pile of long sticks behind Brandy Walsh. She was standing directly in front of it. I realized she was trying to shield it from my view.

I pointed at her ankles.

"Any likely suspects in that pile?"

"I won't know until I show them to my client."

The way she said it, it was clear she didn't intend to give them up.

I smiled and said lightly, "I'm really sorry, but I'm going to have to take them. They're potential evidence. They've got to be bagged and tagged. I promise to make sure you have access to them, though."

The ponytail swung again. "No. I found them. I'm going to take them."

"I'm sorry, Ms. Walsh. I can't let you do that. Finder's keepers doesn't apply at a crime scene."

Now she took her hands off her hips and folded her arms

across her chest. She had a small black tube in her right hand. Pepper spray, I suspected, and almost laughed.

Was this twenty-something surfer-turned-lawyer really about to gas me? She was good-looking all right, but about as mean as a junkyard dog. I waited for her to make her move, and readied myself. If her arms unfolded, I decided I was going to run. There was no way I was going to fight her. Being a sneaky lawyer, she'd probably claim I'd accosted her. Tried to rape her or something. No, she could have the damn sticks.

"Look, I'm just doing my job," I said.

I also felt bad for her. She'd probably been out here all afternoon, gathering her little pile of wood, and thinking about her client in jail and how badly he'd been treated, thinking about all the bad things she'd probably heard about me, and then here I was, in the dark, scaring her to death, and threatening to take her sticks.

"I'm supposed to collect all the evidence and witness statements and hand them over. It's up to you lawyers what happens from there," I tried again.

"Is that right? Just doing your job? Is that why you handcuffed Jonah and put him in jail? Is that why you allowed him to be brutally assaulted in there?"

"Listen, I'm the one who—"

She wasn't listening. Her pretty face, with its high cheekbones and oval shape, wore a very unpleasant expression. She was half smiling and half scowling, every feature loaded with scorn.

"Is that why you and Luke Endow stood around smirking after having him locked up on a no-bond hold?"

"I wasn't—"

"Is that why you're charging him with murder instead of something even remotely related to what actually occurred? Why you're refusing to negotiate a plea appropriate—"

I held up a hand with the palm to her face.

"Whoa. It was you and your boss who didn't want to negotiate yesterday. If Luke is being intractable, it's just because you guys came into town yesterday and busted his balls, and because he's getting a lot of heat from the community. All he's probably trying to do is leverage you guys into a reasonable deal at a more reasonable time. But then you and your professor spit in his face. I know you're pretty new to this, but there's a way these things generally work."

She rolled her eyes.

"Oh? And that makes it right?"

Before I could think of a way to explain the system that wouldn't make it sound too corrupt or me too self-serving, she continued, "While you're trying to answer that one, why don't you tell me why they call you QuickDraw?"

It was said with such sweet venom that if she'd been a man, I would have knocked out her teeth. This was one vicious lawyer.

I took a deep breath. Then another.

Very quietly I said, "Don't call me that." Then, after another moment: "Look, I know you don't like me. You've probably heard some ugly rumors about me." Why did I care? I'd always needed to be liked—it was what had driven me to be so effective undercover, but I'd learned to live without it since Cheyenne and Baja. Now this nasty little lawyer was making me need it more urgently than ever. "But those are just rumors. Unsubstantiated accusations. But they don't matter here. I'm just trying to do my job as best as I can. This whole thing sucks, as far as I'm concerned, but I'm doing what I can to see that Jonah's treated fairly."

"Don't move," she hissed.

Her arms uncrossed from where she'd been holding them over her chest. Startled by the force of her whispered voice, I didn't. Even when the little black tube of tear gas was extended in my direction. *Here it comes,* I thought. But then I could see that her face was tilted up, that she was looking somewhere over my head.

"There's something up there," she said quietly.

Slowly, I turned around and looked up the steep rock wall that led to the top of the boulder. For a moment I couldn't see anything. Then I made out a long snout and two glinting eyes protruding over the edge above us.

I laughed.

"That's my mutt. Mungo, get your ass down here."

She lunged over the edge and came sliding down the slope, landing in a long-legged tangle. As she regained her footing at my side, I noticed Brandy backing away.

"She's harmless," I said.

But Brandy kept walking backward on the stones, holding her little canister pointed at both of us. It was hard to believe this mean, tough lawyer could be so afraid of an animal like Mungo.

"Really," I insisted. "She's friendly. Smile, Mungo."

Mungo dutifully raised her upper lip, exposing long, white teeth. Brandy Walsh's extended arm shook then tightened, and I closed my eyes and winced. I belatedly realized that someone scared of a dog might not see Mungo's sheepish grin as being disarming. But the blast of pepper spray didn't come.

Instead Brandy circled to the side, then launched up a section of the rock wall that was far steeper than the easy section right behind me.

"Hey. I'm sorry. I didn't know you were scared of dogs."

"Now you do, jerk."

Moving fast, she grabbed good edges with her hands and smeared toeholds with her feet. She kept her butt far out from the rock—a counterintuitive move climbers use for maximum traction. But it made her camera swing and bang against the stone.

"You're a climber?" I asked, not really expecting an answer.

At the top, she hesitated. She'd abandoned her pile of sticks. I'd won. I rubbed Mungo's head appreciatively.

"Why do you care?" she demanded. Then: "Some of my friends climb at Vedauwoo. I've watched them a few times."

Vedauwoo. The word was magic to me. Vedauwoo was my

spiritual home. When my father was based nearby at Warren Air Force Base, the whole family had spent many good days there. Before Dad had been forced to resign because of his son's conduct and retire to Mom's family ranch in Argentina. Before all the bad things started happening to Roberto and, later, me.

"That's a really nice place," I said almost reverently. "Good rock. Fat cracks."

Maybe something about my tone, or her position of relative safety high above us, caused her voice to soften just a little.

"Do you still climb?" she asked me.

The question meant that she knew I used to. It also meant she knew more about me than just the lies and innuendo she'd probably read about that long-ago fiasco in Cheyenne. I'd never been anywhere near as famous a climber as my brother, but some of the stuff I'd done did occasionally make it into the climbing mags. At least she couldn't know about Baja—the only thing I had to be really ashamed of. No one had ever publicly connected me to that.

"Pretty much every day. There's a lot of good rock around here. You ought to come out with me. We could talk about Jonah's case. See if we can work out a way to keep Luke and your professor from butting heads to Jonah's detriment."

She remained still and silent, a silhouette before the first faint stars. And I wondered why the hell I'd gone and said that. Maybe it was because I knew that she was, or had been, an athlete, too. Or maybe it was because I wanted to prove myself to her, prove that the rumors weren't true. Or maybe, more pathetically, it was because she was just so damn good-looking and I kind of liked being treated like shit.

When she answered, it was in the flat, disdainful voice she'd been using before.

"Thanks, but I don't think that would be a very good idea."

Then she disappeared. After a minute the Jetta's misfiring engine snarled to life and reverberated down the highway.

* *

Roberto called just as I was plopping two fillets of fresh-caught trout into a pan of butter and garlic. I hesitated, staring at the phone's backlit screen, wondering if I had the courage to answer. My instinct was not to, to just let it chime shrilly until the message system picked up and the flashing light kicked off, then to take the pan off the flames and fire up a bowl instead. I looked up at the sky and saw Orion burning brightly. It was a constellation I'd always associated with my brother. The great, impulsive hunter, drunk and wounded and blind, staggering about in the sky.

I moved the pan to the side and pushed Mungo away when she tried to swipe the fish. Then I hit the button to answer the call.

"Yo, Ant," my brother said in his soft, slurry voice. "How you doing, *che*?"

"I'm doing okay." I couldn't bring myself to ask him how he was. "Just making some dinner for me and Mungo. What's going on? I haven't heard from you in weeks."

"You haven't called, Ant."

I didn't say anything. Mungo grinned at me in the firelight and made another lunge for the pan. I grinned back as I pushed her away again. This was one of her favorite games, waiting for me to be distracted, then stealing the food she knew I'd eventually share with her anyway. I allowed it because it kept me on my toes. Plus I liked seeing the wolf in her.

"Rebecca said you stood her up the other night. The little ankle biter, too. Both of them sounded kind of pissed off about it. Moriah howled like a banshee when I dropped her off—I think she's got me confused with her dad."

"Work," I said too quickly. "It's gotten a little hairy up here lately."

"Yeah? Still hooking and booking, *che*? Been catching those nasty ol' druggies?"

"Something like that. Speaking of druggies, what are you on these days?"

He laughed. "I'm high on life, Ant. You know that."

There was no resentment in his laugh or his comment. That was something that never stopped amazing me. I'd detected absolutely zero bitterness in him since the incident in a Wind River mine that had taken away most of the use of his legs. On the rare occasions I saw him, I would look into his glacier-blue eyes—so out of place with his black hair and high-cheeked Indio features—and see no lit fuse, no impending explosion. The only rage that lingered there, I discovered to my alarm, was the reflection of my own eyes.

"You might not believe it," he went on, "but I've been staying pretty clean. See, lately I've been hanging out at this zendo with these Tibetan dudes. Chanting and praying and all that shit. Can't say I understand any of it, but I like it. It just empties your head, kind of like being way up off the deck. And these monks are the coolest, most laid-back guys you've ever seen."

"Is Mary getting into it, too?"

"Nah. She's way too wound up for any Buddhist bullshit. She's all aggression and guns, running around protecting these corporate big shots in Baghdad and Tripoli. Speaking of Mary, she was in town over the weekend. Between jobs—she flew out again this afternoon. But while she was here, she gave me a little present. It's an old van, and it's got these hand controls on the wheel that let me punch it and brake. Anyway, I need to get out of here for a while. Thinking about heading up your way. I want to check out that secret project of yours. And I need to feed the Rat, bro. It's time."

"Uh, 'Berto, you think you're up for that?" I said it with extreme delicacy, after a long pause.

"I could always climb circles around you, Ant," he laughed. "You know that. Nothing's changed. Did eighty-five pull-ups this morning, and that was just the first set. Now I'm 'bout ready for you to be my belay slave again."

I wanted to say that the only reason he could do eighty-five pull-ups was because he no longer had any meat on his legs. But I knew he'd been getting strong. The last time I'd seen him, his upper body was even more developed than it had been after his federal prison sentence. After months of hospitalization and rehab at the world-renowned Craig Hospital, he'd gotten to where he could hobble around pretty good on a pair of metal canes and had regained enough control of his legs to use them for balance. At home in the small Boulder house he shared with Mary Chang, he used a metal railing that had been installed a foot below the ceiling to get from room to room. But you can't climb rock walls with your arms alone.

"Listen, it's not a good time, 'Berto. Things are really crazy up here."

Now it was his turn to pause. I could picture him in the house he liked to keep dark when Mary wasn't around, staring into space, fighting with every ounce of his formidable strength to ward off the siren song of the hot sap he loved to inject in his veins. I could picture him shrugging off my rejection, loving me, his little bro. I'd once worshiped him, and I probably still did. But if he were to try to climb again and fail, I wasn't sure what would happen. It might break him once and for all. I couldn't even face what I'd already done to him.

He ended the pause, saying, "Hey, man, that's all right. I understand. Come on down and see me sometime, okay? See your little girl, too. She needs a better role model than me—that's for sure."

I abandoned the pan of fish to Mungo as I raced for the wine bottle and the purple-haired Indigo in the back of the truck.

nineteen

While buying donuts and coffee the next morning, I was drawn to the local twice-weekly paper by a crowd of stout donut-stand regulars talking heatedly over the rack. I grabbed a copy and hurried out to my truck. Walking, I had a glimpse of the headline. It read, "LEGAL EAGLE IN TOWN TO DEFEND RIVER KILLER—Says Defendant 'Grossly Overcharged.' "

Well, I couldn't really dispute that. But I still found it offensive, somehow a personal insult, even though I had nothing to do with the charging decision.

And it was annoying that William J. Bogey had already run to the press. He knew full well that the initial charges are *always* overblown—it's simply a starting place for the plea negotiations. Like the sticker price on a brand-new car. And good politics for Luke, too, because it makes him look tough while his electorate is focused on the case. A few months from now, it wouldn't matter as much if he drastically reduced the charges and dealt the case away.

Bogey knew how these things worked, yet he appeared determined to embarrass the county attorney in front of his hometown press. And at a crucial time for him, too. It was a bad move. Bad for everyone—me, the town, the prosecutor, and, I suspected, Jonah. Luke could be a stubborn, vindictive bastard, and this would really make him hit the roof.

Sitting in the Pig with Mungo nosing the donut bag, I read on: "William Bogey, an attorney with a nationwide reputation, said that 'inexperienced small-town prosecutors often overcharge when dealing with accidental deaths,' but that he is certain 'County Attorney Luke Endow will come to his senses once the unfortunate facts of this tragedy sink in.'"

Shit. Luke wasn't just going to hit the roof. He was going to stick to it.

But I found him in his chair when I walked into his office fifteen minutes later. He looked like he'd just climbed down into it. His face was red, his hair and tie askew, his eyes narrow and mean. The paper was open on his desk. It looked like it had been wadded and unwadded a couple of times.

"That prick wants to play hardball, he's come to the right place."

I waited, saying nothing.

"He thinks he's going to bully me into some sweet deal. Well, fuck him. Nobody pushes me around. I'm adding five years to any offer I make."

I still didn't say anything. I could have told him the obvious—that you don't punish a defendant just because you hate his counsel—but Luke knew that. He was just so pissed he wasn't thinking straight. For me to point it out would only make him madder. So all I did was put two chocolate donuts with rainbow sprinkles on his desk.

He looked at them, his favorites from the old days when we were partners. He started to smile, but it twisted on his face.

"Something's wrong with my tummy. I don't think I can eat them."

Someone knocked on the door frame behind me.

"What?" Luke demanded.

His secretary, a blue-haired, churchy-looking woman in her sixties, said, "The judge just called. He wants to see you in chambers."

"Fuck. Tell him I'll come down in fifteen minutes."

She frowned at the obscenity and set her jaw.

"He said he wants to see you *now*."

Luke cursed again and lifted his bulk out of his chair. Breathing hard, he stabbed his arms into his jacket.

"Take it easy," I advised. "What do you think he wants?"

"Probably to ream my ass about something. Or bust my balls for this crap in the paper." Then he winced and stooped a little, one hand massaging his stomach. Seeing me watching him, he snapped, "You're my lead investigator. You tell me."

Because I didn't want to hang out in view of his glowering secretary, and because I was curious, I followed him down a staircase in the back of the building. It led to a corridor behind the courtroom. The door to the judge's chambers was open.

The "chambers" of Colter County's only district judge turned out to be just a small room, maybe twelve feet by fourteen. But it looked nice, with paneled walls of dark wood and shelves full of faux-leather statute books. The fierce old judge sat unsmiling behind a desk facing the door. On the desk's glossy surface lay a single sheet of paper. Perpendicular to the desk, against one wall, was a love seat. And perched on it like a pair of smug vultures were William Bogey and Brandy Walsh.

Seeing them, Luke took in a gulp of air. Then he managed to lift the corners of his whitening lips, but he couldn't do anything about his face, which was turning an even darker shade of red. I half-expected Luke to lose it. If it had been eight years ago, when he was a cop, he definitely would have. In my "training days," I'd seen him berate, threaten, and sometimes even rough up witnesses who refused to cooperate. Several times I'd had to drag him off. Later he always insisted it was just a show—that I'd played the role of "good cop" to his "bad" to perfection. But I'd never been quite sure.

"What's this?" he now tried to joke. "A little ex parte party? Thanks for thinking to invite us on down."

Bogey smiled slightly. Brandy, her hair pulled back tightly, looked aloof and also contemptuous. They both wore suits. She made no acknowledgment of having seen me at the river last night. She just stared at me as if she were an entomologist studying a strange kind of bug that had just crawled into view. To get that expression off her face, I was tempted to do something shocking—like bend down, grab her by her suit's deep brown lapels, and kiss her squarely on her thin lips.

The judge held up the piece of paper on his desk.

"Mr. Bogey, do you have a copy of this for Mr. Endow?"

"I do, Judge."

Bogey bent to the briefcase that was propped against the bottom of the couch and pulled out a single sheet. Despite an apparent attempt at restraint, Luke ripped it out of his hand when Bogey offered it to him.

"What is it?" Luke demanded, leaving him open to the obvious retort from Bogey—*You can read, can't you?* But Bogey was polite enough not to mock him in the judge's presence.

I read over Luke's shoulder. The document was titled "Motion to Compel." It demanded the production of all materials relating to the case, particularly all exculpatory evidence, and concluded by asking for sanctions against the county attorney's office for failing to comply.

I could feel the heat rising off him. One of my arms lifted a few inches from my side, readying to grab the back of his coat. But all he did was say coldly, "The usual crap. That's what this is all about?"

Bogey smiled again, and the judge nodded.

"Mr. Bogey alleges that you have potentially exculpatory material in your possession that you have refused to turn over to the defense."

Luke forced a laugh.

"Judge, about all I got is a report from my investigator here, and another from a couple of state troopers who were at the scene. I already told Boogie I'd be happy to give them to him, just as soon as my girl gets them copied."

"Your Honor," Bogey said, "we met with Mr. Endow and his investigator two days ago. They had these reports with them at the time, as well as access to a copying machine, yet despite my persistent requests, they were unwilling to provide them to me. All I received was the same vague promise you just heard. As you're surely aware, this is an exceptional matter, with extremely serious implications—"

Luke interrupted, "Damn it, Boogie, I told you—"

The judge froze them both with the ice in his voice.

"I don't want to hear any more. Mr. Endow, turn those files over to Mr. Bogey immediately. Mr. Bogey, your Motion to Compel is granted, the Motion for Sanctions is denied. Now, does either of you have anything further to say?"

He stared from attorney to attorney to me, daring all of us to speak. Bogey, apparently, was unafraid.

Still holding on to his polite smile, the lawyer said, "One other matter, Your Honor. When I attempted to speak with my client yesterday, I was turned away. I was told by the deputy sheriff in charge that because of budget shortfalls and staffing shortfalls, attorney-client interviews are not permitted on Sundays. Then this morning at eight I was again turned away—rudely—and told to come back in two hours. Now, as you're aware, under both state and federal law, I have a right to access my client as often as I deem it necessary. I hate to say it, but right now I'm considering a federal suit against Backwater—excuse me, Badwater—both for restricting access and for the beating my client suffered on Thursday night."

The judge's hawkish features tightened, as if they were being screwed down. He was being insulted, too, and he knew it. And I had to give Bogey credit for balls.

I began to suspect that he was one of those attorneys who baits judges into bad rulings, then uses them as grounds for an appeal. Or makes the judge bend over backward to show that he can remain impartial even when being spat upon. What I really didn't like, though, was the way Brandy turned and looked at him with admiration. For some reason, that pissed me off more than Bogey's bullshit tactics.

Now there wasn't just ice in the judge's voice, but icicles. The sharp, cold daggers were thrown with every word.

"You do whatever you feel is appropriate, Mr. Bogey. Mr. Endow will speak with the sheriff about making your client more available, this afternoon at the very latest, but for the time being he's in the custody of the sheriff and this court. You will receive no special privileges no matter how much you threaten or bluster."

After a chilly pause, he added, "This is not Miami, New York, or even Cheyenne, Mr. Bogey. Here we do the best we can, and we all get along. Do you understand? Don't come running in here every time you encounter a minor inconvenience. And don't attempt to try this case in the local newspaper. After hearing about your stunt this morning, if Mr. Endow here were to file a motion restricting interviews with the media, there's a damn good chance I would sign it."

Luke now tried not to show his sudden cheer as he said, "I intend to do that, Judge."

With a final glare at all of us, the judge spun around in his chair to study the papers on the credenza. He dismissed us by announcing, "We're adjourned."

No one spoke as we filed out into the hallway. I raised my eyebrows at Brandy when her eyes swung my way, but they blankly passed right on by. I began to follow Luke up the courthouse's exposed back staircase.

Bogey called after us, "We'll be waiting in the lobby for the discovery materials."

Luke didn't reply.

He did pause, though, at his secretary's station, to curtly order her to copy everything we had on the Strasburg case and deliver it to Mr. Bogey in the court's lobby, and to shuffle it thoroughly before handing it over. I followed him into his office, where he slammed the door behind me. He slumped in his chair.

"What are you going to offer him to make this piece of shit go away?" I asked.

It was the wrong thing to say.

Luke snarled, "There's not going to be any deal. He can plead straight up or go to trial. For once somebody's going to be convicted of the crime they actually committed."

It was something I'd wanted to hear a prosecutor say for a long time. But not in this case.

twenty

I was eager to get back to my camp and Moriah, but instead I was drawn downward toward the jail. There might be a reason other than ineptitude or just plain contrariness in Luke and the sheriff dragging their feet about giving Bogey access to his client. It had already happened once, I knew, remembering Jonah hog-tied, beaten, and terrified on his bunk next to the big, bearded Smit. But I thought I'd taken care of that when I'd ordered Jonah to solitary confinement and warned Luke of the potential repercussions of allowing him to get beaten again. I felt negligent, though, for not having checked up on him again sooner. Hadn't I promised him I'd look out for him? But that was before his rabid attorneys had shown up to defend him.

It was Russell Smit who first greeted me when I descended the concrete stairs into the corridor. He seemed to have been waiting for me—he stood just on the other side of the bars, as if he knew I'd be coming. I stopped on the landing and stared back at him.

Like the other night, he was wearing no shirt and only his orange jailhouse trousers. The exposed area was heavily muscled, hairy, and covered with bad tattoos. He'd plaited his beard into a long braid. His eyes showed that he still didn't like me very much. While I watched, he stuck out his tongue to display for me the spidery black stitches around the missing tip.

"You gonna pay for wat, moffa-fucker," he lisped.

"Well, I might consider paying for some speech therapy," I told him.

He didn't explode, and he didn't respond. He just kept on staring, trying to break me with the intensity of his hate. I've always been pretty good in stare fights, and a few years ago we could have stood there on opposite sides of the bars for hours. But I liked to think I'd long since stopped caring about proving my machismo. So I broke the stare and headed down the hall.

I half expected something to be thrown after me, but no blow or splash hit me in the back. I looked into the rec room as I passed and received sullen but mildly interested stares from the other inmates. I smiled at the eyes I met and nodded. There appeared to be fewer inmates than there had been four nights ago, but then, in the excitement and the dark, everything had seemed much denser. Now, in the daylight that was coming through the windows high up on the walls, everything seemed relatively peaceful.

I didn't see Jonah, though. Not in the rec room, and not visible in any of the cells on the other side. There were just the usual alcoholics, tweakers, wannabe bikers, and illegal farmworkers picked up for minor stuff like traffic violations.

Inside the control room were two deputies I didn't recognize. The looks they gave me weren't any friendlier than those of the inmates.

"Yeah?" one asked.

"Where's Strasburg?"

The deputy jerked his thumb at the ceiling. "In one of the interview rooms. Seeing his punk-rock girlfriend."

I got more of the stink eye but no more lisping threats when I passed Smit again and headed back up the stairs. He did flick his tongue and grin at me, though. On the ground level I found the entrance to the sheriff's office, was buzzed in after a long wait, and found the blonde female deputy—from the swing shift four nights ago—standing in the hall outside the little room where I'd interviewed Jonah after his arrest.

"Hi, Sally," I said. "Thanks for speaking up for me the other night."

She scowled, but it turned into a small smile. "I kind of wish I hadn't. My sergeant's got me working double shifts all this week."

"I didn't mean to get you into trouble."

"Well, I was pissed about it at first. But now it seems kind of funny. Anyway, that big bastard had it coming. He's started thinking he owns the place, that he could say whatever he wanted to me. At least that lisp has shut him up some."

I looked past her and through the little window set in the door. Mattie Freda was inside, talking intently to Jonah. I couldn't see his face—his back was to me—but at least he was still walking and talking.

"I'm sorry I stirred things up," I told her. "I just kind of freaked when I saw what he'd been doing to that kid in there. By the way, how's he doing?"

Sally shrugged. "We keep him locked up at night, but let him into the rec room if he wants during the day. He usually comes out. Smit still gives him a hard time, but nothing like last week. Just pushes him around some. Knocked him down a few times. But that's about it."

I looked in the window again and saw that Mattie had noticed me. Jonah was turned around, too, and was looking back. His face was still puffy with old yellow-blue bruises, but there was a fresh one of dark black around one eye, which was swollen almost shut. And a long red scratch that ran all the way down his cheek.

I felt myself getting mad and tried to choke the anger down.

If the deputies knew about him getting "pushed around" and "knocked down," there was a damned good chance a lot more was happening.

"I thought the county attorney agreed that he should be kept in solitary."

"Well, we can't keep him in there all the time. It's too much trouble. And, like I said, he wants to come out. He does it voluntarily."

Her smile had faded. She could sense that I was getting irritated. So I made myself smile and said, "I guess it's always rough on guys like him, isn't it?"

"Yeah," she agreed. "Skinny guy from out of town. Not to mention a child-killer. Half the guys in there have suddenly gotten morals or town loyalty or something and have decided they want to get a little payback for what he did to Cody Wallis."

"It's understandable," I said. But I didn't say that it was anything but understandable that the deputies would allow it.

"I heard you've been hanging around town. Want to grab a beer or something later?"

She definitely thought I was one of them. A cop who wasn't above meting out a little justice for himself. She might even believe all the QuickDraw bullshit. Well, that was understandable, too—she'd seen me Tase a man who was just reclining on a bunk. But I wasn't flattered by her offer.

"I can't," I told her. "Luke's running me ragged on this investigation."

She accepted my rejection by turning around and shoving open the door.

"Time's up," she announced to Mattie and Jonah in too loud a voice.

I waited while Jonah got to his feet and, with his hands cuffed behind him, came to the door. He was limping, something he hadn't been doing in court three days earlier. Another injury, unseen somewhere under the baggy jumpsuit.

He didn't look like a punk rocker anymore. Just a beat-up kid, probably scared out of his mind. Each minute in the jail, either alone in his cell or being stalked by Smit in the rec room, had to be sheer terror for him. I didn't know how he could stand it. I didn't know how long he would. Men manage to kill themselves in county jails all the time, and I could imagine Jonah hanging from a high bar. Mattie stared at me, and I could tell she still blamed me for all this. If the worst happened, she certainly always would. And I would, too.

"You doing all right?" I asked him softly when he came through the door.

He met my eyes for a minute.

"Yeah," he said tightly. "I'm fine."

I left the sheriff's office without speaking to anyone. With clenched fists, I walked the two blocks to where I'd found some shade in which to leave Mungo and the Pig. I couldn't complain to the sheriff, or to Luke, about how Jonah was being treated. It would make it look like I was siding with the defense. As McGee had reminded me, all it would take would be one call from him to the AG's office and I would be history.

I couldn't help Jonah anymore, but I thought I knew who could.

The Pig was where I'd left it—under a big cottonwood in an empty town park by the river. But someone had taken it upon themselves to touch up the truck's mismatched paint job. On one side was spray-painted "Wolf-Lover." On the other "Sheep-Fucker."

Nice.

The windows were still rolled up except for the two inches of air space I'd left. Spittle and froth, though, decorated the rear passenger glass. A trickle of blood, too.

I threw the door open. Mungo was still inside, cowering between the crates in the far back. Her mouth was bloody, and her eyes were just yellow slits.

"Hey, girl. It's okay. *Tranquilo,*" I murmured when she growled at me. "*Tranquilo, tranquilo.*"

I hesitated before petting her, worried for a second that she might be so traumatized by whatever had happened that she'd snap at me. But she didn't, and soon I was stroking her head.

What had happened was pretty obvious. The broken stick on the backseat made it even more so. The Mann twins had fucked with my truck and my dog again. Mungo had probably gone crazy, raging all over the interior, but they'd just laughed and poked at her with the stick. Just like they'd done out at their ranch. It could have been worse, I told myself. They could have done a lot more damage. But that didn't help the rage that was swelling my chest and my throat.

Cool it, Ant, I told myself as I tried to comfort Mungo. She wouldn't stop growling, though, even as I stroked her. I couldn't stop either. But I had to stay cool. I couldn't go after the Manns the way I wanted, not for something so petty. I had to stay cool. I had to do my job, be the good cop, and not let emotion carry me away.

So I got moving.

I trolled the streets around the courthouse looking for a banged-up Jetta with a mountain bike in the back, the one I'd seen at the river last night. When I didn't find it on the streets, I cruised the tourist motels on the highway just outside of town. I finally found it at a place called the Outrider. I pulled up across the street.

I wasn't sure how to approach her, or how to even make contact. If I started knocking on doors or went to the desk and asked which room she was in, Luke might somehow hear of it. I decided it would be better to try calling on my phone. The motel's number was right there, on a big sign above the office.

I was starting to dial when she came out of one of the rooms. She was dressed in biking gear, like she had been at the river. Tight black riding shorts, a sleeveless jersey. This time she also wore a helmet and a pair of wraparound sunglasses. I tossed the phone onto the seat and put the truck into gear as she started trying to wrestle the bike from the back of her car.

Cutting across the street, I bumped over the curb into the parking lot.

"Walsh," I called.

She straightened quickly, dropping a tire to the pavement. From behind the sunglasses she took in both me and the words now written so prominently on the side of my truck. "Wolf-Lover."

"What do you want?"

"Where's your professor?"

"He's gone out to try and interview Randy and Trey Mann. They refused to speak with me," she said accusingly. "If someone told them not to talk with us, then you can bet we're going to be asking the judge for sanctions."

"Go down to the jail and see your client. Even if he's too stoic to tell you, you should know that they're messing with him down there. Get him out. Get him transferred to another county for his own protection."

"What?" she demanded.

"Just do it. And we never had this talk."

I put the truck back in gear and bumped back over the curb. In the rearview mirror, I could see her staring after me. She could now see what was written on the other side of the truck. I wondered what she thought. I needed to find some primer to cover the graffiti on my truck, and some time for me and Mungo to lick our wounds.

And I still needed to cool down. To get back to being the good cop. I needed to stop swearing to myself, every time I looked at Mungo, that I'd make the Mann twins pay. I'd make them all pay.

twenty-one

Three days later there were only three reporters in the courtroom for the hearing. One from the Casper paper, one from Denver, and a florid woman in a big hat whom I suspected of being the local gadfly. This turnout was kind of funny because for the last two days Luke had been fielding calls from reporters across the country displaying interest in the case. They wanted to know if "anonymous" allegations that Jonah was being scapegoated, that he was being railroaded for political gain, were true. It was obvious Bogey had been out chumming the waters, but wasn't having much success in catching a big shark. Once Luke explained that this was to be a simple bail hearing and that the defendant had *admitted* to practically throwing the child into a dangerous river, the big media sharks swam away.

Bogey had to be pissed off at being ignored like this. But he should have done his homework before making such idiotic allegations and trying to turn the case into an even bigger circus.

The rest of the spectators filling the benches in the small courtroom were locals. Cody's parents were not present, but the combustible Manns were. The whole family, arranged in a grim-faced row at the front of the gallery, looked very determined to act as the parents' proxies in the demand for vengeance. I felt the eyes of the older twins burning into the back of my neck. I wanted a little vengeance of my own.

The only outsider besides the three reporters was Mattie Freda. Undoubtedly she, too, was the focus of a lot of hostile stares. Maybe even some whispered threats. I was pleased that she ignored me just as I had ignored her at the funeral.

Jonah came in from the door at the rear of the court, shuffling in ankle chains but without handcuffs. His jumpsuit hung on his bony frame like a big orange sack. Even discounting the new and old bruises, he didn't look good. He was paler than he'd been before and his skin seemed pulled tight on his face except for where it was darkly bagged under his eyes. I wondered if the harassment had continued. I didn't feel guilty for not having checked on him, though. He had annoyingly combative attorneys to look after his interests now. Surely they'd be screaming to the judge if anyone in the jail so much as gave him a black look.

The clerk came in and called us to order. On her heels, the judge brusquely flew in with robes and thin white hair flapping, almost as if he were trying to take flight.

Within minutes, Luke and Bogey were showboating for the pews of interested spectators and the few reporters.

The only topic of substance was whether or not Jonah should be granted bail. Luke said no. He argued that Jonah had no property, no friends, no relatives, no ties to the state of Wyoming, and no reason to comply with the requirements of pretrial release. He argued that, with the defendant being an out-of-state musician with a high likelihood of being convicted, he was more likely to flee than hang around and get sent to prison. My former partner and friend did a nice job. I had to admit that he made a pretty good lawyer.

Bogey then argued that the charges were ridiculous, that the case would never make it past a preliminary hearing, and that the prosecutor was simply grandstanding before his grieving constituency for political gain. He was then gaveled down by the judge and reprimanded for grandstanding himself and making a personal attack on counsel.

I did my best to tune it all out. I pretty much agreed with Bogey—although I felt Jonah deserved some punishment—but had to be loyal to Luke for both personal and professional reasons. I tried not to think about it. Instead I thought about Moriah, and the way my raw shoulders were burning, and that numerous cuts seemed to be weeping onto one of my only dress shirts and sticking it to my skin.

Unpleasant as this was, these thoughts were really preferable to anything else I could have thought about. Rebecca was pissed I hadn't come down to see my daughter—actually accused me of being chickenshit—plus my job was hanging by a thread, not to mention a handicapped junkie brother wanting my attention, meth labs all over the place, oil and gas rigs tearing up every corner of the state I loved, a war in Iraq, and a deficit that my daughter was going to catch the bill for.

So it was through a deep, dark gloom that I heard my name being called.

The judge had just asked if either party had any witnesses. No one ever testified at bail hearings. But then Luke had for some reason said "Special Agent Antonio Burns" and turned to look at me.

What the hell was he doing? I could see that—as usual over the last few days—his face was pink, his lips white, and his blue eyes all squinty.

"Come on," he urged. "Get up there."

Shit. There was nothing, absolutely nothing, that I hated more than testifying.

I pushed back my chair and headed for the little half-booth that was the witness stand.

I stated my name and job title into the microphone. A glance at the defense table showed the pair of lawyers there sharpening their knives. The shabby trio of reporters behind them, too. I knew at least Brandy had my number. Were they going to mention Cheyenne now? Or wait until trial? From the looks on their faces, it appeared Bogey was ready right now. But would the judge allow that kind of impeachment at a mere bail hearing?

The judge gave me reason to hope my public flaying would be delayed.

"I don't want this case to be tried right here, right now," the judge said. "You'll keep your comments to the issue of bail and whether or not Mr. Strasburg is a flight risk."

Luke nodded, folded his hands behind his back, and assumed his most lawyerly demeanor.

"Agent Burns, how did you first make contact with the defendant?"

"I arrested him. I also spoke to him twice—once before and once after I arrested him."

"Did he indicate that he has any family or friends in this state?"

"No. He said he was traveling in the West while on vacation."

"Did he indicate that he has any property in the state?"

"No. I believe the car he was traveling in belongs to a friend."

"Does he own any property in *any* state?"

"I think he mentioned that he rents the apartment where he lives in New York."

"Does he have family anywhere in the country?"

"I was told his parents emigrated to Israel a few years ago, and I'm not aware of any brothers or sisters."

"Does he have a criminal record?"

"Yeah. He does."

Bogey objected even as I spoke the words. A defendant's prior bad acts are almost never introduced in a trial, but, as Luke now pointed out in response to Bogey's objection, this was just a hearing—there was no jury yet present—and the issue was relevant to the purpose of the hearing.

Luke was being really clever. Usually, the prosecutor would love to shout out a defendant's past crimes but was restricted from doing so. This time, however, Luke was just acknowledging that there were past crimes. He didn't ask me for any of the details. Even if Bogey now tried to take the extraordinary step of revealing his client's past crimes—and how ridiculously minor they were—Luke could object on the grounds that he feared the case being turned over on appeal. It was a nasty little conundrum for the defense.

"Did he show up for court as required when he was charged with those *prior crimes*?" Luke made the priors sound like they'd been sodomy and murder or worse.

"Uh, no. At least not on one occasion," I said, remembering the FTA on the open-container charge. And feeling like shit for being a part of this.

Luke now paused. Preparing for his finale, he gave me a slight smile and a wink, then turned and looked at the room behind him, his eyes finally coming to rest on Jonah.

"Based on what you've just said, and taking into consideration the seriousness of the charges against the defendant, do you believe him to be a flight risk?"

"Objection!" Bogey almost yelled. "The question calls for an opinion, and Agent Burns is no trier of fact—"

Luke was prepared for this. "Agent Burns has had eight years of experience investigating and arresting people in this state. In those eight years he's arrested people from all walks of life, and even had to rearrest them after they violated the conditions of their bail. If anyone's qualified to have an opinion on the likelihood of—"

"Be quiet. Both of you," the judge ordered. "I'll hear what he has to say, but I won't necessarily be swayed by it. Mr. Bogey, you'll have your chance to cross-examine."

Luke beamed at me, awaiting my condemnation of Jonah Strasburg. The Manns all seemed to be leaning forward in their seats, eager to hear me condemn the killer of their nephew and cousin. All I had to do was say yes, then hunker down and ignore whatever would be thrown at me during the cross-examination. That was my job, as Ross McGee so often liked to remind me.

Seeing me hesitate, Luke took the opportunity to repeat, "Based on his lack of familial ties and property, as well as his criminal record, do you consider the defendant to be a flight risk?"

I cleared my throat. Then spoke the truth.

"No. Not really."

The enthusiasm left my old friend's face, and the gleam faded from his eyes. For a moment, as he stared at me, he had no expression at all. The betrayal had apparently stunned him beyond words, beyond expression. He turned his back, murmured, "No further questions," and sat down. He wouldn't look at me.

Bogey bounced up, so eager to tear me apart that he looked like he might float out of his shoes, but now he hesitated, flummoxed. He looked at me, at Brandy, and then at the judge.

Finally he agreed with Luke.

"At this time, I have no questions for this witness."

And I knew I was in deep, deep shit.

2

October 2004

twenty-two

Moriah was getting more and more difficult as the summer ran out, and I was getting increasingly desperate to conquer her. She was harder to hold on to than anything I'd ever dreamed of grasping. I hated to even think it because of her namesake . . . but Moriah was a bitch.

I tried backing off for a while and giving my torn flesh and muscles a chance to recover. Between excursions all over the state while still scouting for meth labs, I had visited Denver twice. While there I held my squalling baby until I couldn't take it anymore, then handed her back and slept on the couch. I went to Cheyenne once, where I had an unhappy meeting with my superiors—who regarded me with a combination of suspicion and contempt. I went to Vedauwoo, the world's Mecca for fat cracks, and practiced an assortment of techniques on climbs like Penis Dimension, Trip Master Monkey, and Squat. I kept returning to my little canyon west of Badwater, swearing each time that I was more determined than ever, swearing I was stuffed full of renewed vigor, but inwardly knowing I was more scared and defeated than I'd ever been in my life.

I tried facing left, then right, tried groping deep into the recess for an edge I could crimp or even a pimple of rock I could pinch, tried running my hands over the underside of the roof for any protrusion that would accept even the most fragile smear, but there was nothing that would allow me to cling to her. All I could do was jam. My muscles screamed, my mouth went dry, and I shook out of the crack again and again, each time falling through space until the rope caught in the cams I'd placed and ripped me out of near-terminal velocity. All I got for my efforts was a hide patchy with raspberry rashes where it wasn't black-and-blue.

Meanwhile, the aspen leaves changed from green to gold. They dried out and started to rattle in the wind like small bones. I spent far too much time lying on my back, staring up and contemplating the bitch while getting high.

I didn't spend much time thinking about Jonah Strasburg. Or at least I tried not to. The guilt I knew he felt was something I too closely sympathized with, and I didn't know how to help him. I'd read in the paper that he'd been unable to meet a $100,000 bond (apparently my opinion hadn't much swayed the judge—either that, or he was worried about his own reelection). I also read in the same article that Jonah had been temporarily transferred to the jail in the next county while awaiting trial in the fall.

That, at least, was a good thing.

The only time the case was mentioned to me was on the single trip to Cheyenne for my semiannual review.

McGee and two suits listened to my report of new meth lab discoveries and their surging abundance with silence and the promise of more inactivity. Then I was told that my performance was being rated as "unsatisfactory." Once my reviews had been consistently stellar, far and away the best among the state's criminal investigators. When I imprudently demanded to know why things had changed, McGee smirked through his beard and one of the suits informed me that a prosecutor had made a formal complaint, accusing me of undermining his most important case—which just happened to be the only case I was currently assigned to.

I was officially placed on probation.

Afterward, McGee had followed me out into the parking lot. As a hot wind blew dust and trash between us, he made no apology, no greeting, and offered no jokes. He simply informed me with a growl that the DEA was interested in having an agent fly up from El Paso to speak to me about the disappearance of drug lord Jesús Hidalgo, and that he'd told them that at the moment I was still unavailable, that I was doing sensitive undercover work exposing methamphetamine laboratories.

The threat couldn't be more clear: behave, or else.

The only other time I thought about the case was when I ran into Brandy Walsh.

I'd finally managed to swallow a taste of the fear and overwhelming guilt that seemed to be drowning me, and had taken Roberto climbing. Or to watch me climb, anyway. I made him promise not to even try.

Rebecca had talked me into it, saying I had to do something for him. "He's using again," she'd told me. "Using heavily. Remember that nice Tibetan monk I told you about, the one who brought him out to see Moriah? He called the other day. They had to ask Roberto to leave the meditation center—they said he was acting crazy. He'd climbed up on the outside of a monument called the Great Stupa and refused to come down." I'd seen the Great Stupa in the mountains outside Fort Collins. It was over one hundred feet high. Not a bad little climb.

In his new custom van, we drove up to Vedauwoo to see if he, or any of the legendary fat cracks there, could suggest a strategy for Moriah. I knew of one called Lucille that Roberto had climbed years ago. An acquaintance of ours named Jay Anderson had spent almost a decade working on this forty-foot off-width roof crack before making the first ascent. I wanted to check it out and get my brother's advice. But the crack sat atop a two-hundred-foot formation, and first I had to figure out how to get up there with Mungo, Roberto and his metal canes, and a packful of ropes and gear. Jay had somehow done it, I knew, with his canine buddy Alobar. I figured there had to be a way. And that it would be a good, and hopefully not too humbling, test for my bro.

We were standing at the base of a beginner's wall with me wondering if Mungo and Roberto could climb and/or be dragged up an easy system of cracks. Another climber was floundering around high above on a steep slab. Roberto pointed out the way his calves were pumping like twin sewing machines. It was obvious the climber was about to fall, that he was going to jitter himself right off the wall. His belayer was a girl in a bikini top who was obliviously reclining on a boulder, more interested in getting a nice tan than protecting her boyfriend. She had at least ten feet of slack in the rope.

I walked over to her and said hi. She smiled up at me and checked out Mungo, too.

"Dude. That's a seriously badass dog."

"Thanks."

Then she checked out my brother.

Women had always stared at him, but not like this. Before the accident, he'd always seemed—to them and to me—half Superman and half wild animal. They'd been mesmerized by his blatant intensity. *Destraillado* was how our mother described it. Unleashed. Utterly feral, utterly free. A kind of noble savage. But now I could see that this girl regarded him as something out of a freak show as he swayed nearby on a pair of metal canes.

He'd come a long way from the romantic poster I'd glimpsed in the Badwater Adventures store. His hair was now shorn, revealing a scarred and dented skull, and his neck was covered with a wide leather collar. Shirtless, his overdeveloped arms, shoulders, and chest mocked the two thin sticks that could barely be called legs. He appeared both monstrous and monstrously pathetic. During the hours I'd spent with him on the drive up, I could barely make conversation. All I'd wanted to do was run away—run back to the wilderness and hole up with my wine, pot, and guilt.

Just as I was trying to think of something nasty to say to break her stare, a scream came down from the sky.

Roberto slammed his cane down on the slack rope as the boyfriend peeled off the rock. The fall was even bigger and more entertaining than anything I could have hoped for.

He plummeted twenty feet before the rope tied to his harness snatched him short, and only then because the weight of Roberto's cane locked it in his girlfriend's belay plate. She was rudely ripped off her boulder and bounced into the cliff by the force of the fall.

What was unexpected was the way his screaming went on and on, even after the fall had been caught. My first thought was that maybe his ankle had struck an edge and been broken. But I reassessed as I saw him gripping his hands to his chest as he howled.

I put my arms around the dazed girl and began to lower him gently using the belay plate on her harness. He was howling so loudly that other climbers, hikers, and mountain bikers were soon scrambling up the boulders toward us. By the time I had him near the ground, a crowd of ten or more people had gathered.

"What happened?" they were all asking. "Is he all right?"

Among them there was a man and a woman dressed in cycling gear. Helmets, sunglasses, CamelBaks, and tights. Something about the woman was familiar. Even more noticeable was the way she seemed to be staring at me through her yellow lenses instead of up at the rapidly descending howler.

It was hard not to curse when I finally recognized her.

Twenty feet off the deck the howler spun around on the rope. His hands were still clutched to his chest, but now I could see that they were running with blood. It was streaming down to drip off his elbows, and there were tears running down his cheeks.

"What happened? Are you okay?" everyone kept yelling.

He was almost to the ground when he moaned, "My finger! I tried to hook the bolt with my finger! It tore my frigging finger off!"

"Which one?" his girlfriend demanded, which seemed like an odd question.

Still descending, he opened his hands to either check or illustrate, and a rubbery little something the size of a .40-caliber bullet tumbled down the rock the last few feet to the ground.

The growing group of us at the base of the climb barely had time to glance down at the thing in the dirt and conclude it was indeed a fingertip, when a gray blur snaked between our legs. I opened my mouth to yell, "Mungo! No!" but knew it was too late before I got the words out. She was playing Snatch, her favorite game. In another two seconds she was running over the boulders along the bottom of the cliff, running with a familiar slinky stride that meant she thought she was being playful.

I kept my mouth shut.

Other people didn't, though. A couple of them vomited, including the male cyclist with the blonde. I managed to get the howler to the ground where he lay, still screaming, in a fetal position in the dirt.

"Was that your dog?" the horrified girlfriend shrieked at me when I finally released her. "Make him give it back!"

But I knew it was far too late. Mungo would have gulped the snack the moment she snatched it up. I heard a clattering noise and saw Roberto speedily hobbling away, the muscles in his back jerking with suppressed laughter.

"No," I said with as much sincerity and outrage as I could muster, "I've never seen that dog before in my life."

The girlfriend turned to make the same shrill demand to other potential dog owners. I turned and looked around, too, hoping I didn't appear too guilty.

Brandy Walsh was staring right back at me.

Behind the dark-yellow lenses, I could see that her eyes were wide. Her mouth was slightly open, too. Either from the exertion of running up to the cliff's base in her cycling shoes, or she was about to shout out an accusation. I gave her a little shake of my head.

She stayed silent. She even lowered her head a little to one side, and I swear it looked like she, too, was trying to hold back a laugh.

I didn't hang around to find out. I picked up my pack and jogged down the boulders in the direction Roberto had gone. I wouldn't whistle for Mungo until we were well out of sight. As I ran, I felt an unfamiliar smile on my face. I think it was the first time I'd smiled all summer.

I did manage to accomplish something constructive after eight weeks of effort, both physical and mental: I got a third Number 5 Camalot fixed in place more than halfway through the roof. The technique I used was a sudden, bizarre inspiration. If anyone had seen me, I probably would have been strapped in a straitjacket and hustled into a white van.

I wiggled more than thirty feet out—passing the two cams I'd placed months earlier. I squirmed with one shoulder, elbow, and knee jammed in the crack, when, as usual, the moment I reached for a third cam on my harness, my legs cut out and I prepared to take another drop and swing.

I resisted the inevitable with a sudden and surprising fury. Kicking at air that offered no purchase, I punched my free arm into the crack just as the rock began to peel another layer of skin off the jammed shoulder. I found myself relatively secure, with my head now inside the crack, both palms smearing, counterbalanced by my back and triceps, both feet pedaling in space. My head was twisted to the side, a cheek pressed to one side, an ear and the back of my skull pressed to the other. A head jam. It took only a few pounds of pressure off my screaming arms and shoulders, but it was enough.

I started to laugh, inhaling rock dust and lichen. But I stayed put.

It was such a ridiculous position that I had nothing to lose by getting even sillier. So I torqued my legs up and out, jackknifing them with a spine-twisting move even farther out into the crack. I somehow managed to jam my feet there, one with the side against a wall, the other foot's heel to its mate, and toes grinding hard into the rock. For a long minute I held it, head in the rock, feet in too, even higher and farther out than my head, and as the lactic acid in my arms and neck began to build, and as the rock began to peel the skin from my cheek and opposite ear, I wondered what to do next.

My arms gave out. My upper body swung out of the crack, tearing some skin from my face. But my feet now held. Suddenly I was a bat, suspended upside-down, three hundred feet off the earth. This was even crazier, but I wasn't laughing now. With numb, shaking hands, I ripped the big cam off my harness, did an upside-down sit-up, and shoved the protection deep into the crack. Shaking even harder, I managed to clip the rope to it. Then I released my feet and dove headfirst toward the ground.

The bone-jarring jerk of the rope snapped me upright. I was hanging out in space, free and easy, half-blinded by light. Actual sunlight, after all the months of groping in the shadows. I squinted up at Moriah and saw that the cam was almost two-thirds of the way to the lip.

I screamed.

The triumphant whoop tore up and down the canyon, sending birds into the air, rabbits diving for their holes, and Mungo into the Pig.

What I screamed was *"Batman!"*

I held the key—all I needed now was to get stronger.

That night I drove to Denver.

Rebecca had a dinner with friends or a date—I didn't ask, I didn't want to know—and she was reluctant about canceling the baby-sitter. I insisted that I could handle our daughter, but my ex-fiancée's face was creased with worry when she left. She wondered out loud how long I'd last before her cell phone vibrated with a panicked call.

"Leave it here," I told her.

"What? Are you sure?" she asked.

"Leave it," I repeated.

She left the phone. For the next two hours I held Moriah even when she screamed and cried and kicked. I held her and cooed and talked and promised undying devotion. I held on and on. I didn't let go. And, after a long while, she actually settled down. She stared up at me with her gray-blue eyes as I wiped away the tears and spittle.

"I'm going to try my damnedest. And I'm not going to stop trying. You can hate me, little girl, but you can't stop me."

Then she burped, pooped, actually smiled, and, after another long stare, closed her eyes.

twenty-three

Buoyed a little by my late-summer successes with the two Moriahs, I stopped by the College of Law in Laramie on my way back to Badwater for the pretrial hearings. For a brief period of time I felt—foolishly, it would turn out—like I could do anything, that I could solve Jonah's case and get it off my back.

Bogey's office was on the second floor of the sandstone building on the University of Wyoming's campus in Laramie. The office wasn't hard to find even though it lacked a nameplate. An expensively framed cartoon by a well-known editorial cartoonist was nailed to the wall next to the door. It depicted an exaggerated Bogey—all chin and hair—dressed in a suit, standing in a courtroom. There was also, incongruously, a feather in his hair, scalps hanging from the belt around his waist, and a bloody tomahawk in his hand. He was grinning a lot of big teeth and saying, "Next witness, Your Honor." Beneath the picture was a caption: "Wyoming Attorney William J. Bogey—For the Defense?!"

It referred, I supposed, to his reputation for brutal cross-examinations, which I'd read about when researching him in Luke's office.

The door was open and he was working at the desk inside. The room smelled of his heavy cologne. Sensing a presence, he held up a finger for patience while he continued scribbling on a legal pad. I studied the framed headlines on the walls—all referring to him—while I leaned on the door frame and waited. He certainly had an ego.

When he finally looked up, he smiled politely and raised his eyebrows before recognizing me. Then the smile became real.

"Oh my. Special Agent Burns. I heard you were lurking in the vicinity. Should I be dialing 911?"

I smiled back. "No. I just wanted to stop by and say hello. I understand Jonah Strasburg got transferred and I wanted to see if he's doing all right."

"Well, this is a surprise. And it's very decent of you. Particularly since it was due to your arrest that he's been held for the last three months, beaten and subjected to shocking harassment, and charged with murder."

I stopped smiling. Already I could tell that this was a bad idea. I'd expected some gratitude for my career-threatening candor at the bail hearing, but it was plain he felt he owed me none.

"Look, I'm just trying to see that he's treated fairly. By everyone involved."

He laughed. "Of course. You're well known for ensuring that suspects and defendants are treated fairly."

I didn't tell him to go fuck himself, but it took some effort. And he was determined to make it even harder.

Lacing his hands behind his head and leaning back in his chair, he said, "This really is quite a coincidence. Just this morning I was reading about you. Brandy and I have been preparing what we hope will be a very revealing cross-examination."

I realized that the papers on his desk included an old photo of me. Some articles, too, downloaded from Lexis. They were the kind of articles that I would never frame and hang on my office walls. If I had an office. But I didn't let myself be goaded.

"You aren't actually going to take this thing to trial, are you?"

He shrugged. "You and your former partner Luke Endow have left me no choice."

"Have you talked to him about a deal?"

"No. Are you here as his proxy to offer one?"

I shook my head.

Brandy Walsh suddenly appeared, squeezing past me through the door. As she had been the day before when I'd run into her at Vedauwoo, she was wearing mountain-biking clothes and shoes, this time with a yellow-and-brown jersey that said "University of Wyoming Cycling Team." She also had a bad case of helmet-head, but for some reason she was almost painfully attractive to me—I had been celibate too long if I was attracted to a lawyer. I could smell her sweat, and the scent of sun on her skin. She must be something more than a casual rider, just as she'd once been something more than a casual surfer. It didn't really surprise me. Most trial lawyers are former athletes and intensely competitive—something that drives them to go far beyond truth-finders and presenters of facts.

She gave me a look but no greeting. I returned the look and said nothing. Except for a small nod in her direction, Bogey ignored her, too.

"It doesn't matter anyway," he continued. "There won't be any deal. The only 'deal' I'll accept is a dismissal of all charges. And a public apology from both of you."

"You know that won't happen. Look, is a trial really in the best interest of your client? This isn't about getting back into the limelight, Bogey. It's not about you. Besides, you lose and you'll just look like an ass. Jonah will get convicted of something. If not murder, then something close. Unless you manage to get a change of venue, the people in Badwater are going to hammer him."

"Oh, I know. That fact's been made abundantly clear over the last few months. I've been wondering if you were responsible for some of it."

"For some of what?"

He stared at me, still smiling, and said, "I expect you know."

I didn't. And I didn't want to prolong what was obviously an ill-advised conversation by asking what the hell he was talking about.

Before I could figure out a way to get out of there, Brandy asked Bogey, "We aren't going to consider *any* offer?"

Bogey turned to her and lost his smile. "No," he said flatly. He looked angry at her for having interrupted our pissing match.

I suddenly liked her a lot better. Maybe she, at least, could be reasonable. And she hadn't mentioned my finger-eating wolf.

"I guess I'll see you in court," I told Bogey as I backed out into the hall.

His smile came back. "I'm looking forward to it. Really."

I looked back once and could only see Brandy inside the office. She was looking after me as Bogey said something sharp to her.

I wasn't entirely defeated yet. I was determined to give it one more try.

"What the hell happened to you?" Luke demanded when I walked into his office in Badwater.

"Climbing."

"You're still trying to kill yourself that way?" He shook his head, probably wishing I had long ago. "Just don't do it before the trial, okay? And do something about your face. You look like you got slapped with a cheese grater."

My old partner was hunched behind his desk, looking more uptight than I'd ever seen him. Gone was the lazy fat man who kicked back in his chair and hefted his boots on a desk cluttered with only fast-food wrappers. He was losing weight, and he sat erect, as if the wound to his posterior was acting up, and the desk was piled high with real work: reports, motions, and law books. More boxes of papers and books were scattered over the floor. He smelled of cigarettes and Binaca, and the white spots on his shoulders showed that he'd been spraying himself to try to hide the odor from his wife.

I wasn't all that surprised that he was so stressed. Coming into town, I'd noticed a lot of signs for his opponent in the coming election, but very few for Luke.

"How's it going?" I asked carefully.

"Fucking Bogey. The bastard's burying me with motions. Motions to change venue, to recuse me and the judge, to suppress all the evidence we've got and a lot that we haven't, all the usual crap and a bunch more. There're more than a dozen separate motions to dismiss. He's probably wiped out an acre of the Shoshone with all the paper he's using up."

"Are you handling it okay?"

"Sure. I can handle him any day of the week," he said with false good humor. It was obvious from the nasty gleam in his eyes that he was still angry about my betrayal.

"But I've evened things out a little," he continued. "Hell, he's getting help, so I figured I'd better get some, too. I've been talking to your office, and I've been getting some help with all this shit—answering motions, making sure my investigator toes the line. A guy who's got a lot of experience. He's gonna come up and ride shotgun during the trial, too."

"Who's that?" I asked, knowing the answer already and not liking it one bit.

Luke smiled.

"I think you know him pretty well. He's about the orneriest bastard on the planet. Your old buddy, Ross McGee. From what I hear, though, you guys aren't so tight these days."

No, we definitely weren't. The man had once embodied everything I believed in about the law—do the right thing and don't fuck it up—and now I wasn't sure who had drifted farther, me or him. Luke had always been way out there. At least he was constant. But it was amazing, and incredibly disappointing, to learn that my mentor would now be collaborating with the man he'd once forced to resign from law enforcement.

"You heard about the threats?" Luke suddenly asked.

"I heard something about them."

"And not just for our defendant, either, although now that he's back in our jail for the hearing tomorrow he'd better be watching his ass. Bogey was too busy filing all this shit to demand any special protection for him."

Having seen Bogey in action, I bet he didn't want any special protection for Jonah prior to trial. He probably wanted Jonah showing up battered and bruised to elicit sympathy in the jury box and outrage in the press.

"Where's Smit?" I asked, alarmed.

"The big freak had served his sentence. We kicked him loose. Speaking of checking six and watching asses, you'd better be watching yours. But no, I'm talking about his ham lawyer. Supposedly, anyway. It's probably some kind of media stunt. Bogey claims he's been getting threatening calls both at the motel he stays at up here and at his office in Laramie."

So that was what Bogey had been talking about. And accusing me of.

"Who's threatening him?"

Luke smirked. "They're anonymous, of course. A muffled voice, he says. Telling him to get the hell out of Badwater or else he'll be raped to death. Shit like that. Most of the calls we traced were made late at night from a pay phone in that little park near the motel. Nobody saw anything, and the clerk who transferred the calls can't remember anything other than being told to forward the call to 'Bill Bogey's room.' The sheriff thinks he's probably making the calls himself—or getting his girl Friday to do it—just so he can crow about it."

"Who's he crowing about it to?"

Now Luke frowned and then winced and touched his stomach.

"Local rag." He burped. "The Casper paper, too. Anyone who'll listen. Been getting into Denver and Salt Lake City a little bit. You didn't see it last week? 'Lawyer Warned to Leave Town'?"

I shook my head. "I've been in the mountains for most of the last three months."

"He got that one in the city papers because he had 'evidence' of the threats. You know what his evidence was? Someone took a big ol' dump on the hood of his Benz SUV in the Outrider parking lot."

I had to return his grin. "You're kidding."

"Nope. He tried to demand that we bag and tag it and submit it to the FBI for a DNA analysis. I told him he could analyze it himself if he wanted, that for all I knew, the poop came from a vulture that's been feeding on all the crap he's been spouting."

Luke managed a bigger smile, adding, "Then he accused me of the dirty deed. I told him I just wished I'd thought of it." He looked at me with renewed sharpness. "I guess you haven't read what he's been saying about you, either."

"Do I want to know?"

"You should know. It might give you an idea what to expect tomorrow at the suppression hearing."

He dug through the pile on his desk until he found a folder full of folded newspapers. He selected one and handed it across to me: "Strasburg Defender Calls Investigation 'Criminal.' "

I didn't react, but I'm sure my face colored. It seemed a little harsh for the guy who'd gone into the river after the kid, who had avenged Jonah for the beating he'd gotten in the jail, and who had warned them to get him transferred.

The lead read: "Jonah Strasburg's defense attorney had sharp criticism for the investigation performed by state agent Antonio Burns, calling it 'criminally deficient.' William Bogey, lead attorney for the man charged in the drowning death of a local 10-year-old child, said Burns's failure to adequately question witnesses to the event and the subsequent charges that have been filed demonstrate a bias on the part of police and prosecutors against his client. 'It shows an intentional or reckless unwillingness to consider the possibility that Mr. Strasburg had committed no crime.'" Apparently Bogey felt I hadn't pressed hard enough in questioning Randy and Trey Mann, and insinuated that they would change their story.

I'd assumed all along they were lying when they denied throwing rocks and that Cody had struck Jonah. I simply wrote in my report what they'd told me. It was an unsurprising defense spin, but also a good one.

"Have you talked to the Manns lately?" I asked Luke.

He shook his head.

"Ed and his wife won't let me talk to them. Even when I threatened a subpoena. Said they'd show up at trial, but that was it. I got an idea, though, what's going on."

I waited while he shuffled through another stack of folders. This time he came up with a couple of typed pages and gruesome photographs labeled "Autopsy."

I ignored the photos. There was nothing in there I wanted to see. I knew they'd be infinitely worse than the memory of the peaceful, cold, and thin young body. Luke directed me to a page that summarized the standard toxicology reports.

Cody Wallis had had methamphetamine in his blood.

I felt a momentary surge of anger and sadness. This was what I'd been fighting all along. This was what my office, my state, had been ignoring all along. A ten-year-old kid high on meth.

It took me a minute to clear my head and to realize what the implications were for Luke. The victim was tweaking. And if Cody was high, his older buddies and cousins Randy and Trey surely were, too. A jury might slam Jonah for killing an innocent kid, but they'd have a much harder time convicting him of killing an aggressive little junkie. And Randy and Trey would probably do anything to keep their parents from learning what they'd been smoking. Even if it meant admitting to the sticks and stones.

In staring at the page and gathering my thoughts, I noticed something else. There was no stamp on the document indicating that it had been discovered to the defense.

"Bogey's seen this?"

Luke stared back at me, stone-faced now.

"Nope. Not yet. I'm going to wait awhile. Until after the hearing tomorrow, at least. Then I'm going to see about making a deal for manslaughter and a stipulated ten-year sentence. Hopefully the thought that those kids could have been high has never crossed his mind, and it had better stay that way."

The last part was definitely a warning. I stared back, trying to decide just how unethical it was for him to withhold this information. I reminded myself that Luke had always been this way, even when he'd been my training officer and friend and had once gotten shot thinking he was saving my life. But his corruption had obviously gotten worse since becoming a politician.

I took a deep breath, and said what I'd come here to say. It was time to get it out in the open and hopefully convince him to get rid of this piece of shit.

"Luke, you've never asked me what I thought about this case."

His eyes narrowed. "What are you talking about?"

"It's not exactly uncommon for the prosecutor to ask his lead investigator what he thinks the outcome should be. Especially when his lead investigator was a witness to the crime itself, or at least its immediate outcome."

He kept on staring.

"How come you haven't asked me?" I asked. "Is it because of Cheyenne? All those years ago?"

He chuckled and said, "That QuickDraw stuff? Nah. Far as I'm concerned, they should have given you a medal. Going in that house all wired up, knowing you'd probably already been burnt. Then wasting those fuckers. That was good work. Rough maybe, but righteous."

"Then what is it?"

"I've been hearing some rumors about something that went down in Baja."

I inhaled and let it out without taking my eyes off him.

He continued, "That dealer, Hidalgo, who you raided with a

bad warrant. The one that the Feds released even after the way he fucked up your brother. People say he's disappeared. And people say you went down to Baja Norte last year just about the time he disappeared."

I did my best to hold his stare.

"So you think that I'm dirty, and that my opinion means shit."

"No, no. I'm not saying that. What I've heard is just rumors—hell, not even rumors really. Just whispered innuendo. And I know something about you, too. Now don't look at me like that, QuickDraw. If it's easier for you, think of it this way: They give me the charging and prosecuting authority because I'm trained in the law. See, cops are too close to their cases. They need someone with some objectivity. Some exterior judgment. Someone who can see the whole thing—the political ramifications, and all that."

I tried to hold on to my cool. I'd come here with a purpose, to defend Jonah, not myself.

"Okay. You may not want my opinion, but I'm going to give it to you. It was an accident. Jonah Strasburg didn't mean to kill that kid. He might not even have meant to push him in the river. You're prosecuting the hell out of him because you want to stick it to your old professor, Bogey, and you want to make a name for yourself as a hard-ass. Win the election and all that. But that's not your job, Luke. You're a prosecutor. Your job's to do the right thing."

But Luke didn't look as if he agreed. He was turning a dark red. It was like all the blood in his body was coming into his face and starting to boil.

"Okay, QuickDraw, now I'm gonna give you *my* opinion. I want you to go down the hall to the third door on the right. It's the men's room. Go on in there and take a good look in the mirror. Then come back and tell me if *you* should be giving *me* advice on law and ethics."

twenty-four

I should have taken Luke's advice and been watching my back, but I was too angry from the way our conversation had ended to be even looking in front of me, much less behind. As a result, I never saw them coming.

My stomach was roiling with bile by the time I got back to Mungo and the Pig. Mungo's must have been, too—she was all over me when I climbed in the truck. I drove to a grocery store, restocked my larder with dog food and some bread and peanut butter, and headed out of town. We didn't make it back to the camp to eat because I was light-headed with hunger and Mungo was drooling down my neck. So I pulled off the highway on a dirt side road and drove a short ways into the Shoshone National Forest.

I was just getting out when they attacked.

The high-pitched whine of a four-cylinder engine torqued to red-line came screaming at me. Turning, I faced a little blue Chevette that was barreling down the road. Someone was hanging out the passenger-side window. It took me a half second to recognize him as Zach Mann—Hairlip—and note that he was waving a two-by-four. Hunched behind the wheel was Smit, from the jail. And squeezed into the back was Ned Mann.

I remember thinking that the car couldn't possibly be Smit's—no red-blooded Wyoming male would own such a car, particularly not a tattooed and bearded giant whose principal interest in life seemed to be intimidating others. Maybe it was his girlfriend's, or maybe it had been borrowed or stolen. The fact that they were coming at me in such an incongruous car was as alarming as the speed at which they were moving. They must be planning something bad. They must mean me real harm.

I didn't have time to think about how stupid I was for having allowed them to follow me unnoticed. There was only a millisecond in which to react. The Pig was parked lengthwise between stout pines and the road, and it would take too long to get around it. Or even to make a dive over the hood. All I could do was press into the Pig's side and duck as the two-by-four came swinging at my head.

I almost didn't duck low enough. I felt the wind in my hair as the piece of wood passed over my head. My shoulder actually bumped the door of the throbbing Chevette as it tore by. There was a cowboy whoop, then a sound like a batter hitting a home run. As I turned to look after the little car and felt its wind and exhaust, I saw my side mirror sailing up into the blue sky. It was a damned good thing I'd already rolled up the windows, otherwise Mungo's head would have been in the line of fire.

I was too startled and too mad to do the sensible thing and get in the Pig and go after them. Or, even more sensibly, just call it in to the sheriff and have the trio picked up. Instead I started running after the Chevette as it bounced down the rutted road. For some reason, just as I started to run, I threw open the Pig's door, too, letting Mungo out.

She might have thought it was a race, or more likely, due to the rumbling coming from her throat that was audible even over the sound of the high-revved engine, she was even more pissed at the Mann brothers than I was. Within a few paces she was outdistancing me.

Through the rising cloud of dust, I saw the Chevette brake just before a turn in the road and start sliding sideways. I finally should have had reason to begin to doubt my choice of actions. They were executing a bootlegger's turn, preparing to come back at us. But I kept running toward them. My blood was up. I'd had enough. And I was only barely aware that my gun was in my hand.

Where was Antonio Burns, the good cop? In action, when you're relying on nothing but gut instincts, is when you reveal yourself. I could have easily slipped into the woods and called for the sheriff. Instead, I wanted a confrontation. I needed one.

The Chevette was facing us now, still sliding, but twin plumes of dirt were rising off the back tires as it tried to get forward traction.

"Mungo!" I shouted as I slowed, and the gun in my hand came up. She was still loping down the center of the road, intent on taking on the car directly. From her point of view, it probably wasn't much bigger than a yearling buffalo, a creature her ancestors had been tackling for millennia.

Someone in the car gave another cowboy hoot.

As I tried to take aim on the windshield over the back of my low-flying wolf-dog, something far bigger than the Chevette appeared from around the corner just behind it. The new object was lime green and moving fast—fast enough to actually plow right into the back of the Chevette with a metal-crumpling, window-shattering crash.

The forest-service pickup never even slowed before hitting the Chevette. The corner it was coming around was blind and the driver was going too fast. The Chevette, which had still been trying to gain purchase on the dirt with its skinny tires in order to come after me again, was shoved into the trunks of stout lodgepole pines, where it collapsed like an accordion. Even if it was still drivable, the forest-service truck held it pinned.

"Mungo!" I yelled again.

This time she veered away, spooked by the truck's sudden appearance and the resulting crash.

"Load up!" I shouted.

She reluctantly turned and passed me on the way back to the Pig.

I approached cautiously. The forest-service worker was getting out of the truck, rubbing his shoulder. Nobody was getting out of the Chevette. It seemed so small and crushed that I wondered if the men inside were dead. But I thought I could see some movement.

"Don't shoot," the ranger called, thinking, I supposed, that I was stalking toward him.

"I'm a cop. The guys in the car just tried to run me over. Use your radio and call the sheriff in Badwater."

The ranger jumped back in his cab.

A groan came out of the Chevette. Then a curse. I could see inside an open window now, and it wasn't pretty. The front seat was a tangle of blood, limbs, and glass. Bad guys don't wear seat belts, so I was expecting it. The limbs were moving, though, and I heard more curses, growing louder. At least someone was still alive. Looking in, I began to sense some order in the mess.

Smit's head was in Zach's lap, twisted and looking up at me. Zach was folded over him, but Smit's bloody face was exposed. Ned, who had been in the tiny backseat, was sprawled on top of both of them. Smit snarled something unkind, which made me laugh. All things considered, for a moment I suddenly felt pretty good.

I smiled at them from behind the sights of my automatic.

"Hey, guys. You having fun yet?"

It took most of the afternoon to see the twins and Smit carted off to the hospital, write the reports, and finally arrange to have the trio booked into the jail. Amazingly, not one of them was seriously injured. Zach had broken his collarbone, Ned one wrist, and Smit just his nose. There were numerous contusions and lacerations covering all three, of course, but the hospital was willing to discharge all of them after a few hours, so the deputies transported them down to the basement jail. My report accused them of attempted assault on a peace officer and more minor charges such as careless driving. Smit, at least, with his lengthy adult record, would not be getting out of jail again anytime soon.

Less fun was the brief run-in I had with one of the paramedics who responded to the scene, Jo Richards. She scorched me with evil looks and muttered insults every time I came into her view.

At one point I worked up the courage to approach her and say, "Hi, Jo. It's good to see you. I'm sorry I haven't had time to call yet, but as you can see, things have been pretty busy—"

I meant it, too. She looked good in her jumpsuit, sober and professional except for the muttering. I'd been without a woman for way too long.

She interrupted me, saying, "Get away from me, you lying son of a bitch. You're going to have to do a lot more than just call if you think I'll ever go out with you."

It would turn out that placating her would require more time and energy than I had to offer. My day wasn't over.

I was in for another surprise that afternoon when I returned to camp. In a way, it was even less pleasant than being accosted by three steroid junkies in a Chevette.

Mungo and I bounced up the canyon trail late in the afternoon. I was eager to get up on Moriah, and I suppose she was eager to eat again. But just as we began the final climb up the steep hillside to the camp, I had to hit the brakes.

There was a vehicle already there.

A big white van was parked next to my tent. It had Colorado handicapped plates and a bumper sticker reading "Bad Cop—No Donut," which, of course, had been put there for my benefit.

"'Berto," I muttered. "Shit."

Clearly pleased with himself for having found me, he was sitting beside a small campfire with his canes laid across his legs.

He was clearly stoned, too. I could see it in the width of his grin and the broadness of his wave.

Mungo was happy to see him. She ran to him and nearly bowled him over in the leaves. Between them, it had been love at first sight. She seemed to view him as the leader of the pack, something that hadn't changed even after Roberto got hurt. In her eyes he was still the alpha male. It had always made me a little jealous, but Mungo probably sensed that I looked up to my big brother despite all his faults, and he was as much a wild animal as she was. Maybe even more so.

"Eh, eh, *chica,*" he was saying in his soft voice as she danced around him. "Cool it now."

He snagged her by the scruff of her neck and threw her onto her back. It was an impressive feat, done one-armed with a 120-pound resisting wolf-dog, especially from a seated man with little or no leverage coming from his legs. And it was meant to be. Looking up at me, he held her that way, rubbing her chest, while she squirmed and whined with pleasure.

"A couple of hours ago you were about to take on one thousand pounds of steel. Now you're acting like a sissy," I told her. But she didn't care.

"You up for a little climbing, *che*?" Roberto asked.

I looked at him. Skinny legs, massive arms, dented skull, scarred throat, and fused spine. I felt the sickness coming over me. The glacial-blue eyes were bright, though, even if the pupils were just tiny black pinpricks. I wondered just how stoned he was. But the need—the hunger—in his face was glaring. I couldn't deny him.

"Yeah," I told him. "I think I am."

He was a free spirit. He'd always made his own decisions, even if they were consistently to his detriment. It wasn't failure or a fall that would finally crush him: it was me telling him what he could and couldn't do.

* *

It wasn't pretty.

His legs would support only a very little weight, so he had to essentially climb the vertical pitch all the way up to the cave with just his arms. One-armed pull-ups, really, off flared hand jams, over and over again for more than a hundred feet. Even Roberto, with his massive arm strength and his former technical abilities, was barely able to pull it off. But he raised his head to gently chide me every time I tried to lift some of his weight with the rope. Still, he was wringing wet with sweat and blowing hard when he finally pulled himself over the edge and into the cave.

I didn't say a word. And I didn't dare look directly at him.

My brother settled in next to me, legs swinging in the void, while his breathing slowed. I stared at the cliff across the canyon and the festively colored aspens below.

Finally he said, "You might've picked something a little easier for my first time back, bro. What was that, 5.10?"

His tone was light, his complaint mocking. A laugh burst out of me.

"First time? I heard about the Great Stupa. What did it go at?"

He started laughing, too.

"Oh, I don't know—5.7, maybe. With twenty feet of bouldery overhang at the start. But it seems a lot harder when there's a bunch of monks in saffron robes swinging brooms and trying to knock you off."

We talked and laughed for a while. I was so relieved, I couldn't shut up. I showed him Moriah, which gaped just over our heads, and he whistled in appreciation and even tried to get up in the crack. But with legs that didn't work very well, even Roberto couldn't do more than hang in it for a minute. He also gave me a professional confirmation that if it went, it would be the hardest wide crack in the world.

Still on my talking jag, I told him all about what I was doing up here other than Moriah. I told him all about Jonah, the river, and the prosecutor's and town's planned semilegal lynching.

Roberto listened intently. He might have been stoned and borderline psychotic, but he certainly wasn't dumb. When I told him about my sympathy for Jonah and what he'd done, Roberto saw the obvious parallel. He knew I was really talking about his accident and how I blamed myself and my overblown ego for having put him there.

Later, after the sun went down, we rappelled out of the cave and down to the ground where Mungo waited.

"You start dinner," he told me. "I'm going to take a little walk and howl at the moon."

I knew what that meant. That he was going to get high. Higher.

I wanted to tell him not to go, not to ruin it. But who was I, a drug-enforcement agent with my own stash in the back of my truck, to tell him what to do? Before I could even sort it out in my own head, my phone started making its electronic chime. Roberto hobbled away as I picked it up.

"What the hell are you trying to do?" Luke demanded. "Make sure I lose the election?"

"What are you talking about?"

"The goddamn Mann boys. What were you thinking, hooking them up? Don't you know that their pa can swing the entire cowboy constituency? And their uncle everyone else?"

"They tried to kill me, Luke. Took a swing at my head that would have taken it off if I hadn't ducked."

"Shit. That's no big deal. I've wanted to do the same thing myself a couple of times recently."

"Fuck you, Luke. It's assault on a peace officer."

"We'll see about that. I already got the twins bonded out, at least. But Ed Mann was not at all happy. You'll be pleased to know Smit's staying inside. There's no way I can cut him loose, not with his record. But he didn't seem too upset about it, since Jonah Strasburg's been transferred back over from Park County." Sniggering, he added, "I gather Smit was pretty pleased to see him.

Now, you be on time for the hearing tomorrow. You're going to be the star witness, QuickDraw. You'd better do a good job—I hear you're awfully close to getting kicked out of DCI."

When Roberto staggered back from "howling at the moon," I was waiting for him.

"Hey, 'Berto. Will you do something for me?"

"I'd do anything for you, *che*. You know that."

That was true. Just looking at his wrecked body, you could see how true it was.

I swallowed hard, then asked, "Then how about going to jail for a week or two?"

So I made my fourth arrest of the day. I handcuffed my brother and took him to the Colter County Jail.

twenty-five

The evidentiary suppression hearing went about like you would expect. The defense filed every bullshit motion imaginable and asserted that every bit of evidence was tainted. There was no reasonable suspicion of a crime for the officers to detain the defendant on. There was no probable cause to arrest him. Any and all incriminating statements I said he'd made were fabrications I made up to implicate him. And, in the alternative, if they weren't lies, then they were involuntary. They alleged that I'd intimidated and beaten Jonah for the confession he'd told me on the beach, that I'd tortured him later in the interrogation room, and that I'd ordered him further tortured in the jail. They argued, too, that the town was only prosecuting Jonah in order to alleviate its own grief at a local boy's death in an accident the boy himself had instigated. This resulted in some outraged shouts from the gallery. The judge had to have several people removed.

They argued all these motions with a straight face, too. And they brought up every rumor and piece of dirt they could about me during cross-examination in order to impeach my credibility. Especially Cheyenne. Sustaining Luke's repeated objections, the judge wouldn't let them question me about it at the hearing, but he did allow them to make their argument in open court—in front of the spectators and the media—that I was beyond unreliable, that the state had settled a lawsuit with the families of the gangbangers I'd killed three years ago for an undisclosed sum, the obvious implication being that I was a murderer being protected by the state's chief law-enforcement agency.

Not only that, but they wrapped the whole thing in a pretty package, too. Brandy Walsh in her elegant chocolate-brown suit did the honors.

So I wasn't in a particularly good mood as I sat in the idling truck just a block from the scene of my annihilation. Bogey was holding forth for his pet press corps—there were a lot more of them now—and posing for pictures on the courthouse steps. His wish for increased media coverage seemed to be coming true. Some townspeople were watching in groups, fanning the flames by occasionally yelling at him and giving outraged interviews. An impromptu protest by angry Badwater residents was forming. Early in the summer, after I'd arrested Jonah, I'd been worried that he might be lynched. I couldn't care less, though, if the mob decided to go after Bogey or Brandy.

Adding to my discomfort was the fact that I hadn't heard anything from Roberto. I couldn't exactly go down to the jail and talk to him, as I'd booked him under a fake name, claiming I'd found him staggering on the highway with a small amount of heroin in his possession. Thanks to Colter County's antiquated computer system, the fingerprints wouldn't reveal his true identity for weeks. The part about the heroin was true, though. Now I just had to wait until he either called me or I picked up some gossip from Luke or the deputies about things in the jail. I was seriously regretting my decision to put him in there. Roberto wasn't a superman. Not anymore. How was a cripple like him supposed to protect Jonah from a monster like Smit?

It was tempting to pull him out. All I had to do was go down, interview him, then claim he'd agreed to act as an informant. I could have him out in an hour. . . .

I noticed my personal executioner slipping away from the crowd in front of the courthouse. She was walking quickly, presumably back to her own car, when I let the Pig creak up beside her. Mungo—who seemed to feel my pain—was glaring balefully out the window.

"Get in."

She looked over with surprise, then suspicion.

"We need to talk," I told her. "In private."

She still just stared at me.

"Get in, damn it. As much as I might like to, I'm not going to hurt you."

She seemed to consider, frowning, then looked up and down the street. She waved to someone, but I think she was faking it. She just wanted me to think someone was watching her in case something happened.

She climbed in and placed her briefcase demurely on her lap. She didn't look at me. I pressed the accelerator and began working through the gears.

"We need to talk about Jonah," I said.

No response.

"The way you guys are making this town look in the media, I sure as hell hope you plan on filing for a change of venue. Otherwise, they're going to hang your client just because of the way you're talking about the people here."

She finally turned and examined me. Her nose seemed to be faintly wrinkled. It was not a look a man wants to see on the face of a beautiful woman observing him. Mungo protectively placed her huge paws on the armrests and thrust her head and shoulders between the seats. Brandy pressed herself against the door, leaning away as far as possible. *Good dog,* I thought. I hoped the lawyer's suit would be covered with gray hair by the time I let her out.

"Bogey's decided there won't be any venue change."

"Why the hell not?"

"That's none of your business. And he doesn't necessarily share every aspect of his defense strategy with me."

"It's so he can make it more of a media circus," I told her. "Take it out of Badwater and it's not a story anymore. He wants Jonah to get nailed, to become a martyr."

"And you don't want to see him convicted?" she asked in the same contemptuous voice she'd used while impeaching me.

"No, damn it. I arrested him because I believed he'd committed a crime. Not murder, but something else. Maybe reckless endangerment, or maybe nothing at all. I thought that would get figured out later. During the investigation. Which I sure as hell didn't think would get assigned to me. As you just pointed out in open court, I'm considered a loose cannon."

"Then why did you allow him to get charged with murder?"

"Jesus Christ. Don't you listen? I didn't charge him with anything. All I did was find, at the scene, that there was probable cause to believe a crime had been committed and that he had committed it. I'm a cop. I don't charge people with crimes. That's a lawyer's job."

"And you want me to believe you don't advise and influence Luke Endow? I know about you two. I know he used to be your partner."

"I don't advise or influence him about *anything*."

She peered at me over Mungo's head, her eyes not losing any of their hostility.

"That's a little hard to believe, Agent Burns. He saved your life once, and you captured the man who shot him. I know about that, too."

"We were partners. That's what you do. But I don't think we ever really liked each other. And he certainly doesn't like me right now. I think he's hated my guts ever since I spoke up for Jonah at the bail hearing. Maybe even before then."

He'd probably been jealous for years of my unearned reputation—"QuickDraw," and all that. That was just the sort of thing he would have loved to be called. And that's exactly the kind of cop he'd been.

"Listen. If it were up to me, Jonah would get a deferred judgment to reckless endangerment with time served and five hundred hours of community service, or something like that."

I hoped that sank in. That she could hear my sincerity. I gave it a minute.

Then I continued, "But you know what? You wouldn't take it. Not even a deferred. You and Bogey are so determined to get yourselves on TV, to go on all those bullshit shows that love to expose supposed government corruption, that you'd insist on a trial no matter what. Bogey is a has-been desperate to get back on top. And you're just as desperate to make a name for yourself. You guys have goaded Luke at every turn to keep him from offering a reasonable plea, and now you're inflaming things as much as you can to keep the media interested. I don't know how you justify it to yourself, but there's no way in hell you're acting in the best interest of your client."

We rode in silence. The radio was off and the only sound was the big tires vibrating on the pavement. Mungo was straining forward between us, peering out the windshield, trying to guess where we were headed.

"Where are you going? Turn around."

Without really meaning to, I had gotten on the highway and was driving us out of town. I wanted to say: *Not until you admit it,* but didn't want to be later accused of kidnapping a defense lawyer. I slowed and obediently turned around.

We rolled along for a few more minutes. She was looking out her window, her shoulder pushed against it, as far away from Mungo and me as she could get.

I wondered if she was considering what I'd said, or whether she was really frightened of me. Maybe the threats the defense lawyers had been getting were for real and she thought I was the one who'd crapped on her professor's car and made those phone calls. I almost hoped she did.

"You lawyers always talk about the trial process," I said. "About the search for the truth. About just making sure your client's side of the story is heard. It's all bullshit, you know. It's only about winning. All those motions you filed, all that stuff you said about me in there, you *know* it's all bullshit."

Now her head turned and she looked at me.

"You should quit while you're ahead, Burns. What I implied about what happened in Cheyenne may or may not be true, but I'm beginning to uncover some interesting things about a botched federal raid in a town called Potash and a little trip you took to Mexico last summer that make those allegations seem pretty minor."

I tried to hold her gaze. To stare her down with a contemptuous look of my own. But I was driving, damn it, and I had to make sure we didn't go off a cliff into the river. I turned back to the road. It wasn't fair. In that gesture I think I made a fatal admission.

"Not that I entirely blame you, after what they did to your brother."

I wanted to grind my teeth. She knew about my brother, too.

We reentered town, passing a gas station, liquor store, and grocery. Her motel was coming up.

"What are you doing this afternoon?" I asked in the calmest voice I could muster.

"I don't know. Pack. Go for a ride. Bogey's doing interviews all afternoon, but I wasn't asked to sit in. Why?"

"Come climbing with me. You said—that night when I took your sticks—that you'd done some. Let's figure out a way to make this thing right. We know our bosses aren't going to get it done."

twenty-six

She was quiet for a long time. I assumed she was refusing to even acknowledge such an outrageous request. For her, a lawyer on the opposite side, to do something alone and in a remote location with a man she'd just accused of being a multiple murderer, not to mention his flesh-eating dog, would be insane.

But then she surprised the hell out of me by murmuring "All right."

I suppose she thought she might be able to get something out of me to help her case, and for that she was willing to take some risks.

I was instructed to pull to the back of her motel. She disappeared around the side of the building and returned five minutes later without her chocolate-brown suit. Instead she wore wraparound sunglasses, baggy khaki shorts, and one of her sleeveless riding jerseys. She had pulled her blond hair back into a ponytail.

"Did you leave a message for Bogey?" I asked.

"No."

I assumed she was lying.

We picked up sandwiches at a drive-through, earning me three more punches on a new card. At least I would get something out of this. Mungo and I were familiar there, and the girl at the window gave Mungo a slice of salami, nervously feeding it to her with her fingers after asking me if it was all right. I thought I heard Brandy snort when I replied that Mungo was harmless.

I passed the sandwiches through onto Brandy's lap.

"Three sandwiches," she commented with what seemed a mocking tone. "Getting dragged over the coals in court must have given you an appetite."

"The meatball's for Mungo," I explained, trying not to sound annoyed.

She had pushed up between the seats again and was now drooling onto Brandy's shorts. Good dog.

"You mean it doesn't just eat human flesh?"

I leaned forward to stare over at her. She was smiling. I had to smile back.

"It's a she. And thanks for not ratting us out at Vedauwoo. I guess she just thought someone dropped a tasty snack."

Now she did laugh. "That was about the grossest thing I'd ever seen. My date tossed his cookies. And he didn't ever ask me to go riding with him again."

Her date. For some reason I cared about that bit of information. Luke had all along assumed she was sleeping with Bogey—made a lot of obscene and illustrative comments about it, actually—but maybe she wasn't after all. Attractive as she was, I reminded myself, she was still a defense lawyer.

I fed Mungo hunks torn from the meatball sandwich as we drove out of town. We had just passed the turnout by the river, where this had all begun, when Brandy abruptly asked, "So what are we going to talk about this afternoon?"

"How to finally get Jonah out of the mess he's in. How to get our bosses to stop playing games and acting like such frigging lawyers."

I could sense her starting to bristle. But all she said was "And how are we going to do that?"

"By telling the truth, for a start."

"The truth about what?"

"Everything. But for the moment, you've got to swear to me that everything we say stays between us until we figure out a way to make this work. Okay?"

"Sure. So tell me the truth," she said, sounding skeptical.

Keeping my eyes on the road, I said, "For one thing, the kid—Cody Wallis—was high on meth. So were the Mann brothers, probably."

I could feel her staring at me. I knew the ramifications for her would be huge. It would make the victim seem not like just an innocent child. It would give rise to a whole new defense. Self-defense was the simplest explanation for what Jonah had done on the edge of the boulder, but Bogey had so far refused to press it either in court or to the media. It wasn't as glamorous as going after a murderous cop and a vindictive, campaigning prosecutor. Self-defense wouldn't make the news the way police persecution did.

"How do you know that?" she demanded.

"It's part of the autopsy report. Luke is holding back on discovering it to you. At least for a while. He's hoping you won't notice until he can force you, on the eve of trial, into a hard-nosed plea. But we both know Bogey won't accept one. No way. His primary concern is grandstanding, getting his name back in the papers and on TV. He wants a trial no matter what. Right?"

I looked past Mungo and met her eyes through the sunglasses. Just before I had to turn back to watch the road, I saw her give a small nod. Relief flooded through me. I was taking a huge gamble by telling her. If it got back to Luke, I'd certainly be fired. And maybe worse. But I could now see that the look she'd given me as I'd walked out of Bogey's office the day before was genuine. She hated what he was doing. I was relieved because I thought I was safe. I knew she could figure out a way to demand the autopsy report without raising suspicion. It would even make her look good to her boss because demanding it was something he'd obviously overlooked.

"What about the Mann brothers?" she asked after a little while.

"Which ones?"

"Those young boys. Will they confess to getting high with Cody? Have they already confessed to you?"

I shook my head. "I haven't seen them since my initial interview with them, way back in June. When they denied throwing rocks. Have you talked to them?"

"No. I tried. Bogey even sent me out to their ranch—he tried to make me dress kind of sexy for it, actually. He thought it would make them more cooperative. It didn't matter, though. They wouldn't talk to me. Their parents wouldn't let them. But he managed to talk to them himself a couple of weeks ago. I don't know how he did it."

I, too, wondered how he'd pulled that off. Ed Mann and his wife certainly wouldn't willingly cooperate with the lawyer of the man who killed their nephew. I guiltily remembered suggesting just that to them, when I'd been out there. But they probably wouldn't be too happy about cooperating with the prosecution, either, now that I'd arrested their older twin sons just the day before. Maybe that was why Luke had gotten their bail reduced.

"Have you met the older brothers?" I asked Brandy.

"No. I just heard there were some. Twins, right?"

"Yeah. Ned and Zach. They're trouble. Chances are, they're the ones who've been hassling you. Making those threats and all that."

"We, uh, thought it might be you," she said carefully.

"Why... never mind. It wasn't me. But this morning, when you had me up on the stand, I would have liked to have ordered Mungo up onto the hood of your car."

I heard her laugh as she pictured it. I laughed, too. Then she said, by way of apology I guess, "That was business."

"It was just the lawyer in you, huh?" I was beginning to see that there was more to her than just being a zealous attorney. She had a sense of humor.

We entered the Shoshone National Forest and bounced along increasingly rugged logging roads. Branches scraped at the sides of the Pig, and we splashed through two shallow creeks before entering the canyon. I paused for a minute to let her see the beauty of the place. From the river in the center, it rose in forested slopes of aspens and pines to the rock walls, which led hundreds of feet higher to a blue Wyoming sky. Twelve-thousand-foot peaks capped with snow were not far off.

"Wow," she said. "You live here?"

"Sometimes."

I put the truck back in gear and headed up the rocky double-track that led to my camp beneath Moriah. Enjoying showing her this place, I'd forgotten about Roberto's van still being up there. When she asked whose it was, I said a friend of mine who'd gone into the wilderness for a couple of weeks. It was close to the truth. She didn't mention the handicapped plates or the bumper sticker. I wondered how much she knew about my brother and whether she'd put it together.

Getting out of the truck, she examined my little blue tent, the ring of blackened rocks, and then pointed up at a green bag hanging from between two trees.

"What's that up there?"

"Dinner. And breakfast. Hopefully the bears around here aren't tall enough to reach it."

She looked around, slightly alarmed. "Bears? What kind of bears?"

"This canyon is the gateway to the Absaroka range," I told her. "Welcome to grizzly country."

"Have you seen any around here?"

"Just some tracks. Bears don't like the way Mungo smells."

"Why not?"

I decided there wasn't too much risk in admitting it. "She's half wolf. Bears don't like wolves."

Brandy stared down at Mungo. She was lying upside-down in the dirt, scratching her back by bicycling her long legs. She couldn't have looked less wolfish.

"Surely she's too small to fight one. What will you do if a bear comes into your camp? Shoot it?"

"My gun's a .40-caliber handgun. It wouldn't stop a grizzly. It would just make it mad."

"Well, what about pepper spray? Do you have any of that?"

She reached in the pocket of her shorts and came out with the little black cylinder, the same one she'd used to threaten Mungo and me that night on the river. It wasn't much bigger than a cigarette lighter.

I repeated an old joke. "If a bear charges, you should use that to spray yourself in the face. You don't want to see what the bear's going to do to you."

But she seemed truly agitated by the threat of predatory bears. This surfer girl, I guess, hadn't had much experience around them. I tried to explain that bears eat mostly roots, bugs, and berries, and they'd be a lot more scared of her than she would be of them. She didn't look convinced, though.

"There's not many left around here," I added, "and they aren't usually dangerous unless you run into a mother with cubs. Or try to feed one a peanut-butter sandwich, like the tourists do in Yellowstone. Grizzlies have killed about ten people in the last decade. Deer have killed more than a thousand, coming through windshields. It's a one-in-a-million chance."

"I bet the odds are a lot shorter when you're out here every day. A friend of mine was bitten by a shark."

"Is that why you stopped surfing?"

Her look was very direct. "You've been checking up on me, too, huh? I guess it's only fair. As you know, I've certainly been checking up on you. No, I quit because I wasn't that good."

"That's not what I read."

"I was good, but only as an amateur. I couldn't compete with the pros. In surfing, there's a huge difference between a good amateur and a true professional. Isn't it the same with climbing?"

I shrugged. "I don't know. I never competed."

"But you were mentioned once or twice in the climbing magazines. I checked on Lexis and read about some expeditions you went on in Alaska and Patagonia. Your brother was mentioned all the time. Before his accident."

"I just climb for fun. My brother, he's another story." I tried to make it pretty clear I didn't want to talk about him, even though I was curious about what she knew. I didn't want to think about him right then. "You might want to turn around, because I'm going to take off this suit."

I was still wearing my courtroom suit. Once her back was turned, I stripped out of it, hung it up in the back of the Pig, and pulled on a pair of cut-off shorts and a ragged T-shirt.

"What are we going to climb?" she asked when I was done changing and busy stuffing a pack with gear.

"See that cliff above us?"

She pointed up at Moriah. "That thing that looks like a hat brim on top?"

"No, not that. Down the canyon a little ways. Where it's not too steep."

"Oh. I see. That looks more reasonable."

"That 'hat brim' is my secret project. I might show it to you later. But like everything we talk about today, it's confidential, okay?"

"Yeah, sure."

I led her a quarter mile along the base of the cliff to where it was only a hundred or so feet high. Here I dumped a packful of rope and gear on the broken rocks that littered the ground. I handed her a pair of shoes.

"These ought to fit."

"You have woman's-size shoes?" she asked.

"They're mine. For climbing hard stuff. The smaller the better."

She looked at my sandaled feet and seemed to be comparing the length of them to the length of the shoes. "That must hurt."

"You get used to it. It's a little less comfortable than surfing."

"I bet," she said dubiously.

After she put the shoes on, I held out the harness for her to step into.

"Just tell me how to do it," she instructed, trying to take it from me.

I suppose she didn't want a killer's hands too close to her waist and thighs. I wasn't planning on groping her, and I felt myself getting annoyed again. She'd been opening up a little, but the window appeared to be closing. I checked the sky and saw that dark afternoon clouds were already massing around the peaks to the west, and knew we might not have much time.

"It's quicker if I do it," I told her. "Step in."

Reluctantly, she complied. She held her body stiff and said nothing as I buckled the harness tight around her waist then tied her in to one end of a rope with a double figure-eight. She sucked in her stomach as I fed the rope through, but my knuckles still accidentally brushed her a couple of times. Each time I felt her make a tiny jump. The hair on her arms was standing up.

She really must be afraid of me, I thought. *Or think I'm really disgusting.* With one eye on the clouds, I gave her a quick course on belaying—protecting my lead up the cliff by managing the rope through a piece of notched metal clipped to her harness—and explained how she'd follow me up to the top, then we'd rappel off. I lifted a sling of gear over my head and one shoulder and then hopped onto the rock.

"Belay me."

I found an easy route on mostly good edges and scrambled up. There was a place or two where she'd have to jam her hands, but I could explain the technique to her while belaying from above. Every fifteen feet I slotted a cam or a nut into a crack and clipped the rope to it for protection. At the top, I built a quick anchor by looping a sling around a stout tree and yelled for her to come on up.

She was hesitant at first. Her limbs trembled with a sewing-machine pace and I could see she was breathing hard and fast. But after the first twenty feet, she just took off. Her arms and shoulders were strong from a lifetime of surfing, and her legs powerful from her more recent passion of mountain biking on hills and in the canyons around Laramie. She was a natural, I decided with mixed emotions. I was still feeling the sting of her barbs in court and wouldn't have minded seeing her humiliated. Now, as she raced up to me, it was hard to believe she was a lawyer. I could see her eyes behind the yellow wraparound sunglasses and they were wide with excitement.

"Having fun?" I asked when she pulled up next to me on the top of the cliff.

She grinned widely. "Oh yeah. Not as good as dropping in on a double-overhead at the Pipe, but yeah, I'm having fun."

My brother called the thrill "feeding the Rat." I thought I could see a hungry little Rat stirring in her rib cage.

I'd taken off my shirt in the afternoon heat, and now she did a double-take when looking at me. She examined the wounds from my summer-long battle with Moriah.

"Jesus. What the hell happened to you?"

"This is what a serious climbing addiction will do to you."

She stripped off her cycling jersey, which was wet with sweat, to reveal a black athletic bra. She pointed to small white stripes that scarred her back on one side from shoulder to hip.

"Coral," she told me. "I got slammed into it during a contest on the North Shore. Surfing's not exactly for sissies, you know."

I tried not to stare too much. Her skin was tan and smooth. Her upper back was covered with small freckles, just like her nose and cheekbones beneath her yellow glasses.

"I can see that," I said.

For the next two hours we barely spoke at all, and said nothing about Jonah's case. I barely thought about it. Through her, I began reliving my own joy in climbing, remembering good days with Roberto and our father when he introduced us to the sport, seeing it all as new and thrilling again. I'd been so grimly focused on Moriah, and the real Moriah, and also my career problems, that I'd forgotten how it was to feel all that air beneath your heels, to feel a hot wind rising up from beneath you, to feel unrestrained by the laws of gravity.

I didn't notice until late in the afternoon, as we climbed our way back toward my camp on higher and steeper walls, that it was getting cooler and that the storm clouds building around the peaks were starting to swing our way.

"We'd better call it a day," I told her.

"One more," she answered. "I want to see that secret project you promised to show me."

twenty-seven

The weather looked bad. There were thunderstorms almost every afternoon at this time of year, but usually they just danced around on the horizon, swinging close but never quite striking my little canyon. Chances were that they'd just put on a show for us, crackling and flashing in the mountains to the west. Threatening like a junkyard dog behind a fence but never doing any damage. But if the storm did come, at least the lower part of the rock was protected from rain by the enormous overhang above.

I led her to the base of the one-hundred-foot hand-size crack that was the only way to get to the cave beneath the roof. Rated 5.9 or so, the crack would be harder than anything else we'd done that afternoon. But she was a natural; I was confident she could make it, even if I had to give her a little tension. Roberto had done it just the day before without the use of his legs.

"This is going to be pure jamming," I advised. "There's really no edges or holds. Just slot your hand into the crack, then twist and flex to expand those two fat muscles in your palms. That's what will hold you."

"Are you saying I've got fat hands?" she asked with a sparkle in her eyes.

Nope. Her hands were small and thin and nicked and bleeding, but there wasn't anything fat about them. Or her. I just smiled instead of answering. All I said was "Belay me." When she nodded, I headed up. The route had become so familiar that I could have climbed it with my eyes closed.

The cave under the roof was a small hole, even smaller than the inside of my truck. The extra ropes I'd cached in the back made a little nest where I would sometimes curl up and nap between attempts on Moriah. I checked the three pitons that I'd hammered into tiny cracks on one side for a bombproof anchor and clipped into them. The wind was rising; the cave exhaled a low moan. It was getting colder, but the cave was cold even on the hottest days—it was a place that had never seen the sun. It had soothed my burning flesh after a hundred tries on the horizontal crack that began from its roof.

I turned around to check the weather but couldn't see anything but the canyon below and the opposite wall across the river. It seemed to be getting dark, though. If I'd worn a watch, I would have checked it. But it couldn't be past five o'clock. At least I'd get in one shot on Moriah, with an actual dynamic belay for the first time. And I'd get to show off a little.

"Come on up," I yelled.

"Okay! Climbing!"

I adjusted my clove-hitched leash to the anchor and sat at the edge where I could peer down between my knees and watch her progress. It was amazing how fast she came up. But just by looking at her it was easy to see she was a serious athlete, accustomed to the burn of lactic acid and all the other stifled discomforts of hard-core play.

Within ten minutes she was ignoring my outstretched hand and climbing over me and into the cave. Sweat-slick skin that glided over my thigh, chest, and shoulder. Her hot breath, too, was coming fast. She smelled of sun-bronzed flesh.

The charge I felt at that moment was so strong that it had to be from the friction of the storms swirling over the canyon—not the brief touch of a lawyer's skin. Then she was past me and hunched and panting in the back of the cave.

"You're something," I told her as I tied her off. "There aren't many people who could climb something like that on their first day out."

She looked at me, smiled, and looked down at her raw hands. When she'd caught her breath, she asked, "So, this is your secret?"

"My secret project. Yeah."

"Where?"

"Right here."

I reached up and patted one side of the flaring crack that bisected the roof over our heads. I pointed out how it ran straight out for forty feet, all the way to the very lip of the overhang. The two Number 5 Camalots I'd placed were visible, carabiners dangling, the farther one almost two-thirds of the way to the lip.

She frowned, studying the inverted crack. "How can you climb that? It's upside-down. And it's too wide to jam with your hand, or even a fist."

"I'll show you. Put me on belay."

I closed my eyes and tried to focus. But it wasn't easy. The wind was still picking up, and I was already chilled from fifteen minutes in the cave. I should have hauled up my shirt. It was getting darker, too. And that electricity I'd felt when Brandy had crawled over me was still giving me a buzz.

I took ten deep belly breaths, stood without speaking or even looking at her, and locked my palms and elbows into the crack. Supported by them, I twisted my knees and feet and hips up into it, too. Then I began inelegantly worming, humping, and panting my way out into space. This wasn't showing off, I belatedly realized. This must appear totally bizarre. Like a contortionist's trick.

And I was flubbing it, barely making the jams. I'd done it alone so often that being watched was disconcerting. Despite the public flaying I'd received that morning in court, I'd also somehow lost the anger, too. It was when angry that I climbed the hardest. For the first time that summer, I didn't feel like I had a fire in my belly.

I was almost to the first cam when it happened—the loudest *crack!* I'd ever heard, combined with a brilliant flash of light. It was as if a grenade had gone off in my head. And the rock all around me rattled as if God had smacked his fist on the top of the overhang. The rock lurched and constricted all around me. Then it opened and furiously shook me out.

I was so stunned I didn't even feel myself falling, or slamming into the cliff nearly thirty feet below. My weight tore Brandy out of the cave, but still she managed to hold the rope locked through her belay device.

When my head finally cleared and the thousand clanging bells in my mind stopped their din, I looked up and saw her hanging, too. A splash of rain hit me. Within seconds it became a torrent. It was raining *up*—the wind wrapping the water under the overhang.

Shakily, I got my hands and feet into the crack to take my weight off her.

"Can you get back in the cave?" I yelled.

It was raining so hard that it was difficult to see or hear. But the rope came taut around my waist, so I was forced to climb a little higher. She must be getting back in. The blurred vision of her kicking legs disappeared. I climbed up the remaining twenty-five feet fast despite how weak I felt. I didn't feel strong enough to stand, much less climb, but I made it.

The cave was misty with blowing water, but at least the wind-blown firehose couldn't reach all the way inside. The wind was howling across the entrance, though. Brandy was huddled all the way in the back, on the nest of spare ropes, gripping the rope through her belay device. She was still belaying me even though her hair was plastered all across her face except for where two huge eyes stared out.

I made myself give her a big grin.

"Just a little dust-up," I shouted. "It should blow over in a few minutes."

She surprised me by smiling back and yelling, "It's like a freaking hurricane!"

Outside, it was so dark it was as if the entire cliff were under water. More *booms!* and *cracks!* could be heard tearing up and down the canyon. I'd never seen a storm like this one. I knew several climbers who'd been struck by lightning, even one who'd died high on Longs Peak, but I'd never imagined this kind of intensity.

I was starting to shiver hard. I put my hand on Brandy's ankle and felt her shivering, too. All of our clothes were a hundred feet below and undoubtedly soaking wet. And we couldn't reach the tent or the car—there was no way I was going to rappel out of the relative safety of the cave.

"What about Mungo?" she asked.

Mungo had always been skittish in storms. But she was half wolf—a species that had been living outdoors in storms for tens of thousands of years. I hoped she wouldn't lose her head. I hoped she hunkered down under the Pig instead of tearing her way into my expensive tent.

"She'll be okay. Are you freezing, too?"

I thought I could hear her teeth chattering when she nodded and said, "Yeah."

"You can take me off belay."

She wiped the hair out of her face. Her grin, although a little nervous, still held.

I squeezed around behind her, seating myself against the cold back wall. I fit my legs and arms around her and pulled her back. She resisted for half a second then, slowly, leaned into me. I held her tightly. Her jumping skin began to heat my chest, stomach, and thighs. I closed my eyes and imagined steam rising from between us. I could smell the remnants of sunlight on her skin.

"How long will it last?" she asked.

"I don't know. Probably not long. I hope."

The wind blew more mist into the cave and we squeezed together even tighter. A blast of light and a *crack!* and *boom!* almost as close as the first, ripped through us and nearly stole my breath.

After its echo faded and I could breathe evenly again, she asked a question that came out of nowhere, just like the storm.

"At the bail hearing, how come you said Jonah wasn't a flight risk?"

"I didn't think he was. I was under oath."

I was speaking through a mouthful of wet hair. It tasted as good as she smelled.

"Okay," she said, then paused, as if wondering why someone like me would be constrained by an oath. She seemed to accept it finally, but a skeptical lawyer's mind was at work.

"But you could have said 'I don't know.' That would have been justifiable, wouldn't it? There's no way you could know."

"But I thought I did. I was asked for my opinion. I gave it."

Another *crack!* and flash of brilliant light and the whole canyon shuddered. The wind moaned louder as it ran across the cliff's face.

She'd pulled her knees up to her chest, and my arms wrapped around them, too. I couldn't feel her shivering anymore. I didn't think I was, either. The way I was wrapped around her, keeping her warm, was allowing her to warm me, too. My core felt so warm that I actually felt hot.

"How about another honest opinion?" she asked. "What do you think about this storm?"

I smiled and touched my mouth against the back of her neck.

"I kind of like it."

"Me, too."

She arched her head back, pressing my mouth harder against her neck. My lips parted of their own volition and my teeth and tongue touched her skin. Now I could taste the sun as well as smell it. The salty tang of the ocean, too. She was a surfer girl again, an outdoor athlete. Her actually being a lawyer seemed outlandish.

My hands rose up and came together around her wet face. My thumbs fit under her jaw and my fingertips touched those prominent, freckled cheekbones. My fingers then found her lips and traced them. Her features were just as delicate and wonderful to hold as I'd imagined the first time I saw her, when I'd wanted to shock the disdain out of her by kissing her on the mouth. But now I was the one getting shocked.

Maybe I turned her head back toward me, but I think she did it herself. A new crash of lightning blew through us—so close it felt like my hair was standing on end.

Just this morning this woman had me in a fury as potent as the storm when she'd ripped me apart on the witness stand. Now she was ripping me apart again. She twisted around within my tangle of arms and legs. I peeled off the wet bra while her fingers slipped under my harness and caressed the lower ridges of my stomach. Our lips and tongues barely touched, but moved continuously and seemed impossible to separate. Her breasts were perfect handfuls, the nipples hard as pebbles in my palms.

Somehow we got the harnesses off, oblivious to the risk of the cave's downward-slanting floor. I slid down onto my back on the ropes and she rose up over me, nipples lightly cutting my chest when I moved my hands south to pull down her tight shorts. Her matted hair, smelling of that hidden sun and sea, fell over my face as she arched her back to help my hands.

Another bolt struck. It was so close and loud it must have hit the canyon's rim directly above us. Her flesh was goosebumped with cold and electricity. I could actually see sparks dancing over her skin. When I touched her the sparks converged on my fingertips and drove into them with a sensation of tiny pinpricks.

"Wait . . . wait," she breathed into my mouth.

Then, "Slow . . . okay . . . okay . . . okay."

Roberto called at ten that night.

I'd taken Brandy back to her motel, dropping her off around

at the rear like she asked. My muddy wolf-dog and I had just gotten back to the canyon and zipped inside the tent when the phone started chiming. A light rain was still falling, but the thunderstorm had moved on. I was exhausted and a little bewildered by all that had happened during the day. At first I thought the caller might be Rebecca. I almost didn't answer. But the number on the flashing screen showed a local number.

"They're letting you use the phone this late?" I asked my brother.

"I'm a cripple, *che,*" he answered in Spanish, chuckling. "Plus they think I'm a bit deranged. They're treating me real nice. Real careful."

They were right on both counts.

"I only have a minute, so let me tell you what's going on."

They'd booked him in the previous night, just like he'd been booked dozens of times before. His portrait was snapped and his fingerprints taken to go along with the fake name and address he gave them. It would take a week at least for them to be posted to Cheyenne and Washington, processed, and matched up to the notorious Roberto Burns. He told me he'd added to the confusion by pretending to speak only a little English—a trick I hadn't thought of, and one he could easily pull off. Roberto had always resembled our Indio mother more than our Celtic dad. He had darker skin than me, higher cheekbones, and a slightly hooked nose. Unless someone was comparing us side by side, there was no way to see a resemblance.

He'd arrived just before lights out and was assigned a bunk in the main room. The other prisoners pretty much ignored him, except for a few illegals working on local ranches, who'd been picked up on minor charges—bullshit charges, according to Roberto—and were only being held because they couldn't raise even a hundred bucks for bail.

Jonah had kept to himself, and Roberto hadn't seen any need to introduce himself as his protector. Some dirty looks were directed at the child-killer, but no one made any moves on him. At least not at first. The big man with the broken nose, Smit, hung out playing cards with the Anglo alcoholics. He'd only spoken to Roberto once, threatening to stick one of his canes up his ass if my brother and his new friends didn't stop yammering in "Mexican."

At lights out, Jonah was placed in a separate cell off the rec room. The deputies closed the door but didn't lock it. Smit was given his own cell, too. The deputy only pretended to lock it. Roberto told me the deputy was an old man with a crew cut. I guessed it was the same one who had jumped all over me for having Tased Smit three months ago. Tom, I remembered. The guards then went into their station across the hall from the main room and started popping popcorn and watching a movie.

An hour later, Smit had slid his cell door open. Roberto faked sleep and watched as the wannabe biker padded over to Jonah's cell and shoved open the door. When he went inside, there was a shout that was cut off. Roberto thought it was Jonah shouting, then Smit clamping a hand over his mouth.

He wasn't sure what to do, which was rare for my brother. But I hadn't given him very good instructions. I'd been too sick with the thought of what I was doing to him to bother with a very detailed plan. He decided that maybe he shouldn't give up the game too soon.

It turned out that he acted with surprising subtlety. He started coughing, then faked a seizure. "A real paroxysm, like I was epileptic or something. I flopped all over the place, yelling and hooting and whacking the bars by the cot with my canes for good measure. You should have seen me, *che*. And heard me." He laughed. "The two cops on duty came tearing out of that office with their hair on fire. They even called an ambulance, and had this sweet little blonde come down to check me out."

I knew that blonde, and knew it was a good thing she didn't know Roberto was my brother. As mad as she was at me, she might have insisted on giving him multiple injections and a rectal exam.

Smit had come running out of Jonah's cell as soon as Roberto had started yelling and spasming. He'd walked back to his own cell and slammed the door. While the paramedics were there, Jonah staggered out. His face was bleeding. But all he'd said to the guards was that they'd forgotten to lock his cell.

"That kid's a stand-up guy. Didn't bitch or moan or anything. Refused to even let that hot paramedic check out his face. He just demanded that they lock his cell properly. You could see he was scared, though. Dude was shaking like a leaf."

The next day there hadn't been any trouble. But Roberto was pretty sure that more trouble was coming. He said Smit had stared at Jonah in the rec room all day long and that he made some threats, too, about how he was going to get "the faggot child-killer" and make him pay.

"But I think everything's cool tonight. This hard-ass chick locked them in tonight, not that old man. Really locked them—I watched her do it. Uh-oh, here she comes now. Take care, *che*. Don't let the fuckers get you down. I got your back in here."

I just wished I were covering his.

twenty-eight

The next morning I learned that I was the one who'd been fucked.

The throwaway newspaper on the rack at the bagel shop proclaimed it. Under an old picture of me, the caption read: "Update in River Killing: Cop Says Victim High."

I felt my stomach try to crawl up my throat, like someone had kneed me in the groin. The betrayal was so unexpected, so total, that I couldn't really get a grasp on the enormity of it. It just couldn't be true. Brandy was tough—I knew that. Dedicated, too, and I knew she could play hard, if not dirty. She'd shown that at the suppression hearing. But she'd seemed straightforward. Sympathetic. Not evil.

And I just couldn't possibly be this frigging stupid.

I tried to read the article but couldn't seem to digest it. My eyes were unable to keep their focus. But behind the counter I could make out similar headlines—less sensational but just as fatal to me—in the regional papers.

I got back in the Pig without my bagels. I'd intended to take them to Luke as a sort of peace offering before making another pitch for lightening up on Jonah. Mungo had to remind me by sniffing then slapping at me with her paw. I climbed back out, retrieved the sack from a scowling bagel-lady, paid, and returned. Turning on the engine, I was tempted to just drive out of town. Head for the hills. The temptation was pretty strong.

I'd been accused of a lot of things in recent years. Of naïveté. Of trickery. Of abuse. Of deceit. Of immorality. Of murder, even. Shit, multiple murders. And a lot of it was true. But I'd never been accused of stupidity.

Now I would be. And it would be one hundred percent true.

But I didn't head for the hills. The only way to face something like this was head-on. My brother had taught me that, and my dad before him. When there's something you fear, you never run and let it chase you. Instead you get in its face. Even if it's going to kick your ass. So I pulled out—nearly getting T-boned by a passing pickup—and headed for the county attorney's office.

The secretary didn't smile or say hello when I walked in. As much as she probably disliked her boss, it was clear she now hated me. I've been given a lot of ugly looks, but the one that accused me of being a traitor was the worst.

Luke had his gun on his desk.

My first thought was that he was going to shoot himself. Then I saw his expression, and decided no, he was going to shoot me.

Ostensibly, he was cleaning it. At least there was a can of oil, a toothbrush, and some newspapers spread on the desk.

He pointed it at me—the toothbrush—and said, "I once saved your life."

"Yeah, you did."

"I'm goddamn sorry I did that. Why the fuck are you trying to ruin me?"

"All I did was tell the truth, Luke."

He just stared.

He needed to let it out. I gave him the opportunity.

"For what it's worth," I told him, "I didn't mean for this to happen. She promised me our talk was confidential. I just told her the truth."

But he didn't accept my implicit offer. He didn't ridicule me, or blow up and start screaming, or call me names. He just kept looking at me as he said, "Your office wants to talk to you after we're through here. And man, are we through."

It was blazing hot outside at nine in the morning. There wasn't a cloud, a breeze, or a sign of yesterday's storm. The black asphalt of the Outrider's parking lot absorbed and intensified it, but it was nothing like the heat I was feeling. That heat was radioactive. My head felt like it was about to explode.

An air conditioner rattled beside the door and the curtain was closed. I beat on the door five times with the heel of my fist.

If I were capable of being surprised by anything anymore, I would have been surprised by who answered the door. It was Bogey. My first instinct was to punch him in the face. My second was that I had the wrong room. Then the first thought was reinforced when I saw Brandy sitting on the unmade bed behind him.

"Good morning, Agent Burns," Bogey said. "I certainly appreciate how you've helped us."

The lawyer wasn't smirking. He appeared exhausted, as if he'd been up all night. Working the phones and celebrating, probably. His hair was perfect, of course, and he'd applied his usual overdose of cologne, but there were bags under his eyes. Oddly, for once he seemed sincere rather than slick. He probably believed I'd kill him if he played it any other way. And he might have been right.

I looked at Brandy again. She looked like she'd just woken up. Her hair was a mess, and she was wearing a T-shirt—the one I'd lent her last night—and that was all. There was a newspaper lying guiltily on the bed beside her. She looked as shell-shocked at being confronted and exposed as I'd been when seeing my own stupidity announced in the headlines. But what the hell had she expected? Did she think the next time we saw each other I'd still be fawning all over her?

All I could do was stare at her. She couldn't meet my eyes. She bent over and covered her face with her hands.

I turned around and walked away.

twenty-nine

The scene of the crime did nothing to cool me down. I paused in the cave only long enough to yank the rope off my back and tie one end into the anchors. After giving it a jerk to check that it was secure, I threaded it through the self-belay device attached to my harness. Breathing hard before even making the first move, I raised my arms and sank them into the cold, wide crack. I launched myself out into space.

I'd never been a grunter, but I was grunting with each explosive exhalation by the time I reached the first cam fifteen feet out. I got the rope clipped to it, but just barely. My whole body was shaking hard, but I was determined not to fall this time. Falling was what I'd been doing all summer. Shit, for the past couple of years. Now I needed to do something different.

With my right arm jammed elbow-and-palm over my head, my left elbow fiercely wedged in the crack out in front, my head twisted in for good measure, and my legs doing only God knows what, I wormed my way under the cam. The hundred feet of empty air below sucked at me, but not nearly as much as the lead weight in my heart.

I made it to where the crack squeezed down. Like I'd done before, I let my legs drop. The shift in weight nearly ripped me out, but I grimly held on. I even managed to kick my feet up and in ahead of me. Grunting louder now, each sucking gasp followed by what sounded like "Fuck!" I worked them in until my heels and toes were fixed in place on opposite sides of the crack. Then I slowly released the pressure on my arms and face and let my torso scrape down out of the crack, until, with a snap, I was hanging upside-down by just my feet. I was Batman again, but this time there was no exultant shout.

I rested for only a few seconds before I jackknifed up with a violent twist of my gut and sank my arms and shoulders back into the roof. Worming again, I burrowed onward though the crack.

Then I froze. It was an instinct more than a conscious thought to place some more protection. But I didn't have any. I'd left it all a hundred feet below. I'd failed so many times that I had unconsciously stopped carrying the extra weight. I couldn't look behind me to see how far I was past the last cam, but I could manage to see in front of me—see just how far I was from the roof's far lip.

It was a distance of only ten feet. I was ten feet away from pulling off the hardest crack in the world.

And I didn't give a damn.

But I fought on, because that's all there was for me to do.

My gasps grew more ragged, and the trembling increased. My muscles were so jam-packed with lactic acid that it felt like they might detonate.

Then, almost unbelievably, there was nothing for my right hand. My arm passing through the air very nearly levered me out of the crack. There was just sky. Blue sky. I reached straight up and my fingers caressed a flat expanse of vertical rock. I was just seconds from total collapse. But there was nothing for me to hold on to now. And there was nothing backing me up.

With my searching arm extended so high that my face was in my armpit, I felt an edge. It seemed huge—at least an inch of positive traction. And it was hot from being in the sun. It was the first sun-touched rock on the entire climb. It felt like the rim of a sacred golden chalice.

I wrapped my fingertips over it, then put my thumb on top of them, crimping for every added ounce of strength. Then I pulled.

Nothing happened. I pulled again, but I had nothing left. My body had maxed out. My heart rate had been red-lined for way too long, the fire in every muscle had burned out, and the blood and oxygen carried through my veins were at a dead stop. Like an engine run at high torque without oil, I became a solid block of cramping. I dropped out of the rock, swung through space, and crashed into the wall.

"It's me," I said into the phone. "I heard you wanted to talk."

The only reply for a solid minute was the ragged breathing of an emphysemic. Beyond it I could hear the sound of wind and tires on asphalt.

"Where the hell have you been? I've been calling you all day."

"I know. When I turned on my phone, I had sixteen messages from either you or your secretary."

"Well?"

"I've been climbing, Ross."

"I figured you'd run for the border. Or maybe that you'd fallen and finally managed to kill yourself. I was kind of hoping. You've let me down again."

"I guess you aren't the only one."

I could hear my boss take a long suck on one of the unfiltered cigarettes he'd started smoking again.

"So where are you?"

"At my camp. About forty minutes outside Badwater."

"I'll be there in two hours."

"You won't be able to get your sedan into the valley."

Especially not the way the suspension on the driver's side was already riding on the pads from the weight of McGee's bulk.

"You're going to meet me in town, QuickDraw. I'll even let you pick the place. The condemned man gets his choice of a last meal. Just make it something good. I'm starving, and eating you alive won't fill me up."

"There's a Mexican place called Cesar's."

I didn't mention that the food was awful. I started to describe how to get there, but found that I was speaking to a dead phone. After tossing it into the tent, I dug around in the back of the Pig until I found my little Tupperware stash. Then I packed a bowl.

One of the messages left on my phone was from Brandy. It wasn't until days later that I listened to it because I recognized her number on the caller ID, but here is what it said:

"Anton . . . I don't know what to say. . . . You'll probably never speak to me again. I don't blame you. But I'm sorry. So sorry. I told Bogey because I thought he was my friend and mentor, and because he promised to keep it quiet until we figured out what we were going to do. I didn't know he'd start making calls, that he'd use it that very night. I just felt . . . I guess I felt duty-bound to tell him. For Jonah's sake. Then he betrayed me, Anton . . . and I guess I betrayed you. I'm sorry."

thirty

Cesar's was busy. And like the last time I was there, it was only at the bar that the crowd was gathered. The restaurant section remained as dark and silent as a cave except for the firefly flickers of a few red-globed candles. I checked out the crowd of mostly oil workers and their dates, wary of again running into the Mann twins. It was a relief that they weren't there. I had enough problems this evening. I was too tired and too angry and too stoned for another confrontation.

Wading into the gloom of the restaurant portion with dark red vinyl booths and black walls, I could spot only one customer ignorant of the restaurant's terrible food. He looked as if he belonged in the darkness.

"Howdy, Ross."

"QuickDraw" came a grumble from the shadows.

Ross McGee was hunched over one of the red-globed candles, his features colored crimson. Both beard and eyebrows bristled with stiff white hair. He resembled a troll king more than a lawyer and now bureaucrat. But I had enormous respect for the man. As a prosecutor, he'd put more people away for life than anyone in the state. He was the go-to guy when someone very bad needed to be put away for a very long time. When he was at the height of his powers, just his appearance at an arraignment could make defense attorneys swoon. But that was before poor health and increasing cantankerousness had forced the office to chain him to a desk. His eccentricities, once considered charming, were now labeled profane. Because of his harmless flirting with every woman he came across, the whole office was forced to go through sexual harassment training annually. For years they'd been waiting for him to quit or die—he knew where all the bodies were buried so he could never be fired. But he just kept hanging on. He would have made a hell of a climber.

"You're looking good," I told him, lying.

McGee was obese, his tobacco breath came in rasps, and his eyes were yellow and watery but somehow still fierce.

"Bite me," he replied.

I slid into the booth. The waitress appeared—the same one as the last time I'd been here, the one with the sticky curls and the four-inch bangs ironed up like a cresting wave. She listened to me order a margarita on the rocks before walking off without a word.

"You must have already shown her your considerable charms, Ross."

"She keeps up that attitude, I'm not going to show her. I'll keep my belt buckled and my zipper high and tight."

"That's cruel, Ross. Really cruel. How long are you staying for, anyway?"

"I'm going to stay in this backwards-ass town as long as it takes. Your little stunt in today's paper was the last straw—probation's revoked. You've got a new baby-sitter, QuickDraw. Until this trial's over."

"What's going to happen then?"

He kissed his fat fingers and then blew on them.

"Then you're gone."

I met McGee's watery stare over the candle.

"Gone? You mean I'm fired?"

McGee shook his head. "No. You're going to resign. You don't, and they're going to make it hard for you. Harder, I should say. Much harder."

For the eight years I had been a cop, McGee had been my protector. He backed up all the agents. He would go toe-to-toe with the administration whenever they tried to scapegoat some legal disaster off on the cops. And he'd win. More important, he would back us up even when we, in his words, screwed the pooch. He only asked one thing in return, and that was loyalty to the spirit and letter of the law. You failed that, and you were gone. Luke had been fired years ago and gone off to law school. I, despite having "screwed the pooch" on numerous occasions, stayed on because McGee had always thought he'd seen something promising in me.

But now it was clear he wasn't seeing it anymore. McGee's words and tone indicated that he wouldn't be backing me up this time. And that stung, even though I'd been expecting it. I doused the pain by getting mad instead.

"Tell them they can go fuck themselves. They don't have the balls to do it."

Like McGee, I knew some of the skeletons in the department's closet. I knew which administrator's wife had gotten off on a DUI, who'd slept with their secretaries, and whose kids had their drug charges quietly dropped.

McGee just grinned at me.

"They're talking about starting an investigation into your activities in Mexico during your leave last summer. They want you to cooperate fully with the DEA. That is, unless you resign and disappear."

I realized the difference between me and McGee—we both knew about the office's skeletons, but the office also knew about some of mine. Or at least suspected their existence. McGee, the decorated former Marine colonel, was too straight to have any rattling bones lying around.

My manufactured anger lost some of its potency.

"Shit" was all I could say. And I could no longer meet McGee's eyes.

The surly waitress appeared with my drink. She ignored McGee when he raised his glass and gestured with it.

When she turned to go, McGee barked, "Hey. Girl. Come back here."

She turned slowly, rolling her eyes. Then she gave him a dazzling fake smile, cocked her head, and said pertly, "You want somethin' else, old fella?"

I felt my anger return—for real this time. I could handle the waitress's rudeness, but not when it was directed at McGee. I wanted to toss my drink right at the pale roll of flesh that spilled over her jeans and say something like "You don't have the right to even *look* at him like that. This old man fought five tours in Vietnam, got wounded twice, served this state for the next thirty years, locked up child molesters and wife killers, stood up to politics and industry, and protected his agents with the ferocity of a wounded grizzly. And he was my best friend, you smug, stupid bitch."

But I said nothing.

When she was gone, McGee said, "I should have fired you last year. You're worse than useless. The only reason I kept you on was for Rebecca. And Moriah."

I slid out of the booth. I started to walk away. Again. Just like I had at Brandy's motel that morning.

McGee's low growl of a voice followed me.

"You're not a cop anymore, QuickDraw. It's unofficial until this trial's over, so you can keep your badge for now, but you're not a cop. So stay out of trouble or else I'll lock you up myself and throw away the key. Understand? You hear me?"

thirty-one

It would be almost twenty-four hours before I would learn that Brandy Walsh's day was even worse than mine, if you can imagine that.

After discovering what Bogey had done—when he woke her up and showed her the papers, begging for forgiveness—she got in her car and drove up into the Shoshone. She wanted to get away from him and from everything and clear her head with a long, long ride. She spent the afternoon on her mountain bike, tearing around on remote trails in the forested hills.

The night came on as a surprise. The sun just dropped like a stone behind the peaks. There were no storms that afternoon, and the sunlight had seemed like it would last forever until it suddenly went out. The looming darkness caught her on top of a ridge where she had to dismount and carry her bike across a knife-edge before getting back on the trail. She realized she was more than five miles from where she'd parked her Jetta at the gated end of a fire road. Suddenly she was a little scared, not sure if she'd make it back before the night became complete. And she was weak and dizzy, too; she'd been too caught up in her guilty thoughts to have bothered with things like eating and hydration.

Clipping a light onto the handlebars, she started riding fast. She rolled downhill, around twists and turns, like she was dropping in on a wave that was a little too big for her abilities, like she was in over her head. She tried to slow down. She had seen only one other rider all afternoon, and if she got hurt it could be days before she would be found. The only other human sign was the sound of four-wheelers tearing around on the logging roads down by her car. But she was racing the dark, and her hands kept easing off the brakes.

After twenty minutes she skidded onto the gated fire road and felt a surge of relief. It was just another few miles to the gate that kept it closed to motorized traffic and her car. She was relieved, too, not to be so closely confined by the trees. The road was wide and graded. It seemed less likely that a bear would jump out at her here.

But soon she could see a hazy orange glow down-valley, about where her car should be, and it alarmed her. A mile farther on, the glow was brighter and she could smell smoke. She wondered if someone had lit a bonfire near the picnic tables by her car. She really didn't feel like talking to anyone, particularly drunken kids roasting hot dogs. But then maybe they'd have a spare hot dog. And a beer. The smoke had a funny smell to it, though. Like gasoline. Without really thinking, she began to pedal faster.

Brandy leaned around a final hairpin turn, saw the access gate across the road glittering in her headlights, and swerved around it. She skidded to a stop.

There were no picnickers, no hot dogs, no party. There wasn't even a fire. There was just a smoldering pile of metal that had once been her car.

She stared at it, shining the bike's light over the blistered paint and blasted windows. Gray smoke trailed up toward the stars from bumper to bumper. The ruin crackled and popped, spitting sparks from the smoldering upholstery. She dropped her helmet on the ground and just stared.

"Lady, do you need some help?"

The voice came from the other side of the road, from a place where she remembered seeing the graffitied picnic tables and fire pits in the daylight. Brandy turned the handlebars in that direction, but the light wouldn't penetrate the darkness far enough to see anything.

"I don't know. That's my car. Do you know what happened to it?"

There was a laugh.

"I got no idea. But it looks like it got cooked."

The voice was that of a young man. It had a strange quality to it, a hysterical edge, that made her wonder if whoever it was might be drunk. Or stoned. Or crazy.

"We can give you a ride into town on a four-wheeler. You're that lawyer, aren't you?"

We? He was walking toward her; she could hear his feet on stones and leaves. But all she could make out in the light were some aspen trees. Brandy put her left foot onto the pedal and clicked it in. Then she had to turn her head when, on the other side of the road, her car hissed out a shower of sparks from the back window. She turned back just in time to see a figure standing close to her. But a little bit behind her, where she couldn't illuminate him with the light.

"Come on. Hop off that bike. We can stash it in the trees somewhere."

Brandy didn't.

"Thanks, but I'll just ride into town."

She pushed forward and lifted her right foot, trying to clip it in, too.

"Hey," the figure said.

One-footed, she pedaled a couple of strokes, picking up speed and still trying to clip in her right foot.

"Hey! Where you going, lady? I said we'd give you a ride."

She could hear his feet scuffing the dirt as he began to run alongside her. She didn't turn to answer him, though. She focused on not running off the road and on getting her shoe to clip into the pedal. She held on tight to the handlebars.

She was suddenly aware of someone else running up on her other side. The "we." They were catching up to her, as was her panic. They were on both sides. She could feel the wind their bodies made on her bare arms. She gave up on clipping in her foot and just began to pedal.

But she'd only made a couple of strokes when one of the shadows lunged forward and jabbed something into her front wheel. A stick. The effect was immediate. The wheel locked and she was instantly airborne.

She hit the hard dirt headfirst. There was a flash of luminosity like a lightning strike and then only blackness.

thirty-two

The blackened car was still warm to the touch, although it might have just been from the sun. But by laying my palm on it, I thought I could picture flames in the night. I thought I could hear a scream, too. And laughter. But my imagination didn't tell me why it had happened or who had done it. It didn't even have any suggestions, either, as to whether or not she was still alive.

I hadn't gotten the call until almost eleven o'clock. The county fire chief and sheriff had left long before I arrived. But even though I was no arson investigator, I could make a few assumptions.

The accelerant had been gasoline. I could smell it. But the gas tank was still intact, so it had come from another source. It had been poured over the hood and roof, because it was there that the paint was the most blistered. The fenders and doors were barely scorched. Also, chips of glass lay all over the cooked interior, but only a few were on the dirt outside, indicating that the car had been vandalized before it was burned. Inside, there were the charred remnants of the biking gear I remembered seeing at the river—I couldn't tell if anything had been stolen. Brandy's expensive mountain bike stood nearby, leaning against a picnic table, covered with gray fingerprint powder. Theft had definitely not been a motive.

"All right, you've seen enough. Now get away from that car," Luke commanded.

Dressed in a suit for the benefit of newspaper photographers and curious locals and tourists being kept down the road, he had been glaring at me with his hands on his hips.

"Don't be a jerk," I said. "Tell me who's in charge. Who's doing the investigation?"

Luke shook his head.

"I'm the goddamn county attorney, QuickDraw. I'm in charge, at least when you're not usurping my authority and conspiring to ruin me. The sheriff's going to assign someone to do the footwork, but I'm running things at the top."

I tried to keep my temper.

"Okay. Just tell me what you've found."

Still glaring, he snapped, "It's right there in front of your face. We've got a burned-out car and a pain-in-the-ass defense attorney who didn't go back to her room last night. That's it. That's the sum total of what we know. Except for the obvious fact that it's probably a big hoax. Now you're going to stay out of it. I'm going to ask you some questions and then I don't want to see your face until the trial next week."

"A hoax?"

"Another bullshit publicity stunt. Trial date's almost here, and old Bogey's not getting enough attention from shitting on the hood of his own car. Or from a certain scumbag DCI agent who's feeding him inside information. So he pulls this. *Lawyer disappears—kidnapped in the town that's trying to frame her client.* Bogey will look great screaming it on TV, don't you think?"

"You've got to be kidding me."

"Screw you, Burns. Why else would someone torch the car? No one's that stupid."

He had a point. Who would kidnap a lawyer and call attention to it by burning her car? Idiots. That was one explanation. You had to be really dumb to light a car on fire when you could simply dump it in the millions of acres of forests. In Wyoming, where something like ninety percent of all crime could be tied to methamphetamine, it was most likely that the idiots were tweaking.

It was either that, or Luke was right and it was some bizarre ploy for media coverage and to possibly influence potential jurors. After the way I'd been screwed—literally and figuratively—by Brandy Walsh, I now believed she was capable of just about anything. But I also knew she was smart, and I just couldn't imagine her participating in such a harebrained scheme.

"We knew a couple of guys once who were dumb enough to torch a car," I reminded Luke.

Almost eight years ago, when we were partners, we'd been flying with a contract pilot looking for a rumored marijuana farm in the Medicine Bow Mountains. We'd seen a lot of black smoke rising from a remote canyon and had flown over it. Below, a van was on fire, and a car was hurrying away from the scene. A swoop over it had given us the license-plate number. It turned out the owner of the car and a buddy had stolen the van from a retirement home and used it for a series of armed robberies in Wheatland. For some reason the idiots had thought burning it would destroy any evidence left inside. Instead all it did was draw attention and get them caught.

Luke looked like he might smile at the memory, but successfully maintained his frown and instead just rolled his eyes.

"You don't come across morons like that more than once in a career. But your remembering that brings up another point: Where the hell were you last night?"

I rubbed my eyes.

"Bite me, Luke."

McGee came slowly stumping up the dirt road from beyond the line of fire-department tape. He was breathing hard, both hands on his cane.

I called to him, "Luke thinks I'm in on an elaborate hoax to make him look bad by burning cars and kidnapping defense lawyers."

McGee grunted out a chuckle.

"Get a grip on yourself, Endow. QuickDraw may be capable of a lot of things, but that's not one of them. If he really wanted to make you look bad, he'd just shoot you and leave your fat ass in the woods to rot."

"Thanks a lot, Ross."

"You're one to talk about fat, McGee. But maybe it isn't a hoax," Luke persisted. "Maybe he killed her last night for revealing his role as a defense plant."

McGee looked at me, considering.

"Screw you both."

I shook my head and walked toward the access gate that blocked the road. Several pieces of paper wrapped in plastic had been wired to one of the bars. The first was titled "Notice: You Are in Grizzly Bear Country." Below was well-meaning but useless information and advice, like playing dead if a charging bear appears to be only protecting its territory, but fighting back if it acts in a predatory manner. How do you tell the difference when it's gnawing on your head?

I wondered if Brandy had seen the notice. She was obviously—and for good reason—afraid of large carnivores. But I knew a bear wasn't responsible for her disappearance. Bears don't torch cars.

Another notice on the iron gate stated that only hooves, knobby bike tires, and boots could touch the ground on the other side. To one side of the gate there was an opening for people and horses to slip through. There was a puddle of mud there, although it was almost dry. Tire tracks could clearly be seen in the dirt. No footprints, though. But more than one bike had been in and out.

I walked back to the car and studied the ground around it. The dirt road was angled just a little to drain water, and well graded. There were no obvious puddles. I couldn't make out any tracks on it—not even those of the car itself.

"Did you have someone come out to look for footprints or tire treads?" I asked Luke.

Luke just squinted at me angrily.

"Are you going to call in the FBI? You should get them in here as fast as you can. You need dogs and planes with heat-sensitive cameras. Are you on top of this?"

He shook his head and managed a bitter laugh.

"Hell no, you fool. That's just what Bogey wants. And I'm not going to do that unless I get some information that this is more than just a stunt. What do you care, anyway?" In a lower voice he added, "Didn't you hear the old man last night? You aren't a cop anymore."

"I've still got my badge. That's more than you've got."

Luke spat in the dirt.

"But you know what? I can have you arrested. For obstruction of justice, if you don't get out of here right now. You're interfering with my crime scene. All I have to do is whistle for those deputies down by the tape and they'll come up here and throw your ass in jail. Where it belongs."

I smiled at him.

"You do that, Luke, and your case will really turn to shit. It's pretty funny. Until the trial's over, McGee can't take away my badge, and you can't arrest me. Fuck you both, then."

While Luke and McGee bickered about what had happened and how it might affect next week's trial, they were allied in giving me dirty looks. I wandered in ever-growing circles around the burned-out shell of the car. The lodgepole pines and stands of almost bare aspens grew close together on the sides of the road, where they fought for light. But just beyond that tight wall the woods opened up into the picnic area. The ground there was rocky, full of pine needles and fallen leaves.

I found a lot of stuff. Beer bottles broken and whole, fast-food litter, soda cans, cigarette butts, shotgun shells, and a washing machine shot full of holes, but nothing that looked relatively fresh.

I was making one last, wide perimeter circle when I found a trail.

It was an old trail, but with fresh tracks. I knelt and examined them where they went through some drying mud. The tires were wide but close-set. A four-wheeler, or maybe more than one.

I walked back to the road. Luke and McGee were still growling at each other over aspects of the case against Jonah Strasburg and how a lawyer's disappearance might affect it. I didn't tell them what I'd found. Screw them.

But I did mention, "Isn't it wonderful, the way I've brought you two together again?"

Under the weight of their combined glares, I headed down the road and ducked under the yellow tape. The Pig was waiting there. I took my H&K from the lockbox under the seat and slid the paddle holster under the waistband of my pants. Then I snapped a leash to Mungo's collar—something she hated—and let her out. She kept shaking herself and tugging in different directions to make clear her objection. But I dragged her into the forest and started to lead her back to the ATV trail I'd found.

"Where do you think you're going?" Luke shouted.

"To check something out. Follow if you think you can keep up."

Luke cursed me but came after me.

I began to jog, still dragging Mungo on the leash. There were more mud puddles and more fresh knobby tracks. There were definitely two vehicles, I decided. I could see where they'd played around, highballing at some corners and tearing up some small meadows. I ran on. The tracks met up with an old logging road and disappeared down it.

thirty-three

The first sensation to return to Brandy was her sense of smell. This was unfortunate, because what she smelled was vomit. Her own vomit, she suspected as her empty stomach heaved again. Something else, too, something cloying and chemical. But as her other senses lit up on the control screen of her brain, she realized that the stench was the least of her worries.

Pain came next. It radiated at first from inside her head, throbbing with each beat of her pulse. It hurt so bad it made her want to vomit some more. Then she noticed the pain around her jaw and wondered if it was broken. And finally there was the sharp pain coming from both her shoulders because of the way they seemed to be twisted behind her. Maybe she'd broken both her collarbones, as well. But how?

"Damn. Damn," she moaned, but the words came out strangled and slurred. Something was holding her mouth open.

It wasn't easy to open her eyes because of the way they seemed to be swollen. And when she did manage to open them, she winced against the light. It took a few seconds to make out her surroundings. She expected the sterile horror of a hospital room—IVs and catheters and anxious parents leaning over her—but what she found instead was even worse.

It appeared to be an abandoned cabin. The walls were made of logs, the gaps between them plugged with decaying mud. All the window frames were empty. The floor was nothing but a pile of planks. Only half the roof remained, hanging precariously over her head. Looking up, she could see blue sky and the tops of two rocky spires. Out the doorless doorway, she peered down on a small lake. The sun was reflecting off it, almost blinding her when she looked at it directly.

She had absolutely no idea where she was, or how she'd gotten there.

Brandy's mud-spattered legs were stuck straight out in front of her from where she sat on some rotting boards. One knee was covered with dried blood, and a lazy fly was working on the wound. She tried to brush it away, but her arms wouldn't move. They seemed to be secured somehow to a corner post behind her.

Her shout was muted by a gag.

For a little while she lost herself to panic. She bucked and fought and wept and screamed. But none of it did her any good. It took a while longer, but she finally managed to calm down by taking huge, sucking breaths around the gag. Only then did she manage to take stock of her situation. She started with a physical assessment of her body, because that was less scary than her surroundings.

She knew she had a concussion. The pulsing headache and the vomit down her shirt were sufficient evidence of that. But she couldn't remember how she'd gotten it. She was wearing bike shoes, shorts, and the soiled jersey, so it must have been while riding. Her mouth ached, but the jaw still worked. It was pried open by what tasted like duct tape that had been wrapped around her head again and again.

She had to pause for more breaths before continuing.

Her arms were pinioned behind her. More duct tape. It was wrapped tight enough around her wrists that her fingers were tingling—she could barely feel them when she tried to wiggle them against one another. They worked, but not well, and they felt as fat as sausages. They were secured around a post that didn't budge when she shoved back with her feet and threw her weight against it.

More deep breaths.

Her bra felt strange. She realized it had been pushed up under her shirt. But the filthy jersey had been pulled back down over her breasts. She wondered if she'd been raped. But that part of her, at least, didn't seem to hurt, and she was still wearing her riding shorts. With her thumbs she could hook the waistband and found that she was still wearing underwear.

What the hell had happened, and how the hell had she gotten here?

She had to work very hard to concentrate. Her head hurt so bad, and her thoughts kept veering off-course toward panic. She could remember being in the cave with Burns during the storm. She could remember how his face had looked in the flash of lightning as she rocked above him. And she could remember how different he looked the next morning, when he stared at her without any emotion in the doorway of her motel room. She could remember Bogey, reeking of his usual overdose of cologne, waking her up in the motel room and showing her the papers, then the fight they'd had. She remembered being incredibly pissed off and going riding. But that was all.

She shivered. It was cold. Very cold. She couldn't tell if the sun was going up or coming down.

She tried again to remember. She had to have been riding, right? She could hear her bike cleats tapping on rocks. She'd been carrying her bike. It was starting to come back. Night was coming. She'd been hurrying, risking a crash. She had to get to the car before dark. And then she remembered everything. Her charred and smoking car, the figure coming out of the trees, the mocking, excited laugh, and the sound of footsteps running alongside her as she tried to flee. Everything but what she most needed to know. How she had gotten here. And who it was who had brought her.

She let out a moan of frustration. Her mouth was dry, her cheeks and tongue swollen. The twists of tape in her mouth tasted and smelled like glue. The stench of the dried vomit on her shirt was almost overwhelming. But again she sensed something else, another scent. That sharp tang of leather and spice. She bit down on the gag and, dry as her mouth was, could actually taste it.

Then she realized what it was. And she knew who was responsible.

Brandy rocked back and forth and kicked her legs. She shouted through the crude gag and jerked at the twists of tape securing her to the log wall until her voice was hoarse and her wrists were raw. She did these things not to free herself—she'd given up on that—but in an effort to stay warm and sane. It wasn't panic that most threatened her now. It was fury.

Bogey.

thirty-four

Late in the afternoon, William J. Bogey stood on the courthouse steps to address the assembled press. There was a bigger crowd today, but it still wasn't the mob of news vans and eager, coiffed reporters shouting questions that he had been gunning for since this whole thing began. But the lawyer was finally getting some national attention. There were just five or six print journalists with notepads and microcassette recorders and three photographers dutifully taking shots with their digital single-lens-reflex cameras.

I hung well back, waiting to ambush the lawyer when he walked to his car. As tepidly interested as the reporters appeared, I worried that a sighting of the much-maligned QuickDraw might be like blood in the water for a school of piranhas. More reporters might flood into town and turn it into the feeding frenzy Bogey was undoubtedly hoping for. I'd dealt with the media enough for this lifetime.

I couldn't hear whatever bullshit Bogey was spreading before them, but I assumed it was something similar to what he'd been shoveling around for three months. Stuff like "The county attorney is scapegoating my client for political gain." "Badwater is using Jonah Strasburg to alleviate its grief." "Jonah Strasburg will never get a fair trial in Badwater." It might be true, but it was still bullshit. He wanted Jonah scapegoated and tried just as much as anyone in this town did.

Added to it now, I would learn later, were statements like "My co-counsel's disappearance can only be the result of elements in this town that will do anything to see Jonah Strasburg, an outsider, blamed for a child's tragic but entirely accidental death." He would also accuse police and the prosecutor of failing to take the disappearance seriously.

I loitered nearly a block away while Bogey finished answering questions from the somewhat dubious assembly. They'd already been briefed on the possibility of a hoax by Luke. The defense lawyer posed for a final picture, shook hands all around, hefted his briefcase, and crossed the street.

Worried that he would run the other way if he saw me coming—or worse, call the reporters to his aid—I waited until Bogey was nearing his Mercedes SUV before stepping out from behind a tree and heading for him.

But Bogey didn't run or call for help. He just scowled and kept on coming.

"I have a few questions for you that those reporters might have forgotten to ask," I said, stopping in the middle of the sidewalk.

Bogey stepped a little to one side and brushed by me.

"You're really something, Agent Burns. I was just asking those reporters, 'How many people does he have to kill before they lock him up?' "

I grabbed his arm. He tried to pull it away, but only halfheartedly. He looked toward the courthouse, hoping someone was watching. I looked, too. No one was.

"Stop for a second. Goddamn it, stop," I told him. "Listen. I'm trying to help your client. I've been trying to help him all along."

Bogey stopped resisting, so I let go. But he didn't say anything. He raised his eyebrows and waited.

In my nicest voice I asked, "I just want to know one thing. Off the record. Is this a hoax? Another publicity stunt? Is Brandy just hiding out, waiting for you to score some points?"

I stared hard into Bogey's eyes, hoping to catch a signal if he tried to lie. Bogey stared straight back. He didn't flinch, or redden, or look away.

"Agent Burns, I sincerely believe that you had something to do with Brandy's disappearance. God help you if I'm right, because I will not stop until you're *finally* prosecuted to the fullest extent of the law. Now, if you'll excuse me, I'm going to go and do what's supposed to be your job and try to find my co-counsel."

On the way out of town, I fell prey to a perverse impulse and pulled off the highway and into the turnout by the river. Mungo and I walked out onto the big rock. Standing on the very edge, I stared down into the sink twenty feet below.

It was clearly visible this late in the season. The river was much lower. So much so that the water was riffled everywhere but in the shadow directly beneath the rock. The dark water down there spun ominously, with foam, sticks, leaves, and other debris riding the current. And if that wasn't enough of a warning, there was a sign posted atop the rock, and another bolted to the side of the rock where rafters coming downriver could see it.

"Warning: Whirlpool!" it said.

I had a bad feeling. If someone was to dump Brandy's body, this would be the most logical place to do it. The only location where you could pretty much guarantee it wouldn't ever be found. Even if her disappearance had nothing to do with the trial, then all the publicity would certainly suggest this place. Hell, even the signs suggested what a fantastic spot this was to hide a body.

I wondered if I would eventually have to go back down there

and take a look. Just the thought made me shiver. I could picture her under the water, laid out like Cody on those coffin-size logs. Or maybe slipping through them and beyond into the most horrible darkness I could imagine.

The possible suspects were few.

There was no chance it was a bear or a mountain lion. Although both species killed someone in the woods around here every few years, they would have a hard time flicking a Bic without opposable thumbs. It was possible that there was some kind of random two-legged predator traveling through or even living nearby. DCI had more than eight open cases of young women who had disappeared without a trace in recent years. One of them, a trail runner, had even vanished in a forest not too far away from here. But that had been almost ten years ago. Unless the perp had been in prison for something unrelated and just gotten released, it was unlikely Brandy had fallen prey to the same killer.

That left the Mann twins, who, despite being related to Cody, didn't have much of a motive other than that they didn't like lawyers—or cops.

Or it was a hoax, set up by Brandy and Bogey.

Despite having proven that she was capable of deceit and betrayal and a willingness to even whore for her cause, I couldn't believe Brandy would do something this stupid. It just wasn't necessary—Bogey had already all but won his case. With the information he had about the victim's intoxication, not to mention the prosecution's withholding of it, he certainly could laugh off the possibility of a murder or manslaughter conviction. Even after having done everything he could to insult and offend the town's potential jury pool.

It just didn't make sense.

I got back in the Pig and headed for the Mann ranch.

thirty-five

Above the high hill just beyond the barbed-wire fence, I could see dark clouds beginning to huddle over the peaks. They looked as intimidating as the day I'd been getting screwed in the cave, just two days ago. I hoped it wouldn't storm all night this time. When you live in a tent, it's hard to sleep when getting pounded by rain, rocked by wind, and bombarded with lightning. Not to mention when a woman who has betrayed you is missing, and your brother is trying to keep the peace in a violent jail.

Once again, there were no cars in front of the Manns' house. I could see several, though, through the windbreak of tall trees. None appeared to be the vehicles I'd seen the mother and father driving, but I could see the jacked-up yellow pickup that was registered to the twins. Good. I came up here hoping the parents would be at work, the younger boys at school, and the twins right here for a showdown.

McGee had said I wasn't a cop anymore, and I intended to take advantage of that. It was weird, but instead of feeling frightened and uncertain, I felt very free. And a little bit scary. I could do whatever I wanted now. As long as I didn't get caught.

Pulling in front of the house, I saw that what little luck I seemed to have for once was on my side. The twins were home. They were recuperating from their car crash injuries by suntanning on towels on the grass to one side of the house. They were also probably trying to burn off their steroid-induced acne.

I drove toward them. Right over the rocks that edged the gravel drive and onto the grass. I stopped just a few yards from them. They both scrambled to their feet with difficulty. Zach's right arm was in a sling, Ned's wrist was in a cast. Blue-black bruises and abrasions showed all over them. Zach wore long denim shorts to hide his chicken legs, and Ned had on those colorful weight lifter's sweats that had been unfashionable in the eighties.

When they saw that I was braking, that I wasn't going to run them down, they both bowed up a little, flexing and trying to look as intimidating as possible. I thought they looked like the most pathetic losers I'd ever seen.

Hopping out of the Pig, I called, "Hi, guys. I was hoping to find you here."

"What the hell do you want?"

"Who gave you permission to come onto our property?"

I ignored the questions. I had my own.

"Are your folks home?"

"No. Now get the hell off our land."

"Where were you shitheads last night?"

"Fuck you," they said in unison.

"Look, you tell me what I want to know, and I'll leave you alone. You mess around, and I'm going to arrest you both. Again."

"You arrested us before and we were locked up for what, two hours?" Zach snickered.

"Yeah, *you're* going to arrest *us*," Ned said. "All by yourself this time. Without a warrant, and on our land."

"Yeah. I am."

My smile and my certainty wasn't what they were used to.

"On what charge?" Ned demanded after a second's hesitation.

"Just for being assholes. And I'll throw in something extra, like providing drugs to minors, or harassing officers of the court. Wait, I've got it—how about resisting arrest and another attempted assault on a peace officer? No, I guess that won't work, seeing as how I came here this time. Hell, maybe I'll just have to shoot both of you. Take you to the morgue instead of the jail."

They looked at each other again, considering. By the way they hesitated, it was clear they knew something of my reputation.

"Now, where were you last night?"

"You can go blow yourself, man," one finally ventured.

I whistled for Mungo, who'd been watching through the Pig's windshield. She put both her enormous front paws on an open side window and vaulted out.

"Get mad," I told her in Spanish, even though she could read the situation for herself and definitely remembered the brothers. She was already wrinkling her nose. At my command, she snapped her jaws twice and turned up the volume of the rumbling coming from her throat.

"Holy shit!" Zach said.

Ned began to back away, turning to run for the porch.

"Stop!" I yelled. "You run, and I'm not going to be able to control her. She'll hamstring you like a deer."

I meant it, too. I didn't know for sure that she wouldn't.

So they stood very still, trying hard to look surly rather than scared. Mungo hunched just ten feet away with a lowered head and all of the hair around her neck and shoulders spiked. She was like a horrible Medusa, turning the brothers to stone.

"Where were you last night?"

Ned spoke up.

"In the Shoshone. But we didn't torch no car. And we didn't kidnap no lawyer. Our brothers were late coming in and our folks sent us out to find them."

"Bullshit."

But before I could continue the interrogation and gauge whether or not they were lying, or even digest the information other than their admission that they were in the vicinity of the crime, the sound of a vehicle crunching up the drive could be heard. I grabbed Mungo's collar before I turned and looked. It was Ed Mann behind the wheel of his big truck, the one with the Randy Weaver bumper sticker and the rifle in the back window.

"Dad!" Zach yelled.

He crunched over the gravel toward us, then got out with the rifle in his hands.

"That's a wolf!" one of the muscle-bound pricks yelled. "Shoot it, Dad!"

"Load up!" I told Mungo, spinning her and shoving her toward the open window of the truck.

Mr. Mann was pointing the rifle but didn't pull the trigger. His sons and I were in the line of fire. Once Mungo was in the truck, he lowered the gun. But he still held it two-handed across his body, ready to bring it up again and fire.

"What are you doing on my land? And what are you doing here with a wolf? I don't recall giving you permission to come out here."

"He threatened to kill us, Dad. Just like he did Randy and Trey!"

"Mr. Mann, I need to talk to your sons. All of them. About the lawyer that's missing. I think they might know something about it."

The father looked at his sons in such a way that I knew he probably had few illusions about their character.

"Do you know anything about it?" he demanded.

"No!"

He turned back to me, and I could also see in an instant that although he might be willing to believe anything about his oldest boys, he wasn't going to let someone like me push them around without some damn good evidence.

I said quietly, "Mr. Mann, I think they're the ones who've been threatening Jonah Strasburg's lawyers. Harassing them. I think they may have had something to do with that lawyer's disappearance."

"Can you prove it?"

"Not yet."

"Then it's time for you to go."

The brothers laughed. I considered arguing, but read the look on the father's face. I also saw the way his hands were white around the rifle. I creaked open the Pig's door and climbed in.

"Bye-bye. *Adiós, amigo,*" the brothers taunted.

"You're on notice, Agent," their father said. "Don't come back on my property without permission or a warrant. You do, and I'll be within my rights to put a bullet in you."

I backed over the rocks edging the driveway and turned around in front of the house. The Pig had a huge turning radius, and I had to circumnavigate the entire drive. At the far edge, I saw two four-wheelers through the trees. I almost hit the brakes. But then I drove on and the brothers waved mockingly and Mr. Mann held on to his rifle.

thirty-six

While I was running around threatening citizens, Brandy was wondering for the thousandth time what was supposed to happen to her.

Then she heard footsteps outside.

The spark of hope was hard to smother. She wouldn't let herself cry out, though. If it was Bogey or whoever had helped him bring her here, she didn't want them to think she was begging. She would never give the bastards that kind of satisfaction. So she determined to wait and listen—she wouldn't try a muffled yell for help unless the footsteps stopped coming toward her and started moving away.

Crunch, crunch, crunch.

The steps came right up to the door frame. The sun was still on the lake, the light reflecting into the cabin, and she'd been staring out so hard that at first she couldn't make out the figure that blocked the light. But she could smell him.

Then slowly Bogey's features became visible. He stared back at her with an expression of surprise.

"Brandy? Oh my God. Brandy! What are you doing up here?"

He rushed inside, still talking. "My God! Are you all right? I can't believe I found you!"

He grabbed her by the shoulders and briefly hugged her, drawing taut the duct tape behind her back. Then he stopped and stared at her face. She knew he was reading the accusation in her eyes. The hatred. She felt it so strongly she wouldn't have been surprised if he burst into flames.

Slowly, his aristocratic face lost the surprised, concerned expression. It creased up into a slight smile.

"Oh well," he said. "You can't blame me for trying, can you?"

He dropped his pack on the debris-covered floor. He opened it and took out a supermarket-wrapped sandwich and a bottle of water. Taking out a pair of pliers, he crouched beside her and clipped the gag.

Suddenly Brandy couldn't get enough air. She gulped and gulped at it. God, it felt so good to have that thing off. For an odd moment she felt grateful to him. Then she caught herself and hated him all the more.

She desperately wanted to rub her mouth, to knead its torn corners, but Bogey didn't make a move toward the tape that bound her wrists.

"First we need to have a little talk," he said.

"You sick bastard!" she shouted at him, only it came out slurred. The gag had been in so long it had molded the shape of her mouth. "You goddamn—"

"Shh. Shh. Be quiet and listen to me, Brandy. You need to understand something. This is all an accident. A mistake that's snowballed far beyond anyone's intentions. The boys only intended to spook you last night. To keep up the pressure of threats and harassment. I had no idea they would burn your car."

"You're a goddamn liar," Brandy shouted at him.

"Shhh. Just listen to me now. According to what they told me, you showed up later than they expected. For all they knew, you were camping somewhere in the woods. That's apparently why they burned the car. Just to do something. Then you showed up, and they tried to chase you off. Just to scare you, nothing more. But you fell off the bike and hit your head. They didn't know what to do—they were frightened. So they brought you up to this old cabin they knew about from hunting trips and tied you up. At some point late last night they realized things had gone too far and decided to call me, to see if I could help them. And you. Do you understand? I'm going to get you out of here, but we've got to help them in return. Keep them out of trouble. I promised them that if they told me where you were, I'd make sure they didn't get in trouble."

Brandy watched him for a moment. Then she spoke slowly and carefully, enunciating every word.

"I'll tell you what I'm going to do, Bogey. As soon as I get back to town, I'm going to call the police. Then the university. Then the state bar. And then all of your favorite reporters, and let them know exactly what kind of man you are."

Bogey shook her shoulders.

"You need to listen to me, Brandy. You do that, and Jonah Strasburg will go to prison for the rest of his life. It won't just ruin my defense strategy, it will turn it into a bomb against us. Everything I've done has been for Jonah. I told you at the very start—this is war. You say anything, you do anything, to keep the state from convicting your client. You want to be a defense lawyer? Then you've got to be a warrior. You've got to understand why I did this, and play your part. When we get back into town, you tell the authorities that you were kidnapped by a bunch of locals. That you didn't see who they were, but they told you this was in retaliation for what happened to Cody. I found you only after getting an anonymous tip. You'll be famous. And Jonah will be saved."

Brandy stared at him in disbelief.

"You're really sick," she said. "No, you're not just sick, you're fucking insane."

"I'm really sorry to hear you say that," he replied.

He looked very sad all of a sudden, like he was disappointed in her. *He'd better be sad,* she thought. *He's about to lose his job, his license, his reputation, and his freedom.*

Shaking his head, Bogey reached behind her and grabbed the tightly wound strips of tape that held her wrists. He tugged on them, hard.

"Ow!" Brandy yelped. Her wrists were bloody and bruised.

Bogey tugged again.

"Take it off!" she ordered him.

"Just checking that they're secure."

He backed away, brushing then plucking at the creases of his pressed jeans. He bent to pack up the food and water he hadn't given her. Suddenly he lunged toward her again, ripping an arm's length of duct tape from a roll. Her scream of outrage was cut off as he wrapped the tape crookedly around her head.

"I don't know what I'm going to do with you, Brandy. You disappoint me. Maybe you just need some quiet time to reconsider."

He started to walk out the door, then turned back.

"Think about this: If I let you go, no one will believe you. They'll think that you were just part of the hoax. Or that the whole thing was your idea, and I refused to go along. Yes, that's what I'll say. I refused to participate, and now you're angry and trying to blame it all on me. They might suspect me of being involved, but there's no evidence other than your word. But for you, you're finished. You'll be disgraced. You'll never practice law again."

thirty-seven

I drove back through Badwater looking for McGee's car. I knew it was a state vehicle, a shiny black four-door Buick, usually filled with fast-food litter and the stench of cigarettes. I had ridden in it many times in better days. I'd laughed a lot in it, too.

I found it outside Cesar's. I parked next to it in the lot and went inside. McGee wasn't at the bar, which hadn't yet filled with the after-work crowd. Instead he was exactly where he'd been the last time—in a booth in the empty restaurant portion. Despite the bad food and surly service, he evidently liked this place. Something about the black walls and the blood red upholstery must have appealed to him.

Spread across the table was a copy of Luke's files on the Strasburg case. McGee was studying the pages in the light of the table's red-globed candle. I had a partial view of an autopsy shot. I averted my eyes. I had always hated seeing that stuff.

"Speak of the devil," McGee said by way of greeting.

"You're talking to yourself now? Don't tell me you're getting senile already."

I slid into the booth without being asked. McGee began closing up the files. I saw that there was also a fat folder labeled "Antonio Burns." My personnel file. When he had them all in a disorderly stack, with the personnel file buried beneath those about the Jonah Strasburg case, he leaned back and sipped his signature drink of rum and Diet Pepsi.

"What are you doing with all that stuff? Are you baby-sitting Luke, too?" I didn't mention having noticed my file.

"I'm consulting with him."

"He really agreed to that? To taking advice from the guy who fired him as a cop eight years ago?"

"I had to exert some influence. He's going to at least hear me out if he wants the endorsement of the AG come election time."

I felt suddenly sad. McGee was hawking the AG's endorsement? Since when had he become a politico? Through the years of our friendship, he'd always railed against politics as the greatest threat to the impartial rule of law, which had seemed to be his religion. Over the last year, as our relationship fell apart, I'd noticed more and more times when he'd had to compromise for what I supposed he saw as the greater good. It sounded like now he'd crossed the line, just as I seemed to be heading in the other direction. It made me sad, but it also made me want to hurt him.

"Oh. That's just great. So the two of you are going to work together now to sacrifice this kid."

McGee bristled. "That's not how I'm looking at it. I'm going to talk to Luke about a reasonable plea offer."

I snorted.

"What? Plead to the top count, and you'll promise to stand silent at sentencing?"

It was a joke, an ugly one. Murder had only one sentence when the death penalty wasn't invoked—life in prison.

"I thought a deal was what you wanted. Isn't that why you've been running off at the mouth to the defense? Or is it just because you wanted to shag the co-counsel?"

I ignored that. "What is it? The deal? Another media ploy to make you guys look generous? You know Bogey won't take anything. All he cares about is the attention. Fuck it. I don't care about the case anymore, Ross. I just don't want the girl to get hurt. I don't give a shit about anyone—or anything—else in this state."

I felt too much emotion raising my voice. I never did that. I slouched lower in my seat.

McGee scoffed. "She's in no danger. It's a publicity stunt."

I shook my head and said, "No, it's not. I know her."

"Carnally, I assume?"

He didn't mention his goddaughter's name, but it was implicit in the way his eyes blazed as he spit the question. As if I could still somehow wrong Rebecca a year after she had ended our romantic relationship.

"Yeah. That's right. Brandy Walsh might have screwed me and then stabbed me in the back for her client's sake, but she wouldn't pull something like this."

"Oh, no. She'd just whore herself out to the lead investigator for information. But she's a moral person. She certainly wouldn't dirty her hands."

I didn't reply. I knew I couldn't win. After all these years, McGee should trust me. Trust my instincts, at least. But those days were long gone.

The chubby waitress walked by without looking our way. When she passed again, still pointedly without looking, McGee raised his glass and rattled his ice cubes but to no avail.

After a few minutes of silence, he asked, "Have you been keeping out of this? Leaving it to the professionals?"

I sat up a little straighter. The insult stung—the fact that I wasn't really a cop anymore.

"Not really."

McGee's scowl intensified.

"What have you been up to?"

"Nothing illegal. Well, nothing *too* illegal, anyway. Just sort of out there on the line without quite crossing it. Arguably, as you lawyers say."

"What have you done?"

"Do you really want to know?" I asked. "You might have to fire me before this case goes to trial. It will screw things up for you and Luke. Screw up the election."

"Don't fuck around with me, QuickDraw."

"Well, I used Mungo to intimidate some citizens. It kind of went along with my threatening to arrest or maybe shoot them if they didn't answer my questions."

Instead of exploding, McGee just glared harder. He had a major-league stink eye, even in a dark restaurant. But I sustained it and gave right back my best brown-eyed version.

"I thought we had an understanding, QuickDraw," he growled. "Your probation's been revoked."

"Yeah, I'm not a cop anymore. Just a private citizen. An unindicted felon, isn't that pretty much what you called me? If you want to believe bad things about me, the least I can do after all these years of friendship is prove to you that you're not entirely senile yet."

McGee's face was turning a darker color of crimson than the red-globed candle could account for. I decided, *Why the hell not?* I was as disappointed and as angry as he was. My onetime best friend and mentor was spurning me; why not give it right back? I laid all my cards on the table.

"You might find it interesting that I plan on stepping all the way over the line tonight. I've never done it before, at least not on this side of the border. But it might be the only way to find her. See, I know the Mann twins had something to do with Brandy's disappearance. They know where she is. They all but admitted it—they were in the forest last night. Before I could finish my questions, though, their father drove up and booted me off their land. Pointed a gun at Mungo, too. So I need to talk to them again, and this time I'm not going to be so nice."

"How are you going to do that?" he demanded. "You said you already threatened to shoot them."

"That's something that, I swear, Ross, you *really* don't want to know."

* *

Roberto called again. Things were still peaceful in the jail, but something was definitely up. Tom, the prick with the crew cut, was on duty tonight. He was the one who'd been so upset when I Tased Smit, and the one who'd only pretended to lock Jonah's cell the other night. Roberto thought he and the deputy working with him—a young male I didn't know—were disturbingly sociable with Smit and his little crowd of Anglo inmates. And disturbingly hostile to Jonah.

Not only that, but the Anglo inmates had been giving Jonah a particularly hard time throughout the day. Smit had taken his food while the guards chuckled and pretended not to see. Someone had tripped him when he was trying to get back to his cell. There'd been talk all day that tonight was the night he was finally going to get it.

"Okay. Just try to stay out of it," I told him. "Fake another seizure if you can. I'm not sure what else you can do. See what happens and I'll try to make sure that the perps are prosecuted."

It was a hollow promise, given my current status. But I didn't know what else I could do. The county attorney didn't give a damn if his prized defendant was attacked in the jail—he'd made that very clear. Jonah's own lawyer would love it if he was seriously assaulted. It would make his client a martyr, and make things even more of a circus. The sheriff had hated me from the night I'd Tased Smit. In fact, he might be listening to a complaint right now from one of his leading citizens, the head of the County Cattlemen's Association, about how I had trespassed on his land—accompanied by a banned predator—and threatened his eldest sons.

Roberto, though, had never been particularly good at following orders.

thirty-eight

I sat in my truck with Mungo restlessly prowling the backseat for nearly an hour. I'd pulled down a side street where I could see Cesar's parking lot, but where it was unlikely I could be seen. We listened to the Clash on the CD player. "I Fought the Law" was playing when the Mann twins pulled into the lot in their raised crew-cab truck with the naked-woman decals on the rear mud flaps, and I wondered what kind of omen the song suggested. The brothers drove to the far dark corner of the lot and got out. Despite their injuries, they were laughing as they walked toward the bar. They didn't notice my truck.

Mungo seemed to want another meatball sub, so we drove to the sandwich shop for dinner. Then back to our surveillance point to eat. As usual, Mungo finished her sandwich before I could take the first bite of mine.

When I was done with my roast beef on wheat, I pulled on a pair of grease-stained leather gloves. I didn't think it would matter if I left fingerprints, but I knew the gloves would look intimidating.

"Sorry, Mungo, but I get to have all the fun tonight. You can watch, though."

I got out of the truck and walked down to the parking lot, then to the brothers' truck. The doors were locked. I jumped into the bed and tried the sliding window. It was locked, too. So maybe they weren't quite as dumb as they looked. I smacked the edge of the glass hard with the heel of my palm and it cracked open. Maybe not.

It was a tight squeeze, but a hell of a lot easier than Moriah. I wormed through and crawled into a pile of litter, tools, muscle magazines, and beer cans in the backseat. I took a pen flashlight out of my pocket and began to go through the trash, checking the rear door of the bar every ten seconds.

I found a lot of interesting stuff. A set of hypodermic needles, several vials of human growth hormone from Mexico, a marijuana pipe, a bag of cheap shake to fill it with, and a beat-up but loaded .45 revolver.

After a while I got bored. They didn't seem to be coming out, not even for a toke. I lay down on the floor of the backseat and covered myself with jackets and debris. It seemed like a ridiculous place to do it, but I began the meditation exercises Rebecca had taught me. The purpose wasn't to relax, or even focus. The purpose was just to empty my mind. Anything to keep from thinking about what I was doing.

I was totally relaxed and totally remorseless when both front side doors opened. I was my brother's brother, my grandfather's grandson. Generations of bad men flowed in my veins, for all I knew.

The dome light didn't come on, although I expected it to. I was low enough and covered enough that it wouldn't have mattered. The brothers staggered up and slumped together on the front bench seat, giggling. They talked as they filled their pipe with the dry weed.

"Did you see that ho? Man, I think she likes me."

"Her boyfriend didn't, that sawed-off little freak."

"Next time he looks at me like that I'm going to knock his teeth down his throat."

"Uh-uh, dude. We beat someone's ass in there, they won't let us in no more."

"Yeah, yeah. Speaking of beating ass, are you keeping your eye out for the motherfucker Burns? I'd love to run across that little spic tonight."

"Like Dad says, we got to stay away from him. But I say we kill his dog."

That cracked them up.

In the backseat, I felt a chill. It wasn't so much the threat to Mungo, but the fact that they weren't talking about Brandy. I was sure it was them. It had to be them.

They were debating ways of torturing and killing Mungo, as well as sucking on the glowing pipe, when I sat up.

"Surprise," I said.

Then, as they both jumped and turned to look behind them, I grabbed their heads and smacked them together.

They rebounded off each other with a solid *thunk*. I wondered if I'd done it too hard when there was no immediate reaction—the brothers just swayed woozily in their seats for a couple of seconds. I worried I might have knocked them out. Then, belatedly, they both made horrible grimaces and grabbed their heads. Tears began to stream out of their eyes.

"Oh fuck, man. Oh fuck. My head!"

Relieved, I lifted up the big .45 I'd confiscated from the glove box and loudly cocked the hammer.

"Eeny, meany, miney, moe," I said, pointing the gun at first one and then the other. "Which one of you losers should I shoot first?"

I chose one—Zach, in the passenger's seat, with the broken collarbone—and shoved the gun into his neck. I held the other side of his face with my free hand, and felt his body jump when I screwed the cold, wide barrel against warm flesh. I shuddered myself. Someone had once done that to me, and I still remembered the total weakness that had washed over my body at the time.

"Where is Brandy Walsh?"

"Oh my God! Oh my God!" Zach began gasping.

"We don't know, man. We don't know!" his brother chorused.

"You were in that forest last night. Tell me what happened there."

"We already told you! Mom sent us to look for our brothers. They'd gone out riding on their four-wheelers and didn't come home until late. But we didn't see them. They came home on their own!"

I used the butt of the gun to put some pressure on Zach's broken collarbone. He howled, but didn't try to pull away.

"I'm going to pull this trigger in five seconds. Blow your spinal cord right through this window if you don't tell me. Where is she?"

A bad odor began to fill the cab. Zach was slumping despite my tight grip. I pressed the barrel into his neck harder to keep him upright.

Ned was screeching, "We don't know! We don't know!" just two feet from my ear.

They were the wrong guys. The wrong brothers. Suddenly I was sure of it.

Oops.

thirty-nine

It was dark when Bogey returned.

The late-afternoon storm had put more than an inch of snow on the ground. The sky was clear now, all stars, but the cold hadn't relented. If anything, it had gotten colder. Brandy had been shivering uncontrollably for more than two hours.

Even without the crunch of hiking boots on snow, she could hear him coming from a long way off. She could hear him because he was making a lot of noise. He was huffing and puffing, and there was a strange sliding sound, as if he was dragging something heavy.

She listened for a long time before he poked his face into the doorway. His skin was slick with sweat, his breath blowing steam. He stepped fully into view.

"Well, Brandy. Have you been reconsidering?"

She'd been reconsidering since he'd left her two hours earlier. Why not just tell him she'd go along with his plan? Sweet-talk him a little, tell him how brilliant he was, how she understood that things had gotten a little out of control. And that he was right—their client was the most important thing. She'd certainly keep quiet for Jonah's sake.

But she couldn't do it. There was no way she could pull it off. Just seeing the man, the heat filled her eyes. He'd betrayed her, betrayed their client, led two young kids to commit a felony, destroyed her car, kidnapped her, and basically tortured her by chaining her up in these conditions. And he was doing all of it to promote his own celebrity. She knew there was no way she could go along with that. There was no way she could fake it. She was no actress. And Bogey was not an idiot.

She'd have to ride it out. Like going over the falls on a wave you weren't ready for. You just hold your breath, take the pounding, and hang on, knowing that sooner or later you'll pop up out of the giant washing machine and be able to grab a breath.

"Fuck you," she mumbled around the gag.

The man wouldn't leave her up here forever. She could wait him out. She could last at least another day or two.

"I'm sorry you feel that way. I'm sorrier that you're backing me into a corner this way."

He ducked under the doorway and came inside, his amused eyes studying hers. He crouched down in front of her.

She wanted to spit in his face. But she didn't have any saliva, and even if she did, she wouldn't be able to get it around the gag.

"Last chance," he said.

He took a tape recorder out of his pack and held it up.

"All you have to say is that it was your idea, that I didn't want to have anything to do with it. Now, I know what you're thinking—it might not be admissible if you can prove it was made under duress. But it will be your word against mine. And as we've discussed, in our trial process the judge must do all he can to favor the defendant. Better to let ten guilty men go free than to convict one innocent man, right?"

She raised a foot to try to kick him. But he saw it coming and easily blocked it. She was getting weak, she realized. He'd better give her something to eat and drink or she wouldn't last the night.

"I've got something for you. Hang on a sec."

He ducked back outside. She heard the sliding sound again.

The back of his Gore-Tex jacket became visible as he pulled something very, very heavy. She couldn't see what it was.

"Remember," he grunted as he tugged, "what you told me after your romantic interlude with Burns? That he lives in the wilderness like a wild animal? That he lives with wolves and bears?"

She couldn't imagine why she'd ever told the bastard something so intimate.

"Well, I've arranged for you to meet some of his friends."

Then she could see what he was dragging. It was a long, thin leg that he was pulling by the hoof.

Bogey maneuvered through the doorway again and backed into the cabin, tugging on the hoof. It was the hindquarters of a deer. A dirty, bloody mass of muscle, exposed bone, and fur.

"Don't worry about this guy. He's already dead. It's the animals his corpse is going to attract that you ought to be worried about."

He sat down on part of the collapsed roof and wiped his face with a bandanna.

"I'm just a lawyer, Brandy. I thought about it, but decided I don't have the courage to kill you. Not even to shoot you. I didn't know what I was going to do. And as I was hiking down out of here, I came across this guy. Someone had shot him—poached him, probably—and cut off his head.

"Now, I don't know if you know much about bears, but they hibernate all through the winter. About this time of year, they're desperate to eat anything they can find to put on fat so they can make it through the winter. There's no guarantee any bears are around here. But I suppose we'll find out. I figure your chances are pretty good. But if I'm wrong, then as far as you're concerned, I'm really wrong. Anyway, I'm going to give you until tomorrow to change your mind. You can either change it, or not. Either way, eventually my problems will be solved."

She couldn't speak. She couldn't even look at him. All she could do was stare at the headless carcass in absolute horror.

"Have a good night, now."

forty

TV lights flickered in an upstairs window. I watched the blues and greens through binoculars from the edge of the forest a few hundred yards from the house. After an hour, the lights went out. And I still didn't have a plan.

This time I'd screwed myself. But maybe it was fatal only in a moral sense. I doubted the twins would go to the police. After all, they were both drunk despite their bond conditions, smoking pot, and they'd been humiliated. I didn't think their machismo would allow them to admit to an outsider—especially not to the local police—what I'd done to them. Especially not in a case that had become so public. No, they'd be recovering with drugs and alcohol. Talking up their courage and what they were going to do to me. And there was no doubt about one thing—they'd be gunning for me even more now. I'd need to really watch my back. I needed to stay away from them.

But after climbing out of their truck—using the door this time—I'd driven west on the highway then turned off on the county road that led to the Mann ranch. There was nowhere else to go. I'd already crossed over, so I might as well stay the course. I was pretty sure I'd figured it out.

The meth in Cody's blood, and the likelihood it had been given to him by his slightly older cousins, evidenced that they weren't as young as their years. Then there were the four-wheelers I'd seen by the house, the tire tracks I'd seen near the burned-out shell of Brandy's car, and the fact that the boys had been out late last night.

It was the brats.

I'd done the driving equivalent of a tiptoe onto the Manns' property. Creeping along, with the headlights off. I even paused before turning onto their land to hop out and pull the wires that operated the brake lights.

There was a full moon, though, and I was nervous. I didn't know if the older brothers were headed back to the ranch or not. It would be very bad if they came up behind me while I was trying to feel my way to the house. By now they'd be recovering, getting high and getting angry. Really angry. And I'd left the .45 in the backseat after spilling the shells onto the pavement. That might have been a bad move. But I wasn't a thief. I couldn't have just stolen it.

I'd rumbled past the fence and over the cattle guard. Then, instead of taking one of the high roads that led in the general direction of the house, I'd veered left and followed double-tracks leading into the forested valley, and left the Pig in there.

I tried to formulate a plan, but all I could think about now was Brandy. She was out there, somewhere. If dead, her killer or killers needed to pay. If alive, she'd be praying for someone to do all they could to find her. I would be that one, whether she deserved my help or not. I wasn't doing it for her, though. I was doing it because, whether or not it was official, I was at heart a cop. And I was fed up with all the bullshit surrounding the case. Thanks to intractable lawyers, the whole thing had snowballed into an avalanche of shit. If there was one thing I was going to do before my badge was finally taken from me, I was going to clean up the mess I'd made when I arrested Jonah.

The upstairs light went off. The whole house was now dark, and it was only eleven o'clock on a Friday night. Maybe the boys were staying at a friend's, or maybe they had a generous curfew and someone else's parents were going to drive them home. I kept on waiting. If worse came to worst, I knew what I'd have to do.

Break into the house.

But a tiny beam of light spared me from that ludicrous danger. The light appeared in another upstairs window. I checked it through the binoculars and saw that the window was open and the beam was pointing at the ground. Something was hanging out the window, too, other than a black-clad arm and the flashlight. It was a line of knotted rope.

These guys thought they were ninjas.

The big one—Randy—came first. I suspected he weighed as much as his older brothers, although his mass was in the form of fat, not muscle. I hoped he'd secured the rope to something really sturdy. He must have, because he made it down. Once he was safely on the ground, his little brother, Trey, followed. Together they slunk across the lawn and made for the windbreak. As they entered it, both of them flicked on flashlights.

The brothers reappeared, stealthily pushing their four-wheelers down the hill. I followed.

They picked up speed going down the hill and jumped into their seats. I had to start jogging to keep up. The Pig was concealed down there, but I knew I would give away too much if I tried following them in the truck. I just hoped they weren't going far, and that I wouldn't trip over anything or step in a hole. Thankfully the moon was bright enough that I could see my shadow.

At the bottom of the hill we entered the trees. The woods were open, interspersed with meadows. Here the brothers both fired their engines and flicked on their headlights. They gunned their engines toward the Shoshone National Forest boundary. I began to run. Mungo loped along easily at my side, but I was breathing hard. More from anxiety that I'd lose them than anything else. At least the noise from their engines made me stop worrying about being detected.

Fifteen minutes later they crossed the boundary into the national forest. They were a half mile ahead of me now, but not gaining too much ground. I could hear the engines and sometimes see the glow of their headlights in the distant trees. I didn't need Mungo to do the tracking, because the rough trail was obvious in the moonlight, as was the smell of untreated exhaust. Even when we crossed an old logging road, we didn't hesitate. We veered left as one. I was running so easily now I almost felt like a stalking wolf myself.

The road was familiar. After five minutes on it, I realized I'd been down it before. A minute later I remembered when. Four months earlier, on the day when it all began. I even remembered where to cut off into the trees. I could hear the river now. I could almost hear the screams that had attracted Mungo that day.

On the double-track, I hissed for Mungo to slow. She immediately dropped into hunting mode. Lowering herself, putting head, chest, and tail all closer to the ground. I did my best to emulate what a millennium of woodland hunting had taught her ancestors.

Ahead through the trees I could see some thin lines of light. Up there was the meth lab I'd been looking for at the beginning of the summer. The meth lab—one of so many—I'd stopped bothering to follow up on.

At the same time I was stalking through the woods, Roberto was faking sleep. As he'd predicted when we'd talked earlier, tonight was the night. He could sense the violent energy all around him, swirling in the air like pheromones at a rave. The entire jail was aware of it. The two deputies kept peeking out of their station and chuckling in low voices. He could see the glint of dark eyes among the three illegals he'd befriended as they, like him, feigned sleep. The gringos were whispering and giggling like little girls at a slumber party.

Roberto felt like laughing, too. He loved this shit. He couldn't help it. For the last two days he'd been enduring headaches, the shakes, and cold sweats as the withdrawal symptoms set in. He desperately needed to have some fun.

It was almost two hours after lights out before anything happened. Everything started then, when Smit slid back his cell door and held up his finger in a shushing motion toward where the gringos had grouped their cots. Roberto could see him quite clearly because of the emergency lights in the hallway beyond the bars and because he was the closest to the gringos. The other illegals all had taken cots as far from the gringos as they could. From his position, Roberto could see the cells, but not the gringos. But he wasn't disturbed when a barefoot Smit padded silently out of his view to confer with his buddies. He would be able to see when Smit tried to enter Jonah's cell.

Despite my instructions to him, Roberto had no intention of faking another seizure. He was going to take care of Smit directly. He had one hand on top of the blanket, gripping his twin canes. He was ready for it. He was looking forward to it.

The big man had been hassling him for the last two days. Almost as much as he hassled Jonah. When Roberto just stared back at him, pretending not to understand the insults that were made in English, Smit had threatened time and time again to take one of his canes and stick it up his ass. The guy was obviously an asshole with an asshole fixation. Every time he made the threat, Roberto just went on staring. He knew from the way Smit turned away that the big man was afraid of him.

Imagine that—afraid of a cripple. He almost laughed again.

But the urge was choked off when big hands clamped—simultaneously—over his mouth and throat.

forty-one

At the same time, Brandy couldn't stop shivering. And she couldn't stop staring at the carcass. At times she was shaking so hard she thought she saw it move. A portion of the spine was exposed, reaching toward her from the open cavity of the neck. Bits of flesh clung to the white bone.

But at least she wasn't alone.

Two mice had appeared early in the evening. They'd darted in and out of the doorway for maybe an hour. Looking at her with glassy black eyes, then the carcass, then her again. Having finally chewed through the duct-tape gag, she tried talking to them, but it just made them scurry away. So she shut up and just smiled. She badly needed their company.

They slipped in and began nibbling. After a while they even stopped glancing her way. But then they suddenly fled in terror as a red fox leapt in the door.

After her initial surprise, she played the same silent, smiling game with the fox. It, too, soon accepted her as harmless and began to nibble, tearing delicate chunks from the huge wound where the deer's head had been sawed off. Brandy barely made a whisper at first, careful not to raise her voice too much until the fox grew used to it. After a while, as the sky darkened and finally turned black, she could speak at an almost normal volume. But her speech was impaired when she tried to compliment its pointed ears and clean, fluffy tail by the fact that her tongue was swelling hugely in her mouth from thirst.

It was only when the fox fled that she began to really get scared. Its flight from such a smorgasbord could only mean something bigger and badder was on the way. Her teeth began to chatter. She couldn't clench her sore jaw tight enough to stop it.

The change in smell was the first thing she noticed. It wasn't the sickly sweet smell of the rotting meat, or even the now-familiar odor of her own vomit, sweat, and fear. It was something heavier, more powerful, and tremendously rank. She brought her quivering knees up to her chest and squeezed as hard as she could into the corner of the wrecked cabin.

She never heard its footsteps, but she could hear it huffing toward her from a long way off. Every now and then there came a low groan, like wind through rock. The two sounds kept coming—regular huffs like a steam engine climbing a steep grade punctuated by groans.

Even though she had lots of time—far, far too much time—to prepare, she was in no way ready when the head swung around the door frame. It was as big as a truck tire. But its eyes were small, shiny buttons. The moonlight silvered the honey-brown fur.

The head swung from side to side twice as the massive snout seemed to suck all the air out of the ruined cabin. Then the nose and the eyes locked in on her and everything became very still. Brandy stared back with her mouth open as the black lips lifted and revealed broken yellow teeth as long as knives.

forty-two

The moon was just hanging there in the sky, so bloated and bright that it cast shadows from every upright object in the woods. The shadows were still except for when an easy breeze ruffled needles and leaves. In all of the Shoshone National Forest, only two of these shadows were moving fast. One was made for night running—it glided along, low to the ground, smooth and straight as a bullet. The other was far more awkward. It ran erect, its spine straight, frantically pumping limbs that never connected to the earth or the feet of the man who cast it. Every now and then it crashed to the ground, only to rise again, spitting curses.

I was gasping like a bellows from the climb. We'd ascended more than two thousand feet from the road, up through pines and aspens and steep fields of scree. Sometimes we were on the rocky four-wheel trail, and other times we lost it entirely. My route might have been foolish, but I was determined to take as direct a path as possible toward the saddle between the two peaks in the night sky.

One of the sobbing brothers had pointed out the peaks. The

other one was facedown on the dirt floor of the hut, Mungo's jaws clamped around the back of his neck. It had taken less than a minute after kicking through the door for them to tell me what and where.

The what was Bogey. The where was an abandoned cabin in the looming mountains.

Through their frantic squeals that were muffled by the dirt, I was told that everything had gotten out of hand. They'd only meant to scare her. But she'd fallen off her bike and hit her head. They'd gotten scared themselves and brought her to the shed. Unsure what to do next, they'd called Bogey. He was pissed. He told them to take her someplace more remote. He'd assured them he'd take care of her, bring her food and clothes, and talk her out of getting them in trouble. In return they'd never, ever mention his name, or else they'd spend the rest of their teenage years in a boot camp in Utah.

My heart had long since red-lined—it was pounding as hard as it was willing to; any harder and it would explode. I really should have borrowed one of the ATVs. But just driving one of the damn things was such anathema to me that the idea hadn't occurred when it would have counted. Besides, I was in the best shape of my life thanks to Moriah, and was certain I could run the distance over rough ground in the dark faster than I could maneuver a machine. I supposed now that I was wrong.

"Wait, Mungo," I croaked, sounding like McGee climbing a flight of stairs. "Slow down."

Mungo turned and glanced at me. She was panting lightly, barely winded. Her look said, *What? Not again.*

I doubled over with my hands on my knees and took huge belly breaths. I tried to walk a little, but my legs were so stiff with lactic acid that they'd barely follow my commands. But I managed to force them back into a reasonable jog rather than the all-out sprint that kept creeping over me. I kept thinking how every second might count, how if I'd been just a little faster in reaching

Cody Wallis, the boy might have lived and none of this would have happened in the first place.

Up, up, and up, we soon passed into a forest of far smaller trees. These were stunted by the altitude and twisted by the wind. Their shapes were bizarre, their long shadows even more so. It couldn't be much farther now—the brothers had tearfully claimed it was just above the tree line.

After just a few more minutes I topped out on a rise and saw a headwall before me. It protected the hanging valley between the two peaks, nestling the cabin in its bosom. Somewhere was the four-wheel track, but damn if I could find it.

Approaching it, I finally commanded my muscles, heart, and lungs to apply the brake that they'd been screaming for. As great as my need for speed was, I couldn't just go charging in. Someone could be there—maybe even Bogey.

It wasn't hard to pick a route up the wall even without spotting the track. Down its middle spilled a great field of talus. Large blocks—their sizes ranging from dishwashers to SUVs—that wouldn't likely move or slide from the weight of just one human and a light-footed wolf-dog. Here I had the advantage. Pushing with my legs and pulling with my hands, I gained elevation at an even pace. Mungo was now the graceless one, forced by her anatomy to lurch from stance to stance.

Within fifteen minutes we crested the top of the wall. Before us was a small valley that widened into a lake, then narrowed again into a dirty gray glacier, which then climbed into a saddle between the two high peaks. I couldn't see a cabin. But based on the geography, I could guess where it would be: on a safe knoll above, but not far from, the glacial lake, and on the north side to best catch the light.

"Whoa, Mungo. *Tranquilo,*" I hissed.

Mungo turned again to look at me. This time I didn't see disgust for my slow pace in the way she held her body. Her head was very low, and her tail was held straight out and stiff as a board.

Her shoulders looked huge in the moonlight, like she'd slipped a pair of shoulder pads under her fur. I realized that all her hair was standing on end.

Something very bad had happened—or was happening.

The ground at the base of the hanging valley was floored with scattered rocks and high-alpine tundra. We made our way together over and through small hillocks, Mungo staying by my side. So close, in fact, that she kept nudging me off-balance. But I didn't reprimand her. I was just glad she was with me.

We came to the foot of the lake. The cabin had to be somewhere to the right. Mungo darted ahead—then froze before I could try to call her back. She lowered her head all the way to the ground and took a tentative lick. I approached and knelt, pushing her away. I examined the ground in the moonlight, touching it. I found sticky blood and flecks of skin and hair.

"Oh fuck."

Before I could stop her, Mungo darted ahead again. This time she didn't stop, not even when I hissed. She ran a straight course to the north side of the lake. When she was a hundred feet away, showing no signs of stopping, I cursed again and started to run after her.

I came over a rise and saw, just ahead, the outline of a small cabin. And the gray ghost shape of Mungo flying toward it. The cabin looked tiny, no more than twelve feet wide and seven feet high and probably missing its roof. It had a long-abandoned aspect to it. A few steps closer and I could make out the door, or at least the black hole of where a door should be, just as Mungo shot into it.

I didn't know what to expect, but what happened was the last thing I could have imagined in my worst nightmares.

A sound that was like the boom of thunder broke the night sky wide open. But it was longer than thunder, more animated, and full of rage. It was a roar that no human could make. It lifted all the hair on my head. I actually felt the vibrations blast through me. Then an enormous head and shoulders rose above the walls—the body that supported it had to be eight feet tall. I almost believed I was witnessing some monster from a nightmare, until I saw the profile of the snout, and my brain screamed *bear!*

What followed was total chaos. The bellowing roar continued, and another voice from a hell's chorus joined in. It was Mungo, snarling louder and more ferociously than I knew she was capable of.

Running again, I automatically touched the gun on my hip. But the .40-caliber now felt as deadly as a cap gun. I was fifty feet away when Mungo scampered back out the doorway. She was running fast on just three legs.

She was limping to the left, so I broke right. If the bear came out after her, I'd have a better chance to drill it with a full law-enforcement clip if I wasn't right in front of it.

But the bear didn't come out. I found myself circling the cabin, listening to the huffing and scratching and growling from within. With the exception of one final bellow, the roars had stopped with Mungo's hasty exit.

I couldn't decide what to do. Approaching the cabin seemed like a very, very bad idea. Finding Mungo and getting her the hell out of here seemed infinitely easier and wiser. Then going for help and a bigger gun. But I knew that the hard choice is usually the right one. One way or another, I had to see what was inside the cabin. If there was a one-in-a-million chance that Brandy was somehow still alive in there, being mauled, being eaten alive, I had to risk it.

I approached the cabin from the rear. Each huff or scratch sent a buzz of alarm racing down my spine. I held my gun ahead of me in a two-handed grip while my mind frantically debated target options. Heart or head? Would the thick skull deflect bullets?

Coming up behind the cabin, I could see how rickety the walls were. They were barely standing. They seemed to vibrate with each noise from the interior. There appeared to be gaps several inches wide between the logs that formed the walls.

Crouching low, I crept up and settled down behind one of the gaps. Just on the other side of the wall were ungodly loud groans and slurps.

The stench was the first thing that struck me. Over the powerful body odor of the bear was the stench of rotting meat. It almost made me gag when I couldn't help but realize the likely source of the latter smell. And it almost made me creep away. But I had to look. I had to know.

I put my face against a large seam and stared into the darkness. Because most of the roof was missing, the moonlight blazed straight down inside. The massive shape of the bear, with its humped shoulders and swayed back, was moving side to side as it pulled at something on the ground.

And then I heard it. A tiny, rasping voice just on the other side of the wall. Singing what sounded like "Twinkle, Twinkle, Little Star." Serenading the bear.

The voice wasn't coming from where the bear was pulling and tearing on the opposite side of the cabin. It was coming from just inches from my face, down low. I had a vision of a disembodied head chanting the song.

Then the song changed. An improvised song began. "Mungo, Mungo, if that wolf was you, I wish you'd come back to me. And bring your master, too." Sung in the same small voice.

"I'm here," I whispered, so quietly I didn't even hear myself.

Instantly, the song stopped. And the bear responded, too, letting go of the carcass and raising its great head. It seemed to be staring straight through the crack at me. I knew I was shadowed by the wall, but I wondered if that was enough. The bear sniffed the air while I held my breath.

The singing started again, a little louder. This time it was "Hush Little Baby."

The bear stared, then reluctantly, growling sulkily, went back to feeding. I could now make out the rotting carcass as that of a big mule deer. Something was sticky when I touched the wall. I ran my fingers gently over it and recognized a twisted wrap of duct tape. Above and below it were two filthy, swollen hands.

The fingers moved. Very carefully, I took hold of one of the hands. It squeezed back with a strength that startled me. Its touch conveyed some kind of triumph, some kind of victory over psychic and physical agony.

I leaned a little to the side and tried to see to the right, the direction the wrists seemed to run. I could make out a pair of lips moving, the ragged voice coming from them, and pale, dirt- and blood-streaked skin.

The hand wouldn't let go. I had to set my gun down carefully between my knees in order to dig my knife out of my pocket. Holding it tight, I opened it one-handed. Carefully, awkwardly, while the voice connected to the hand continued to sing, I sawed through the tape with the razor-sharp blade.

The bear raised its head again at the sound of the tape parting. This time it didn't hesitate or sniff the air. It lunged forward a single step, crossing the entire diameter of the cabin. Its head was enormous. It opened jaws from which swung thick ropes of saliva and bellowed right into Brandy's face.

I felt the sticky saliva cover my face as it sprayed through the crack. I felt the shattering vibration of the sound rattle through my bones. But the hand holding mine didn't even flinch. And when the roar was finished, the singing continued, never having stopped. "I'm not going to hurt you, I'm not going to eat your dinner, I'm just a silly human, no threat to anyone." I couldn't see any fear on her wet face, with the bear's open jaws just inches from it. There was none of my own terror reflected there.

For the first time in my life, I felt awe.

From the doorway of the cabin came a higher-pitched growl. The bear swung around, stretching out one paw and slapping the air. The paw caught the side of the door frame and shook the whole cabin but missed Mungo.

Now she snarled again and darted forward, like she was going for the meat. The bear lunged for her. Its huge shoulders completely filled the door and made the wood crack.

I didn't hesitate. It was now or never. Letting go of the hand,

I scrambled over the crude wall and fell inside. The bear's hindquarters were so close I could have touched them. Brandy was trying to rise, but her legs didn't seem to be working. I grabbed her, lifted her to her feet, and threw her over the back wall.

A quick glance at the bear showed that it was pushing its way out of the cabin. Maybe so it could turn around and come back in. Jumping up, I grabbed the top log of the wall and vaulted over. I landed on top of Brandy with one knee, but she didn't cry out. I found my gun, lifted her again, and began dragging her away from the cabin as fast as I could.

With Brandy beginning to recover the use of her legs, we ran across the rocks and the tundra heading for the end of the valley. Behind them, it sounded as if Mungo and the bear were locked in mortal combat. A fight that could only have one outcome.

"Keep running," I yelled, letting go of Brandy.

But she didn't listen. She stopped, too.

In the open space in front of the cabin, the bear was standing on its hind legs, bellowing and swinging its paws. Between swings Mungo darted in to snatch bites at its legs and belly before darting out again.

I pointed my gun in the air over the cabin and fired. The shot cracked out just as the bear caught Mungo with a mighty hook. My wolf-dog was thrown through the air, spinning, and landed in a heap. The bear dropped to all fours.

I fired again. And again. The bear swung its head as if dodging bullets in slow motion. Then it turned and shambled over the hill at a sideways lope.

I ran for where Mungo lay still.

"Good girl," I said, scooping her up in my arms. She didn't seem to weigh much at all. Or maybe it was just that the adrenaline throbbing through my veins was giving me superhuman strength.

With Brandy following, trying to help by holding Mungo's haunches, we hustled out of the valley.

* *

The hands clamped around Roberto's mouth and throat were strong. They held his head pinned to the cot. He gripped his canes and brought them up to sweep the air behind him, but other hands grabbed hold of them. Grinning faces appeared over his torso. He fought for control of the canes for just a second before deciding he'd be better off without them. Releasing them, he heard one go skittering all the way across the rec room floor. The other began to beat at him. He ignored the blows, though, which were mostly on his numb thighs. He focused instead on punching behind his head with all his considerable strength.

One fist connected solidly with a smacking sound. It felt like he'd hit solid bone, probably a forehead. The other fist just struck air. A bellow of pain sounded just behind his ears. For an instant the hands gripping his mouth and throat released. But just as Roberto started to lift his head to begin a roll off the cot, they clamped down securely once more. My brother was startled that the man behind him—it had to be Smit—had recovered so quickly. But then without his feet on the ground, and without any strength in his legs, he knew the force of his punch had been greatly diminished.

Being crippled sucked.

The other hands were flailing all over his chest and stomach and groin, punching and trying to grab hold of his arms now. Roberto punched around him indiscriminately, but with much better effect. He had the leverage of the cot beneath him when he punched at the men above. He'd get in a good shot and a face would go reeling back into the darkness. But he was taking three punches to every one he fired off, and the faces kept returning. Sometimes bloodied, but they kept on returning to join the others.

If his fucking legs worked, he'd take them all out. But his legs didn't work.

Smit's face wouldn't come into view. The man had to be

crouching behind his head, forcing it down, and ducking the punches my brother threw that way. Roberto was sliding up the cot, the back of his head against the metal rail, then over it, so that the cold steel bar was pressing into the back of his neck. With his head arched all the way back, and his throat cruelly exposed, he could finally see Smit. The big man's upside-down face was covered with blood, but he was grinning. His eyes—still swollen from the broken nose he'd received in the car crash—were slitted with brutal ecstasy.

"Gonna take care of you first," he grunted as he arched my brother's head even farther back.

In this position Roberto couldn't see the other men on top of him to punch at them, and his arms and shoulders were losing their strength. One arm got pinned to his side, and then the other. He tried to roar in frustration, but Smit's huge hand over his mouth choked down the sound. His fucking legs just wouldn't work.

A bandanna was looped over his throat and the rail at the head of the cot. It was cinched down over the scar where his throat had been slashed just a year ago. Someone yanked it tight, then tighter still. My brother's breath was getting cut off. He could feel his eyes starting to bulge, his lungs starting to strain. When Smit finally took his hand off Roberto's mouth, my brother didn't have the wind to shout. Strips of cloth torn from sheets and pillowcases were used to secure his wrists and ankles.

"I told you, spic. Told you I was gonna stick the cane up your skinny ass."

Behind Smit, Roberto could see the three illegals he'd gotten to know. They were huddled together against the bars closest to the guard station. One of the gringos was standing in front of them. He had one of Roberto's canes. He was swinging it like a baseball bat each time one of the illegals so much as flinched. The door to the guards' station was closed for the first time in the three days Roberto had been in the jail. The bastards had to be in on it.

The illegals were keeping quiet. The gringos were whispering gleefully. Roberto couldn't make a sound.

Smit stood up and walked to his side. "Where's the other goddamn cane?" he hissed.

Everyone stopped talking and giggling and looked around.

"What did you do with it, you shitheads?"

Everyone kept looking around in the darkness.

"Well, give me that one," he demanded to the gringo who was holding off the illegals.

The man turned to hand it over when another gringo voice from near the cells said, "No, I've got it."

Out of the corner of his rapidly fading vision, Roberto could see a man taking two quick steps toward Smit, one of his glittering metal canes held high in triumph. As Smit turned to face him, the cane was raised even higher. Then it came swinging around so fast my brother could hear it slicing the air.

The cane connected solidly with Smit's already broken nose. Without a sound, the big man reeled back and collapsed on the concrete floor.

"Who's next, you motherfuckers!" Jonah Strasburg screamed.

One of the illegals floated forward in a perfect boxer's crouch and nailed the man who'd been herding them with a three-punch combination.

forty-three

Getting down the talus that spilled from the mouth of the hanging valley wasn't easy in the dark. Especially not while carrying 120 pounds of limp canine, and while expecting a thousand-pound bear to come charging down the slope after you, as it followed the trail of blood.

I remembered hearing during a campfire conversation on a climbing trip that if you run from a bear, you should run downhill. Their foreshortened legs made a steep slope awkward for them. But then, unfortunately, I could also remember hearing someone laugh and say that it was an old wives' tale. The laughing friend was majoring in wildlife biology. He pulled on the jug of wine and mentioned that grizzlies can run thirty-five miles per hour—almost as fast as a racehorse over a short distance—and that instead of running, you should just bend over and kiss your ass good-bye.

Trying to push away these thoughts, I focused on not falling as we scrambled from boulder to boulder. Brandy helped me as best she could. She was gaining strength. But we were moving painfully slow.

Only at the bottom of the slope did I allow myself to rest. Surely a bear that big would make a hell of a racket pursuing us.

Still holding Mungo cradled in my arms, I collapsed on a low stone and was able to take her weight off my burning shoulders and biceps.

"Are . . . you . . . okay?" I asked Brandy.

She was bent over, gasping, her hands on her knees. I saw that she was wearing dirty biking clothes, and the hair that spilled over her face was knotted and tangled.

"Hungry. Cold . . . until we started running. Freaked out." She raised her head and looked at me. "And really, really pissed."

I nodded and went back to just trying to get enough air into my lungs. I'd been operating beyond red-line for far too long. My body was starting to lock up. The oxygen I was gulping just wasn't getting to my muscles. I anxiously looked back up the dark slope behind us. But I could see no sign of the bear.

After another minute, Brandy stood and gently patted the matted fur on Mungo's shoulder. Her palm was dark when she held it up to the moonlight. I probed it too while Mungo whimpered. There were four deep punctures, but they seemed to be clotting.

"You're a good dog. I mean wolf," Brandy told her.

Mungo was still conscious—she licked her clenched teeth as I probed deeper. There wasn't any swell that might indicate internal injuries, and there didn't seem to be any obviously broken bones, so I thought she'd be okay. Wolves are tough.

"I'm going to buy her the biggest steak I can find," I said. "And keep buying them until she's better."

Brandy cupped Mungo's face in her hands and kissed her muzzle.

"You saved my life," she said.

What about me? I thought. Then, *No steak for you, wolf.*

I looked behind us again. Still no sign of the bear. If it wasn't chasing us by now, it would probably sulk for a while then go back to what it was eating.

"What was that, in the cabin?" I asked.

"A headless deer. Bogey dragged it in. He said it would attract bears. I think he meant to come back after I'd been eaten and remove the duct tape. Everyone would think I'd just been hiding out, pretending to have been kidnapped, when I got attacked by a bear." She shivered and hugged her arms around herself.

"Jesus. He planned this all along?"

She shook her head.

"No, he seemed to feel bad about it. At first, anyway. He said things just kind of snowballed. You know about the kids?"

"That's how I found you."

"He threatened to expose the fact that Cody had meth in his blood. Get them in trouble, too, because it would be obvious he hadn't been the only one smoking it. They said they'd do anything to keep him from telling. So he had them try to scare me. When they couldn't find me, they burned my car. And when I came up and caught them at it, then wiped out on my bike, they thought I was going to die. So they felt they didn't have any choice but to kidnap me. Bogey fit it all into his publicity plan. Then, when I wouldn't go along and told him I was going to expose him—that's when he brought in the carcass."

I looked up the slope again. Still nothing. I was pretty sure we were safe. But Bogey wasn't. He was in a hell of a lot of trouble.

"What do you want to do to him?" I asked.

"Make him pay," she said simply.

forty-four

At close to two in the morning we finally made it to my camp beneath the great overhanging cliff. Brandy had insisted we come here; I'd tried to make her go to the hospital, but she wouldn't have it. She said she didn't want to have to explain what had happened to her before she could prove it. She was scared of how Bogey would twist the situation, scared that she wouldn't be able to prove his culpability, and scared of the potential ramifications to Jonah's case.

First I took care of Mungo. I laid her down on a blanket and dumped a bottle of hydrogen peroxide on her shoulder. It bubbled and hissed while Mungo growled and kicked. She even snapped, but always carefully so as not to actually bite me. Brandy had to help me hold her down. The wounds looked more or less superficial—still no signs of internal swelling, although she was sore as hell. But I was pretty sure she was going to be all right.

I fed them both from a can of rice and refried beans that I cooked up on my camp stove. After that, I used the stove to heat my "winter shower," which was a five-gallon black bag of water. I hung it on a tree branch once it was sufficiently hot. Brandy washed immodestly in the dark—she was too filthy and exhausted to care. She'd even let me wash her hair when her stomach cramped and suddenly she was too weak to raise her arms and her knees kept buckling. I wrapped a beach towel around her and held her while she shivered. I led her back to the tent, stuffing her naked into my sleeping bag.

"When did you last sleep?" I asked.

She tried to answer but stopped herself, shaking her head.

"Just give me the phone. Let's do it," she told me.

I lit a candle lantern that hung from the highest point of the little tent. Mungo raised her head and gave Brandy a concerned look.

"It can wait. Until tomorrow night, at least," I told her.

But she'd shaken her head again.

"No, we've got to do it now. Get your phone."

Brandy said, "Hi, asshole."

There was no response from the other end of the line.

"Can you hear me? Maybe this transmission from the grave isn't so good. Maybe we have a bad connection."

She was sitting in the tent, Indian-style, with my sleeping bag pulled up over her chest. Only one arm was exposed to the cold in order to hold the cell phone to her ear. Above her head my candle lantern swung back and forth, casting weird shadows.

Bogey cleared his throat.

"Brandy?"

"That's right. Your co-counsel who was kidnapped and left to die. Correction—that you kidnapped and attempted to murder. As you've probably noticed by now, I'm still alive, and you're in some very deep shit, Professor."

There was another pause.

Then, "Brandy! I don't know what you're talking about, but I'm so glad that you're all right! Where have you been? What happened to you?"

She looked at me and shook her head. Her freckled nose wrinkled with disgust. I smiled and shrugged, as if to say *Well, what do you expect from a lawyer?* Still, I kept on holding the microcassette recorder to the earpiece. But I knew it wouldn't do any good.

"Brandy! Can you hear me?" the fake-ebullient Bogey yelled.

"Meet at the river, asshole. Where that boy was killed and your slimy career was revived. Be there in two hours, at four A.M. I've got some instructions that you'd better follow if you don't want to spend the rest of your life in jail."

I nodded at her, letting her know she was doing well. The river was an important part of the plan. It was symbolic, where it all began. I also believed the scene of Cody's death might cause a psychological weakening of even an egotistical psychopath like Bogey. "You use any advantage you have," I'd explained earlier. Another was speed. To confront him now, as soon as possible. If things went well, it might work. It might get him to say something incriminating. Neither of us mentioned the possibility that he would try again to kill her. But that, too, would certainly be incriminating.

"Brandy?" Bogey said. "Where are you? I'll go anywhere you want me to, but I don't understand—"

"You bring any of your new friends and you're finished," Brandy added. "Four A.M. The rock above the river, you unbelievable prick."

I took the phone away from her and clicked the END button.

"How did I do?"

"Great."

"Sorry about the bad language. I know that wasn't part of the script. It just kind of came out."

I smiled. "It was authentic. The most important rule of working undercover is to be yourself, even when you're not. Understand?"

"I'll have to think about that."

"I did mostly undercover work for eight years. That's how

long I've had to think about it." I added lightly, as a joke, "Now I don't know who the hell I am."

"Is that what you're going to go back to doing? After you arrest Bogey?"

I smiled one more time and shrugged, but I could tell my eyes didn't transmit the smile very convincingly.

From my crate of clothes, Brandy chose a gray long-sleeved polypro shirt that fit her well enough—it had been Rebecca's—and a pair of baggy shorts I secured around her waist with a piece of webbing. I didn't have a bra so she couldn't place the tape recorder there, and her old clothes were far too filthy to use. I improvised with more webbing, making a kind of chest harness that placed the recorder between her breasts. Then I gave her a threadbare aloha shirt to wear on top in order to conceal the lines.

"An original Reyn Spooner," she said with a wan smile, reading the label on the old shirt. "I'm impressed. It reminds me of home."

We were going over what I wanted her to do and say at the river when my phone started chiming. It was a local number, but not Luke's, or the jail's, or anyone I knew. After hesitating, I pushed the button.

"Burns?" a voice said.

Who the hell would be calling me at this hour? Even though I was wide awake, I answered sleepily, worried that it might be Bogey checking to see if I was a part of Brandy's plan.

"Wha?" I groaned.

"Burns? Is that you?"

"Yeah. What? Who's this?"

"Jo. Jo Richards. Danger Girl, you bastard. I'm the paramedic you never called after I flirted with you shamelessly and gave you my number."

This wasn't a good time to try talking to an angry woman. There was way too much going on. But she sounded more concerned than truly angry—there was a note of amusement in her voice, so I didn't hang up. Brandy was watching me with a puzzled expression. In the confined space of the tent, she could hear both ends of the conversation.

"Look, Jo, I'm sorry. I told you I was really busy."

"Yeah, I remember that. And it seems that you weren't just busy riling up the town by arresting Jonah Strasburg, either. You're apparently somehow mixed up in a riot we had at the jail tonight."

Oh shit.

"What happened?"

I was starting to feel the weakness and nausea that always overwhelmed me when I thought of what I'd done to my brother. A year ago, and again just three nights ago. I couldn't seem to stop hurting him, couldn't stop putting him at grave risk. I turned away from Brandy so she couldn't see my face.

"Like I said, there was a riot. A bunch of people were hurt—"

"Who?"

"Hang on, I'm telling you, you son of a bitch. A bunch of people. A couple of them pretty bad. One guy, Smit, our town bully, has got a cracked skull. He's in a coma, being Life Flighted to Salt Lake. Two other local guys got broken jaws and some other small bones in their faces. There's an epidemic of broken ribs, too. And then there's one guy sitting here on the bed in front of me who says he's both a super-secret undercover agent and, believe it or not, your flesh-and-blood brother."

"How bad is he hurt?" I demanded. "What happened to him?"

"Jesus, Burns, you are a real pain in the ass. He's fine, except for some contusions and some old, uh, injuries. He wants to talk to you. But before I put him on, I want you to know something. He's a hell of a lot cuter than you. A lot friendlier, and a lot more fun, too. Your loss, Burns. His gain."

forty-five

With typical arrogance, Bogey arrived at the river at 4:30 A.M., a half hour late. No matter what he'd said on the phone, how he'd pretended to be delighted that she was "back," I guess he had to demonstrate to Brandy that, even now, he wouldn't be pushed around. And that was okay with me. I was fine with everything just as long as he showed up at the river.

I'd placed her out on the rock, near the pile of mildewing stuffed animals, the survivors that hadn't been blown into the river along with the flowers by the violent storm two days earlier.

Her back was to the single small tree that grew from the crack in the rock. From her position, she could see the headlights that swept through the trees by the highway as Bogey pulled into the turnout. She informed me of this in a whisper. I was hidden in a bush just twenty feet away. Although the moon had disappeared, I could see her face clearly in the starlight. She didn't look scared, but I was.

The river gurgled ominously behind and below her. I could almost feel it sucking me in.

I watched silently as she felt through her two shirts and hit the RECORD button on the microcassette. A little earlier, she'd wondered why I was having her do this. She said it couldn't possibly work. Bogey had been aware she might have been trying to record him on the phone and had avoided saying anything incriminating. Why was I so sure he'd fall apart at the sight of her and start babbling?

"Like I told you before," I'd said. "I've been building cases for eight years now. Before all that QuickDraw stuff started, I was the best investigator in the state."

I said it without modesty, simply stating a fact. It was true. But I could read her mind: *Yeah,* she'd wanted to say, *but the last three years you haven't done anything but fuck up, right? After what I heard about Mexico, I think an argument could be made that your judgment might be a little suspect.*

She did what I asked, though. I think she trusted me. And she sure as hell owed me.

An engine died, a car door snicked shut, and footsteps could be heard coming down the trail, led by a bobbing flashlight. Ostrich-skin cowboy boots crunched on leaves and gravel.

I saw her take a deep breath then stand up.

"Hello?" a voice behind the flashlight called.

"Right here, dickhead."

Language, language, I wanted to chide her. Until tonight I'd never heard her use an obscenity. I was feeling almost giddy with relief about Roberto and tremendous excitement about what was happening right here. Finally, I believed, I could get Jonah Strasburg's case off my back. Justice, or at least the closest thing to it, would be done.

He came closer, warily, turning and shining the light around him, saying, "Brandy? Are you okay? How did you get here?"

"Never mind how I got here. All you need to know is that I got out of that cabin you left me in. Tied up and freezing to death."

"I don't know what you're talking about, Brandy." He played the light over her, slowly, down from her face to her feet. "Where did you get those clothes?"

"Shut the fuck up, Bogey. You're going to listen to me now. Here's what you're going to do. You're going to publicly apologize for demonizing this town and insulting its county attorney. Then you're going to go to Luke Endow and beg him for the very best deal he can offer Jonah. If it's fair, commensurate with what we know of the facts, then you'll convince Jonah to take it. If it's not, you recuse yourself from the case and have me assigned. Solo."

"I can't do that," Bogey said. "You've never tried a case, Brandy. It would be depriving our client of the best defense available, something I recall you believing is an intrinsic right. He's entitled to a no-holds-barred defense, something only I can offer him."

"If you don't do as I say, I'll expose you."

Bogey turned all the way around again. He shined the light at the bush I was hiding behind, but then it moved on, probing others.

"Who brought you here? I'm guessing it was Burns, and that he's your co-conspirator in whatever stunt the two of you are trying to pull. Where is he? Why don't you ask him to come out?"

He was getting closer to admitting something. That was one reason for this whole setup, but only a minor one. I wanted to backdoor Bogey into talking about what he'd done to Brandy by getting him to agree to follow her instructions about the case. His agreement would imply that he was guilty—why else would he follow her orders? I hadn't been able to tell her this. If we'd planned this too hard, she might have come off fake.

"There's no one here but us," she lied, and we both knew that *he* knew she was probably lying. "Are you going to agree to my conditions, Bogey? Or am I going to have to take you down?"

"Come on out, Agent Burns," he called. "Come out, come out."

Brandy now said exactly what I had coached her to. "He's not here. He saw you at the cabin, though. And he saw you dragging that carcass inside. Now, do you agree to my terms, asshole?"

Bogey stopped calling and studied her again.

"Brandy, what you ask isn't in our client's best interest."

"Kidnapping and trying to kill me wasn't in *my* best interest, you scumbag. You agree to my conditions or I'll tell the police, the press, the university—everyone—about what you've done. Either beg Endow for a deal and apologize publicly, or else you're going to be exposed."

"Oh, are those all of your conditions?" he asked sarcastically. "Just end my career?"

She gave an evil laugh.

"Oh yeah, thanks for reminding me, shithead. That's another one. You surrender your license to practice law as soon as Jonah pleads to a reduced charge. God knows you were worthless at it anyway—you always had to cheat, didn't you?"

He shined the light in her eyes, moving closer. I knew what he was doing. He was blinding her.

"You bitch," he hissed.

She'd finally gotten to him. Just as I knew she would.

"Get away from me," she started to say. But only got as far as "Get—" before his hands were on her shoulders. The afterglow of the flashlight would still be in her eyes, looking like a red sun. He started to swing her around. She tried to resist, but she didn't know where the edge was anymore. She didn't know which way to fight—she might fall right off it. The way Cody Wallis probably had.

I stood up and starting walking. I should have shouted something, but I didn't. I couldn't. The words "stop" or "freeze" just wouldn't come out. As I took those few quiet steps, I felt eight years of law-enforcement training and rigid self-constraint fall off me. Even though I suspected it was coming, Bogey's sudden violence—and his obvious intent—turned something in me loose. I let go of all the controls, allowing myself just a few seconds of living in my brother's world.

Brandy did her best to force him—and herself—down onto the stone, where he would have a harder time pushing and swinging her. But he was too strong. He was holding her up now, dragging her.

Brandy screamed. She flailed at him with her arms and feet, and even tried to bite the arms holding her. But the stone kept sliding beneath her shoes.

That was when I hit him. I hit him in the small of the back, giving it all the strength I'd amassed from a summer of clinging to Moriah, from a summer of frustration, guilt, disappointment, and overwhelming disillusionment. I put it all into that single kidney shot; it was a blow of pure, undiluted rage.

Bogey went rigid, rising up on his toes. He made a sound like a low groan but couldn't shout or scream as the air whooshed out of his lungs.

Brandy threw herself flat on the ground as Bogey's hands released her. She spread her arms and legs over the rock to hold herself still. Bogey was toppling forward, over her. With agonizing slowness, he lifted a leg to catch himself. But the leg just wouldn't seem to work right. I suspect his kidney had exploded, releasing toxins throughout his body and permanently jumbling all his nerves. The foot snagged on Brandy's body, the pointy toe of the cowboy boot catching in the baggy aloha shirt.

He went down like a tall tree. But he didn't strike the ground with a thump. Instead he kept on falling. He just disappeared into the blackness. A second later there was a splash. And after that, nothing.

Her eyes beginning to clear, Brandy crawled frantically away from the edge. I could see that she was unsure what had happened, who was in the water. I got myself back under control, forcing myself into the role of Antonio Burns, the good cop, again. But I wasn't sure which face was the mask anymore.

"Anton?" she asked hesitantly.

"Yeah."

"What happened?"

"I was trying to get him to let go of you. He fell off the cliff."

The flashlight was lying on the rock a few feet away. She pointed at it.

"Quick! Get the light! Shine it down there!" she said.

"Okay," I told her.

I took a step and bent down, reaching for the flashlight. But I somehow managed to clumsily kick it with my toe just before my hand could grab it. The flashlight rattled over the edge and plopped into the blackness below.

"Oops," I said.

"My God! We've got to do something. He's going to get sucked into the sink!"

I made my voice very gentle and almost apologetic.

"Sorry, but there's no way I'm going in there again. Not now. Not ever. I'm afraid he's fucked."

I moved closer to her and pulled her to her feet. I held on, worried she might try to dive to Bogey's rescue. But she wouldn't let me embrace her. When I tried, she pushed me away. I felt off-balance, though, and kept holding on. I needed her support.

She began to realize that I wasn't going to help Bogey. There wasn't any help I could offer, anyway. It was too late. We both listened intently for another minute and heard nothing but the swirl and suck of the river below.

"Oh my God," she said. "He's gone."

Then, after a long, long silence: "We'd better call the police."

I had managed to regain my equilibrium. I let her go.

"I am the police."

"Come on, Anton. Who do we notify? There're procedures and laws about this kind of thing, aren't there?"

I shook my head.

"No. Not for him. He was a lawless man. He didn't believe in it, only in manipulating it. The law doesn't really apply to him."

I moved to hold her again, but she pushed me away a second time.

forty-six

Luke didn't hold his press conference in any of the scenic or symbolic places that had been so carefully chosen by the opposition. Not the courthouse steps, not the parking lot in front of the jail, not even in his own office. Instead he did it in the concrete hallway behind the courtroom, with just a handful of reporters in attendance. They were the same ones who'd been Bogey's tools over the course of the summer, stubbornly refusing to believe that they'd been conned by the lawyer.

They were about to be rewarded for their obstinacy.

Luke spoke without any lawyerly flourishes; his manner only showed tired surrender.

"Brandy Walsh has been found. She is dehydrated and exhausted but otherwise unharmed. It appears that her two-day disappearance was the result of a publicity stunt by William J. Bogey, her supervising attorney. We don't believe Ms. Walsh is in any way culpable. However, a warrant has been issued for the arrest of Mr. Bogey. The charges include kidnapping, false imprisonment, and false reporting. We hope to have him in custody soon. Ms. Walsh is declining to speak with the media at this point."

Usually there would have been an outpouring of questions at this point, but instead there was only a stunned silence.

Luke cleared his throat.

"Additionally, Jonah Strasburg has been offered a plea agreement that I expect him to accept. Ms. Walsh will continue to represent him. After a lengthy investigation that has continued even while the trial has been pending, I've determined that the murder charge that was initially filed against him is unwarranted. Because of outrageous and insulting statements by the defense recently, I would love nothing better than to take this case to trial. Believe me. However, I wasn't elected to this job to conduct vendettas, or to go for the maximum penalty in every case. I was elected to do justice. Even when it means reevaluating my case after filing initial charges. And that's what I'm going to do. Jonah Strasburg did an irresponsible, thoughtless thing. It caused the death of a young boy. He needs to be punished for it, but a life in prison for him is not just. If the people of this community don't like my decision, they can vote me out of office next month. I'll sleep well at night either way, knowing I represented the people of this county and the laws of this state to the best of my ability."

The reporters just stared. And I tried not to laugh.

"I won't be taking any questions, so don't bother asking."

Ten eyes swung toward me.

"He won't, either," Luke said, suddenly sounding angry rather than defeated.

He turned his back on all of us without another word. He walked up the stairs and I headed down. I wondered if that symbolized anything.

Jonah was still being held in the jail, but he wore his own clothes instead of an orange jumpsuit. The sleeveless black T-shirt seemed to fit him a little better now. Maybe he'd put on a few pounds thanks to all the fast food we feed Wyoming inmates in county custody. The tattoos and the tough look fit him a little better, too. When he saw me standing in the hall, he got up off a cot and walked over. He was smiling a little shyly.

"You getting out today?" I asked him through the bars.

"Yeah. So they say, anyway. The county attorney says he won't object to a personal recognizance bond until I plead and get sentenced."

"Are you okay with it?"

He shrugged. "I did what I did."

"I want to thank you. For what happened in here last night. I don't know if you heard, but the guy they were beating and going to sodomize was my brother."

Jonah laughed. "Yeah, man. I know. I know. I knew from the moment he was brought in. All summer long my lawyers had been telling me about what a bad guy you were, and how you even had this brother who was some kind of psychotic killer who'd lost the use of his legs. They said they were trying to draw some connection between what had happened to him and some drug lord who disappeared last year. So when this guy comes in, all buffed out and kind of crazy-looking like you, a guy who can't use his legs too well, I made a guess. I had nothing else to do but sit around and think about things. Only I didn't know if you'd put him in here to kill me or to save me. When he had that seizure right as Smit was starting to pound on me the other night, I knew it was to protect me. So I felt kind of obligated to protect him."

"Thanks. You did a good thing. Thank you."

I shook his hand through the bars and turned to walk away.

Jonah stopped me, saying, "Hey, Burns. You did what you had to do. I don't blame you for arresting me. You're a cop, man."

I gave him a wave and kept walking.

forty-seven

The dark booth at Cesar's had become McGee's office. It fit him well, as did the red candlelight that made him appear a little satanic. He'd even somehow managed to melt the cold, cold heart of the waitress. She now brought him fresh drinks just as the ice cubes began to rattle and called him "sweetie."

"I just came from an interesting press conference," I told him while sliding in.

"Oh?"

"Luke gave a little song and dance about the principles of justice, then announced a deal. Jonah's agreed to plead to involuntary manslaughter, and Luke won't object to a sentence of probation and community service."

McGee didn't appear terribly interested. He was busy snapping chips in two, plunging the halves into hot salsa, and gnashing them with his teeth. His beard was littered with crumbs.

"You're complaining?" he asked.

I considered it. Yeah, I was disappointed. After all Jonah had been through, I would rather have seen him totally exonerated.

But he really didn't deserve total exoneration. He had been responsible for Cody's death. The crime, arguably, had been involuntary manslaughter. If things were to work as they were supposed to in the statute books I had once venerated, then that was exactly the outcome that should have resulted. That's what I'd bitched and moaned about for years—plea bargains by prosecutors to avoid the effort and uncertainties of a trial, sweet deals for those with political connections, reduced sentences to relieve overcrowded prisons, the surrender of the system. How could I complain when it was what I'd been dreaming of for years? But not this case. Not this defendant.

"No. It's cool," I said. "Did you make that happen?"

McGee shrugged. He was watching me as he crunched. Waiting.

I stared off into the darkness. Yeah, that's the way it's supposed to work. Ironic that it should happen just now. Was bad luck following me, or did some kind of karmic power just require that I pay full price for every little bit of good luck that passed my way?

"You want a drink, QuickDraw?"

I shook my head and stared back at my boss. He had lost faith in me, but I'd compounded it by losing faith in him, in the whole system. All the complex mechanizations we'd tried to drive in the right direction for eight long years despite a hundred opposing forces. He'd been doing the right thing all along—he wasn't here as a political flunky but to force Luke to do the right thing. Me, too. And to give me one last chance, which I'd squandered. There was too much distance between us now to ever be closed. He still believed, and I didn't. My nature wouldn't allow it any longer. There was too much Roberto in my blood, and I'd spent too much time alone with a half-wolf.

"What about the kids? The Manns?" he asked. "Luke say anything about them?"

"No. But they've probably suffered enough for their complicity and stupidity. Unless the office wants to be embarrassed by having allowed a rogue agent to run around torturing children, I suggest you tell him not to pursue it. They'll probably come to the same bad end all by themselves."

And what I'd done to them would probably help them along.

McGee was still watching me with his penetrating eyes. Only now he looked impatient. He was waiting.

I took out my wallet, opened it, and pried the seven-pointed gold star out of its holder. I spun it across the table to McGee. The old man plucked it up with stubby fingers and it disappeared into a pocket. As quick as that, and it was over.

"You sure you don't want a drink?"

"Actually, yeah. I think I do."

McGee had barely glared toward the bar before the waitress stepped up.

"Anything I can get you, sweetie?"

"A shot of tequila for my friend. The best you've got."

"Chinaco Reposado okay?" she asked.

I said, "Yeah, that'll be great."

She came right back with it. It wasn't just a shot, but a wide snifter filled almost halfway. McGee thanked her with a satyr's wink. I took a couple of quick sips and tried to feel the burn. No luck.

"Where's Bogey?" McGee asked.

I felt an unpleasant smile twist my lips that didn't come from the tequila.

"Where do you think?"

"As the Bard says, 'that fell arrest without all bail.'"

"That's good. I really like that."

McGee wasn't smiling back.

"How did he get there?"

I began telling him about the morning at the river. There was no point in refusing, as someone would be checking phone records eventually, after getting the requisite warrants, and they would find that the call to the motel came from my cell phone. Questions would be asked from there, of both Brandy and me, and answers would have to be given. I was careful now to detail our intended purpose: to get Bogey to incriminate himself on tape.

"You thought that would work?" McGee asked. "When did you become such an amateur?"

I felt the smile again on my face. I shrugged, then continued with the story.

"Anyway, Brandy provoked him too far. She said he was a shitty lawyer, and that he'd only made a name for himself by cheating. His ego couldn't handle it. He tried to throw her in the river. I intervened, to save her life. He fell in during the struggle."

McGee pulled on his drink until the ice clattered into his lips. He wiped his mouth with his coat sleeve and started to say something, but the waitress arrived with another double rum and Diet Pepsi. He waited until she had walked away and then some.

"And you didn't report it?"

"Nope."

"And she didn't report it?"

"She *did* report it. To me. I was a cop at the time, you might remember. I was a cop until just a few minutes ago."

"Unfortunately, I do. Having you investigated again and maybe even eventually arrested is going to be a real black eye for the office."

"I don't think you want to do that, boss."

"Why the hell not?"

"Well, if you conclude that Bogey's dead, that he couldn't have swum to safety, then you certainly should do an investigation. And you'll have to charge me, too, because of the way Bogey was always spewing to the press about what a bad guy I am. That's going to be a pretty big black eye. But imagine how much bigger it's going to be when the press starts churning up all the same stuff about how I should have been fired years ago. And it will grow into a colossal black eye when you can't touch me. You wouldn't have a chance in hell of convicting me of anything. Remember, I was only trying to stop him from killing a young lawyer.

For the second time. A simpler, less painful way for you to look at it is that we don't know *for sure* that Bogey drowned. He might just have swum away, then fled. He would have had to run. We had what basically amounts to a confession at that point, plus the fact that he was trying to kill her. And it was too dark to see anything. And there's no body, of course. No corpus delicti, as you lawyers say."

McGee was still staring, boring into my head.

"You set him up. And then you killed him."

No. He was wrong. But in a way, he may have also been right. I didn't want to look that deep into myself to find the answer. So I just said, "I know you're good, boss. You taught me everything I know. You're still the best in the state. But can you prove it beyond a reasonable doubt?"

forty-eight

I drove to the Outrider Motel, but Brandy was long gone. She'd probably moved to another tourist place to avoid the media. What there was of it, anyway. They'd never have all their questions answered about why Brandy had been kidnapped, what had happened to Bogey, and why the county attorney had done a sudden about-face and given Jonah such a generous deal. There was a presidential election going on, with a vice-presidential candidate from Wyoming, and other issues were taking precedence, like increased logging in the national forests, federally encouraged drilling for oil and gas on every bit of land that wasn't capable of growing profitable trees, the status of the state's few wild wolves, and snowmobiles in Yellowstone. As usual, politics trumped all. But in this case I really didn't mind. The whole thing would die a relatively quick death.

I could have checked the other motels in town, but I was spared the effort by a message that must have landed on my phone while I was talking with McGee.

The message sounded rehearsed. It said:

"I don't know who you are, Anton. When this all started, I

thought you were a bad guy, a rogue cop. A felon and a killer like that brother of yours I'd read about. Then I began to see that maybe you weren't so bad. You seemed to be trying to do the right thing about Jonah. Especially that day when we went climbing. In that canyon, on that rock, I decided you really were a nice guy. Someone who was willing to risk his career and everything for a good cause. That's why I slept with you up there. It wasn't to get you to tell me more about the prosecution's case, and it wasn't just the storm and hormones, you know. I liked you up there. A lot. And then you came and saved my life when I was tied up in the cabin. I need to thank you for that."

There was a long pause. I would have hung up, thinking that was all, but before I could hit the button, she said in a quieter voice, "And so I'm saying thank you. But after last night, I just don't know about you. And I'm sorry, Anton, but I don't think I want to know. Good-bye."

My impulse was to find her and explain. But, despite what she'd said, she did know. She knew it all. There was nothing to explain.

Feeling hollow, I drove to the hospital instead. Roberto was being kept in a small room there.

The last time I'd seen him in the hospital—a year ago—he'd looked like a dog's breakfast. His entire body had been bruised and battered, his eyes had been swollen shut, and there'd been tubes running out of him from every orifice. I remembered the metal cage that had been bolted to his skull, the black stitches like a necklace of spiders across his throat. All of it and more done to him because of me. I remembered wanting to throw up, to kill someone, and, mainly, wanting to run. But this time I didn't do any of those things. I swallowed the bile that rose up from my stomach and kept my balance.

He was sitting up on the bed, and there were no tubes or machines connected to him. The bruises looked no worse than the ones he'd gotten in school when he'd taken on a pack of boys three years older who were determined to kick my ass.

"Where's Jo?" I asked. "The paramedic?"

He shook his head sorrowfully.

"I had to tell her about Mary. That girl was *pissed*, Ant. I think it would be a good idea if we blew this town. What do you think, *che*?"

So it was just me, my wolf-dog, and my brother who drove up to the canyon in the Absarokas to retrieve my tent and gear. While stowing it, I couldn't resist taking one last shot on Moriah. This time, with my brother bellowing encouragement so loud it set Mungo to howling, I held on to the sunlit edge at the far end of the hideous roof crack and didn't fall off. I crawled on up and stood, for the first time, on top of the overhang beneath nothing but a clear blue Wyoming sky.

There was no real joy in having climbed the hardest fat crack in the world. I felt satisfied, that was all. And free. Unleashed, just like Roberto and Mungo. I'd finally slipped the collar and it was all behind me now.

We finished loading the Pig and headed for Denver. It was time for me to spend some time with my daughter, the real Moriah. And figure out what the hell to do with the rest of my life.